"We are lifemates."

Marguerite choked, spitting wine out as she coughed and sputtered.

"Are you all right?" Julius asked.

She nodded.

"Not the most delicate approach, was it?"

They stared at each other, his expression assessing, hers wary.

"What are we going to do about it?"

She swallowed. "Do we have to do anything about it for now? I mean, there is no need to really do anything at all. We are immortals and appear to be lifemates."

"We *are* lifemates, Marguerite. There is no 'appear' about it," he growled.

His eyes were blazing, the silver consuming the black of his eyes.

She licked her lips nervously and paused when his gaze followed the action. The air in the room was suddenly electric. Her heart rate sped up, blood moving swiftly through her veins as her breathing became shallow . . .

By Lynsay Sands

LYNSAY SANDS

Vampire, Interrupted

AN ARGENEAU NOVEL

AVON
An Imprint of HarperCollinsPublishers

This is a work of fiction. Names, characters, places, and incidents are products of the author's imagination or are used fictitiously and are not to be construed as real. Any resemblance to actual events, locales, organizations, or persons, living or dead, is entirely coincidental.

AVON BOOKS
An Imprint of HarperCollins*Publishers*
10 East 53rd Street
New York, New York 10022-5299

Copyright © 2008 by Lynsay Sands
ISBN: 978-0-06-122977-0
www.avonbooks.com

First Avon Books paperback printing: March 2008

Avon Trademark Reg. U.S. Pat. Off. and in Other Countries, Marca Registrada, Hecho en U.S.A.
HarperCollins® is a registered trademark of HarperCollins Publishers.

Printed in the U.S.A.

20 19 18 17 16 15 14 13 12 11

For Dave, thanks for all the help, Mr. Spice.

And special thanks to Daniela Brodner for help with naming Lissianna's baby.

Vampire, Interrupted

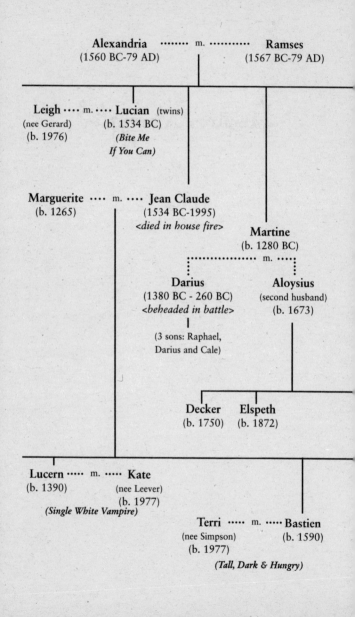

Alexandria ········ m. ··········· **Ramses**
(1560 BC-79 AD)   (1567 BC-79 AD)

Leigh ···· m. ···· **Lucian** (twins)
(nee Gerard)   (b. 1534 BC)
(b. 1976)   *(Bite Me
                     If You Can)*

Marguerite ····· m. ····· **Jean Claude**
(b. 1265)   (1534 BC-1995)
                              <died in house fire>

                                        Martine
                                        (b. 1280 BC)
                                        ····················· m. ····
                              Darius   **Aloysius**
                              (1380 BC - 260 BC) (second husband)
                              <beheaded in battle> (b. 1673)

                              (3 sons: Raphael,
                              Darius and Cale)

                              Decker   **Elspeth**
                              (b. 1750)   (b. 1872)

Lucern ····· m. ····· **Kate**
(b. 1390)   (nee Leever)
                   (b. 1977)
(Single White Vampire)

                   Terri ····· m. ····· **Bastien**
                   (nee Simpson)   (b. 1590)
                   (b. 1977)

                   (Tall, Dark & Hungry)

Argeneau Family Tree

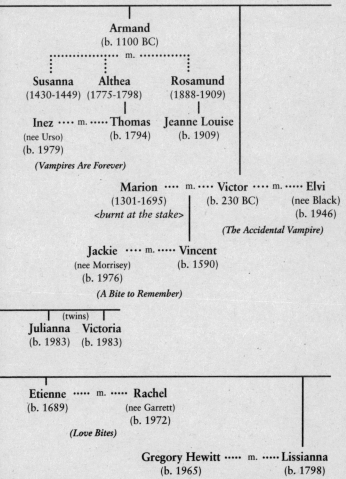

Armand
(b. 1100 BC)
······················ m. ··············

Susanna   **Althea**   **Rosamund**
(1430-1449)   (1775-1798)   (1888-1909)

Inez ····· m. ····· **Thomas**   **Jeanne Louise**
(nee Urso)   (b. 1794)   (b. 1909)
(b. 1979)

(Vampires Are Forever)

Marion ····· m. ····· **Victor** ····· m. ····· **Elvi**
(1301-1695)   (b. 230 BC)   (nee Black)
<burnt at the stake>   (b. 1946)

                                    (The Accidental Vampire)

Jackie ····· m. ····· **Vincent**
(nee Morrisey)   (b. 1590)
(b. 1976)

(A Bite to Remember)

(twins)
Julianna   **Victoria**
(b. 1983)   (b. 1983)

Etienne ····· m. ····· **Rachel**
(b. 1689)   (nee Garrett)
                (b. 1972)

(Love Bites)

Gregory Hewitt ····· m. ····· **Lissianna**
(b. 1965)   (b. 1798)

                (A Quick Bite)

One

Marguerite wasn't sure what woke her; a sound perhaps, or the crack of light from the bathroom being momentarily blocked, or maybe it was simply an instinct for survival that dragged her from sleep. Whatever caused it, she was alert and tense when she blinked her eyes open and spotted the dark shape above her. Someone stood at the side of the bed, looming like death. That thought had barely formed in her mind when the dark shape used both hands to raise something overhead. Recognizing the action from her youth when broadswords and weapons of its ilk were more common, Marguerite reacted instinctively, rolling abruptly to the side as the assailant's arms started their downward swing.

She heard the weapon slam into the bed just before tumbling off the bed. Marguerite landed on the floor with a thump and a shout that became a frustrated curse as she found herself tangled in the sheets. Glancing up, she saw her attacker jump onto the bed to follow. When he swung the sword again, she promptly gave up on the sheets, snatched the lamp off the bedside table, and swung it around to block the blow.

Pain vibrated up her arm on impact, eliciting another shout. Marguerite turned her eyes away from the flying sparks as metal met metal, and spared a bare moment to be grateful that the Dorchester was a five-star hotel with quality—and fortunately—metal-based lamps that didn't snap under a sword's blow.

"Marguerite?" The call was followed by a knock at the connecting door to the rest of the suite that made both she and her attacker pause and glance toward it. In the next moment, her attacker apparently decided he didn't wish to take on two of them and leapt off the bed to race for the balcony doors.

"Oh, no you don't," Marguerite muttered, dropping the lamp and lunging to her feet. She wasn't the sort to allow someone to sneak up and attack her in her sleep, then run off to do so again another day. Unfortunately, she'd forgotten about the sheets tangled around her legs, and crashed to the floor with her first step.

Gritting her teeth against the pain vibrating through her, Marguerite peered toward the balcony doors as the curtains were tugged open. Sunlight immediately poured in, and she saw that her attacker was encased from head to toe in black: black boots, black pants, long-sleeved black shirt, and all of that covered by a black cape. He also wore black gloves, and even a black balaclava covering his face, which she saw as he turned to look back at her. Then he slid out onto the balcony, allowing the curtain to drop back into place as her bedroom door slammed open.

"Marguerite?" Tiny rushed toward her, concern on his face.

She waved him toward the balcony doors. "He's getting away!"

Tiny didn't ask questions, but immediately changed direction, rushing for the doors leading onto the terrace. Marguerite stared after him with amazement. The man wore nothing but a pair of gold silk boxers with a big red heart on the backside. The sight made her mouth drop open in surprise, but the moment he disappeared through the billowing curtains her surprise turned to concern. She'd sent an unarmed, nearly naked man after her attacker—who had a sword.

Cursing, Marguerite concentrated on the sheets wrapped around her legs. Of course, they fell away easily now that she was no longer under threat. Muttering with exasperation, she scrambled around the bed and hurried to the balcony doors, charging right into Tiny's bare chest as he stepped back into the room.

"Careful. It's daylight," he rumbled, catching her upper arms and moving her back away from the curtains. He turned to close and lock the doors.

"Did you see him? Where did he go?" Marguerite asked, trying to peer around his large frame as he pulled one of the heavy curtain panels into place. The action blocked out the worst of the sunlight and most of her view of the terrace.

"I didn't see anyone. Are you sure you weren't

dream—?" Tiny paused mid-sentence as he glanced back and caught a glimpse of her in the bit of sunlight slipping between the gap in the curtains.

Marguerite raised an eyebrow at the sudden widening of his eyes as they traveled over her in the short pink silk nightie she wore. His stunned gaze moved slowly down all the way to her pedicured and red-painted toes and then just as slowly back up, skimming her shapely, bare legs, her rounded hips, and then skipping up her stomach to her breasts, which she knew were more revealed than not by the low neckline. His eyes stopped there, the dazed look turning to a concerned frown.

"You're hurt." Tiny caught her by the chin and tipped her face up and to the side so he could get a better look at her neck. After a second, he released her with a soft curse.

"What is it?" she asked as he took her by the arm to hurry her across the room.

Marguerite glanced down at herself. There was a line of blood dripping down her upper chest and soaking into the lace neckline of her nightie. Frowning, she felt around on her throat until she found the nick in her neck. Apparently the sword had caught her as she rolled away.

"Tell me what happened," Tiny ordered as he ushered her into the en suite bathroom and flipped on the light.

"I woke up to find a man standing over the bed. He had a sword. I rolled off the bed as he swung it," Marguerite said simply, her gaze shifting out toward the bedroom and the balcony doors as he snatched up a clean washcloth and turned on the taps to wet it.

Her adrenaline was still pumping and she now found she had itchy feet. She wanted to pursue the man who'd attacked her.

"Roll faster next time," Tiny muttered, reclaiming her attention as he began to wash the blood away from her skin. He scowled as he worked, and then relaxed a little and said, "It isn't too bad. Not deep I don't think. Just a nick."

"It will heal quickly," Marguerite said with uncon-cern as she moved away from him and back into the bedroom. She wasn't used to being taken care of and wasn't comfortable with it.

Her feet took her to the balcony doors, where she shifted the curtain to peer out on the bright terrace. There was no one there, and no rope or anything else to suggest how they'd got onto her balcony either.

She scowled out at the skyline. They were on the seventh and top floor. Her attacker must have climbed down from the roof.

"He was aiming to cut off your head."

Marguerite released the curtain and glanced around at that comment. Tiny was at the side of the bed, ex-amining the slice across the mattress right where her neck had been.

She shifted on her feet, her thoughts starting to take order in her head. Her attacker had used a sword. That told her he was definitely an immortal. Mor-tals usually killed each other, with guns or knives. If they were trying to kill an immortal they went for the classic stake. Beheading with a sword was usually the sign of another immortal.

"Do you have enemies here in England that you forgot to mention?" Tiny asked suddenly, straight-

ening from examining the bed to spear her with a
frown.

Marguerite shook her head. "It must be connected
with this case."

He raised a doubtful eyebrow. "Why? We haven't
found out anything yet."

Marguerite grimaced, disgusted by their inability to unearth even a bit of information regarding
their case. They were here to help Christian Notte, a
five-hundred-year-old immortal, find out the identity
of his dead birth mother. It had sounded an easy task
in the beginning, but it wasn't turning out that way.
A lot of time had passed since his birth, and Christian had little information he could offer them except
that he'd been born in England and his father had
returned home to Italy with him when he was only
two days old.

Tiny and Marguerite had started the search in
England, spending the last three weeks searching
through dusty church archives looking for mention
of his birth or even of the name Notte. They began
in the southernmost part of the country, working
their way north until they'd reached Berwick-upon-
Tweed. It was there that Tiny had finally suggested
they question Christian again to see if there wasn't
some bit of information he could give them to help
narrow the search to one area, or at least one half of
the country.

Relieved by the suggestion, Marguerite had promptly agreed. She'd expected private detective work to
be much more interesting than it was turning out to
be and was seriously reconsidering her career choice.
But she'd promised to help Christian find out the

identity of his mother and intended to do her best to accomplish that.

Tiny was the one who called Christian in Italy and arranged to meet in London. Rather than wait and catch a train the next morning and have to travel during daylight, Marguerite rented a car and they drove through the night, arriving at the hotel shortly before dawn. Christian had already arrived and checked in.

They'd met briefly with Christian Notte, and his cousins Dante and Tommaso on arriving, but only long enough to arrange a meeting at sunset to discuss the case. They'd then parted to go to their rooms.

"No, we haven't found out anything," she agreed now, pursing her lips as she peered at Tiny and then added, "But I can't think of any other reason someone would try to kill me. Perhaps the very fact that we're here and looking is enough to worry someone."

Tiny didn't look convinced. He did look worried though so she wasn't surprised when he suggested, "I think we should switch rooms . . . possibly even hotels."

Marguerite was frowning at the thought of having to dress and pack and move when Tiny suddenly added, "It *was* an immortal, wasn't it?"

Her startled eyes shot to his face, though she knew she shouldn't be surprised. She might be a newbie at this detective business, but Tiny was the real thing. She should have realized he'd put it together.

Sighing, Marguerite ran a hand through her hair and nodded. "Yes. I am sure he was. And, yes, we should switch hotels and even use a different name. But not this morning," she added firmly. "I am sure he will not try again this day and I'm exhausted."

Tiny nodded and then asked, "Did you leave your balcony door open?"

"No."

"Was it locked?"

Marguerite hesitated and then shrugged. "I did not open it when I came in, so have no idea."

Tiny frowned at her answer, and then announced, "You aren't sleeping in here. You can take my bed."

"Well, you are not sleeping in here either," she said firmly.

"No," he agreed. "I want to stick close to you until we move hotels. Jackie and Vincent would never forgive me if I let you get killed under my nose."

Marguerite smiled faintly at the mention of her nephew, Vincent Argeneau and his lifemate, Jackie Morrisey, who also happened to be the owner and president of the Morrisey Detective Agency, Tiny's boss . . . and hers now too, she supposed.

"I'll nap on the window seat in my room while you take the bed," he decided.

"You'll not get any sleep there." Marguerite moved to the door leading to the rest of the suite. "You can sleep in the bed with me."

Tiny snorted at the suggestion as he followed her through the sitting area to his door. "Like I'd get any sleep there."

Marguerite glanced back and grinned when she caught him watching her behind as he followed her into the second bedroom. It didn't take her ability to read his mind to know he found her attractive. She'd been aware of that from the beginning of their friendship. And she found him attractive as well;

tall, handsome, built like a line-backer with one of those lovely, wide chests a gal could spend hours exploring . . . and he could cook too, a skill Marguerite had never acquired. The man was practically perfect. There was only one flaw to him as far as she could tell, but it was a big one. Marguerite could read and control him. Having spent the last seven hundred years trapped in a marriage with a man who could read and control her—and couldn't resist doing so at every opportunity—she wasn't willing to visit that on someone else.

"You are perfectly safe with me," she assured him solemnly as she crossed the room to his bed.

"Marguerite, honey, no man is safe with a woman who looks like you," Tiny muttered as he closed the door. He watched her climb into bed and added with a shake of the head, "Especially in that nightie. What the hell did they make it out of? A hankie and some lace?"

Marguerite peered down at herself. The nightie wasn't really that revealing. Or at least, it wasn't as revealing as some of her other ones. And she liked pretty lingerie, it made her feel sexy. Single gals like herself had to get that feeling somewhere. Besides, she hadn't expected anyone would see it.

She raised her gaze to Tiny again to find him settling on the window seat. It wasn't long enough for him to stretch out on, so he sat himself on it, back against the wall at one end, arms crossed over his chest, expression grim as he avoided looking at her.

"You are not going to get any sleep like that," Marguerite said with a sigh.

"Yeah, well, I don't need a lot of sleep," he muttered, his gaze sliding to her and then quickly dancing away.

Marguerite stared at him for a moment and then shook her head and lay down in the king-sized bed. She closed her eyes and tried to sleep, but after a couple of moments, she opened them again to stare at the ceiling overhead and then finally turned a scowl in Tiny's direction. This was just stupid. He wouldn't catch a lick of sleep on that window seat, and she was never going to sleep knowing *he* couldn't sleep. Besides, it was a huge bed, with plenty of room for both of them.

Narrowing her eyes, Marguerite gave in to temptation and slipped into his thoughts. It took little effort to take control of the man, bring him to his feet, and direct him across the room to the bed. She made him lie down beside her and then took a moment to ease him into an untroubled sleep before slipping free of his mind with a little sigh.

Marguerite peered at him for a moment, and then turned out the bedside lamp, scooted under the sheet and blankets, and closed her eyes . . . only to have them pop open a moment later. She peered at the dark outline of the man in bed beside her, a frown curving her lips as she realized that she'd just done to him, what she'd so resented her husband doing to her throughout their marriage. She'd made him do what she'd thought was best rather than what he wished.

Marguerite tried to excuse herself by pointing out that it was late and they were both tired and he really would sleep better in the bed, but that didn't ease the guilt she was feeling. Tiny wasn't the first mortal she'd controlled during her seven hundred years of life, and normally she didn't have any guilt over it, but Tiny was a friend and friends didn't control friends . . . just as her husband, Jean Claude, shouldn't have controlled her.

Grimacing, Marguerite sat up in bed again, turned on the light, and nudged Tiny's arm to wake him. His eyes immediately shot open.

"Wh—What's happened?" He peered around a bit wildly, then spotted her in the bed beside him and appeared confused. "What?"

"I put you in bed so you would sleep comfortably, but then realized that it wasn't right for me to control you. So, if you really want to sleep on the window seat . . ." She shrugged.

Tiny stared at her blankly, and then slow anger crossed his face. "You controlled me?"

Biting her lip, Marguerite nodded apologetically. "I'm sorry. I realized it was wrong, that's why I woke you up."

Tiny's anger slid away, leaving him deflated as his gaze slid to the window seat. He didn't look particularly eager to leave the bed, but sighed and started to shuffle out of it, only to pause when he realized he was under the comforter, but on top of the sheet.

"I thought if you woke up before me it might make you feel better if you were on top of the sheet and I was under," she explained when he glanced her way.

Tiny relaxed and nodded. "It does. I guess it's okay if we sleep like this. But next time don't control me. We're partners, Marguerite . . . equals. I need to be able to trust you, but I can't do that if you're going to control me any time we disagree on what to do."

"I won't," she promised.

Nodding, Tiny lay back in bed and Marguerite turned off the lamp and followed suit. They lay there in silence for several moments, and then Tiny sighed.

"I can't get back to sleep. Do you think you could do that control thing and *make* me?"

Marguerite turned her head to peer at him with surprise. "You *want* me to control you?"

"Just to put me to sleep," he muttered.

The last of her guilt slipping away, Marguerite slid into his thoughts and put him back to sleep, and then lay back with a small smile. She liked Tiny. He was a good man. It was really a shame she could read and control him. He would make a good lifemate for some lucky gal.

Perhaps she should see if she couldn't find him a lifemate, Marguerite thought. It would be nice for her nephew's wife, Jackie, to have her friend with her in the future. She knew the woman would be shattered when he died whether it was next week or some time in the far distant future when he'd reached his dotage.

Marguerite closed her eyes, her mind filling with immortal after immortal she knew that may suit Tiny. He was a big, sweet man, a gentle giant. He deserved a sweet, kind wife who would appreciate him as he deserved to be appreciated. She drifted off to sleep while still considering the matter.

Julius Notte looked down at the empty bed and frowned. It wasn't even five o'clock yet, more than an hour from sunset. Marguerite Argeneau should be snug in her bed, but wasn't. He knew he had the right room. The scent of a woman's perfume—sweet and musky like fruit at harvest time—assured him that this was her room. And she'd obviously been sleeping here earlier, but now the room was empty.

Scowling, he glanced over the mess around him, taking in the rumpled bed with its sheet and comforter trailing onto the floor, the broken lamp next to it, and the shattered glass that had been knocked from the bedside table.

Concern replacing his annoyance, he retraced his steps, instinct sending him to the door of the other bedroom in the suite. It should be where the private detective, Tiny McGraw, was staying, but when he inhaled he caught a faint whiff of that sweet and musky perfume. Marguerite was in there, or had been at some point.

Julius opened the door and moved silently inside.

Two

Marguerite's eyes snapped open, muffled sounds jerking her from sleep. She was immediately alert. Even so, she had to blink several times before her mind accepted the sight before her. Tiny dangled in the air, caught by the throat and held above the floor by . . . Christian Notte? Eyes locked on the two men, she reached back blindly to feel around until her hand knocked against the bedside lamp. Finding the switch, she turned it on and squinted against the light that exploded into the room.

"Good evening, Marguerite."

Stiffening in the bed, she stared at the man presently dangling Tiny in the air. It wasn't Christian Notte. This man was several inches over six feet in height, with wide shoulders, handsome features, and deep silver-black eyes. All of which described Christian, but this man had short black hair and wore a business suit. Christian's hair was long and auburn and she'd never seen him in anything but black leather or black jeans.

"Who are you?" she asked, glancing worriedly at Tiny's face. Much to her concern the mortal was turning blue, his struggles becoming less frantic. She scowled at the man holding him and said, "Stop being so bloody rude and release my co-worker. We're friends of Christian's and he won't be pleased if you kill Tiny."

"Co-worker?" He dropped Tiny and perched his hands on his hips to scowl at her. "Is that what they call it now?"

Marguerite didn't respond, her concerned gaze was on Tiny. The detective was gasping and coughing and struggling to get to his knees. But he was alive. That was something, she supposed, finally turning her attention back to the angry man looming over the bed.

It seemed obvious he was somehow related to Christian, who was technically their employer, but . . . really this situation was somewhat beyond her. This was her first job. How did one deal with these things? She wanted to snap at the man to get the hell out of her room—well, Tiny's room, she supposed. However, she wasn't sure if that was the most professional approach. Perhaps she was supposed to be polite.

Marguerite glanced to Tiny, wondering if he was recovered enough to give her some guidance in the matter. Her eyes widened with alarm as he lurched to his feet and—still struggling to get back his breath—launched himself at their visitor.

The attack seemed to suggest she didn't have to be polite, Marguerite decided with satisfaction, and then

winced as the immortal responded to the assault with
an impatient flick of one hand that sent Tiny flying
backward into the bedroom wall.

"Hey!" she cried out. Her gaze flickered between
the man and Tiny until she saw that the mortal
seemed all right. At least, his expression was grim,
not pained, and he was moving himself into a sitting
position where he'd fallen.

Scowling, Marguerite turned back to the attacker,
mouth opening to berate him, but she paused when
she noted that he was no longer looking at her. His
attention was on the bed. She followed his gaze to see
what fascinated him so.

The comforter had slid to the floor and while she
clutched her half of the sheet to her chest, the other
half still lay in place on the bed, wrinkled and flat
where the large detective had slept on it. The sight
seemed to fascinate the man, though she didn't know
why. Before she could even try to sort it out, Tiny
distracted her by tackling him again.

Marguerite clucked impatiently at his foolishness
even as the intruder simply responded by tossing him
against the wall once more. She winced at the thud
as he slammed into it, and then decided enough was
enough. It was time to intervene before the sweet but
apparently not-as-bright-as-she'd-thought detective
got himself hurt.

Reaching out, Marguerite grabbed up the bedside
lamp and swung it around. She'd expected the plug to
pop from its socket as the one in her room had when
she'd used it to fend off that attacker's sword. Her
intention had been to smash it into the man's chest.
Instead, something about the angle and the table be-

ing close to the wall prevented that happening and rather than hit him, she nearly dropped the damned thing in her lap as the cord pulled tight and brought it to a halt.

Muttering impatiently, she turned and began tugging the cord this way and that above the table, trying to get it free.

Honestly, if she'd had this problem when the man with the sword had attacked, she'd be dead right now, Marguerite thought with disgust, then cried out as she was grabbed from behind and pulled backward against a hard chest.

Of course, *now* the damned cord decided to give way and the lamp popped her in the eye as it flew free. Cursing, Marguerite ignored the sting of pain and quickly shot her hand out with the lamp as he tried to grab for it.

Her attacker immediately switched his hold on her, his right hand dropping across her chest to hold her in place as the left hand—previously at her waist— now reached for the lamp.

Marguerite squawked in shock as his right hand closed over her breast. She didn't really think he was even aware of it in the struggle. *She* was, however, and wasn't at all happy to be groped by a complete stranger, accidentally or not, and somehow-related-to-their-boss or not. That was about the end of her patience right there.

Gritting her teeth, she swung the lamp up and over her shoulder, smashing it into her attacker. Marguerite wasn't sure where she hit him, but it had the desired effect. The man cursed, his hold on her loosening in surprise, and she burst from his arms and began to scramble off the bed. She had one foot on the floor, the other folded under her and pushing her off the bed when he suddenly grabbed that ankle and tugged.

Pulled off balance, Marguerite tumbled to the floor with a grunt, and then rolled onto her back to sit up, only to fall back with another grunt when he started to get off the bed, got caught in the sheets and fell on top of her, the impact forcing the air from her lungs.

That's when the door opened. The room had gone dark when the lamp plug had pulled from the wall, but the moment the door opened, light from the hall splashed into the room again. Then the overhead lights by the door came on, brightening the room further.

"Tiny?"

Recognizing Christian's voice, Marguerite struggled out from under the intruder who had gone suddenly still on top of her. Once free of him, she sat up and peered over the bed. The first person she saw was Christian's cousin, Marcus Notte. Her eyes widened in surprise. Marcus hadn't been with Christian when they'd met up just before sunrise that morning. He was here now, though, and with a woman in a maid's uniform. Judging by the concentration on his face and the blank expression on the woman's, she knew he was wiping the memory of this incident from her mind.

Marguerite's gaze slid around the room then until it landed on Christian. The second immortal was kneeling beside Tiny, checking him over. He glanced around now, though, eyes widening when he spotted her.

"Marguerite?" Standing, he started to move around the bed, but froze, his eyes widening with shock when her attacker suddenly sat up, popping into view as well. "Father?"

"*Father?*" Marguerite echoed, turning an amazed gaze on the man she now knew was Julius Notte.

"Yes," Christian said, his mouth hardening with displeasure as he hurried forward to help her to her feet. Once he had her upright, he glanced around, then grabbed Tiny's robe and quickly bundled her into it.

Marcus had finished with the maid and closed the door by this time, and as she slid her arms into the robe, he hurried past them to approach the father who was getting to his feet. She saw Marcus whisper something in his ear, and while she didn't catch what he said, she did hear Julius hiss, "What? Are you sure?"

"Yes, and you would be too if you'd taken the time to read his mind," Marcus said a bit impatiently. "I told you to wait until—"

"I know, I know," Julius muttered, interrupting him. "But I couldn't."

"There." Christian's voice made her glance his way, and then down to see that he'd tied the sash of the robe for her. She smiled her thanks, and then looked curiously back to the two older immortals. Christian did too, but while her expression was now curious, his was annoyed.

"What the hell were you doing, Father?" he asked shortly.

The senior Notte peered at his son, and then avoided his gaze by straightening the cuffs of his business suit as he said innocently, "Nothing. I just stopped in to have a word with your detective."

Marguerite's eyes widened incredulously. "A *word*? You attacked Tiny!"

He shrugged. "I thought he was attacking you."

Marguerite snorted with disbelief. It was Christian who asked with interest, "Why would you think that?"

"Her room is a mess," he explained calmly. "There is a broken lamp, glass everywhere, and the sheets and comforter are strewn across the room. I naturally assumed she'd been forced in here against her will."

Christian glanced to her in question. "Is that true?"

"Well, yes," Marguerite admitted, and then frowned and scowled at the man again as she asked, "How did you get in?"

"The maid," he answered promptly, and—she felt sure—honestly for the first time. "When I received no answer to my knock, I knew something was wrong. It wasn't yet sunset and you should have been in. So, I got the maid to open the door with her card key."

Christian nodded. "That's how I got in here just now. My bedroom backs onto this one and all the racket in here woke me up. I hurried out to see if everything was okay and met Marcus in the hall. When no one answered our knock, we had the maid open the door." He glanced from Marcus to his father and shook his head. "If you're both here, who's running the company?"

Marguerite glanced to Julius. Notte Construction was a very successful, family run company that had become international with job sites all around Europe and North America. She knew Julius headed the company and that Marcus was the second in charge.

"Your aunt Vita," Julius murmured, and when Christian's eyes narrowed and he seemed about to ask something else, the man quickly glanced at Marguerite and asked, "So what *did* happen in your room? Were you and this Tiny person—?" He froze abruptly. "There's blood on your nightgown."

Marguerite glanced down to see that the robe Christian had wrapped her in had slipped, revealing the blood-stained neckline of her nightie. Sighing, she pulled the collar of the robe back into place and said, "Someone broke in and tried to cut off my head."

"What?!" The three immortals squawked at the same time.

She nodded. "That's why I am in here. Tiny didn't want me staying in my room in case my attacker returned, and I didn't want him sleeping in there for the same reason, so . . ." Marguerite shrugged. "He offered to sleep on the window seat, but he's much too large for that. So we shared the bed."

A moment of silence passed as the three men turned and peered at Tiny. Marguerite rolled her eyes, knowing they were probably reading his mind, seeing if sleeping was all they'd done. She found it vastly annoying. It was really none of their business. She could have an orgy in here and it would be none of their business.

Tiny groaned and Marguerite hurried around the bed to kneel before him. He'd managed to pull himself to a sitting position and leaned weakly against the wall, eyes squeezed shut in pain.

"Are you all right?" she asked with concern

"I'll live," he muttered.

Marguerite smiled at the grumbly tone he was using and stood up, catching Tiny under the arm and lifting him to his own feet as she did.

"Whoa," he muttered, grabbing for the wall to help stay upright. He then grimaced and said, "Stop doing stuff like that, Marguerite, you'll give a guy a complex."

"Stuff like what?" Christian asked with amusement.

"Stuff that proves she's stronger than me," he admitted with a wry smile. "I'm not used to chicks who can bench press me."

"You're exaggerating," she said with a chuckle and urged him to sit on the side of the bed. Once he was seated, she stepped between his legs and grabbed his head in both hands to tilt it down so she could examine the top and back of his scalp.

"What are you doing?"

Marguerite glanced to the side and gave a start when she found Julius Notte looming beside her, a scowl on his face as his gaze shifted between her and Tiny.

"Checking for head wounds," she answered with irritation. "You were tossing him about like a Frisbee and I want to be sure you didn't do him serious harm."

"I'm fine, Marguerite," Tiny rumbled, forcing his head back up. "My back took most of the punishment."

"He's fine," Julius echoed, catching her arm and tugging her from between Tiny's legs. "Leave the mortal alone. They're weak but not that fragile."

"Tiny is neither weak nor fragile," she snapped, tugging her arm free of Julius Notte's hold.

"No, I'm not," Tiny agreed, his chest puffing up as he got to his feet. Marguerite almost expected him to beat his chest, but apparently his ego wasn't *that* threatened by Julius Notte's insults.

"I gather you're what kept hitting the wall and woke me up," Christian commented as the mortal began searching for something among the comforter and sheets.

"Yes. I woke up to find your father holding me up by the throat," Tiny muttered, distracted by his search. "Where the hell is my robe?"

"Oh, I'm sorry, Tiny. I have it. Here, you can have it back." Marguerite began to shrug out of the robe Christian had wrapped around her, but glanced to Julius when he suddenly sucked in a deep breath beside her.

Her hands froze with the robe half off when she saw the way his eyes were moving hungrily over her pink nightie and all it revealed. Tiny had looked at her the same way earlier, and it had made her feel attractive and even a little sexy, but this was different. Silver flames had burst to life in the immortal's black eyes, and Marguerite could almost feel their scorching trail over her body. A shiver slid along her body under her skin in the wake of his gaze. When his eyes stopped on her breasts, her nipples tightened and stood at attention as if he'd bent forward and rasped them with his tongue. When his eyes finally moved lower, dropping over the gentle swell of her stomach, the muscles there rippled under her flesh as if in response to a caress. And when they then shifted to settle at the apex of her thighs as if he could see through the delicate silk to the treasure that lay beneath, liquid heat pooled there and she began to ache.

Marguerite had never reacted to a man like this before and the fact that she was now, and with a complete stranger, sent confusion rolling through her mind, infecting every corner.

"No, no." Tiny was suddenly at her side, tugging the terry cloth robe back up her arms and distracting her from Julius. "That's okay. You keep it. I'll just put on my pants." Patting her shoulder, Tiny glanced over her head to give Julius a narrow-eyed look and then walked over to pick up the jeans he'd apparently hung neatly over the back of a chair before retiring that morning.

Julius Notte cleared his throat, drawing her reluctant gaze away from Tiny as he asked, "What about this attack business? Did you see who did it?"

Marguerite's confusion fled, chased out by irritation as she recalled the events of the evening. Eyes narrowing, she asked sweetly, "Which attack? Yours or the first one?"

She'd meant to insult him. However, the man's lips merely twitched with amusement at her sass. Marguerite scowled in response, then glanced to the door as a knock sounded.

"That'll be my breakfast. I ordered it before I went to bed," Tiny muttered, doing up his pants as he hurried to the door. They all stood silent as he opened the door to a liveried employee who rolled in the trolley of food. The server's eyes widened as his gaze slid over each of them as well as the mess in the room, and Marguerite supposed it must look odd. Three fully dressed men, Tiny in only his pants, and she, in the oversized robe, surrounded by signs of a struggle. The man was probably abuzz with questions, but too well trained to ask them.

"That's fine," Tiny said as the man was rolling the trolley of food past Marguerite. The server paused at once, offering her a nervous smile before turning away to cross back to the door Tiny was still holding open.

Despite the silver plate cover, delicious aromas were wafting off the food on the trolley and Marguerite glanced toward it, and then lifted the silver cover to peer at the food beneath. Apparently, the hotel would send breakfast any time of the day. It was a proper full English breakfast of eggs, bacon, sausage, black pudding, fried mushrooms, fried tomatoes, beans, and a fried bread slice.

If he ate like this all the time, Tiny was likely to have a heart attack before he could be turned, Marguerite thought, taking a piece of sausage before returning the cover. She'd bit into the juicy bit of meat before realizing what she was doing and then glanced guiltily around. Fortunately, everyone's attention appeared to be on the man Tiny was tipping and ushering out the door.

Shaking her head, she popped the rest of the sausage into her mouth and chewed quickly, thinking that she'd obviously been spending too much time around Tiny. Immortals, or vampires as—much to her disgust—mortals liked to call them, tended not to eat after a hundred years or so of living. Food had the propensity to become both boring and bothersome after indulging in so many meals, but she'd kept Tiny company while he had his meals these last three weeks. Marguerite hadn't been tempted to indulge before this, but it had obviously affected her if she was going to start pinching food off his plate.

"I suppose I should see to introductions," Christian said as Tiny closed the hotel room door.

Marguerite swallowed the sausage in her mouth and turned what she hoped was an innocent, interested gaze Christian's way as he said, "Father, Marguerite Argeneau. Marguerite, my father, Julius Notte."

"Julius? Now, why does that name sound so familiar?" Tiny asked.

Marguerite glanced at her partner with confusion as he shrugged into his shirt. She knew he knew the man's name. They'd been searching for it in archives for weeks now.

"I've got it!" he said suddenly, snapping his fingers. He glanced to Marguerite and asked drolly, "Isn't your dog's name Julius?"

Marguerite's mouth pulled into a grin. "Yes, it is."

"He's a big dog," Tiny announced to the others, though his gaze was on Julius as he added, "Fur as black as your hair. A Neapolitan Mastiff. That's an Italian breed, isn't it?" he asked and then shrugged and added heavily, "He drools a lot."

Marguerite turned away and coughed into her hand to hide the laugh that she couldn't hold back. She wasn't surprised by the choked quality to Julius Notte's voice when he asked, "You named your dog Julius?"

Making her expression bland, she turned back and admitted, "I've named every dog I've ever had Julius.

The first was a couple hundred years ago. I've taught a lot of Juliuses to heel over the years."

A choked gurgle slipped from Christian's lips that sounded suspiciously like stifled laughter. Tiny grinned widely and gave her an approving nod. Marcus bit his lip, turned his head to the side, and coughed . . . once. However, Julius Notte didn't look annoyed as she'd expected. Much to her confusion, the man again looked amused.

Deciding she would never understand men, Marguerite shook her head and turned to head for the door leading to the rest of the suite. "I am going to take a bath."

"Just a minute," Julius Notte protested. "You haven't yet explained about the other attack."

"Tiny can tell you about it," Marguerite said calmly. "I am taking a bath."

She didn't wait for further protest, but sailed out of the room.

Julius watched Marguerite Argeneau go, a small smile claiming his lips as his gaze slid over her long, wavy chestnut hair with its red highlights, the robe trying to slip off her shoulder, and down to her shapely legs and cute little bare feet. She was magnificent. Beautiful, intelligent, sexy as hell, and sassy to boot, he thought with admiration, but came to earth with a bump when Christian snapped, "Stop looking at her ass, Father. She's *my* detective."

His mood of a moment ago ruined, Julius turned on his son and snapped, "Marguerite may be your detective, but she's my—"

"Your what?" Christian asked curiously when Julius abruptly cut himself off.

"My responsibility," he finished, avoiding his gaze. "As the head of our family, everyone is, including you and anyone working for you."

Christian opened his mouth to respond, but Julius quickly turned to Tiny and ordered, "Tell us about the first attack."

It was enough to distract Christian. He closed his mouth and turned to peer at the mortal expectantly.

Tiny hesitated and then muttered, "I need a coffee."

Julius shifted impatiently, but waited as the mortal crossed to the food trolley with his cup and then prompted, "The earlier attack?"

Tiny nodded, but reached out with his free hand to shift the silver plate cover off his food. He grabbed a piece of bacon and popped it into his mouth, chewed, swallowed, and then finally said, "Someone broke in and tried to cut off Marguerite's head."

Julius closed his eyes and prayed for patience.

"Er . . . Tiny, that's pretty much what Marguerite said," Christian pointed out.

"And that's what happened," the detective said with a shrug and picked up another piece of bacon.

When Julius began to growl, Christian moved a little closer to the mortal in a protective manner. "Yes, but surely you can give us more detail?"

"Was the attacker mortal or immortal?" Julius snapped. "What did he look like? How did he get in? Was he armed? *Was* it a he?" He arched his eyebrows with exasperation. "You're the detective, mortal, surely you noticed details you could pass along?"

Tiny peered at him calmly, a small smile tugging at the corners of his lips and it seemed obvious his obtuse behavior now was payback for the earlier attack.

Just when Julius thought he would throttle the man, he answered his questions.

"I suspect he was immortal, but I can't tell you for certain and can't describe him because I didn't see him. Obviously he was armed, he couldn't cut off Marguerite's head with his hand. He had a sword. Marguerite seemed to think it was a he, but I can't say for sure because—as I said—I didn't see him."

Julius let his breath out slowly as the man continued.

"He'd fled out onto the balcony by the time I reached her room. Marguerite was tangled in her sheets on the floor. She'd apparently woken up to see the sword coming down and rolled out of the bed. She had a nick on her neck and blood on her nightgown and pointed to the open terrace doors when I ran in." He shrugged again. "The assailant was no longer out there when I got outside. He must have come down from the roof and escaped the same way."

Julius's mouth tightened. Marguerite Argeneau had nearly been killed. Someone had tried to kill her before he'd arrived in her room.

"Marguerite thinks it has to do with the case," Tiny added.

Julius's head snapped up at those words. "What?"

The detective shrugged. "She says she has no enemies, but pointed out—and rightly so—that there *is* someone who doesn't want Christian to know who his mother is."

Julius winced. The man wasn't even trying to hide his ridiculous suspicions. Not that they were really ridiculous, he acknowledged. After all, he *had* done everything in his power to keep Christian from finding his mother. No doubt both Tiny and—more importantly—Marguerite would think him behind the earlier attack as well. *Hell*.

"Did you do it?" Christian asked.

Julius's head reared back with affront. "No!"

"Don't look so offended, Father," Christian muttered impatiently. "You don't want me to know who my mother is and have turned away every detective I've hired until now to ensure I don't. But Marguerite and Tiny aren't from Europe and Marguerite's family is powerful. You can't use threats to make them quit like you have the others."

"You know about that?" Julius asked with surprise.

"Of course I know," he said with disgust. "Most of the immortal detectives I set to the task were younger than I. I could read them. They were *telling* me they couldn't find anything and thought it a waste of time, or that they had 'urgent matters needing attending' and couldn't afford the time for such an extensive search, but their minds were usually screaming, *"Oh shit, I have to get out of this or Julius Notte will crush me like a little bug."*

Julius turned a scowl Marcus's way when a bark of laughter slipped from the man's mouth.

"So, did you attack Marguerite?" Christian asked, then added encouragingly, "Maybe not with the intent to kill her, but just to scare her off?"

"No," Julius repeated, holding his gaze.

Christian looked like he might believe him but then sighed and shook his head. "I want to believe you, but . . ."

"Can't you read him?" Tiny asked. "I thought you guys could read us and each other so long as you aren't lifemates. Marguerite was constantly reading Vincent in California."

"Marguerite is older than Vincent," Christian explained. "I can't read my father unless he opens his mind to me."

"So, have him open his mind," Tiny suggested.

Julius glowered at the mortal, but then went still as Christian turned an arched eyebrow his way.

"Will you open your mind and let me read it to be sure," Christian asked.

Julius didn't even bother to speak, he merely sneered at the very suggestion.

"Just what I thought," Christian muttered with disgust. "You did come here to—"

"Perhaps we should discuss this elsewhere," Marcus suggested, reminding them of his presence. When they both glanced his way, his gaze slipped meaningfully toward Tiny who had pulled the food trolley in front of one of the chairs by the window and was settling down to his breakfast.

"Don't mind me," the detective said with amusement. "I'll just eat while you talk."

"We'll get out and let you eat in peace," Christian growled and then glanced to Julius and said, "We can talk in my room."

When he nodded agreement, Christian turned to head for the door.

Julius glanced from his departing son to the mortal and hesitated. He'd wanted to rip off Tiny's head when he'd found him in bed with Marguerite. In fact, he'd wanted to right up until Marcus had whispered in his ear that he'd read the man and he and Marguerite hadn't done anything but share the bed, that they didn't have the kind of relationship he'd assumed.

Of course, as Marcus had also said, Julius would have known that himself had he taken the trouble to read the man rather than just assume the worst. Now he felt kind of bad about the whole thing. The detective had just been trying to ensure Marguerite's safety. Julius considered apologizing for his earlier behavior, but then recalled that if Tiny hadn't opened his big mouth about his opening his mind for Christian to read him, his son wouldn't be pissed at him right now. The two deeds cancelled each other out, he decided. He didn't owe him an apology.

Scowling at the mortal, Julius turned on his heel and followed his son.

Three

Marguerite's gaze slid over the mess in her room as she headed for the rack where her suitcase sat. Flipping up the lid, she retrieved what she'd need for a bath, and then grabbed fresh clothes to wear afterward, grateful she hadn't unpacked when they arrived that morning. It saved her having to repack everything.

Turning, she moved into the bathroom and set her things on the gleaming marble counter before moving to the huge tub. Marguerite poured in a liberal amount of bubble bath, pushed the button to drop the drain plug into place, and then switched on the taps before sitting on the side of the tub with a weary little sigh.

She was tired and would have liked a couple more hours sleep. It had been a long drive from Berwick-upon-Tweed . . . but then it had been a very long three weeks.

Her mouth quirked with irritation as she thought of the time they'd spent going through book after book of ancient, spidery writing in now faded ink, searching for mention of the Notte name.

So much time wasted, Marguerite thought with ir-ritation, *and all because the stubborn, stupid man in Tiny's room refused to simply tell the name of the woman who had given birth to his son.*

She shook her head in disgust. Julius Notte was an attractive man, far too attractive for his own good. In all likelihood, the truth was probably that he slept around with so many women—mortal and immortal alike—that he had trouble keeping track of the names. Which one of those had given birth to Christian was probably a mystery to him too. She'd probably dumped him on Julius's doorstep while he was out.

Wrinkling her nose at her own catty thoughts, Mar-guerite leaned over to turn off the taps, acknowledg-ing to herself that she was obviously in a very bad mood. Hoping that a nice, relaxing bath would help improve it, she disrobed and stepped carefully into the warm, bubble-covered water, releasing a little sigh of pleasure as she sank into its soothing embrace.

Marguerite loved bubble baths, and had never un-derstood the attraction of showers. She liked to soak, and did so now. It gave her time to relax and think, and she had a lot to think about.

Christian had told them at the start that Julius Notte refused to reveal who his mother was or dis-cuss anything about her. Indeed, the whole family re-

fused to discuss his mother, saying only that she was
dead and he was better off without her.

The few slivers of information he'd gained over the
centuries were just tidbits that had slipped out over
time, nothing that would tell him where to start a
search, he'd told them. Until the day when he and
one of his aunts were looking at a portrait of him as
a child, and she had smiled and commented, "You
were only a few weeks old there. Your father had it
commissioned right after he returned with you from
that year in England."

Finally having somewhere to start the search, Christian had immediately hired detectives to try to find
out his mother's identity. The problem was that any
detective for such a search had to be an immortal,
and all of the immortals in Europe were easily scared
off by Julius Notte and the power he wielded. All it
took was one phone call from the man and the detectives would back off the case.

Until now, Marguerite thought grimly. She liked
Christian and felt he deserved to know who his
mother was. She also wasn't afraid of Julius Notte or
his power. She would continue the search so long as
Christian wished. It would just be so much easier if
Julius Notte simply told them who the woman was.
It would save them all this schlepping around, going
through dusty old books.

Marguerite grimaced. So far, she was very disappointed in her new job. She found this research business boring and was definitely considering seeking
out a different career after this case was done.

Lifting her leg out of the bathwater, Marguerite ran

the soapy washcloth over it and then set it back and lifted the other to do the same as her thoughts turned to Julius Notte.

Marguerite had no idea why the immortal was so set against his son knowing who his mother was. Were she to guess, she'd say Christian's mother had probably hurt him terribly. Or, since the family kept telling Christian she was dead, perhaps her death was what had hurt him. The loss of a lifemate was a crushing blow to an immortal, she'd been told. She couldn't say how crushing, she'd never had a lifemate, but she did know it took some immortals centuries to recover from the loss . . . if they recovered at all.

Still, while Marguerite could understand that this may be the reason he refused to discuss the woman, Christian had a right to know his mother's identity.

Marguerite let her second leg slide back into the water and lay back in the tub to run the washcloth over her arms. When she then slid it over her breasts, she found her hand slowing as she recalled the brief, odd reaction she'd had to Julius Notte when she'd started to take off Tiny's robe and had caught him looking at her.

Just the memory of the way his eyes had slid over her body brought about a response in her and she frowned as her nipples pebbled as if he were there now, looking at her again.

Biting her lip, she dropped the washcloth on the side of the tub and forced herself to relax, hoping to calm the low hum of excitement suddenly running through her again. In her seven hundred years of life, Marguerite had never before had such a reaction to a man just looking at her, and it troubled her to have it now. The man was a complete stranger. One she wasn't even sure she liked!

What kind of barbarian broke into your room and started throwing around the mortal in it? He claimed he'd thought Tiny was attacking her, but they'd both been asleep. At least, she'd been sleeping and she assumed Tiny had been as well. And really, Tiny was a mortal and she an immortal. He *couldn't* make her do anything she didn't want to do.

Julius, however, might be able to, Marguerite acknowledged. He was an immortal, like herself, and she already knew from their earlier struggle that he was stronger than she. *He* could have forced her from her room and into that bed.

For some reason that thought sent a shiver of the earlier excitement down her back and Marguerite scowled at the response. She had just been freed from seven hundred years of marriage to a horrible, controlling husband and had no desire to get tangled up in *any* kind of relationship with another man at the moment. She wanted to enjoy her freedom, have a career, live life a bit . . .

Marguerite had been alive for more than seven hundred years, but felt like she'd been in a deep freeze all that time, her emotions bottled up to keep in the rage of being controlled. Her children had been the only part of her life where she'd allowed herself to feel anything, and she'd poured all her caring and passion into them and their happiness.

It had left her wholly unprepared for the excitement that had rolled over her when Julius Notte's eyes had caressed her body. Marguerite hated being taken by surprise, and had no desire to pursue the attraction the man had stirred in her. In fact, as far as she was concerned, the best thing in the world that could happen was to get Julius Notte and the disturbing effect he had on her out of her life as quickly as possible.

The easiest way to ensure that was to solve this case quickly and fly home to Canada, she thought, and wondered if she might be able to read the man. If she could read Julius Notte's mind, she could find out who Christian's mother was and bring this case to a quick and satisfactory close.

Pursing her lips, she wondered how old the man was. Christian was only five hundred and she already knew he was an only child, so it was wholly possible that Julius Notte was younger than her. If that were the case, she might be able to read him.

Unfortunately, Marguerite had a feeling he was much older than that. She wasn't sure what made her think so, but she could usually judge these things pretty dependably and her instincts were telling her he was older. And if he *was* older than she, reading him would be much more difficult, if not impossible . . . unless he was distracted. When distracted, older immortals could sometimes be read by younger ones.

Marguerite supposed she'd have to wait and see . . . unless she got lucky and Christian was—right that moment—convincing his father to give him his mother's name. Or—alternately—convincing him to leave. Either option would get the man out of her hair, and she'd much rather spend another three weeks combing through dusty old archives than have to spend another moment around Julius Notte.

However, if he was still around when she finished her bath, Marguerite would try to read him to get the information. If she couldn't, she'd just have to learn to deal with the effect he had on her. She was old enough to be able to handle such situations with dignity and grace.

"Yeah, right," Marguerite murmured with wry amusement. Shaking her head, she settled back in the water and closed her eyes, intending only to relax for a moment.

"Now, would you mind telling me what the hell is really going on here?" Christian asked as he led the way into his hotel room.

Julius hesitated, his gaze sliding to Marcus for help in handling this issue.

Before the other man could speak, Christian added, "Don't bother trying to come up with a lie. I know what's happening. You got wind that I'd hired the Morrisey agency to find my mother and flew over here to make them drop the case, didn't you?"

Julius's eyes widened. "I—"

"Don't bother to deny it," Christian interrupted. "You must know that, as an Argeneau, Marguerite wouldn't be easily scared off. You probably intended to send her packing. You would have tried to slip into her thoughts while she was sleeping and vulnerable to find what argument was likely to work best."

"Er . . ." Julius glanced at Marcus who grimaced and moved to lean against the dressing counter.

"But that earlier attack on Marguerite ruined things," Christian went on. "You probably did go to her room first, but when she wasn't there, you went to the other room and found her and Tiny in bed and . . ." His voice faded, his expression becoming considering as he finished, "and for some reason you freaked out. Why is that?"

Julius stiffened, and clamped his mouth shut, refusing to answer.

It didn't matter. Expression brightening with realization, Christian guessed, "Even though she was sleeping and vulnerable, you couldn't get into her mind. Could you?"

"Don't be ridiculous," Julius muttered. "She's younger than I, centuries younger . . . and was sleeping."

"That's right, and you should have been able to read her, but couldn't!" Sure, he was right, Christian was practically crowing. "That's why you attacked Tiny. You were jealous!" He shook his head with amazement. "As long as I've known you, you've been a cold, hard, emotionless bastard, but when you found you couldn't read Marguerite you couldn't stand the fact that she was in bed with Tiny and just *lost* it."

"I thought he was attacking her," Julius insisted staunchly, but his mind was taken up with wondering if he really had been a cold, emotionless bastard all these centuries. He knew he'd been a bit grumpy maybe, but Christian's description seemed a bit harsh.

"Attacking her?" Christian snorted. "You didn't think that for a minute. They were both sleeping when you went in. You freaked because Tiny was in bed with the woman who was a true lifemate to you!"

Shoulders slumping, Julius moved past Marcus to take one of the chairs on either side of the small table by the window. Once settled, he slid his gaze back to his son to see him grinning widely. Julius scowled. "Why are you smiling like that?"

"I'm happy for you," Christian said simply.

"Right . . . well . . ." Julius shifted uncomfortably.

"And now you need me," he added with delight. "I have a bargaining chip."

Julius stiffened. "What do you mean?"

Christian grinned, seeming to savor the moment, and then his expression became more serious as he said, "While in California I found out that Marguerite suffered horribly in her marriage to Jean Claude Argeneau. She has absolutely no interest in finding herself caught in another relationship that might turn out so badly." A troubled expression crossed his face as he added, "I'm quite sure that if she even suspects you might be a lifemate, she'll drop everything and head back to Canada so fast your head would spin."

Julius released a heavy sigh. Marcus had already told him something similar.

"On the bright side," Christian went on, sounding more cheerful. "You need me to keep my mouth shut about your not being able to read her. *And*, you need an excuse for staying near her that won't reveal you think you're lifemates."

"Blackmail, son?" he asked dryly.

"Not blackmail. A bargain," Christian insisted firmly and pointed out, "You don't have to take it. You could try telling Marguerite that you think she's your lifemate and have her try to read you and see how she reacts if she can't."

"I may not be able to read her, but she *may* be able to read me," Julius pointed out, trying for nonchalance as he reached out and plucked a grape from the fruit bowl and popped it in his mouth. "She may not be my lifemate at all."

Christian shook his head, and then pointed out, "You're both eating."

Julius stopped chewing the grape in his mouth, eyes widening as he recognized that he was, indeed, eating. But then he realized that his son had said, "You're *both* eating." Quickly swallowing the grape, he asked, "Marguerite has eaten too?"

"She pinched a sausage from Tiny's breakfast when she thought no one was looking," he announced with a slow smile.

Julius sat back, a smile coming to his own lips. He'd been through this before, but had forgotten that an immortal's appetite for food returned when they met a lifemate. He had no idea why that happened. Marcus and he had once discussed it and the only conclusion they'd come to was that the awakening of one appetite brought the others back to life. Sex was glorious, life was grand, and food suddenly had more flavor. Where once it had seemed boring and a waste of time to eat, everything tasted delicious.

"I'm more than happy to help you out," Christian announced, drawing his attention once more. He then added, "But I want to know who my mother is."

Julius considered him silently, and then said, "Fine. But—" he added firmly before Christian could speak. "The deal is that you keep your mouth shut and help me with a cover story to stay close to Marguerite *until everything is sorted out with her*, and *then* I will tell you about your mother."

Christian narrowed his eyes and tilted his head. "So . . . after five hundred years of refusing to even talk about her, you're willing to tell me who my mother is to get Marguerite," he said slowly and then asked, "Does this mean you're over my mother?"

Julius hesitated and then said in a gruff voice, "I'll never be *over* your mother, Christian. But I want Marguerite."

The words didn't seem to surprise Christian. He accepted them with a solemn nod and said, "All right. It's a deal."

When the younger man then crossed the room with hand held out to seal the bargain, Julius didn't shake it, but used it to pull him into a hug.

"I'm happy for you, Father," Christian said sincerely as he slapped him firmly on the back. "I like Marguerite."

"Thank you," Julius murmured.

"And now that we've made the bargain," he added with a grin as they stepped back from each other. "I can tell you that I would have helped you anyway, even if you hadn't agreed to tell me who my real mother is."

When Julius raised one eyebrow, Christain shrugged and added, "You forget I'm not as ruthless as you. I could never stand between you and someone who might help you forget my mother and be happy again."

Laughing at his expression, Christian stepped away and moved around the table to settle in the second chair. "So, with Marguerite in the bath, we have at least an hour to come up with a good excuse to have you stick close to her. She liked long baths when we were in California and I doubt that's changed," he added for Julius's sake, as he set a pad of hotel stationery in front of him on the table.

Nodding, Julius moved to reclaim his own chair as Marcus snagged the chair at the dressing table and brought it over to join them.

"The easiest way to handle this is probably to stick as close to the truth as possible," Christian said thoughtfully. "Obviously it will have to include the attack on her."

Julius watched him warily, but didn't comment.

"We can tell her that you suspect the attack was perpetrated by my mother's family, that the Morrissey agency's taking on the case and leading it into England has made them nervous and they will try to stop it any way they can."

Julius's eyes widened incredulously. "How did you—?"

"I'm not an idiot, Father," Christian interrupted dryly. "The attack has to do with the case and since I know you wouldn't sink so low, that leaves my mother's family. Obviously, someone besides you doesn't want me learning my maternal origins. Besides, the only good reason for you to keep the secret all this time is to protect me."

"Your mother ordered you killed at birth," Marcus announced quietly.

Julius turned a glare on the man for revealing that and then glanced back to his son. Anger and pain for the lad mingled in his own heart as he saw the stark expression on his face, and then Christian quickly looked down to the pad he was doodling on, hiding it. After a moment, he cleared his throat.

"Right, so it's probably her family behind the attack on Marguerite. Unless my mother's really still alive, then I guess it could be her."

When he raised a questioning glance, Julius hesitated, but kept silent in the end, unwilling to reveal if that was the case.

"At any rate," Christian continued on a sigh when his father remained stubbornly silent. "I'll tell Marguerite that—out of fear for me—you finally revealed that my mother tried to kill me at birth and you suspect her people are behind the attack earlier. That despite this, I want to continue the investigation and that while you refuse to reveal any more, you have decided to remain with us to ensure our safety until we give up, or to be on hand should we solve the case."

Christian paused and considered the plan and nodded. "That should ensure she stops thinking you're a stubborn ass for not telling me who my mother is."

Julius stiffened at these words, but Christian was still talking.

"And paint you in a more favorable light, as well as give you a reason to stay close to her." He paused and eyed his father. "The rest, unfortunately, is up to you."

"Unfortunately?" Julius echoed in a warning growl.

"Well," Christian grimaced. "Father, I don't know what you were like when you were younger, but you aren't exactly a Romeo type now, are you? I mean, the maids at the house and the secretaries in the office are terrified of you, and—"

"I do know how to woo a woman," Julius interrupted dryly. When Christian didn't hide his doubt, he scowled and insisted, "I do."

"Hmm," Christian murmured doubtfully.

"I do have some experience with the opposite sex, Son," he said condescendingly. "I haven't lived like a monk *all* my life. In fact, I used to be something of a rogue in my day."

"I'm sure you were," Christian said soothingly, and then added, "But *your day* was a hell of a long time ago, Father. Times have changed, women have changed . . ." He shrugged. "You might need a little help is all I'm saying."

Julius frowned as the words began to raise uncertainty in him. It *had* been a long time since he'd wooed a woman. In fact, he hadn't since his son's birth, instead, concentrating on keeping him safe and being a father as well as running the family company. But surely things hadn't changed that much?

"Don't worry, Father. I'll help out," Christian said encouragingly. "And I'll really build you up to Marguerite. I'm sure it will be fine."

"I'll help too."

Julius glanced around in surprise as Dante pushed himself away from the frame of the door leading into the rest of the suite. He'd obviously been there listening for some time, Julius realized with irritation as he watched him lead his twin, Tommaso, into the room.

"How long have you two been standing there?" he asked with irritation as Dante dropped onto the bed and leaned his back against the headboard.

"I think we heard most everything," Tommaso admitted as he took the other side of the bed. He crossed his legs at the ankle, clasped his hands on his lower stomach, and recited, "Marguerite's your lifemate. Christian's mother tried to kill him and is probably behind an attack on Marguerite that we apparently missed. And you need help wooing Marguerite. I don't think we missed anything."

"No, you didn't," Christian agreed with amusement. He then smiled at Julius and said, "See? We're all on your side. You'll have lots of help wooing Marguerite."

"God help me," Julius muttered, scrubbing one hand wearily through his hair.

Marguerite opened her eyes and grimaced as she immediately became aware of the unpleasant chill to her bathwater. She'd fallen asleep in the tub and it seemed obvious from the temperature of the water and the lack of bubbles remaining that she'd slept for a good length of time. Her guess would have been that she'd slept for half an hour, though she didn't have a watch to see if she was right.

She did feel better for the sleep, though it made up for the disturbed night she'd had, thanks to the first and second attack.

Humming to herself, Marguerite turned on the hot water to warm up the bathwater and then quickly finished her bath, shampooing and applying cream rinse to her hair before running a soapy washcloth over all the bits she'd missed earlier. She then got out, toweled off, dressed, and quickly dried her hair.

Marguerite didn't bother with makeup except to apply some lipstick. She then gathered her things together and carried them out to put them in her suitcase. She paused when it came to Tiny's robe, considering returning it to him so he could pack it with his things. After a moment, however, she decided she could return it to him when they got to the new hotel, and threw it in her suitcase as well. After a quick check to be sure she had everything, Marguerite zipped up the suitcase with some relief. She was oddly eager to finish and get out of the room. For some reason, being in there was now giving her the creeps.

Strange, she thought, *since she hadn't felt that way when she'd first returned to the room to collect things for her bath.* But right now, she felt as if someone was watching her.

Marguerite started to glance toward the curtained wall facing the terrace, but caught herself. She was suddenly sure there was someone there, peering through the small gap where the curtains didn't quite meet, and she didn't want them to know she knew.

Leaving the suitcase for now, she moved to the table and chairs set in front of one side of the terrace doors, but didn't sit. She bent and pretended to write a note on the hotel stationary, scribbling nonsense in the hopes of relaxing anyone who might be outside her balcony doors. Marguerite then straightened as if to head back the way she'd come, but instead, lunged for the curtain and jerked it open.

Even though she'd suspected someone might be out there, she still took a startled step back, a surprised shout slipping from her lips when she spotted the dark figure peering at her through the window.

Marguerite wasn't the only one startled. When the curtain was pulled back allowing light from the hotel room to spill over him, the figure on the terrace leapt back as if scalded. The action sent him bumping into a chair, knocking it over. He reached for it as if to straighten, but then whirled away to run to the right. Marguerite stared after him until the curtain still in place blocked her view, and then realized he was getting away and lunged for the terrace doors.

Four

"Marguerite?" Tiny's shout made her glance over her shoulder to see the mortal rush into the room, hard on the heels of the slightly swifter Christian, Marcus, and Julius.

"There was someone on the terrace," she explained. Marguerite had barely started to pull the door open when strong hands grabbed her by the upper arms and lifted her out of the way. It was Julius Notte she saw as he set her down out of the way.

"Stay with her," he barked.

Marguerite blinked in confusion at the order as he whirled to follow the other three men out onto the terrace. It was a shuffle of sound by the door that made her glance around to see Dante Notte and his twin Tommaso crossing the room toward her. Apparently she'd taken so long at her bath that all the men had packed and met in the living room to wait for her.

Marguerite didn't stay to ask, though; instead she hurried out onto the terrace after the others.

"There's no one here," Christian said as she joined them in the warm evening air.

Marguerite glanced around, ignoring the two mountains, Dante and Tommaso, as they caught up and stationed themselves on either side of her.

"Are you sure you didn't just see a shadow?" Julius asked quietly.

Marguerite clucked her tongue with irritation. Tiny had thought she'd imagined an attacker that morning until he'd seen the nick on her neck and blood on her collar. And now Julius was questioning what she'd seen as well. Honestly! Why was it men seemed to think all women were hysterical twits? Or was it just her?

"He knocked over that chair when I opened the curtain and startled him," she said impatiently, gesturing to the chair on its side. "I didn't imagine anything."

All five men glanced to the chair then, but it was Tiny who walked over and set it back on its legs. As he straightened from the task, he said, "This wasn't on its side when I came out here after Marguerite's attacker this morning."

The men immediately spread out, looking over the railing along the edge of the terrace as well as peering up toward the roof of the building in search of some sign of the man she'd seen or where he might have gone. Knowing they wouldn't find anything, Marguerite shook her head and moved back into her room. She was extremely annoyed that it had taken Tiny's saying that the chair hadn't been disturbed earlier for them to believe she'd seen someone. She wasn't the sort to imagine things.

Movements stiff and jerky, Marguerite collected her purse and slid it over her shoulder. She then wheeled her suitcase out into the living room, leaving it by the door to the hall with the other suitcases. It looked like everyone had packed up and brought their luggage with them when they'd come to meet in the sitting room of the suite she and Tiny shared. Obviously, she and Tiny weren't the only ones switching hotels, though she was hoping only Christian and the twins were coming and that Julius and Marcus had been convinced to go home and not interfere. Or to simply tell Christian who his mother was.

Wondering which it was, Marguerite walked to the refrigerator, opened it, and then scowled when she saw that all it held was food and alcohol. Mortal food and alcohol.

Her gaze slid to the small red cooler on the table, but she didn't bother to look inside. She'd finished off the last bag of blood in it just before they'd left for the long drive down to London. Marguerite had called Bastien before retiring the morning before they'd set out on the drive. She'd wanted to check on how her daughter, Lissianna, was doing as well as ask him to arrange for more blood to be sent to the hotel she'd be staying at. But, of course, it hadn't yet arrived. They'd arranged for it to be delivered around eight P.M. to be sure she was up and around. Marguerite had suspected she'd be so tired after the drive that she'd probably sleep late tonight. Of course, Julius had prevented that.

Glancing at her watch as she straightened, Marguerite grimaced when she saw that it was only a little after seven. The delivery would probably arrive right after they checked out, she thought gloomily. That just seemed to be the kind of day she was having.

"There you are."

Marguerite turned at those words to see Julius leading the rest of the men into the living room.

"Did you find anything?" she asked dryly, already suspecting she knew the answer. Marguerite wasn't surprised when he shook his head.

"Tiny mentioned earlier that the two of you decided to switch hotels today and I think it's a wise idea," Julius announced as he crossed the room toward her. "Marcus says Claridge's is a nice hotel, so I reserved rooms there for all of us."

"Us?" Marguerite asked, eyebrows rising.

Julius took in her expression and met her gaze as he said, "Us. I understand your concern, but I assure you I had nothing to do with either the attack on you this morning or the man skulking on the terrace just now."

Marguerite tried to slip into his mind to see if he spoke the truth. She would have tried to find out the name of Christian's mother at the same time, but she came up against a blank wall in his mind. She couldn't read the man. Marguerite wasn't terribly surprised. Her instincts had been telling her all along that he was much much older than herself.

Of course, her instincts might be wrong and her inability to read him could mean something else altogether. Were he a mortal, or an immortal but younger than she, the fact that she couldn't read him would have been a sign that he was her lifemate. But he wasn't mortal and reading immortals was a tricky business. She might not be able to read him, but it didn't mean he couldn't read and control her. And she wouldn't touch that with a ten foot pole. It looked like they would have to find Christian's mother the hard way.

Julius waited another moment, but when she didn't comment, he said, "Shall we go?"

Marguerite wanted to argue that she'd rather he stayed here while she and Tiny moved, but merely picked up her purse, slung it over her shoulder, and moved toward the door.

"Dante will take your luggage," Julius said quietly, taking her arm to stop her when she paused at the door and reached for the handle of her suitcase.

Marguerite stilled at his touch, her stomach giving a little jump. She took a deep breath to steady herself, then nodded and turned toward the door when he urged her that way. He held it open for her and walked her up the hall, leaving the others to follow.

They walked in silence, striding at a quick clip that came to a stumbling halt when Julius tried to steer her past the elevators and she dug in her heels.

"We will take the service elevator," he announced, urging her forward.

"Why?" she asked suspiciously as they continued up the hall.

"Because someone may be watching the lobby and it does little good moving from one hotel to another if we let them follow us to it," he explained patiently.

Marguerite's mouth tightened with irritation . . . at herself. She should have thought of that. She was supposed to be a detective. Of course, she could say she was a concert pianist, but that wouldn't give her the skill to be one. Perhaps she should have looked into P.I. training before taking on a case. *Is there a P.I. school?* she wondered.

"We have a car here," Tiny announced, distracting her.

"They probably know about that too and will be watching it as well," Julius said. "Who did you rent it from? I'll arrange to have it collected by the agency when we get to Claridge's."

While Tiny answered the question, Marguerite's eyes narrowed with displeasure at the thought of losing their transportation.

Catching the look, Julius ran what appeared to her to be a frustrated hand through his hair. She thought she must have been mistaken though when he calmly pointed out, "You can call another agency and rent another car."

Marguerite nodded and forced herself to relax as they reached the service elevator. They were inside and the doors were closing when Tiny asked, "What if they have someone watching the service entrance too?"

Julius frowned at the suggestion and began to drum his fingertips against his leg. She suspected it was an unconscious action he committed when thinking, because after a moment the drumming stopped and he said, "Give the keys of your rental to Dante. He and Tommaso can take the car out for a spin to hopefully lead anyone away and give us the chance to slip out the service entrance unnoticed."

Dante turned to Tiny expectantly, but it was Marguerite who handed him the keys, retrieving them from her purse.

"She rented a Jaguar," Tiny muttered, appearing embarrassed that she had been driving during this trip. "It was manual. I don't drive stick."

"I do," Dante said with a grin as he took the keys.

The grin died, however, when Julius announced, "You'll have to take the luggage with you. I want us all in one taxi and the luggage won't fit. Besides, if they happen to see you get in the car and spot the luggage, they'll assume you are moving us all to other accommodations while we could just simply be on a jaunt. Hopefully, it will make them follow you."

Dante and Tommaso groaned at the announcement, but didn't protest and simply began to relieve the others of their luggage.

"I want you to call us if you're followed once you leave the hotel," Julius added. "We'll wait here until we hear from you."

Dante nodded, and then glanced to the doors as the elevator slowed to a halt and the doors slid open. He and Tommaso disembarked first, taking the luggage with them. They were quite weighed down, and Marguerite peered after them with sympathy as they trudged off with their burden, heading for the parking garage.

"They will be fine," Julius said, urging her to move.

Marguerite nodded but remained silent as he walked them to the service entrance to await the call to let them know the twins had left in the car.

The men all began to pace as they waited: Julius, Tiny, Christian, and Marcus doing a small circuit before her. Marguerite simply leaned against the wall, absently tapping one toe as she watched Julius pace. He reminded her of a caged tiger.

They all stilled and looked to Julius when his phone finally rang. He slipped it from his pocket, flipped it open, listened briefly, and then said, "Get the license plate number and drive around for about ten minutes, then park back here and catch a taxi to Claridge's. Use the service exit when you leave."

"Were they followed?" Marguerite asked curiously.

"Yes, they were."

She nodded but didn't comment as they stepped outside.

Julius paused briefly, his gaze moving around the area and Marguerite found herself watching him again. His expression was grim, his eyes alert as he looked for any threat, and she knew without any doubt that he had once been a warrior of old. She could imagine him on horseback, hand on his sword, that very same expression creasing his face. He would have been formidable, she was sure.

"Wait here, I'll hire a taxi."

Marguerite blinked as Julius urged her to the side. While she had been gawking at him, he'd led them away from the service entrance. They were on the sidewalk, a little distance from the hotel and a line of taxis waited just ahead.

Irritated by her own fascination with him, she scowled and asked, "Do we really need a taxi? Surely, the hotel can't be more than ten minutes away on foot?"

They'd passed Claridge's on their way to the Dorchester that morning and she knew the hotels weren't far apart. It seemed silly to hire a taxi for such a short walk when it was a lovely night, the evening air retaining its warmth from the day.

"Ten minutes on foot, two by taxi," he acknowledged. "But the longer we're out here, the better the chance of being spotted and I'd prefer to avoid that." On that note he turned to walk to the first taxi in the line, Marcus on his heels.

"Father had nothing to do with the attack on you," Christian said, drawing her attention his way. "The first one I mean, when the man tried to cut off your head. Or the guy you spotted on the terrace," he added and then his lips twisted. "As for his dragging Tiny out of bed, that was just . . . a misunderstanding."

Marguerite raised her eyebrows at the younger immortal. It seemed important to him that she not think badly of his father and she had to wonder why he cared.

"Of course, I don't blame you for thinking that, if you did. Even I wasn't positive at first, but . . ." His eyebrows drew together and he shook his head. "My father doesn't do sneak attacks. He has too much honor. His first approach would have been a face-to-face meeting to try to threaten you into leaving. In fact, that was probably his original intent when he went looking for you in your room."

Marguerite nodded solemnly, accepting his words. She wasn't sure if she agreed, but she wasn't going to argue the point. "Why is he coming with us?"

"The attack upset him," Christian said with quiet assurance. "It's made him reconsider some things. I will explain everything at the new hotel, but the good news is, we can continue the investigation to find my mother without his interference. I know you'll succeed."

Marguerite wrinkled her nose. Obviously, Christian had more faith in her abilities than she did. Sighing, she admitted, "Christian, I'm not at all sure we can help you any more than your previous detectives . . . unless you know something more that might help us?"

He shook his head regretfully. "I've told you everything I know. I was born in England in 1491. That's it."

"That's all you think you know," Tiny said, joining the conversation. "You might be surprised at what else you know that might be useful." He let the man absorb that and then said, "We'll talk more when we get to Claridge's."

Christian nodded and then asked him curiously, "How did you end up in the detective business?"

Marguerite listened absently to the deep rumble of Tiny's voice as he responded. She already knew the answer to the question and found her attention drifting to where Julius leaned in the window of the first taxi in line, talking to the driver. Realizing that she was standing there staring at the curve of his perfect behind that his dress pants seemed to emphasize, Marguerite forced her gaze away and turned to the store window behind them, but it only displayed shoes, hardly very interesting.

Resisting the temptation to just peek back over her shoulder at Julius, she moved on to the next window instead. Marguerite's eyes brightened as they fell on a cute little outfit in the center of the next display. Leaving the quietly talking men, she moved closer to get a better look.

Marguerite had spent nearly seven hundred years of her life in nothing but dresses. For most of her life, women hadn't been allowed to wear anything but gowns and usually long ones. Of course, fashion had changed this last century. Women now wore pants all the time.

However, Marguerite hadn't yet. She tended to wear more modern dresses or skirt and blouse sets. Jean Claude had always insisted on that. Now that her husband was dead, she was considering changing that and had gone as far as trying on ladies' pants in dressing rooms, but everything she'd tried on felt restricting and uncomfortable in comparison to dresses. She was used to having her legs naked under a skirt, the evening breeze caressing them. She was not used to having them encased in a heavy material that made her feel like a sausage.

These pants, however, looked like they might be more comfortable. The legs were flared and she suspected would look very like a long black skirt when she wasn't moving. They shouldn't feel quite as restrictive as the more fitted jeans and dress pants she'd tried previous to this.

Marguerite nodded. She'd come by and try them on before she left England and—if they weren't too uncomfortable—she might even go so far as to buy them. Marguerite smiled faintly, knowing herself well enough to acknowledge that she was as slow at change as she was at getting started in the morning. Even if she bought a pair of pants, she probably wouldn't feel comfortable wearing them for a good year or so, at least not in public. Maybe she could wear them around the house at first, though, and—

"Marguerite!"

She whirled away from the window in surprise when Julius shouted her name. Marguerite saw the alarm on his face and turned to follow his gaze. Her own eyes widened as she saw the motorcycle roaring up the sidewalk, heading straight for her.

Marguerite instinctively plastered herself against the wall to get out of the way of the oncoming motorcycle. But she wasn't prepared when the passenger on the back of the bike shot his arm out, catching her purse as the motorcycle roared past.

The motorcycle immediately swerved back to the road. Julius leapt into the path of the bike, but they simply swerved, clipping him and sending him to the pavement as they shot up the street. Christian gave chase, but even an immortal couldn't outrun a motorcycle and he turned back after several car lengths to return to them.

"Are you all right?" Marguerite asked, hurrying to Julius's side as he got back to his feet.

"Yes," he muttered impatiently, brushing down the now dirty and torn pants of his expensive designer suit.

"I'm sorry, Marguerite. They got away from me," Christian said as he reached them.

"It doesn't matter. It's just a purse. I can replace everything," she said, waving the apology away and then glanced at Tiny. "I'll replace your phone too, Tiny."

"That's where it was," Tiny muttered. "I forgot you had it. I was going to call the office and check in while we were waiting for you to finish your bath and couldn't find my phone." He sighed and then shrugged. "Ah, well, at least you weren't hurt. Phones are replaceable and no one's going to panic if they don't get a call for a day or two."

Marguerite managed a guilty smile. She'd forgotten to charge her own phone the day before they'd left for London and had asked to borrow Tiny's mobile phone, intending to pay him back for the charge. But when she'd finished her call, she'd automatically dropped it in her purse.

"Do you think this was connected to the attacks?"

Marguerite glanced up as Christian asked the question and found him glancing up the street with worry.

When Julius merely shook his head to say he didn't know, Tiny commented, "I don't think so. They've had a rash of such purse snatches in London lately."

"They have?" Marguerite asked with surprise. "How do you know?"

"I watched the morning news show," he explained. "They had a big story on it. A woman was seriously injured yesterday when she was dragged behind the bike for a few feet before getting free of her purse strap. The police are supposed to be making catching these guys a priority."

"Just bad luck, then," Julius muttered, taking her arm and leading her toward the still waiting taxi. "You seem to be having a run of that."

"Or good luck," Marguerite countered. When he glanced at her in surprise, she shrugged. "Well, I woke up in time to avoid having my head cut off this morning, and I wasn't dragged by my purse strap just now. That seems more like good luck to me."

Julius smiled faintly at the words and seemed suddenly to relax as she stepped into the taxi.

Marguerite glanced around as she entered the vehicle. It was nothing like taxis in either Canada or America. Those were generally cars with a normal backseat. This vehicle had a high ceiling and seemed incredibly spacious with a wide cushioned bench seat at the back and, facing, two cushioned fold-down seats against the backing of the driver's front bench seat.

Marguerite bent at the waist, and actually walked to the backseat, settling herself in the far corner. Julius was immediately sitting beside her. She swallowed thickly as he squeezed up close to her side, then forced herself to watch Christian take the fold-down seat across from her. Marcus laid claim to the other, leaving Tiny to try to squeeze himself into what was left of the bench seat on the other side of Julius. It forced him to shift even closer to her. Marguerite took a deep breath to try to calm the sudden excitement leaping through her, and then let it quickly out as she found her nose filled with the spicy scent of his aftershave.

Not knowing what else to do, she turned her gaze out the window and tried to pretend she wasn't there. In truth, it was a good thing that the luggage wasn't there. The five of them *and* luggage would have been impossible, and she now understood why Julius had dumped it all on the twins.

As predicted the ride took all of two minutes, most of that due to traffic, and then they were spilling out onto the sidewalk in front of the hotel.

"Aren't you going to pay him?" Marguerite asked as Julius took her arm and urged her quickly into the lobby.

"I paid him quite handsomely just before your purse was snatched. Why do you think he waited for us?"

"Oh," Marguerite murmured, her gaze sliding over the elegantly cast lobby. Like the Dorchester, it was all rather magnificent and her gaze slid from the beautiful glass chandelier overhead, to the wide and beautiful staircase, and then to the black and white checkered marble floor at their feet.

"It's busy."

That comment from Marcus drew her attention away from the elegant surroundings and to the people lined up waiting to check in.

"There's no sense in all of us waiting," Christian pointed out. "Why don't the rest of you go on into The Foyer and relax while I check us in?"

"Someone has to wait here at the entrance for Dante and Tommaso," Julius said quietly.

"Marcus can do that," Christian volunteered. When the man nodded, his gaze then shifted to Tiny, and Marguerite got the strangest impression he was trying to think of a chore for him as well, but he was distracted when Julius held out a credit card.

"I booked the rooms on my card," Julius explained. "Make sure they give us at least three rooms with two single beds in each as I requested."

Nodding, Christian took the card and turned away.

"Shall we?" Julius asked, gesturing for Marguerite and Tiny to lead the way.

The Foyer was a restaurant on the main floor. Marguerite stopped at the entrance, her eyes wide as she peered over the glass room. The ceiling was a good eighteen feet high with a silver and glass chandelier at its center that could better be described as a piece of art. The restaurant was decorated in whites, clear glass, and muted silver, the tables all sporting a pale silver tablecloth and napkins. It was quite lovely and definitely a place where one was expected to arrive in the "proper attire."

Marguerite would be fine in the dark blue dress she'd put on after her bath, but—

"Maybe I'll just go keep Marcus company while he waits for Dante and Tommaso," Tiny muttered, glancing uncomfortably down at the T-shirt and blue jeans he wore.

"Oh, I'm sure it's all right," Marguerite began with alarm, but he was already abandoning her. She stared after him with dismay and then glanced to Julius when he took her arm.

"He'll rejoin us as soon as Dante and Tommaso get here. They shouldn't be long," he said reassuringly and urged her forward.

The maitre d' was there the moment they stepped through the door. He greeted them and arranged for a table that would fit all seven of them when the rest of the men joined them. In the meantime, it was just the two of them at the huge table and she wasn't surprised when Julius took the seat next to hers.

Marguerite accepted the menu the maitre d' handed her, relieved at the distraction. She opened it and spent the next few minutes pretending to read the offerings to avoid her table mate, but finally had to set it down or make it obvious that she was trying to avoid talking to the man.

The moment she set it on the table, the maitre d' was at her side.

"Just tea, please," she murmured, managing a smile.

Julius ordered coffee, then asked for a plate of sandwiches, and she couldn't hide her surprise.

"You eat?"

"It's a recent habit I've picked up again," he said calmly, and then asked, "You?"

Marguerite shook her head at once and assured herself she wasn't lying. The sausage she'd pinched that morning was an aberration, she was sure. An uncomfortable moment of silence passed. She tried to think of something to talk about to fill it, but the only thing that came to mind was the case she was working on. That made her pause and raise her eyes back to him again. Julius was peering around the restaurant, so Marguerite wasted another few moments trying to read his mind, but again came up against a blank wall.

Sighing unhappily, she turned her own attention to the restaurant décor as well.

"Jean Claude Argeneau was your husband and life-mate."

Marguerite turned back, eyeing him uncertainly. It hadn't exactly been phrased as a question, but she treated it as such and answered, "No."

"No?" Julius frowned. "'No' what? You *are* Jean Claude Argeneau's widow."

"Yes, I am," she admitted. "But we were not life-mates. Just husband and wife."

Julius sat back in his seat, his expression unreadable. After a moment, he said cautiously, "I have never heard of two immortals who were not lifemates marrying and living together . . . happily."

"Neither have I," she assured him.

"It was an unhappy union, then?" he asked quietly. Marguerite glanced away, her dissatisfied gaze sliding over the other patrons. She normally disliked talking about Jean Claude, her marriage, or anything having to do with the last seven hundred years of her life if it wasn't her children, but she found words she'd never said bubbling to her lips and trying to slip out. Keeping them in was actually causing a painful knot at the base of her throat. Finally, she blurted, "It was seven hundred years of hell."

Marguerite hesitated a moment and then finally glanced back to see how he was taking this revelation. His expression was unreadable. Mouth twisting wryly, she said, "You do not look surprised."

Julius shrugged. "As I said, I have never heard of two non-lifemates living together happily."

Marguerite nodded and glanced away from him again and then had a thought and glanced back. "Were you and Christian's mother lifemates?"

"Yes," he said solemnly.

"Oh." For some reason she found that news depressing, but forced her own feelings aside and said, "I realize it's very painful to lose a lifemate, and that it's probably difficult for you to talk about her, but Christian does have the right to know—"

"You've had a lifemate, then?"

Marguerite blinked at the interruption, thrown off her stride. Frowning, she admitted, "Well, no, but—"

"Never in seven hundred years?" he pressed.

Mouth tightening, she glanced away, muttering, "I fear, my life while married was rather . . . restricted."

A moment of silence passed and then he said, "You were born in England."

She glanced back with surprise. "Yes. I was born to a maid in a castle that was not far from London, actually."

"Was?" he asked with interest.

Marguerite shrugged. "It's gone now. Just rubble I should imagine."

"And is that where Jean Claude met you?"

She scowled. "I would really rather not talk about my life with Jean Claude. In fact, I do not wish to talk about myself at all. I am here in England to find your son's mother. You could help with that."

"I'm afraid I can't, actually. I suggest we agree not to talk about either subject. I will refrain from bringing up your husband, if you resist asking me about Christian's mother."

Marguerite was saved from having to respond by the arrival of a waiter. She found her gaze sliding over the plate of food with unaccustomed interest as he set it on the table. The small sandwiches looked and smelled delicious . . . and she didn't even eat. Though, she probably should, Marguerite thought suddenly. It would help her to build up her own blood until she was able to contact Bastien and ask him to forward the cooler of supplies on to her at Claridge's.

"Would you like one?" Julius asked, lifting the plate and holding it out to her as the waiter set his coffee on the table.

Marguerite raised a hand, about to reach for one of the sandwiches, but froze when she noticed the way he was watching her. Something about the expectant gleam in his eyes made her lower her hand and sit back in her seat.

"I do not eat," she repeated her earlier words. The

sausage really didn't count. Normally, she didn't eat. In fact, she couldn't recall the last time she had before the stolen sausage that morning. But then she couldn't remember the last time she'd been without blood for this long either and suspected her hunger was getting confused.

Marguerite watched silently as he picked up one of the sandwiches and took a bite. Her mouth immediately began to water, and she thought perhaps she'd call down to room service when she got to her room and order something small . . . a sandwich maybe, to tide her over until the blood arrived.

"They're really quite good," Julius said. "You should try one."

"I—No, I really do not eat," Marguerite said stubbornly.

"We have lovely teacakes, if you'd rather something sweet," the waiter said as he set a small teapot and cup before her.

"No, thank you," Marguerite murmured.

Nodding, the waiter turned to leave, but paused as he found himself facing a newly arrived Dante and Tommaso. Marguerite had to bite her lip as the waiter's eyes widened on the pair. Truly, the twins were an awesome sight. Side by side they were a wall of black leather and threat, without even trying.

"Er . . ." the waiter said, his eyes shifting frantically from the pair to the table.

"They are with us," Marguerite assured him, taking pity on the man.

Nodding, he moved swiftly to the side to make way for them, and then nervously backed away.

Marguerite shook her head as she watched him go,

and then turned an affectionate smile on the twins. She'd got to know them well in California when they were all staying at her nephew's home and had been glad to see them when they'd met with Christian at the Dorchester and found they'd accompanied him. The pair looked frightful, but really they were sweethearts. They were still quite young, barely over a hundred years old, and still ate . . . a lot. The only person she knew who came close to being able to put away as much as these two were Tiny and her own son Lucern.

"Where are the others?" Julius asked.

"There's a pub on the other side and they're waiting for us there," Tommaso answered, eyeing Julius's sandwiches.

"Tiny warned us that The Foyer was fancy dress," Dante added as Julius noted the hungry looks both men were giving his food and lifted the plate to offer it to them. Both twins took a small sandwich each as Dante added, "We just came to report in."

Julius nodded. As he set the plate back on the table, he asked, "You managed to lose your tail?"

Tommaso nodded as Dante stuck his sandwich in his mouth to free his hands. He pulled a small notepad from his pocket and tore off a page. He then held it out and took the sandwich out of his mouth with his other hand, saying, "This is their license plate number. I think it was a rental, but you might be able to find out who rented it."

Nodding, Julius accepted the slip of paper and slid it into his suit pocket, making Marguerite frown. She and Tiny were the private detectives. Holding out her hand, she said, "I'll look into that if you give it to me."

Julius shook his head. "I have it. You already have a job."

Marguerite narrowed her eyes. He didn't sound the least angry as he mentioned the case to find his son's mother. Considering how long he'd kept the secret and the fact that he'd come here to try to convince them to head home, he was being rather pleasant. It just made her suspicious.

"These are good," Tommaso commented.

Marguerite glanced his way in time to see him pop the last of his sandwich into his mouth. Her gaze then moved back to the plate, noting that there was only one left. She forced herself to look away from the temptation.

"Christian said to give you two these," Dante said and handed a card key to Marguerite and another to Julius, listing off the room numbers as he did.

"We already delivered the luggage to the rooms," Tommaso added, accepting the last sandwich when Julius held out the plate.

Marguerite watched enviously as he consumed half of it in one bite, and then couldn't stand it any longer and stood up.

"I would like to go to my room."

"Of course," Julius said, getting smoothly to his feet. "I shall see you up."

"No, no," Marguerite waved him off, eager to get to her room now. "I know the room number. I can find it. You go ahead and join the boys in the pub. I'm sure Dante and Tommaso have more to report."

She turned, then, to walk away, but paused when he said, "We're sharing a suite."

Turning back, she raised an eyebrow.

"I arranged for two suites next to each other," he explained. "I thought the boys could take the two bedrooms of one suite, and Marcus and I will share one bedroom in the second suite, while you take the other."

Julius looked as if he expected her to be upset by this news, but she wasn't. The fact was she had her own room, and she *was* the only one with her own room. And she really wanted to get up there and order something to eat.

"Fine," she said quickly and glanced to Tommaso and Dante. "I'd like an hour to unpack and rest a bit, but could you ask Tiny and Christian to meet me after that so we can discuss matters?"

She waited for both men to nod, and then left the table to find her room.

Five

Marguerite let herself into the room using the key Julius had given her, and then paused inside the door to peer around. She'd entered the suite through the door leading into the actual bedroom she would be using, but there were two open doors leading off of it. One led into the en suite bathroom, the other led into the sitting room between the bedroom she occupied and the one Marcus and Julius were to share. It was nice, but all art deco and she'd actually preferred the décor in the Dorchester.

Closing the door between her room and the sitting room, she picked up the book listing the hotel's available facilities and leafed through until she found the room service menu. She scanned it briefly, then moved to the phone and quickly punched the button for room service. Her gaze slid around the room as she waited, and Marguerite wasn't at all surprised to find her luggage there. Dante and Tommaso had seen to it as efficiently as expected, no doubt leaving it at the desk when they'd arrived, to be delivered to all of their rooms while they went to the restaurant.

Marguerite straightened as her call was answered and placed her order, requesting that it come directly to her door, not the sitting room door, then hung up and stood to walk to the window. Tugging the curtains open, she peered out on the city at night, noting that while her room had a balcony, they weren't on the top floor. She suspected Julius had arranged it that way to increase safety, bypassing the penthouses on the top floor for superior suites on the fourth floor, halfway up the hotel, overlooking Brooks Mews. The man was obviously used to handling matters and was good with details . . . like her son Bastien.

The thought made her turn and move to the phone again. She had to call him and have the blood forwarded to her new hotel. She also wanted to check on her daughter. Lissianna was in the last weeks of her first pregnancy. She could go into labor at any time and Marguerite was almost as excited and nervous for her daughter as Lissianna no doubt was herself.

Before leaving for England, Marguerite had made each of her sons, nieces, and nephews promise to contact her the moment her daughter went into labor. If that happened before she finished this case, Marguerite would drop everything and fly home at once. Christian had waited five hundred years to find his mother and surely wouldn't mind a delay of a week or so if necessary. She hoped. It was a shame if he did mind because nothing was going to keep her from her daughter's side in her time of need.

The phone had barely begun to ring when Marguerite noticed the digital clock on the bedside table and saw the time. It wasn't even nine o'clock at night yet here in England, which meant it wasn't even four o'clock in the afternoon back home. Bastien would still be in bed, she realized, and quickly hung up, hoping that the half ring hadn't roused him. She'd just have to wait another couple of hours and then try again, Marguerite thought with a little sigh, but then wondered if she couldn't call the UK office of Argeneau Enterprises herself to arrange for the blood to be brought here. Bastien had given her a contact number for the UK offices just in case something like this arose.

The number was in her address book in her purse. She just had to—

Marguerite's thoughts died abruptly when a knock sounded at the door. Standing, she crossed to the door and pulled it open, a smile curving her lips at the sight of the attendant with the food trolley standing outside her door.

There were three shiny silver covers on her trolley. One hid a bowl of pea and mint soup, another covered a plate holding salad and a steak cooked rare, the third protected an English trifle. Admittedly, it was more than a light snack, but Marguerite hadn't been able to make up her mind about what she wanted. Besides, she didn't plan to eat it all, she assured herself. Just a little of this, a little of that . . .

Half an hour later Marguerite had pretty much laid

waste to the food and was just finishing off the luscious trifle when someone knocked at her door. Stiffening, she glanced guiltily at the table of food, then set down her trifle and moved warily to answer the door. She relaxed a little when she saw it was Tiny and stepped back, pulling the door wide for him to enter.

"Hi." Tiny grinned as he stepped into the room. "Christian should be here soon, we—" He paused abruptly, eyes widening incredulously as he spotted the food trolley across the room. Shock on his face, he said with confusion, "You're eating. You don't eat."

Marguerite sighed and urged him out of the way so she could close the door. The whole hotel didn't need to hear this. Sheesh!

"Sit down," she ordered as she moved back to the table.

"Marguerite. You don't eat. The whole time I've been with you, first in California and then the three weeks here, you do not eat. What is going on?" He paused before her, his eyes suddenly widening. "You've met your lifemate!"

"Don't be ridiculous," Marguerite snapped and gave him a push to make him sit down when he continued to loom over her. She scowled at him briefly for even making such an indecent suggestion. Met her lifemate? Never! She'd been married once and while Jean Claude hadn't been a true lifemate, he'd certainly been an excellent teacher and Marguerite had learned her lesson well. She would never willingly marry again. Even if she met a proper lifemate, she was sure she wouldn't ever allow a man to have power over her again.

"Well, then why are you eating?" he asked, eyes narrowed with suspicion.

"I ran out of blood before we left Berwick-upon-Tweed yesterday," she reminded him grimly.

Tiny frowned. "You said you'd called Bastien to arrange to have some sent to the hotel?"

"We left before it arrived," she murmured and then shrugged at his concerned expression. "I will be fine. I was going to call Bastien to arrange to have it sent on, but it's still daylight back home and I didn't want to disturb him if he was still sleeping. Then I was going to call the London office of Argeneau Enterprises myself, but room service arrived and I got distracted."

"Call now," he urged.

Nodding, Marguerite stood and moved to the phone, then realized she needed her address book and turned to glance around the room.

"What are you looking for?" Tiny asked.

"My address book, I put the contact number Bastien gave me in it. It's in my—" Marguerite paused as she recalled that her purse had been stolen. Her gaze met Tiny's with alarm. "My address book was in my purse. So was my cell phone with all the children's numbers programmed in it."

Tiny frowned. "Don't you know their numbers by heart?"

"Yes . . . No . . . Damn," she breathed with frustration. "I know Bastien and Etienne's numbers, but Lissianna's just moved to a new house because of the baby and I haven't got her's memorized yet. I know Lucern's home phone number, but I've never bothered to learn his mobile number and he's off traveling with Kate."

"Well, don't worry. Bastien can give you the numbers when you call him," Tiny said soothingly.

"Yes, of course, you're right," Marguerite said glancing at the clock. It was nearly ten. Five o'clock in the afternoon. Still too early. "I'll try to call around midnight," she decided. "And I'll ask if he'd mind canceling my credit cards too and arranging for new ones to be sent out to me."

"Hmm." Tiny nodded. "Makes more sense than trying to do it yourself from here. Probably faster in the end too. Bastien is a whiz with these things."

Marguerite smiled, recalling that the Morrisey Detective Agency had been doing work for Bastien for years. Tiny's partner, Jackie Morrisey, was her nephew's lifemate, and it had been her father who had founded the detective agency they both worked for. Argeneau Enterprises had been one of her father's first customers. Jackie ran the show now with Tiny as her right-hand man and continued to do jobs for Bastien.

"That'll be Christian," Tiny said, getting to his feet when another knock sounded at the door.

He let the other man in and led him back to the table and chairs where Marguerite sat.

The younger immortal greeted her with a smile and then eyed the food trolley and sent a grin Tiny's way. "So this is why you left us all early. It wasn't to come up and unpack at all, you wanted to try room service." He gave a laugh. "I can't believe you're still eating. You're as bad as Dante and Tommaso."

Tiny glanced toward Marguerite, but when she sent him a pleading look, he kept her secret and merely rolled the trolley out of the way to the side of the room.

"I've been racking my brain trying to think of anything I might know that would help the two of you with the search, but haven't come up with anything specific. At least, no actual clues," Christian said as he pulled the chair from the makeup counter to the table. "However, as I mentioned earlier, Father and I had a talk. The attack on you upset him . . . enough that he's unbent a bit about this business."

"Has he told you who your mother is?" Tiny asked with interest.

"He hasn't unbent that far," Christian said with a wry smile.

"Then what?" Marguerite asked curiously.

Christian hesitated, and then said, "He told me a little more about my mother . . . she tried to kill me when I was born."

"Jesus Christ," Tiny breathed.

Marguerite was silent, but purely out of horror. She had four children herself and could not imagine doing anything so heinous as trying to kill one of them at birth. Dear God, children were so small and defenseless, so sweet and beautiful. . . . How could anyone kill a child? Why would they even want to? What possible offense could a child be guilty of to deserve to have its head hacked off in the first moments of its life?

"I suppose he told you that hoping to end your desire to find her?" Tiny said grimly.

"It was actually Marcus who said it. Of course, those two are thick as thieves, so it may be by Father's design, but . . ." He shrugged.

"So your father has kept the secret of who your mother was all these years because he wanted to protect you from finding out that she tried to kill you?" Marguerite asked quietly, the man going up several notches in her opinion.

Christian nodded.

"What will he do now that he knows you still want to find her?" Tiny asked.

"Nothing," Christian assured him. "At least, nothing to try to stop or interfere anymore. I think he's come to realize that he just has to let me do this."

Marguerite reached out and covered one of his hands with hers, squeezing sympathetically as she saw the welter of emotion in his eyes. She couldn't imagine any mother not wanting him for a son. He was handsome, strong, intelligent, and quite charming when he wasn't growling and grim. Christian had a tendency toward being more dour. She'd noticed that in California, but—having met his father—she now understood where the tendency came from. Julius Notte was as cold and grumbly as her brother-in-law Lucian Argeneau. She supposed it was a common characteristic among the older immortals. So much time had passed and they had witnessed so much, a lot of it unpleasant. The unpleasant could eventually seem to outweigh the good, especially without a true lifemate to help weigh down the good side of life.

"Are you sure you still want to pursue this?" Marguerite asked quietly as she realized that there may simply be no chance for a happy ending here. If the mother had wanted to be rid of him so badly she'd wished him dead, she wasn't likely to welcome him with open arms. And, even if she'd had a change of heart and did open her arms to him, could Christian really forgive her abandonment and murderous intent?

"I don't need to have a relationship with my mother," Christian said. "I won't force myself on someone who doesn't want me, but I need to know. Just knowing who she is and where I get some of my traits that aren't my father's would be enough."

Marguerite squeezed his hand and nodded in understanding. "So we will continue the search."

"And you're sure your father won't continue to try to stop us and convince us to go home?" Tiny asked warily.

"Yes, I'm sure," Christian said with certainty. "In fact, he's decided to help in a way. He intends to stay with us. He wants to be on hand to ensure none of us is harmed and to be there for moral support should we find her."

"I'm surprised," Marguerite admitted.

Christian shrugged. "The violence of the attack on you surprised him. It was an all-out murder attempt rather than just an act of violence to warn us off. I don't think he expected such a violent reaction after so many years. He's decided that since you are the target, he'd best stay close to you."

"He thinks it was your mother again?" Tiny asked, trying to understand.

"One of her people, I think," Christian said.

"But he definitely thinks it was an attempt to put an end to the investigation?" Tiny asked.

"Yes," Christian admitted and then glanced to Marguerite and added, "which makes me wonder."

"What?" she asked curiously.

"Well, I've hired other detectives before and nothing like this has happened. Of course, Father sent them packing pretty quick, but . . ." He tilted his head. "Why you? Why not Tiny?"

Marguerite's eyes widened at the question. Why indeed, she wondered.

"It made me wonder if perhaps you might have known my mother, or might at least have a better chance of finding her."

Tiny shook his head at once. "I considered that at the start, Christian, but Marguerite's marriage—"

When he paused and glanced apologetically her way for nearly spilling a confidence, she shook her head at him, and then took a moment to phrase her words carefully before admitting, "I fear I had little social life throughout most of my marriage. I visited occasionally with family members; Lucian, Martine, Victor, and so on, but, other than that, I knew few of our kind except through the gossip Martine or the others shared."

"So Martine and the others *did* know more immortals?" Christian asked.

"Yes." Marguerite glanced to Tiny with surprise when he cursed.

"I should have thought of it," he muttered apologetically to Christian, and then explained to Marguerite, "This may be why *you* were the target. *You* may not know Christian's mother, but Martine or one of the other members of your family might."

Her eyes widened with realization. That hadn't occurred to her either, but . . .

"You could be right," she said, a slow smile spreading her lips. "In fact, you probably are. Martine knows everyone. Literally. She's a member of the council over here. She's a member of the council in North America too. She is our best bet."

Marguerite gave a delighted laugh at this first bit of hope they'd had for solving this case, and then her eyes widened with realization. "This means I can see her and the girls while here after all, and without having to play hooky from work. I was very sorry to miss them when we were in York."

Tiny frowned at her words. "You could have taken the time to visit them, Marguerite. I wouldn't have protested."

"Oh, they weren't in town at the time. Martine had taken the girls to Spain for a vacation before school started up again. The girls are both in university now," she added and then shook her head and sighed. "It seems like just yesterday that they were a pair of giggling teens at Lissianna's birthday. Time passes so quickly."

"More quickly for some than others," Tiny said dryly and then added, "I guess if we wish to speak to this Martine, it means a return trip to York."

"Yes." Marguerite smiled at the very idea. "Perhaps this time you'll get more of a chance to look around."

Tiny had been enthralled by the city with its roman walls, medieval buildings, and cobbled streets and snickleways, but hadn't let it distract him the last time they had been in the city. This time she thought he should take the time to tour around and see the city. After all, she didn't need him along to talk to Martine. She could manage that herself.

Julius glanced up from the cards in his hand at the sound of the door opening. He and the others had been waiting for well over an hour in Christian's room while he went to talk to Marguerite and Tiny and put their plan into play. It was Dante who had suggested a game of cards to pass the time. Julius suspected the younger man had known he'd be distracted and therefore an easy target. They were playing poker for money, and Dante and Tommaso were taking turns raking in his sterling. At this rate he'd have to find an ATM and withdraw more British currency, or he'd have only Euros and debit and credit cards to work with.

"So?" he asked, setting his cards down as Christian reentered the room. "What happened? How did it go?"

"It went well, I think," Christian said as the door closed behind him. "They both seemed to accept what I said without suspicion. And Marguerite definitely doesn't seem to think you're as much of an ass now as she did before. She believes you've been protecting me and intend to continue to do so."

"Of course I was protecting you," Julius growled. "Did you think I put up with your constant harassment as you tried to wheedle the information out of me for my own good?"

"I do not wheedle," he said in a growl.

"Hmm," Julius said dubiously.

When Christian merely scowled at him, Julius said,

"So what are the plans now? Do they have any idea what they intend to do next?"

Christian nodded. "We discussed our next move. Tiny and Marguerite think it would be beneficial to talk to people who may have been around at the time of my birth. So, they're planning to talk to her husband's sister."

"Martine," Julius said with a sigh.

"How did you know?" Christian asked, eyebrows rising.

"She is the only sister. Everyone knows that. The Argeneaus had all boys and one daughter, like my parents had all girls but me," he said absently, his mind on Martine and what information Marguerite might gain from her.

"Hmm," Christian said, but then shrugged and added, "we're heading to York tomorrow night. But in the meantime, since there's nothing to do on the investigation here, we decided we should have a night out, visit the clubs maybe, go dancing."

"Go out?" Julius glanced up sharply. "Are you mad? Someone is trying to kill Marguerite. It isn't safe for her to go out. No. We are staying here."

Six

Marguerite tapped her foot restlessly to the loud and lively music, her gaze moving enviously over the people having a good time on the dance floor. She'd thought that a night off after three weeks of slogging through archives would be a welcome and relaxing change. She'd thought wrong. It was boring as hell and she placed the blame squarely on the men surrounding her.

Her irritable glance slid over Tiny and the five immortals with displeasure.

Since none of them were familiar with London, they hadn't known where to go to find the immortal night club they knew must be somewhere in the city. They'd been forced to resort to the mortal clubs. After half an hour and one club, Marguerite was ready to call it a night.

Her eyes moved over the men again, a little unhappy sigh sliding from her lips. Marguerite hadn't, at first, been uncomfortable or upset to find herself a lone female with six good-looking men. No, she'd thought it would be fun. Ha! Had she got that wrong. Truly, she'd never met such a group of stick-in-the-muds in her life. The music was too loud to allow talking, which would have been fine but when Marguerite had announced a desire to dance and headed out on the dance floor, she'd found herself enclosed in a circle as the men surrounded her. Even that wouldn't have bothered her had they danced, but they hadn't. Instead they'd stood facing into the circle, arms crossed as they watched *her* dance . . . including Tiny. They had been a living breathing wall of men watching her with grim determination.

Marguerite had lasted perhaps two minutes on the dance floor before self-consciousness had made her give up and head back to the table with exasperation. Since then she'd simply sat tapping her foot restlessly to the music, wishing she could join the dancers, but knowing it would just be a repeat of the protective circle scenario.

Marguerite gave another unhappy little sigh, and then glanced to Julius when he touched her arm. She watched his lips move, but even with an immortal's extra-sensitive hearing, she couldn't hear his words over the music blaring at them.

Seeming to realize the problem, Julius made a gesture with his hand, and then pointed them toward the door. Apparently he had noticed her boredom and was asking if she wanted to leave, she realized with relief and nodded at once. When she and Julius stood, the other men immediately followed suit and moved to form a circle around them as they moved toward the exit.

With the wall of men around her, the only way Marguerite knew they'd left the club was because the music was abruptly cut off and the temperature had risen from the cooler air-conditioned interior of the club to the warmer evening air. Julius urged them all several feet to the side of the entrance before coming to a halt. Marguerite immediately turned to tell him she thought they may as well give up on the idea of a relaxing night out and return to the hotel, but paused when he pulled out his cell phone and began to push buttons.

Closing her mouth, she moved a few feet away to give him privacy for the call, scowling at the others when the five of them also left Julius behind and moved with her, retaining their protective circle.

They were worse than her sons, Marguerite decided and turned to Julius with relief when he'd finished his call and rejoined them.

He moved through the circle of men to her side to announce, "I called Vita, and she told me where the immortal night club is."

"Vita is our aunt," Dante informed her.

"She's always spent a lot of time in England," Tommaso added. "If anyone would know, she's the one."

Marguerite nodded, recalling the name of the woman running the family business while Julius and Marcus were away. Her eyes followed Julius as he slipped away to approach a line of taxis parked a bit up the road as she murmured, "I'm surprised you haven't been here before and didn't know yourselves."

Dante shrugged. "We've never had any call to come to England until now."

"And we'd hardly come for pleasure. It's supposed to rain a lot here," Thomas added with a shudder.

"Julius didn't encourage them to visit England," Marcus explained.

"Hmm." Christian nodded. "I never really considered his hatred of the country as important until I found out it was where I was born."

They were all silent for a moment, then Dante asked curiously, "You were born and raised here, weren't you, Marguerite? I'm surprised you don't know where one is."

Marguerite smiled faintly. "We moved out several centuries ago and never returned. Jean Claude didn't much like England either. He thought it was too damp, too gray, and too boring." She shrugged. "As far as I know they didn't have immortal night clubs back then. Although my niece and her friend Mirabeau have mentioned an immortal night club in London, but as I didn't expect to have the time to go to one, I didn't ask for the address."

A sharp whistle made them glance along the sidewalk to see Julius holding open the door of a taxi and waving them over.

"I hired these first two taxis," Julius announced as they approached. "We'll split up, three in one, four in the other. Marguerite you're with me in this one. The rest of you pick your ride."

Marguerite managed not to scowl at the command. After all, Christian had already warned her that his father intended to stay close to her so long as she was on this case and under threat. She should really be grateful he was looking out for her, she supposed, but found that after seven hundred years of Jean Claude's less than dazzling attention, it felt uncomfortable to be looked after. Still, she managed to force a thank-you as Julius handed her into the cab. She settled on the bench seat and soon found Julius joining her. Tiny and Christian took the fold-down seats, leaving Marcus to join the twins in the second taxi.

The moment the taxi pulled out onto the road, Marguerite turned her head to peer out the window. However, rather than watch the passing buildings and traffic as she'd intended, she found herself instead fascinated by watching the reflection in the glass of the men in the cab. Christian was making odd faces and gestures at his father that she thought were about her, though she couldn't fathom what he was trying to tell him. Apparently, Julius couldn't tell either, he was staring at the younger man with a blank expression. Tiny was watching the whole thing with an obvious curiosity the two immortals didn't notice.

Marguerite was distracted from the pantomime when the taxi pulled to the curb and stopped. Glancing around, she saw that they were in front of what appeared to be a private residence. There were no signs to advertise the address as anything other than just another townhouse squeezed between two others.

Marguerite stepped out of the taxi to find the men once again crowding around her and sighed with exasperation. "I should be safe enough here."

"It was an immortal who attacked you, Marguerite," Julius pointed out. "If anything, we will have to be more vigilant here, and then careful that we are not followed on the way back. You were probably safer at the mortal club."

She glanced at him curiously. "Then why did you bring us here?"

"Because you were not having a good time," he said simply and urged her toward the entrance ahead of them.

Marguerite moved forward under his urging, her mind distracted with what he'd said. Despite the fact that the men would have to be more vigilant and remain on the alert, he'd brought her here because she hadn't been having a good time and he—presumably—thought she might enjoy herself more here. Her mind was having trouble accepting the claim, her thoughts running around in confusion looking for the motive behind the seeming kindness. Her husband, Jean Claude had never done anything nice without a motive behind it, or something he wished to gain from it.

They reached the door and it was promptly opened by a man even taller than any of the ones accompanying her. It wasn't his height or size that caught and held her attention, however, but the twelve-inch green Mohawk he sported on his head and the dozens of piercings in his face. The man was a living porcupine of silver and green.

"This is a private club," he growled.

Marguerite could feel Julius bristling beside her, but before he could say anything, a soft chuckle slid from her lips. When the Mohawk man turned his scowl on her, she grinned and shook her head. "I'm sorry. I've just realized you must be G.G. Mirabeau was telling me about you."

His scowl immediately disappeared, rolled under by

the waves of a wide smile. "You know Mirabeau?"

"She's a dear friend to my daughter, and niece and nephew," Marguerite said with a nod.

His eyes narrowed on her speculatively, and then he asked, "Marguerite?"

She nodded, eyes widening when he suddenly let loose a loud roar and grabbed her up in a bear hug that lifted her off the ground.

"Welcome!" he roared jovially as he set her back on the ground. He then drew her arm through his in an almost courtly fashion and turned toward the door. "Mirabeau and Jeanne Louise were here just a couple weeks ago."

"Yes, I know. That's how you came up in topic. The girls were at my home to have lunch with me and my daughter and began talking about the trip. Jeanne Louise didn't want to bother including England in the excursion, but Mirabeau was insisting she had to bring her to meet you," she explained, glancing over her shoulder to see that the men were hard on her heels with varying expressions ranging from Tiny's amusement to Julius's disgruntled look.

"I'm worth the trip," G.G. announced, drawing her gaze back around as he led her up a long hall. "Jeanne Louise had a good time here."

"I'm sure she did." Marguerite patted his tattooed arm.

"And you will have a good time too," G.G. assured her. "I will be at the door if you need me, but whatever it is you want is yours. You just tell them G.G. says so."

"That is sweet, thank you, G.G.," she said, touched at his kindness.

The man shook his head. "Mirabeau and Jeanne Louise think the world of you, and so, then, do I."

Marguerite squeezed his arm gently, and then settled in the seat he stopped before when he waved her to it.

"I'll send a girl over to get your orders. The first round is on me," he announced and moved away as the men quickly filled up the seats around her.

"G.G.?" Christian asked as soon as the man was out of hearing.

"Short for Green Giant because of his green Mohawk," she explained with a grin.

"It is hard to believe they would hire someone who looked like that to work here," Dante said, shaking his head with amazement as he peered around the quiet room where G.G. had settled them. Marguerite glanced around now too, taking in the soothing atmosphere of the room they were in. There was a Victorian fireplace along one wall, large comfy leather chairs and sofas arranged in groupings, as well as hardwood floors with various throw rugs strewn around.

"From what Mirabeau said, there are other, less soothing rooms here," she informed them as she turned back to face the others, and then added, "and he doesn't work here, he owns it."

"What?" Julius asked with shock. "A mortal owning and running an immortal night club?"

"That guy is mortal?" Tiny asked with surprise.

Tommaso nodded. "The tattoos and piercings should have tipped you off. Our bodies will not accept either.

"Oh right, I suppose the nanos would see them as foreign bodies or something and shed them."

"How did a mortal come to own an immortal night

club?" Julius asked, still having trouble accepting it.

"More importantly, why the heck is he guarding the door?" Tiny asked dryly, and then pointed out, "If he tries to turn away the wrong immortal, they might turn him into cream cheese or at least lunch."

"According to Mirabeau he has back-up if he needs it," Marguerite told them, and then she explained what she knew. "Apparently his mother was mortal and he is from a mortal marriage, but when that dissolved she found she was a lifemate to an immortal. She wanted G.G. to be turned, but he refused, so his new stepfather financed this club for him in the hopes that if he was constantly surrounded by immortal women day in and day out, he would meet an immortal who would be his true lifemate and change his mind, thus making his wife happy."

"Hmm." Julius sat back and then glanced at Christian. "Perhaps I should finance a club like this for you in Italy. Then you would find a lifemate and start giving me grandbabies."

"Why don't you concentrate on getting your own lifemate first," Christian suggested meaningfully.

Marguerite frowned as more of the pantomime from the taxi followed. It was a wiggling of eyebrows and jerking of eyes in her direction that really looked quite unattractive. Leaning forward with concern, she asked, "Are you feeling quite well, Christian? You seem to be having spasms."

Dante and Tommaso burst out laughing, but Christian just sighed and stood up. "Father, I have to go to the bathroom."

Julius glanced at him with surprise, and then

peered around, pointing when he saw a sign that said "gents." "Oh, there it is there, son."

"Yes, I know. I saw the sign," Christian said with exasperation. "I thought perhaps you might have to go too."

"No, I—Oh! Yes. I'll just . . ." Julius stood and began to squeeze through the small space left between her chair and his. When he saw Marguerite peering at him with raised eyebrows, he muttered, "I have to . . ." He waved vaguely and then hurried off with Christian without finishing saying what he had to do.

Marguerite watched the men go, noting that Christian appeared to be lecturing Julius as they went, then turned back to see that Dante and Tommaso were trying desperately not to laugh, Marcus was shaking his head with apparent despair, and Tiny was looking thoughtful.

Leaning closer to Tiny who sat beside her on the opposite side from the chair Julius had occupied, she asked quietly, "Do you have any idea what is going on?"

Tiny hesitated, and then murmured, "If they were mortals, I would say that Christian is trying to get you and his father together. But since they are immortals . . ." He glanced in the direction the two men had gone, then back to her to ask, "Have you tried to read Julius?"

Marguerite stilled in her seat, wariness creeping through her. She had, but suddenly didn't think she wanted to admit that.

"You have, haven't you?" Tiny asked. His eyes narrowed on her face and he guessed, "And you don't want to admit it because you couldn't read him."

Marguerite blew out an irritated breath and glanced away.

"And you're eating."

She stiffened, and scowled. "That doesn't mean anything. I told you, I'm out of blood and it helps build my own. Besides I've been sitting with you at each meal for three weeks, I have probably just picked up the habit."

"You didn't eat in California when we all did," he pointed out.

Marguerite blinked at his words, then sank weakly back in her seat. For a moment horror overcame her, but then she rallied and—positive he didn't know about the sausage—lied shakily, "It was just one meal, Tiny."

"One meal *and* you can't read him," Tiny pointed out.

Marguerite waved that away as unimportant. "He's obviously older than me. It's difficult to read immortals older than oneself. And," she added grimly as he opened his mouth to speak, "Just because *I* can't read him, doesn't mean *he* can't read me."

Tiny closed his mouth on whatever he'd been about to say at that comment. He knew about her relationship with Jean Claude. Nodding in understanding, he let the subject go and sank back in his seat.

Marguerite bit her lip and was silent for a moment, her gaze sliding toward the men's room, and then she leaned toward Tiny and whispered, "If it turns out you're right—about Christian encouraging Julius, I mean—could you . . . er . . . run intervention."

"You mean interference?" he suggested dryly.

Marguerite nodded. "I would appreciate it."

Tiny nodded.

"Thank you," she murmured.

"Don't thank me. We work together, and you're really in training. It's kind of my job to look out for you."

Marguerite blinked at the words as she realized how ridiculous it was for her to even put him in that position. The truth was he couldn't possibly look out for her against an immortal like Julius. Of course, she didn't hurt his pride by saying as much, simply sinking back in her seat and forcing a smile as a waitress appeared to take their orders.

"What are you doing?"

"What do you mean?" Julius leaned against the counter in the men's room, his eyebrows drawing together as he watched Christian check the stalls to be sure the room was empty.

Finished with his search, Christian paused and propped his hands on his hips, looking for all the world like a parent confronting a naughty child. "I mean what are you *doing*?" Christian repeated with exasperation. "You're supposed to be wooing Marguerite. Getting her to like and trust you so she won't run when she realizes the two of you are lifemates."

"I *am* wooing her," Julius said defensively, turning away to peer in the mirror. He didn't really see himself, he was just trying to avoid having to meet his son's gaze anymore, but ran a hand through his hair as he watched his son's reflection.

"You aren't wooing her. You're staring at her. You've been staring at her all night. You should have danced with her when we were at that mortal club."

"Danced?" Julius asked with horror.

"Yes. *Danced*. Why did you think I was elbowing you on the dance floor? Jesus!" He turned away with disgust and paced the length of the stalls and back.

"I *don't* dance," Julius said with dignity. "At least not the kind of dancing that was happening there. Marguerite dances well, though, doesn't she?" he added with a small smile as he recalled the few moments she'd danced before throwing her hands up with exasperation and returning to their table. She'd been incredibly agile, her hips swaying, body undulating, and breasts jiggling as she'd—

Julius blinked and scowled at Christian when he snapped his thumb and finger in front of his eyes.

"Snap out of it," Christian growled. "This is no time for mooning."

"I was not mooning," Julius said stiffly and turned away from the mirror. Crossing his arms over his chest, he glared at the younger man resentfully and wondered if Christian really was his son at all. *He* never would have been so disrespectful to his own father.

"Okay," Christian said with a great show at maintaining his patience. "So you don't dance. But you could at least talk to the woman."

Julius frowned and avoided his gaze. "I am talking."

"You aren't," Christian insisted. "You haven't said more than a handful of words."

Scowling, he admitted, "I'm practicing in my head."

Christian blinked at this. "Practicing?"

"Well, you don't just blurt out the first thing that

comes to mind," Julius said with exasperation. "I have to approach this carefully, so I'm practicing."

"In your head?" Christian clarified.

"Yes." Julius nodded. "In my head."

"Right . . . Good, good," he nodded, and then said, "but you know what would be even better?"

Julius raised his eyebrows with interest. "What?"

"Talking to her *out loud!*" Christian snapped. "Jesus Christ, Father, you're as old as the earth. You run a huge corporation, dealing with people—even women—day in and day out. Surely you can string a couple of words together and manage a little conversation with the woman?"

"I am not as old as the earth," Julius growled. "Besides, you're the one who said that I scare all the maids and secretaries and—"

"Oh, hell," Christian interrupted with a sigh.

"What?" Julius asked warily.

"It's my fault, isn't it? I shook your confidence with those comments."

Julius glared at him briefly, then let out a slow breath and nodded the admission. "I was fine until you and the twins started spouting that nonsense about how long it had been since I'd bothered with women and that I— Are the maids and secretaries really scared of me?" he interrupted himself to ask with a frown.

Christian avoided his eyes as he assured him, "No, of course not."

"You're lying," Julius said with a heavy sigh. "You never could meet my eyes and lie, and you won't meet my eyes now. They *are* scared of me."

Christian shrugged helplessly. "You can be a bit

sharp and grumpy. I'm sure you wouldn't be with Marguerite, though. In fact, I think she can help you find the fun, laughing, jovial guy you used to be before I was born."

"How would you know what I was like before you were born?" Julius asked, his eyes narrowing on his son with suspicion.

Christian shrugged. "The aunts talk. When you're at your grumpiest, they shake their heads and lament how 'wonderful and easygoing and happy' you were before 'that woman' ruined your life. They like lamenting a lot," he added dryly. "I'd say it's an Italian thing, but most of them weren't born in Italy."

Julius smiled at his grimace, but said quietly, "She didn't ruin my life. She gave me you and that was a hell of a gift."

Christian's eyes widened slightly, and then he glanced away, uncomfortable with the emotional moment. "Yeah, well," he said after allowing several minutes of silence to pass. "Too bad she didn't agree, but instead tried to kill me."

"She didn't try to kill you," Julius said quietly, troubled by the pain he saw flash on his son's face.

Christian glanced up sharply. "But Marcus said—"

"She told her maid, Magda, to kill you," he explained.

Christian considered this news. "The maid told you this? Could she have been lying?"

Julius hesitated and then shook his head. "No, Marcus and I both read the memory in Magda's mind. Your mother definitely told her to kill you and bring your remains to me with the message that she never wanted to see me again."

"Magda?" Christian said the name slowly. "But she didn't kill me."

"No. She brought you straight to me . . . and your mother killed her for the act of mercy."

Christian's eyes widened incredulously. "You didn't take the woman in? You let her go back to be killed?"

"Of course I took her in," Julius said with irritation.

"Then how could my mother kill her?"

Julius shifted uncomfortably and then admitted, "The day after Magda brought you to me, we found her dead at the bottom of the stairs . . . with you in her arms. Your mother was seen at the house and the maid was clutching your mother's pendant in her hand when we found the two of you. She'd obviously ripped it from her neck as she was pushed."

"She pushed the maid down the stairs while the woman was holding me," he repeated dryly. "What a charmer."

"Yes, well, the fall wouldn't have killed you so at least she didn't try to kill you herself."

"Oh, thanks for pointing that out, Father. It makes me feel loads better," Christian said sarcastically and shook his head. "Honestly, the more I hear about the woman, the less I really want to find her."

"I *told* you, you were better off without her," Julius said with exasperation. "But did you listen? No. You just *had* to find your mother. If you had only listened to me—"

"Marguerite wouldn't be here," Christian interrupted dryly.

Julius grimaced, but nodded. "True."

"So . . ." Christian tilted his head and said, "You

never told me how it went in The Foyer. Surely you two talked then? You didn't just sit there silent, did you?"

"No, of course not," he growled, but then admitted, "It didn't go very well, though. I asked her about Jean Claude and she—"

"Definitely not the right topic to inspire a happy conversation," Christian interrupted with exasperation and then sighed and shook his head. "Okay, why don't we practice your talking with Marguerite? *Out loud.* I'll be her."

Julius stared at him blankly. "Now?"

"No, I was thinking maybe next April. Then you could maybe give her a call, arrange a date . . ." He arched an eyebrow in question, and snapped, "Yes, *now.*"

"Oh, right," Julius glanced around uncertainly.

"Just pretend I'm her," Christian suggested. "I'm sitting at the table out there and you and I come out of the bathroom. You take your seat, lean to her and say . . ."

Julius waited, and then frowned and asked, "What? What do I say?"

Christian's shoulders slumped and he leaned back against the counter. "*You* were supposed to tell *me* what you would say to her."

"If I knew what to say to her, I wouldn't have been sitting staring at her all night," Julius pointed out impatiently.

"Right," Christian sighed. "Okay, well let's try a different tactic. We'll think of subjects you can discuss with her."

Julius nodded and then asked, "Like what?"

Christian cursed with exasperation. "Father, you aren't this stupid. There must be something you want to know about her."

"Of course there is," he said with frustration. "I want to know what her life has been like all these centuries."

"Well, there you are!" Christian brightened.

"No. *There* I'm not," Julius corrected. "If I ask her that, it will bring up her unhappy marriage to Jean Claude and—as I've discovered—that will hardly encourage her to relax and consider another relationship."

"Well, maybe you could ask about her children then. She loves her children."

"Yes, her children with Jean Claude, which will remind her of their unhappy union and—"

"Her job, then," Christian interrupted desperately.

Julius looked doubtful. "It will be a very short conversation. Your case is her first."

"Yes," he sighed and ran a frustrated hand through his hair. "Well, we have to think of something."

They were both considering the matter when a deep voice growled, "It sounds to me like you'd be better off letting *her* talk."

Julius and Christian glanced sharply to the door to see G.G. watching them with amusement.

"How long have you been there?" Christian asked with irritation.

"Long enough to know that—as old as you both probably are—you two don't know a thing about women," G.G. said with amusement. Pushing himself away from the wall where he'd been leaning, he crossed the room to the urinals.

"And you do?" Christian asked dryly.

"Yep." He spoke to the wall as he unzipped and began to relieve himself. "Tons of them pass through this place every day and it's always the same thing. Take a look around when you go back out. The men all stand or sit around in little groups looking serious and saying very little, but *maybe* making the odd comment that *sometimes* brings a round of nods or laughter. But the women?" He finished, gave himself a shake, tucked himself away and moved to the sink to wash his hands, glancing at them as he added, "The women talk. And it's like a dance to watch."

"A dance?" Julius asked with interest.

G.G. nodded, his tall green Mohawk unmoving on his head. "They lean forward, they reach out to touch a hand, an arm, or a knee, then they lean back to laugh before leaning forward again; eyes sparkling, smiles wide as they chatter on with whatever story they are telling."

The man was speaking with great admiration. For all his scary looks, he obviously loved women.

"Women like to talk," he continued. "Men don't. It works out very well because then they are not both trying to talk at once. The woman talks, the man grunts every once in a while and everyone is happy."

Christian was staring at him with wide, rather horrified eyes, but Julius nodded and admitted, "I was hoping that she would speak, but she is showing a distressing reluctance to do so. She is quieter than I re— would expect."

G.G. nodded as he turned off the taps and moved to dry his hands. "You have to get her alone. She's a lone female with six silent men and she's old enough to know men aren't big talkers. Besides, from what Jeanne Louise and Mirabeau have told me, she was dominated by that Argeneau she was married to. It's not a natural state for her to be submissive, but it was forced on her. She's only started to come out of her shell and start managing things since his death. That's more natural for her, but new at the moment and she will be intimidated by so many males. Get her alone. Ask one question and she will bloom for you."

Julius frowned. "I have talked to her alone, and did ask her questions and she shut down."

"You didn't ask the right question, then," G.G. said with certainty.

"What *is* the right question?" Julius asked.

G.G. considered the possibilities briefly, and then nodded as he came to a decision. "When Jeanne Louise mentioned her aunt was coming here, she said it was to do work for a detective agency. That helping to solve a case in California made her decide to be a detective."

"Yes," Christian said. "That's how I met her and hired her."

G.G. nodded and told Julius, "Ask her about that. How she liked California. About her nephew Vincent and the lifemate she helped him with. It's a safe topic. It's about her family, which from all accounts she loves, but far enough removed that it won't touch anywhere near her marriage."

Finished dispensing advice, he nodded and turned to leave the room.

"I like him," Julius said as the door closed behind the man. "For a mortal with green hair, he is . . ."

"Interesting?" Christian suggested dryly.

Seven

Marguerite picked up her drink and finished off the last sip with a little sigh of pleasure. It was an immortal Bloody Mary—blood mixed with tomato juice, Tabasco, pepper, lemon, salt, and Worcestershire sauce—and had gone a long way to improving her mood. She'd sat fretting over what Tiny had said until her drink had arrived, but just the one drink had made her feel better able to cope with matters. Obviously, the lack of blood was affecting her, she thought and suspected she could do with several more of the drinks to make up for the lack of straight blood in her system.

That thought in mind, she glanced around for a waitress and then stilled when she saw Julius and Christian making their way across the room. Julius was closing his cell phone and dropping it back in his pocket when she spotted him and she wondered about that. The two men had been gone a rather long time, but the interesting thing to her was that while Christian had looked exasperated and Julius worried when they'd left, Julius now appeared cheerful and Christian worried. Curious.

"We have to go," Julius announced as he paused beside her chair.

"What?" Marguerite asked with dismay.

Julius nodded. "I've called for two taxis and they assured me they'd be here right away so we'd best move."

"But—" Marguerite's protest died as everyone else got to their feet, even Tiny, she noted, though she shouldn't have been surprised that he was happy to go. He'd turned a little green when the drinks had arrived. There was just no way to mistake them as being anything other than blood mixes.

Sighing, she gave in and got to her feet, remaining silent as Julius took her arm and walked her out of the club. They didn't wait long out in front of the Night Club before the taxis arrived. Julius led her to the first one and Marguerite slipped inside when he opened the door. She settled herself on the bench seat, sliding into the corner to make room for others, but no one followed right away. Julius was standing in the door, his back to her, talking to Tiny and Christian.

Marguerite frowned and started to slide back along the seat to try to hear what was happening, but just as she did, Julius turned and ducked to enter. Moving quickly, she scooted back along the seat to make room and glanced sharply back when she heard the door close.

"Isn't anyone else riding with us?" she asked anxiously as Julius settled on the seat next to her.

He shook his head and explained, "I had them all take the other taxi. I wanted the chance to talk to you alone about . . . things."

"Oh." She sat back against the seat as the taxi pulled away, and waited, wondering what he would have to say. Christian had already told her that Julius intended to stick close and keep an eye out for any more attacks, but Julius might not know that and intend to tell her himself, so she waited . . . and waited. Marguerite finally gave up waiting and decided to prompt him, but she'd barely opened her mouth when the taxi pulled to a stop.

"Where are we?" she asked, glancing around with surprise. The car had pulled over in front of a Starbucks, not the hotel.

"I thought we could talk here," Julius explained, handing several pound notes to the driver and opening the door.

Marguerite hesitated and then followed him out of the car and allowed him to see her inside. He settled her at a table in a corner away from the few other patrons and then asked, "What would you like?"

"Nothing, thank you. I'm fine," she answered.

Julius peered at her silently for a moment, and then said, "I suspect we'll have to order something to sit here. I'll pick something."

He headed off to the counter and she watched him place and wait for their order, fretting over why he'd brought her here. When he returned to their table, her eyes widened incredulously on seeing that he'd purchased not only two large, foamy drinks, but two triangular pastries as well as two square ones she recognized as brownies.

"I couldn't make up my mind," Julius said with a shrug as he placed one of the drinks and a plate with one of each of the desserts before her. He then settled in the chair across from hers and fetched several packets of sugar out of his pocket, offering her two.

"Thank you," she murmured.

"These are mocha, frappa-cappa something or others," he said as he opened two packets and put them in his own coffee. Smiling wryly, he admitted, "The girl picked them and assured me they were good."

Marguerite smiled faintly and opened her own sugar packets to pour in. She stirred the drink then, fascinated by the foamy top. They hadn't had drinks like this when she was still eating and drinking. Her gaze slid to the brownie on the plate and then back to her drink before returning. She could smell the sweet chocolate and her mouth was watering again.

"I wanted to tell you, Marguerite," Julius said, drawing her attention away from the brownie. "I really appreciate what you did for my nephew Stephano in California when he was attacked."

Marguerite shook her head. "I did very little."

"You helped save his life," he said solemnly.

"I merely helped watch over him during the turn. Vincent is the one who saved his life."

Julius nodded solemnly. "I was impressed when I heard what he'd done. "Few immortals would have."

"Vincent is special," Marguerite said proudly and then found herself telling him about her nephew; about how talented he was, and about his business and the plays he produced. Somehow that led to talk about her stay in California, which led back to her children and their lifemates.

Julius, in turn, told her some tales of his trials in raising Christian alone. His love for his son was obvious as he spoke. She could hear the pride in his voice and see it in his face, along with his desire—like most parents—to keep his child safe from harm and pain, though he didn't say that outright. Each of them kept to their own tacit agreement not to talk about either Jean Claude or Christian's mother.

Despite skirting that issue, Marguerite began to realize that she'd misjudged the man. It quickly became obvious that he would do anything for Christian, and that his reasons behind keeping knowledge about his mother from him must be purely protective, not selfish as she'd first thought.

Somehow, while not paying attention, Marguerite found herself eating both the brownie and the lemon cranberry scone that was the triangular pastry. Both were like manna in her mouth. She had never tasted anything so good. They also went through several of those mocha-frappa-cappa drinks as well, both of them going up to the counter together to purchase them so they didn't have to stop talking, and so they could both pick out other pastries to try.

Julius was telling her about Christian's musical abilities when Marguerite reached for her drink and lifted it to her lips only to find her cup was once again empty. She shouldn't have been surprised, she supposed, talking and laughing was a thirsty business.

"I, of course, don't know a thing about music, that's something he got from his mother's side, obviously," Julius said dryly, drawing her attention from her empty cup. "But the minute he picked up that violin and started to play it by ear, I was sure he was the next Chopin or Bach."

Marguerite bit her lip on a laugh at his self-mocking expression.

"So I spent scads of money, hired the best teachers in Europe, all the while imagining that one day my son would play in the world's premier orchestras. He would compose music that would last through the centuries. The name Notte would resound through the music world."

"But he didn't get accepted into an orchestra?" she asked sympathetically.

Julius snorted. "Oh, yes. He did. He was accepted to several over the centuries, but he never stayed long at any of them. He found most of the music he was made to play too staid, and the stuff that he did like he soon got bored of playing over and over." Julius shook his head. "Finally, he seemed to give it up. He worked for the company and kept his music as an enjoyment on the side."

"What a shame," Marguerite said sadly.

"Hmm." Julius nodded his head. "I was terribly upset at the time, but now, all these centuries later, he's found the music that stirs his passion. He's actually composing. I can see the difference when he plays it. Even I, musically retarded as I am, can tell that before this, while he was technically perfect, his heart was not in it. But now, he's excited, vibrant, alive . . . playing with his heart rather than just playing by rote."

"But that's wonderful," Marguerite said, and then tilted her head uncertainly at his wryly amused expression. "Isn't it?"

"I guess it is," he said with a laugh. "I just find it . . ." He shook his head. "Ironic."

"Why? What is he playing?"

"My classically trained, world-class violinist, prodigy of a son is playing . . ." He raised an eyebrow. "Hard rock."

Marguerite blinked. "You mean he's switched to guitar?"

"No. He plays violin . . . in a rock band."

Marguerite sat back in her seat with a bump. "Really?"

Julius nodded.

"Well, that is . . ." She paused, at a loss for words. She'd never heard of a violin rock player.

Julius chuckled at her expression and then lifted his cup to his mouth, only to pull it away and peer into it with a frown as she had moments ago. "I'm empty."

"So am I," she admitted.

"Shall we try something new this—" He paused and glanced toward the window beside them. "Is that birdsong?"

Marguerite glanced out the window. The sky was still dark, but now that he mentioned it, she could hear what sounded like birds chirping their morning call.

"The sun will be up soon," he said and Marguerite glanced over to see him peering at his watch with an expression that was half surprise and half disappointment.

She glanced down at her own watch, shocked to see just how late it was . . . or how early depending on your point of view. The sun would indeed be up soon. They'd spent the entire night in that Starbucks talking.

"I guess we'd better head back," Julius muttered.

Marguerite nodded reluctantly, her eyes slipping over their table laden with countless empty cups and half a dozen empty plates that had once held pastries. The aftermath of a night that was the most fun she'd had in a long time . . . perhaps in her life. She didn't ever recall laughing as much as she had tonight, and she was sorry to see it end.

"Yes, we should go back to the hotel," he said more firmly, as if—despite his words—he'd considered not doing so. "We have to get some sleep. We're catching the seven P.M. train to York tonight."

Marguerite nodded and stood. They started to collect their cups and plates, but the fellow behind the counter who had served them all night was immediately there, waving them off and assuring them he'd get it. He wished them a good morning as they left.

It was much cooler than it had been earlier in the evening, but not uncomfortably so. A mortal might have wished for a coat, but immortals' bodies weren't as affected by temperature as mortals were. After so many hours spent doing nothing but talking, the two of them were oddly silent on the short walk back to the hotel, but it was a companionable silence that neither of them seemed to feel the need to fill.

The hotel lobby was nearly empty when they passed through it to the elevator, with just one couple dragging luggage to the reception desk to check out and catch an early flight.

"Here we are," Julius murmured, stopping at the door to their suite.

Marguerite remained silent as he unlocked the door, and then stepped inside when he held it open for her. The lights were on in the sitting room, but there was no sign of Marcus.

Marguerite hesitated, her eyes moving to the door to her bedroom, but then turned back, uncertainly, to Julius. "Thank you. It was fun."

"Yes, it was," he agreed. He raised his hand to gently brush her cheek and for one moment, Marguerite was sure Julius was going to kiss her. Despite her long-held determination not to risk involving herself with another relationship after what Jean Claude had put her through, at that moment, Marguerite wasn't at all sure she *didn't* want him to kiss her, but then he merely offered a crooked smile, let his hand drop away, and whispered, "Good night."

Marguerite slowly let out the breath she hadn't realized she'd been holding and turned away to walk to the door to her room. She paused there to glance back, and smiled slightly when she saw that he had reached his door and done the same. When he smiled back, she slipped into her room and eased the door closed.

It was only as she was undressing for bed that Marguerite realized that he had never brought up the "things" he'd said he'd wanted to talk to her about alone. If there had been "things," she thought, her mind mulling over what had just taken place. As far as she could tell, she'd had a very enjoyable nothing-to-do-with-business sort of date with Julius. And both of them had eaten food and drank several caffeine-rich beverages.

Both of them.

She was eating. He was eating. She couldn't read his mind. Could he read hers?

Marguerite didn't know, but she did know that Jean Claude hadn't eaten when he'd met her. He hadn't displayed that sign of having met a true lifemate. Not that she would have recognized it as a sign at the time. She'd been mortal then, a simple servant in a large and rich castle, completely ignorant that there were immortals walking among them, beings who fed on blood, were stronger and faster and could survive long, long lives while non-immortals dropped around them.

Wincing as she recalled her naivety, Marguerite slid into a long black satin nightgown and moved to the window seat, settling herself there to peer out over London. She really hadn't known much of anything when she'd met Jean Claude. She'd barely been fifteen; young and impressionable and easily swept off her feet by a simple smile from the handsome warrior on horseback. She'd thought her infatuation was love, and had been foolish enough to equate his desire with his loving her as well. She hadn't known until much later that she looked so like his long-dead and well-mourned lifemate that he'd been driven to sweep her off her feet, claim her as his own, and turn her. By then it was far too late to change anything.

But, in all the seven hundred years of their miserable union, Marguerite hadn't *ever* seen Jean Claude eat as Julius had.

Marguerite was almost afraid to consider what this might mean. Perhaps the man made himself eat all the time. Some immortals did, usually the men wishing to keep up their muscle mass. Her own son Lucern had always eaten for just that reason, though he'd taken little pleasure in it until meeting his lifemate Kate. Perhaps Julius was the same way. But Marguerite knew that—despite her fears—in her heart of hearts she was hoping that wasn't the case. She was hoping that she too could find what her children had found and experience what life with a real lifemate was like. The idea of having a true and proper mate to love and care for you and share the burden of this long, sorrow-filled life made her heart ache. Surely she had paid for such happiness in advance with all the misery Jean Claude had dealt out to her? Surely she deserved some happiness too?

As much as Marguerite ached for it however, she was reluctant to risk another relationship that might turn out like the one she'd had with Jean Claude. One would think it wouldn't be a concern; that no immortal would willingly bind to someone who was not a true lifemate, but it had happened. Hers was not the only such match where a naïve mortal was lured into a life-long binding to an immortal who could and did control them. She'd even heard of it happening between immortals, who should know better but—weary of being alone—settled for a union with a non-lifemate. They were usually temporary relationships, however, because it was rare for one immortal to be able to control another as wholly as Jean Claude had controlled her, and they were usually able to break free. Marguerite thought his power over her must have come from the fact that he had turned her, though she would never know the truth.

Whatever the case, while she was attracted to and

was coming to like Julius Notte very much, if he wasn't a lifemate, she wouldn't accept such a relationship, a temporary affair that would eventually go wrong when the stronger one could no longer resist and tried to dominate the other. The truth was she wanted an equal partner such as her children had . . . which meant she should probably avoid being alone with Julius for now. If he hadn't been able to read her, she was quite sure he would have said something, so either he could read her or he hadn't yet tried.

Either way, it seemed better to avoid being alone with him as much as possible until she knew whether he could read her or not. She already liked the man more than anyone else she'd met in her long life, and she was attracted to him as well. She could be very badly hurt if it turned out he could read her.

Marguerite came to that decision before finally dropping off to sleep curled up in the window seat of her room. She awoke a few short hours later to pounding on her door.

Gritty-eyed and exhausted from lack of both sleep and blood, Marguerite uncurled from the window seat and stumbled to answer it.

"Marguerite!" Tiny cried. "Everyone is waiting in the lobby for you. Julius is checking us out this very minute and you aren't even dressed yet!"

She could just make out his scowl through her sleep encrusted eyes and grimaced in response. Honestly, why was it men were always so grumpy? Or was it just her who seemed to bring about this exasperation?

"Move, woman," he ordered, turning her from the door and pushing her across the room to the en suite bathroom. "You shower, I'll get your clothes."

Marguerite paused abruptly in the bathroom door, suddenly wide awake and digging in her heels. "I'll get my own clothes."

"Marguerite," he said with exasperation.

"You are not rifling through my panties," she snapped.

"Oh." Tiny stopped trying to push her at once. "Yeah. Okay, you get your clothes."

Was she not now in a bad mood, she would have laughed at his sudden discomfort.

Shaking her head, she gestured to the door. "Out. I'll be downstairs in ten minutes."

Tiny hesitated and then grumbled, "You'd better be or we'll miss our train."

Marguerite waited until he left, then burst into action, rushing to her suitcase to snatch up clothes, then hurrying into the bathroom. She took the very first shower of her life, cursing when she got shampoo in her eyes, and then cursing again when she realized that she'd been so distracted the evening before that she'd never managed to call Bastien about the blood. Was it once again too early to call him? she'd muttered to herself with irritation as she ran a towel quickly over herself to dry the worst of the water, then stepped—still half wet—into her clothes.

She brushed her wet hair while throwing her nightgown and other items in her suitcase, threw the brush in last and zipped it up. She was ready. Or as ready as she had time to be, she supposed, applying lipstick as she dragged her suitcase out of the room and wheeled it to the elevator.

She stepped off the elevator to find Julius, Marcus, Christian, and Tiny waiting for her near the elevator doors. The relief on their expressions when she stepped out made her feel guilty, but then she noticed that Dante and Tommaso were missing and began to frown.

"Where are the twins?" she asked, dragging her suitcase off the elevator.

"They're on the way to the airport. There's some business back home that needs tending," Julius answered as he took the handle of her suitcase from her. Passing it to his son, he then caught her arm and urged her toward the doors to the street.

Julius already had two taxis waiting. They divided the luggage between the two and Marguerite, Tiny, and Julius rode in one, while Marcus and Christian followed in the other. Traffic wasn't too bad by London standards, which was a good thing since even with that advantage, they arrived at King's Cross just seconds before their train was to leave. A mad dash followed as they raced through the station to reach and board seconds before it pulled away.

Julius had booked the tickets, reserving two sets of table seats for their party of five. One table was a four-seater, the other, which was across the aisle, sat two. Julius explained this as he stowed the bigger suitcases on the rack. Marguerite followed as he then led the way up the aisle to their seats. He paused on reaching them, stowed a black overnight case overhead, and then slid into the nearest window seat of the grouping of four. However, when he then glanced at her expectantly, she—firm in her determination to distance herself a little from him until she knew which way the wind blew and whether he could read her—took the far window seat of the two-seat table on the left so that they were kitty-corner to each other across the aisle.

She saw the surprise that flashed across Julius's face, followed by disgruntlement. Much to her relief, however, he didn't say anything. Tiny was directly behind Marguerite and—after a hesitation—moved to drop into the seat across from her, leaving Christian and Marcus to take the two seats opposite Julius.

Marguerite was at first satisfied with the arrangement, until she realized that Julius's position seemed to put him exactly in her line of vision . . . and she seemed unable to keep from looking. Her gaze drifted over the man and she noted how the overhead light gleamed off his shiny black hair, how his features were almost noble, how deep and mysterious his eyes were, how soft and full his bottom lip looked in comparison to the thinner upper lip— That thought made her wonder what it would be like if he kissed her and she could almost picture it, his strong, nicely shaped hands gliding through her hair, pulling her face closer as his mouth descended—

"Something to eat or drink?"

Marguerite blinked and sat up abruptly as her view of Julius was suddenly blocked by a cart. Glancing up, she found herself staring at a redhead with a healthy sprinkling of freckles on her face that no amount of makeup would hide. Despite that, it didn't detract from her attractiveness; her wide smile and sparkling eyes made up for it.

"I'll have a sandwich, please," Tiny said, drawing the woman's attention.

Marguerite waited until Tiny had finished his purchases and when the woman then turned to her asked, "You don't have anything to read, do you?"

"There was a women's magazine left on my seat, Marguerite," Tiny said as the server shook her head apologetically.

"Thank you." Marguerite accepted the magazine as the girl turned her attention to Julius and the others. She glanced over the cover, grimacing at blaring headlines that read, *"Lose Two Stone In Four Weeks Without Dieting!" "Health Worries—SOLVED!"* and *"100 Secret Sex Techniques To Drive Your Man Wild!"* That last one made her pause and she opened the magazine, flipping through to the page listed on the front. It had been a while. A refresher course couldn't be bad. Not that she expected to have sex any time soon, Marguerite assured herself.

The sound of the cart moving on distracted her and she glanced up, finding herself looking at Julius again. He was saying something to Marcus, gesturing with his hands as he did, and she couldn't help but notice how strong and nicely shaped they were.

Shaking her head, Marguerite forced her eyes back to the magazine in her hands, and managed to read a whole sentence before her gaze slid back to settle on Julius once more.

Really, this was just ridiculous. She couldn't seem to stop thinking about the man.

Now that she felt sure he'd kept Christian's mother's identity a secret to protect him, her judgment had softened considerably. A good parent protected their child as much as possible and that was what he'd been doing. Even more impressive to her was that for five hundred years Julius had allowed Christian to think he was simply being annoyingly autocratic, and had preferred Christian to be angry with him for not telling rather than cause him the pain that knowing his own mother hadn't wanted him and had actually ordered him dead would bring.

Marguerite thought it a very caring thing to do. Most men would have happily revealed the truth and probably delighted in painting the mother a bitch while presenting themselves as the saintly parent who had saved them from her clutches and raised them with love. Instead, he had neither told the truth of the matter nor painted her as anything and Marguerite thought Christian had probably benefited from it.

Julius glanced up from the newspaper he was reading and Marguerite immediately looked away, groaning inwardly as she felt a blush creep up over her face. She was seven hundred years old, not a schoolgirl, for heaven's sake. She had no business blushing. Next she'd be giggling and holding pajama parties.

"I should have picked the cheese and onion sandwich."

"What?" Marguerite glanced at Tiny. He was making a face as he opened his sandwich and spread it out on the table between them.

At first, she didn't think he'd answer. His concentration was on the serious business of scraping off the brown relish from his Ploughman's sandwich, but then he sighed with disgust as he got the last of it off. Slapping the two parts of the first sandwich half together, he explained, "I don't like this brown stuff they put on their ham sandwiches over here. I should have picked an onion and cheese sandwich."

"Why didn't you, then?" she asked with amusement.

"I wanted meat," Tiny muttered.

"They had shrimp salad," she pointed out.

"Shrimp is not meat," he said with disgust and then added, "And who ever heard of putting shrimp on bread?"

Marguerite smiled faintly at the comment as she reached over to take one of his chips and popped it in her mouth. Salt and vinegar. Mmm. The flavor burst in her mouth, almost painful in its sharpness.

"Why didn't you get something for yourself if you're hungry?" he asked with disgruntlement.

"I don't eat," she reminded him.

"Yeah, right," he said on a sigh.

Ignoring his ill-temper, she took another chip and popped it in her mouth. She then sat back in her seat and tried to concentrate on her magazine article. So far, she wasn't seeing any new and wondrous techniques. It seemed nothing had changed much in that area in the more than two hundred years since she'd got pregnant with Lissianna. Good to know, she supposed.

"You look pale, Marguerite. When was the last time you fed?"

Marguerite glanced up with a start, cursing the blush that returned to her cheeks as she saw that Julius had stood and crossed to stand in the aisle beside her. There was a concerned look on his face.

She snapped her magazine closed before he could see what she was reading and answered honestly. "I ran out just before we started the drive to London the night before last."

His eyes widened incredulously. "But you had a

cooler in the hotel. Dante brought it with your suitcase."

"The cooler is empty. I was supposed to receive a delivery at the Dorchester but we left before it arrived. I never got around to calling Bastien last night," she said with a shrug.

"You should have said something. We have plenty to share," Julius said with exasperation as he reached up to shift through the bags in the overhead rack until he found and pulled down the small black cooler bag he'd stored there. Taking the bag, he turned away, ordering, "Come."

Marguerite's natural instinct was to refuse the order, to rebel where she hadn't been allowed to rebel against Jean Claude. But she would only be spiting herself. Her body was aching at the very idea of the blood in the cooler he carried, and she couldn't feed in front of a trainload of people. Sighing, she got to her feet and followed him up the aisle and out of the carriage.

Julius led her to a door and opened it, revealing a small bathroom. Her eyebrows rose at the tiny cubicle, but when Julius stepped aside for her to enter, she stepped inside. Marguerite then turned to accept the bag of blood she expected him to hand her, but instead she found him following her inside.

Eyes widening incredulously, she quickly scuttled to the side, trying to make room for him, but there was really little room to make. In truth, the tiny cubicle was probably too small for him to sit in comfortably alone. It was positively claustrophobic with both of them standing in there. Not that it seemed to bother him, Marguerite noted as he set the small cooler bag on the sink and moved in front of it. She heard the sound of his unzipping it, and then he turned to offer her a bag of blood.

"Thank you," Marguerite said, her fangs sliding out as she took the bag. Leaning against the wall to brace herself against the sway of the moving coach, she popped the bag to her teeth and met his gaze, only to glance self-consciously away as she waited for her teeth to do their work.

Julius didn't take the opportunity to berate her further for not mentioning her need. This rather surprised her. Jean Claude would have. Instead, he simply waited until the bag was nearly empty, and then turned away briefly to retrieve another bag. When the bag on her teeth was empty and Marguerite pulled it free, he held out both hands, one offering her a fresh bag, the other waiting to take the empty one, and they swapped.

Marguerite had never needed as much blood as Jean Claude and the boys, but that need had seemed to lessen as the centuries passed, until now she could go three or four days without feeding if necessary before the need became unbearably painful. She knew it was unusual for an immortal, but it was the way she had always been.

Jean Claude had once said it was the sign of an exceptionally strong constitution. That was way back at the beginning of their marriage when he had still troubled to complement her on occasion. That period hadn't lasted long. His ability to read and control her had soon quashed whatever little bit of respect he'd held for her when they'd first married. It had made her weak in his eyes, less . . . and not deserving of respect.

Pushing these unpleasant thoughts away, Marguerite removed the second empty bag and shook her head when Julius offered her a third. The first two had taken the edge off her hunger and she didn't want to deplete the men's supply when she intended to call Bastien and have him arrange for someone at the UK branch of Argeneau Enterprises to deliver her own supply once she knew where they were staying in York.

"Take it," Julius insisted, giving the fresh bag of blood a shake. "You're still pale."

Marguerite gave in less than gracefully, even performing something of a restricted flounce as she accepted the bag and popped it to her teeth.

For some reason, that made Julius smile. He didn't comment, however, but simply waited patiently for her to finish and then tucked the empty bag away in the cooler when she was done.

Relieved to finally be able to leave the cramped space they were sharing, Marguerite stepped out from beside the toilet the moment he closed the bag and turned to the door. However, the train began to slow then and rather than exit, he turned to speak, and then paused as he found himself face-to-face with her.

Julius's eyes became hooded as he peered down at her expectant face and then he murmured, "We'll have to wait. The aisles and corridor will be crowded with people disembarking. It's best to wait until the train starts to move again and everyone is settled."

"Oh," Marguerite breathed, her gaze somehow finding its own way to his lips.

She felt his fingers brush over the skin of her arm and shivered slightly at the tingle the small touch sent through her. Her gaze returned to his eyes then and she saw the silver of his eyes flicker as if he too had felt the shock of attraction she'd experienced, then his hand was curving over her shoulder to wrap around the base of her neck. He used his hold to draw her forward and tilt her head at the same time as his mouth lowered to hers.

The first touch of Julius's mouth on hers was a revelation. Marguerite may have felt something the first time Jean Claude had kissed her. She'd been infatuated by the man after all. But seven hundred years of pain and cruelty had followed those days and by the end, she'd felt nothing at all when he'd touched or kissed her.

Her reaction to Julius was a stark contrast. Marguerite felt almost too much as his soft lips brushed over hers, then settled firmly and urged her own open. Suddenly breathless, her body humming, she moaned into his mouth and slid her arms around his neck, pressing close as his hands ran over her back urging her closer still.

Julius was not unaffected. His hold on her neck tightened almost painfully before his hand suddenly slid up, his fingers tangling in her hair. He used that hold to direct her head as his mouth became demanding on hers. His tongue filled her and his hips ground into her so that she felt the proof of the effect she had on him. But she didn't need that to tell her what he was feeling, she was experiencing it herself, his excitement and pleasure and need rushing into her, joining her own and bouncing back to him, only to return doubled again.

Heat roaring through her, Marguerite curled the fingers of one hand into the hair at the back of his neck and tugged in demand while with the other she clawed at his shoulder.

The train shuddered as it came to a halt and they both stumbled, breaking the kiss, then Julius urged her back against the wall, pinning her there with his weight as his lips traveled across her cheek to her neck. Gasping, Marguerite tilted her head back briefly, moaning as his teeth grazed the tender flesh. She didn't notice that he'd set to work on undoing the buttons of her blouse until he suddenly pulled the sides apart and leaned back to look at what he'd revealed.

Marguerite bit her lip as his eyes slid hungrily over the black silk under her blouse.

"This has been driving me crazy since we met in the lobby of the hotel," he growled, running two fingers of one hand lightly over the curve of one black silk encased breast. "What is this?"

"A chemise," she whispered, flushing and starting to feel embarrassed and uncomfortable as the passion and their connection began to slip away.

"I could see it through your blouse," Julius growled.

Marguerite opened her mouth to explain that it was supposed to be visible through the blouse, but gasped instead as his hand suddenly closed over one breast. Then his mouth was on hers again and passion leapt in her once more.

Moaning into his mouth as he tugged the soft cloth

of the chemise aside so he could touch her breast un-hampered, Marguerite pressed herself into his leg, raising her own slightly to rub it against his groin at the same time. In the next moment, Julius had turned them both until the small sink counter was at her back. Pressing her against it, he broke their kiss and ducked his head to replace his hand at her breast, drawing the nipple into his mouth and lavishing it with attention as his hands reached for the hem of the short black skirt she'd donned that morning. He quickly began to draw it up her hips.

Excitement coursing through veins too long denied, Marguerite immediately reached to cup his erection in her hand and squeezed encouragingly, then cried out as Julius bit down on her nipple lightly in response. Raising his head at once, he kissed her again as his hands finished with her skirt, raising it almost to her waist so that one hand could slide between her legs. This time it was Marguerite who bit down, grazing his tongue briefly before she controlled herself and began to suck on it instead as his fingers brushed against her through her panties. Then he tugged the delicate cloth aside and found the warm, wet spot waiting for him.

By the time he lifted her onto the tiny counter, Marguerite had forgotten where they were and that people could be outside the door. Her legs wrapped around him automatically and she reached between them to help with his belt and the unfastening of his dress pants when he reached for them.

"Marguerite?" Tiny's query was followed by a knock on the door that made both Marguerite and Julius freeze. A second knock made them break apart.

Marguerite stared into Julius Notte's ebony eyes, watching the silver fire recede, leaving them mostly shadowed black . . . and wondered what on earth she thought she was doing. She'd nearly had sex in a cramped little bathroom on a moving train between London and York, for God's sake. What had she been thinking? This was not keeping her distance.

Another knock sounded at the door, drawing her from her thoughts as Tiny said, "Marguerite? Are you okay?"

Biting her lip, she avoided Julius's gaze and began to tuck herself back into her clothes, doing up buttons and pushing her skirt back down over her hips.

She heard Julius breathe a curse, then he eased away from her and began to straighten his own clothes. They finished at about the same time, then he reached around her to grab the black cooler, his mouth thinning when she shrank from his touch.

Pausing, Julius peered at her and said quietly, "I would never hurt you, Marguerite. You have nothing to fear from me."

Then he turned and opened the door, murmuring something to Tiny as he stepped out and headed back into the train carriage.

"Are you all right?" Tiny asked, eyeing her with concern through the open door.

Marguerite let her breath out on a sigh, but nodded. "Yes. I'll be there in a minute, just . . . give me a minute," she said wearily.

Tiny hesitated, then nodded and closed the door, leaving her alone.

Closing her eyes, Marguerite stood still for a minute, then turned to peer at herself in the mirror. She may have straightened her clothes, but the signs of what had happened were all over her, written in her rumpled hair, her swollen lips, and—Dear God, was that a hickey? She ran her fingers lightly over the barely visible mark, then lowered her head and closed her eyes, forcing herself to breathe deeply.

Everything was fine, she assured herself. Everything would be fine. But she was having trouble believing it. She'd just indulged in a necking session and almost-sex in a cramped and really not very clean—she noticed now—train bathroom.

Everything wasn't all right. She was in trouble. She'd fallen in at the deep end and was sinking fast. Marguerite was not the promiscuous sort to go jumping men at every turn. Jean Claude had been the only lover she'd ever had, though lover was a kind description. It just wasn't her nature to be indulging in a sordid little bit of hanky-panky in a train toilet. It seemed to her that her best bet was to solve this case as quickly as she could and then scurry back to the safety of her home and family.

And that was that, Marguerite thought determinedly as she turned to open the door of the bathroom to head back to her seat.

"There you are," Tiny rumbled as she settled back in her seat. "I nearly came to blows keeping your seat for you when everyone got on this last time. These Brits are quick bastards."

Marguerite managed a shaky smile knowing that was the only reason he'd said it. He was just trying to make her smile. He wouldn't have had to fend for her seat, their seats were reserved. "Thank you for guarding it for me."

"No problem." He eyed her and then asked under his breath, "Are you all right?"

"Yes. Thank you for coming when you did," she answered and meant it. She was sure he'd saved her some heartache by interrupting what had been happening. Leaning over, she gave him a grateful kiss on the cheek, then picked up the magazine she'd been reading, raising it in front of her face to hide from the three pairs of male eyes she could feel on her; Christian, Julius, and even Marcus were all staring at her as if she had sprouted a third nose.

Ignoring them, Marguerite forced her gaze back to the magazine she'd been pretending to read because it had an article on York in it. Since she'd never been to the medieval city, she hoped to learn something about their destination. She hadn't learned a thing yet. Not because the article wasn't good or informative, Marguerite couldn't say if it was or not. She hadn't absorbed a word of the damned article, her attention had kept slipping to Julius. Now, her eyes were staying firmly on the magazine in her hand, but her mind was slipping back to those heated moments in the bathroom.

Trying to distract herself, she glanced out the window, watching the nightscape roll by. In the dark it looked not unlike Canada, and she found herself thinking of home and her daughter and worrying. This was the second night she hadn't contacted her family. They'd have started to worry when she hadn't called the night before. She'd called every night since landing in England.

Of course, Tiny would have called Jackie to check in and she'd let the others know they were fine and what was happening, Marguerite assured herself, letting that worry go. It still left her worrying about her daughter, but Tiny would have told her if anything was happening at that end. Maybe. Vincent probably wouldn't be the first to hear if his cousin went into labor. He and her son Bastien used to be close and seemed to be rebuilding that old friendship, but he really didn't know Lissianna well.

"Tiny, would you trade seats with me? I'd like a word with Marguerite."

Marguerite glanced up in surprise to find Julius standing in the aisle next to them. Tiny hesitated, his questioning gaze moving to her, and Marguerite could have kissed him for his loyalty. He wouldn't move unless she said it was okay. The problem was, it would be incredibly rude of her to say no, especially when the man had shared blood from their supply with her. As for what had taken place in the bathroom, she hadn't been fighting him off. He hadn't forced her, so that gave her no excuse to be rude.

"Marguerite?" Tiny asked quietly when the silence drew out.

Sighing, she gave a slight nod of her head. He nodded back and then stood and the two men shuffled around each other in the narrow space afforded as they switched seats.

Marguerite eyed Julius warily once he was settled in Tiny's seat.

"Are you feeling better?" he asked with stiff politeness after a moment. When her eyes widened incredulously, he quickly added, "From the blood."

A cough from Marcus made them glance his way. When he raised his eyebrows at Julius, Marguerite didn't know what he was trying to say, but then she realized that Julius had been speaking in a normal voice when he'd mentioned the blood. She glanced at Julius to see that he was just grasping the meaning behind Marcus's expression as well. His eyes widened as he realized what he'd done, then he looked angry with himself, and then confused as if he couldn't understand how he could have done something like that and finally he just looked defeated. She almost felt sorry for him.

"Marguerite?" he said quietly after a moment.

"Yes?" she asked reluctantly.

"Did I offend you in some way last night?"

She blinked in surprise at the question. "No, not at all."

"Good," he said, nodding solemnly. "It's just that when you met us in the lobby you wouldn't even look at me, and I noticed in the taxi and then on the train you chose to sit as far from me as you could."

Marguerite stared at him silently, her mind awhirl. How was she supposed to answer that? What could she say? "*Oh no, I'm not offended at all, I simply can't read you, am eating and fear I'm falling in love with you and while twenty-four hours ago that would have horrified me, I now find that I'm quite wishy-washy on the subject and am hoping that you can't read me either so we could have a true relationship as lifemates. Would you mind trying to read me right now so that I can either jump across this table and kiss you if you can't read me or get myself as far away from you as I can if you are able to read me?*"

Marguerite was rolling her eyes at her own thoughts, when Marcus suddenly leaned across the aisle and hissed at Julius, "Tell her you can't read her."

Eyes widening, Marguerite glanced from one man to the other in question. Marcus was looking grim and insistent, Julius was looking startled. He stared at the other man with shock, then jumped up, grabbed him by the arm and dragged him from the seat and along the aisle out of the carriage.

"Did I hear that right? Did Marcus just say that Julius can't read you?"

Marguerite turned to look at Tiny as he dropped back into his own seat. She nodded slowly.

He considered her expression. "You don't look as horrified as I expected."

Marguerite breathed out a little sigh and confessed, "I'm a bit confused. I don't think I'm as afraid of relationships as I thought, just non-lifemate relationships."

"Like the one you had with Jean Claude," Tiny suggested.

She nodded.

"But if Julius can't read you and you can't read him, and you're eating . . . is he eating too?" he asked curiously.

Marguerite nodded.

"So . . . he's your lifemate, which would be an okay relationship. Right?"

"I think so," she said uncertainly.

"That's what I thought," Tiny said sounding relieved. She understood why when he added, "So, I guess I don't have to run interference any more, right?"

"I—" She shook her head helplessly, unsure what anything meant at the moment, but he took it as agreement that he didn't have to and released a breath of relief.

"Good. Cause I thought Julius was going to kill me when he came out of that bathroom."

"Really?" Marguerite asked with surprise. She hadn't noticed anything at the time.

Tiny nodded solemnly. "Trust me, if looks could kill, I'd be vampire fodder right now."

Marguerite patted his hand gently, "I'm sorry. Thank you."

Tiny chuckled. "You can still say that now that you know he can't read you? Seems to me if you'd known that at the time you wouldn't have been thanking me at all."

She blinked in surprise at the words, but realized they were true. If she'd known Julius couldn't read her in that bathroom, as worked up as she'd been, Marguerite might very well have been tearing his clothes off and telling Tiny to get lost, she thought wryly, her gaze shifting to the carriage door.

Marguerite watched through the window with interest as Julius appeared to berate Marcus in the corridor outside the carriage door. She had to wonder why he was so upset at her knowing he couldn't read her, but then thought perhaps he didn't know she couldn't read him either. Or maybe he had some fears of his own.

Tiny followed her glance and teased, "I'd say it's not too late, that you have ten or fifteen minutes before we get to York to drag him back in the bathroom, but it doesn't look to me like he's in the mood at the moment."

"No it doesn't," Marguerite agreed quietly as she watched the men.

"I can't believe you said that," Julius growled as the pneumatic doors closed behind him and Marcus, sealing them in the corridor between trains. Turning, he glared at the man who had been his best friend since the cradle. "Especially after you're the one who assured me it would be a bad idea to get into the whole lifemate deal because she was gun-shy after Jean Claude and wouldn't react well."

"That was Christian," Marcus argued.

"You said something similar in Italy before we flew over here," Julius insisted grimly.

"Yes, well, I was really more concerned about resolving the problems of the past than that. And she won't run," he assured him firmly. "I wouldn't have said what I did otherwise. She is afraid after her experience with Jean Claude, but her mind is turning. You are lifemates, and she can't fight it any more than you."

Julius scowled at the words. Knowing it was true. Despite everything he wanted her, loved her, felt like he needed her. He should be moving cautiously and even angry at her, but instead he wanted to love her and coddle her and give her everything she wanted and needed. Like his hunger for blood, his hunger for her was just as impossible to ignore. It had tormented him for all these centuries they'd been apart, filling his dreams with memories of her laughter, her smell, and her taste, leaving him miserable and lonely on awaking to find her gone, nothing but bitter memories in her place.

"It's true, Julius," Marcus said, apparently thinking his silence was denial. "You're confused and distracted and your mind is an open book to me at the moment. I know you've fallen in love with her all over again."

"I never stopped loving her," Julius admitted grimly. "Despite everything, I couldn't make myself stop loving her."

"Yes," Marcus said sadly, and then shrugged and said simply, "you are lifemates."

Julius turned away and paced to the door of the carriage, his eyes finding Marguerite at once. She was talking to Tiny, her expression uncertain and confused. It made him want to hurry in there, take her in his arms and comfort her, tell her everything would be all right.

"She will not run, but we still don't know what happened when Christian was born," Marcus pointed out quietly.

Julius's mouth flattened unhappily. "Why doesn't she remember me? Us? Our meeting before and loving each other." He turned to Marcus and asked, "I take it you haven't found anything in her memory to help us figure that out?"

"No." He shook his head with regret. "I've searched her mind several times and there is nothing. Just as I found in California, the memories of that time are simply gone. If I didn't know better I would say she wasn't the same woman."

"She's my Marguerite," Julius said firmly.

"Yes. Of course, but . . . Why has she no memory of you? If she were mortal I would say a three-on-one had been done to her to wipe her memory, but that isn't possible with an immortal."

Julius's mouth compressed stubbornly. "It doesn't matter. As I said when you first told me this on returning from California. . . . Obviously something was done to her. Things are not as we had thought."

"I agree something was done to her, but what? And when? And, more importantly, is she innocent?"

Julius sighed unhappily at the questions he could not answer. "I hope to God she is Marcus. I love her enough that I could forgive her almost anything . . . but not for trying to kill our son."

Eight

"We're here," Tiny announced as the train began to slow.

Marguerite looked out her window, eyes drifting over twinkling lights in the darkness and then they were pulling into the large, well-lit train station. The sound of the pneumatic door drew her attention and she glanced around to see Julius and Marcus returning inside. Julius offered her a reassuring smile as he paused at the luggage rack just inside the door and began lifting down their luggage.

They obviously weren't going to get the chance to discuss things for a while, Marguerite realized and was almost relieved. She needed time to adjust to everything that was happening.

She stood and joined him at the rack. When he pulled down her suitcase and set it on the floor before her, she caught it by the handle and then followed him into the corridor to wait for the doors to open so they could disembark.

Marguerite had never been to York and found herself peering around with wide-eyed delight as they left the train station and walked the short block to pass under the arched entrance of the wall surrounding the city. It was like stepping back into her past and she felt a sense of homecoming as they made their way along the sidewalk running parallel to the old roman wall that surrounded the city.

In her mind, she could see the guards who would have been minding the entrance and the wall, and imagined the people moving about in medieval dress. This feeling intensified once they'd crossed the bridge over the river that wove its way into the city. Here the buildings crowded together, an eclectic mix of modern, Victorian, and even medieval buildings. When the cobbled roads and snickleways began to appear, she knew they had arrived in the city center and found herself unaccountably happy, the feeling wiping away the last of the confusion and concern she'd been suffering when leaving the train.

"Here we are," Julius murmured, glancing from the notepad he held in his hand to the brass number beside the door of a townhouse as he came to a halt.

Marguerite's eyebrows rose as she glanced around. She'd expected a hotel, but it seemed they were staying in a proper townhouse. An expensive luxury she was sure. It would not be cheap to own a home in the center of the city and the owner would charge an exorbitant fee for renting it.

"This place is supposed to sleep eight to twelve.

I rented it before I realized Dante and Tommaso wouldn't be with us," Julius explained as he led them to the door. It was opened just before they reached it and a small, florid-faced man smiled out at them.

"Mr. Notte?" he asked, his smile widening even further when Julius nodded. He immediately stepped back to allow them entry. "Come in! Come in! My, the train must have been on time for a change. A miracle that with the state of our trains nowadays, they're forever breaking down and causing delays and switches."

"Fortunately that didn't happen this time," Marguerite said when Julius merely nodded as he retrieved a prewritten check from his wallet and handed it over.

The man beamed at her as if she'd said something clever, and then peered at the check. Apparently finding everything in order, he handed Julius an envelope. "There are two keys in there. I'm afraid it's all we have. Heavy curtains have been placed in all the bedrooms to block out the sunlight as you asked, and the groceries you ordered were delivered earlier so I put them away for you. My home and mobile number are in the envelope in case you have any problems and need to contact me."

"Thank you." Julius accepted the envelope.

"Now I'll get out of your way and let you settle in," the man said with a nod. "Enjoy your stay."

Marguerite followed Julius farther up the hall, taking her suitcase with her so that the men behind her could make way for the man to leave, then left her suitcase there and followed Julius on a quick tour of the main floor. Despite Julius's claim that it was supposed to accommodate eight to twelve people, it was all very small and compact. A door on the right led into a living room with sofas arranged against two walls. A fireplace took up the third wall, and a big screen television filled the other. It wasn't very roomy but the décor was tasteful.

Moving up the hall, Marguerite peered into the kitchen, noting that while there was a lot of cupboard space and all the modern gizmos, the refrigerator was a mini-fridge and the dining table only sat four. It seemed the eight to twelve were expected to eat in shifts. Hearing Julius grunt with displeasure behind her, she bit her lip on a smile of amusement and then stepped around him to open the last door in the hall. This led into a small half-bathroom, again, tastefully decorated.

"I'm almost afraid to look upstairs," Julius admitted, peering over her shoulder into the tiny room.

Chuckling, Marguerite closed the door and retrieved her suitcase to take it upstairs.

"This is England," she reminded him as she led the way upstairs. "An island smaller than the lower half of Ontario but with twice the population of all of Canada. Everything is small and compact here."

"Hmm," Julius muttered, peering over her shoulder as she opened the first of four doors leading off the landing. It led into a small bedroom with a double bed taking up most of the space, the rest of the room was filled with a wardrobe and dresser. There wasn't room for anything else. The second door led to another bedroom, the same size and set-up. The third door was to a bathroom, this time a full bathroom with a tub, sink, and toilet, though they were crammed in pretty tightly. The last door led to the largest bedroom. This one held a double bed, wardrobe, and dresser like the other two, but also had a bunk bed.

"This is supposed to fit eight to twelve?" Julius asked with disbelief.

Marguerite shrugged. "Two in each double bed, two in the bunk beds . . . and probably the sofas in the living room pull out into beds."

"Thank God Vita called this morning and asked me to send the boys back to Italy to help her," he muttered with a shake of the head. "As it is, Marcus won't be happy stuck in here with Christian and Tiny."

She grinned. "Going to stick him with the boys, are you?"

"Well, I can hardly make you share a room with them, and I'm paying for it so I'll be damned if I bunk with them," Julius said with a shrug, but he was grinning too. "Which room do you want?"

Laughing softly, she turned and rolled her suitcase to the first bedroom they'd looked at. "I'll take this one."

Marguerite slipped into the room and closed the door as the others started up the stairs. She set her suitcase on the bed and began to unpack, chuckling when she heard the exclamations of horror as the men discovered they would be bunking together. They had been spoiled by the suites in the hotel. But then so had she, she admitted.

Once again, being the lone female was a benefit, she thought with amusement. Her room was small, but it was all hers.

Once she'd finished unpacking, Marguerite made

her way back downstairs. The living room was empty, so she followed the murmur of voices to the kitchen, smiling faintly when she entered to find Tiny chopping up vegetables and cursing Julius for eating them as quickly as he could clean and cut them. She wasn't at all surprised to find Tiny cooking again. The man loved to cook and had done a lot of it in California. She knew these last three weeks of hotel and restaurant fare had probably been a trial for him.

"Marguerite," he said with relief when she walked into the room, "get the guys out of here so I can cook in peace."

"I'm not doing anything," Christian protested at once. "Neither is Marcus. It's all father."

"I am trying to be helpful," Julius said calmly, pinching another mushroom as soon as Tiny finished cleaning it. He then turned to Marguerite to explain, "The refrigerator is jam packed with food and there's no room for blood. We need to make room. The more I eat, the less has to go back in and the more room there is for blood."

Marguerite laughed at his perfectly logical explanation as she joined him to peer down at the vegetables available.

"What are you making?" she asked Tiny.

"Spaghetti Bolognaise," he muttered, scowling when she pinched the next mushroom he finished and popped it in her own mouth. Heaving a long-suffering sigh, he said, "Marguerite."

"Sorry," she apologized and then taking pity on him glanced around at the three immortals and said, "I wouldn't mind taking a walk to see a little bit of the city."

Julius nodded at once and straightened away from the table, asking Tiny, "How long until it's ready?"

"Take your time," the detective said with obvious relief. "The longer it simmers the better. A couple of hours would be good. I won't start the noodles until you return."

Julius's eyebrows rose, but he nodded and took Marguerite's arm to lead her out of the kitchen.

"Wait!" Marguerite said, glancing over her shoulder with alarm when neither Christian nor Marcus made any move to join them. "Aren't you two coming?"

"They have to see if they can get their hands on something to keep the bagged blood in," Julius answered for them as he led her out of the townhouse. Once the door was closed behind them, he explained, "There really isn't room in the mini-fridge."

Marguerite glanced back to the townhouse unhappily, but merely sighed and said, "It could be difficult. We've found during our three weeks here in England that most stores seem to close early, around five or six o'clock."

"You say it as if that's unusual. What time do stores and offices close in Canada?" Julius asked curiously.

Marguerite shrugged. "Usually until nine, sometimes even ten o'clock. And a few grocery stores remain open twenty-four hours. It's much more convenient for our kind."

"It would be," Julius agreed.

They continued to talk about the differences between England and both their homes, Julius sharing some details about life in Italy while she spoke of Canada, neatly avoiding any discussion about what was really on both their minds, the fact that they were lifemates. However, it was like a big pink elephant walking behind them, impossible to forget or ignore.

They turned down a perfectly preserved medieval street, the cobbled lane narrow and curving. It was lined with half-timbered buildings, their second stories hanging out quite a distance over the ground floor. Marguerite found it hard to believe they still existed and in such good order, but was delighted that they had survived.

Julius noted her expression and smiled, then suddenly caught her arm and tugged her quickly off the road and into a narrow snickleway between buildings.

"Is something wrong?" she asked with surprise, glancing out to the road in an effort to see what had made him draw her here out of the way. Perhaps a delivery vehicle was trying to negotiate the small amount of space afforded by the narrow lane. Certainly, they had to make their deliveries at some point in the day and doing so in the evening when the shops were closed and the streets less busy seemed reasonable, but there was no vehicle. The road was dark and quiet, with just a few people hurrying along, making their way home or to wherever they were going.

"It's like stepping back in time," she whispered.

"Yes," Julius agreed, a strange tautness to his voice. "I can imagine you in a long dress and cape, a silly bonnet on your head, smiling at something I said and that smile moving me to draw you here, to the privacy of the shadows to kiss you for the first time."

When she glanced at him in surprise for the moment of whimsy, he did kiss her, his lips soft and sweet as they brushed across hers.

Marguerite opened her eyes when he ended the gentle caress to find him peering at her almost expectantly. Raising her eyebrows, she pointed out, "But this wouldn't be our first kiss. That was on the train."

His breath slid out with what almost seemed disappointment, and he nodded. "Yes, of course."

She peered at him quizzically, but he managed a smile and urged her back onto the street. After several moments passed in silence, Marguerite tried to start up the conversation again by saying, "I have always wanted to come here."

Julius glanced at her sharply. "Surely, you've been here before."

She shook her head, "Jean Claude refused to come."

"And you never came by yourself?"

"I've never been by myself . . . well, until he died. I was fifteen when we met and he tended to prefer to make all the decisions," she said grimly, then changed the subject by asking, "Have you been here before?"

Julius nodded solemnly. "It is where I met Christian's mother."

Marguerite's eyes widened at this admission, her mind immediately shifting to the case as he took her arm to urge her to turn right. Coming here to speak to Martine had obviously been the perfect move. Her sister-in-law had always loved the city and maintained a home here even when she could not live here herself but was forced to move elsewhere for several decades to prevent her lack of aging from raising questions. Other family members often stayed in the home while she was away, enjoying the city for a number of years before they were forced to move on themselves.

"You met Christian's mother here," Marguerite said thoughtfully, quite sure that Martine would be able to help them after all. Christian had been born in 1491. She couldn't recall if Martine had been in York during that time, she herself and Jean Claude had been on a European tour. She would have to call Martine the moment they returned to the townhouse and arrange a visit. Marguerite was suddenly quite sure they were very close to finding Christian his answers.

"I can see your mind working on that one," Julius said with wry amusement.

Marguerite glanced at him, her eyebrows drawing together. "I understand that you're trying to protect Christian by keeping his mother's identity from him, but surely he now knows the worst of it? Surely there is no longer a reason to keep her identity a secret?"

"It is complicated," Julius said evasively.

"And dangerous if that attack on me truly was an attempt to end the investigation," she pointed out. "Once he knows the truth the danger may be at an end."

Julius frowned, but shook his head helplessly. "I *can't* tell."

"Why?"

"It is difficult to explain," he said, sounding frustrated and then muttered, "she was not who I thought she was."

Marguerite frowned trying to understand. "You mean she gave you a false name?"

"Something like that," Julius muttered and suddenly turned her toward the door of a café. "I am hungry."

Despite his claim of hunger, Julius only purchased

a cookie to go with the cappuccino he ordered. Marguerite followed suit and, finding all the tables occupied on the main floor, they took their trays with them to look for seating on the upper floor.

The café was obviously a popular spot, serving both caffeinate drinks and alcoholic beverages. A corner building, it had two walls that looked out onto the streets on the upper floor. They were made up of long rows of glass offering a view of the city lights sparkling in the darkness. The seating was comfortable, split between wooden tables and chairs and groupings of overstuffed chairs and couches.

Marguerite and Julius settled themselves in one of the corner groupings, Julius settling in a plump leather chair while she curled up in the corner of the sofa beside him and began to sip at the frothy drink she'd chosen. It had been a long time since she'd partaken of food as she was now doing and Marguerite didn't recall anything like this from that period in her life, but it was surprisingly good, she decided, especially with loads of sugar added.

They stayed to talk for quite a while at the café, but were on their way back and nearly home when Julius's phone rang. Pulling it from his pocket, he flipped it open and listened briefly before closing it and slipping it back in his pocket.

"Tiny just wanted to be sure we were on our way back. Dinner is ready," he announced.

They returned to the townhouse to find Tiny's sauce bubbling on the stove. Water was boiling in a second pot, but the men were nowhere in sight. Spotting a letter beside the stove, she moved to pick it up, eyes widening as she read it. The other three had already eaten and gone out to look around York. They planned to tour the pubs and see what the nightlife here was like, as well as find the aforementioned storage for blood. Tiny had left instructions on boiling time for the spaghetti noodles. All they had to do was dump in the noodles then wait eight or ten minutes, drain them and serve with the sauce over it, he'd instructed.

Marguerite lowered the note and peered toward the table. It was already set for two, including candles and a bottle of wine corked and left to breathe. It all looked terribly romantic. Her gaze slid to Julius, then away. "I'll start the noodles."

"I'll pour the wine," Julius offered.

Picking up the box of noodles, Marguerite ripped it open, and then poured the contents into the pot, wondering as she did if there would be enough for the two of them. It didn't seem like much. Shrugging inwardly, she stood stirring them as she waited for the suggested time to pass. Marguerite wasn't sure if she needed to stir them, Tiny hadn't said so, but she was suddenly terribly uncomfortable with Julius and was glad of the excuse to keep herself busy.

It turned out there was more than enough spaghetti. Marguerite feared a good deal of it would go to waste when she drained the pot and saw how much the noodles had swollen in the water. There was little she could do about it at that point, however, so she left half of them in the pot, splitting the rest between the two plates and spooning the sauce over it, her mouth watering as the chunks of meat, mushrooms, and other ingredients in the spicy tomato sauce spilled over the noodles.

"Let me get those," Julius offered, taking the plates when she picked them up. Marguerite followed him to the table, took the seat he indicated, and closed her eyes as she inhaled the smells wafting off the plate. Tiny was obviously a good cook. She hadn't appreciated that in California, but now that she was eating again, the smells wafting off the food he'd made were almost making her dizzy with delight. It tasted just as delicious as it smelled. Marguerite ate several bites before trying her wine. She'd barely lifted the glass to her lips and taken a sip when Julius spoke.

"We are lifemates."

Marguerite choked, spitting wine out in every direction as she coughed and sputtered.

"I'm sorry," Julius muttered, jumping up to grab a dish towel to wipe up the mess she'd made. He began mopping up the table with one hand, while thumping her back with the other.

"Are you all right?" he asked with concern.

Marguerite nodded, but her continued hacking rather negated the action. When the fit finally ended, she sagged back in her seat and eyed him with disbelief. He'd just brought the pink elephant into the room and dropped it on her lap. For heaven's sake!

"I'm sorry," Julius muttered, dropping back in his own seat with a sigh. "Not the most delicate approach was it?"

A small laugh burst from her lips, and Marguerite pressed them tightly closed, aware the sound had verged on hysteria. They stared at each other, his expression assessing, hers wary.

"What are we going to do about it?" he asked finally.

Marguerite swallowed, her eyes dropping to her

glass of wine. She ran one finger nervously over the round base of the glass as she sought a response, but finally asked, "Do we have to do anything about it for now? I mean," she added quickly when his eyes narrowed. "There is no need to really do anything at all. We are immortals and appear to be lifemates."

"We *are* lifemates, Marguerite. There is no *appear* about it," he growled.

"Okay," she acknowledged on a sigh. "But I am here on business. I have to concentrate on Christian's case. Once that is done, perhaps we could take the time to get to know each other and . . ." Her voice trailed away as she saw the expression on his face. She'd been trying to be calm and logical, gain herself a little breathing space to deal with it. He wasn't looking terribly calm or logical. Julius's eyes were blazing, the silver flaring and consuming the black of his eyes. They had looked the same way in the bathroom on the train she recalled.

Marguerite licked her lips nervously, and then paused when she saw his eyes follow the action. The air in the room was suddenly electric and she was unexpectedly flooded with an overwhelming need she was sure had come from him. Her heart rate sped up, blood moving swiftly through her veins as her breathing became shallow. It was all too much, too sudden, too intense.

Standing abruptly, Marguerite turned away from the table, unsure where she was even going except that she couldn't breathe, there seemed to be no oxygen in the room, she needed air. She hurried out of the kitchen and up the hall, hearing the crash of his chair overbalancing as Julius leapt to his feet to follow.

Marguerite reached the foot of the stairs before he caught up and then suddenly he was in front of her, filling her vision.

Julius started to pull her roughly against him, but paused when he saw her face. His expression was both surprised and concerned as he growled, "You're afraid. Why?"

She shook her head helplessly. "I have not been with anyone but Jean Claude. What if I—"

Julius silenced her with his mouth. Marguerite could feel the violence in him as he claimed her with that kiss, but while his mouth and hands were demanding, they were not mindlessly so. She had no fear that he wouldn't stop if she asked and, at first, balanced on the edge between asking him to stop or kissing him back. Marguerite didn't stay there long. His hands were roving over her body and she began to kiss him back, her arms creeping around his neck as he pressed his hands along her back, sculpting her to him. She then gasped into his mouth as they reached her behind and cupped there, lifting and pressing her against his hardness, grinding their bodies together.

Marguerite groaned with disappointment when he eased her back on to her feet, and then again when he broke their kiss, but her heart leapt in her chest and she jerked slightly in his arms with startled pleasure as he suddenly lowered his mouth to close it over her nipple through the silk of the blouse and chemise. She withstood the heated sensations that caused for a moment, but then tugged on his hair, bringing his mouth back to hers.

Marguerite kissed him passionately then, her need mingling with his and swirling inside her as he turned them both and pressed her against the wall. When he broke their kiss to trail his lips along her cheek, she sought out his ear, finding and licking the hollow behind it and shivering as it sent pleasure radiating through them both.

She felt him tugging at her blouse, pulling it from the waist band of her skirt, and immediately set to work on his shirt buttons, suddenly eager to feel his naked flesh against her own. In the next moment she gasped and forgot the buttons, her legs going weak as his hand slid beneath her untucked top and chemise, sliding over her flesh to close around one taut breast.

Sensing her weakness, Julius slid his thigh between both of hers to help her stay upright, and then returned his mouth to hers, thrusting his tongue inside as he toyed with one erect nipple. It set off a clamoring inside her that radiated through her body as if she were a tuning fork.

Clutching at his shoulders, Marguerite bit lightly on his tongue and shifted her body, grinding herself against his thigh, then reached down to find him through the cloth of his pants.

Julius immediately gave up toying with her breast and began to pull her short, tight skirt up until he had it bunched around her waist. He then reached between them, sliding his hand inside her panties and caressing her briefly. Moaning as the need overwhelmed her, Marguerite quickly undid his trousers and tugged him free of his boxers, her hand encasing and squeezing him encouragingly.

Growling, Julius immediately slid his hand from between her legs, caught her by the upper legs and lifted her, urging her to wrap her legs around his waist. Marguerite did, her hand releasing him to catch around his shoulders to help hold her weight as he lowered her, driving into her.

They broke the kiss, both crying out as he filled her, then stared at each other, panting as he slowly withdrew a little then pressed back into her. Pinned against the wall by his weight, Marguerite moaned and closed her eyes as she was assaulted by both the sensation of his body entering hers and her own closing around him and drawing him in. And then he kissed her again, his tongue thrusting into her as his erection did, the kiss quickly growing frantic along with his actions until the tension broke, taking her mind with it. She knew they were falling, but darkness reached up to claim her before they hit the floor and she never felt the landing.

Marguerite didn't know how long she was out. She wasn't surprised to realize she'd fainted, she'd always heard that true lifemates tended to for their first hundred or so times together. She had even passed that bit of wisdom on to her daughters-in-law, but this was the first time she'd ever experienced. When she opened her eyes it was to find that she was in Julius's arms and he was carrying her up the stairs.

"I thought it might be best if we weren't found naked and unconscious at the foot of the stairs when the boys come home," he said with a small smile when he noticed that her eyes were open.

Marguerite blushed, but nodded shyly.

Julius chuckled softly at her expression. "How can you be shy after what we just did?"

"I hardly know you," she whispered wryly as he

carried her into his bedroom. "We only met each other a few days ago."

His expression became solemn and he released her legs, allowing them to drop to the floor so they both stood facing each other. "We are lifemates, Marguerite. I knew you from the moment we met. And you knew me. Somewhere, in some part of your mind or body, you recognize me as one would recognize a long-lost love."

Marguerite stared at him silently, knowing that was true. She had felt his passion and his pleasure as a lifemate did, not something she'd ever experienced with Jean Claude, but her body had also seemed to know instinctively what to try, what would excite him and had done so confidently. Her hands had caressed where they were sure he liked it best, the excitement that then bled from him into her proving her right. Her lips had sought out the hollow behind his ear with assurance, again proven right when she'd felt the tingles of excitement radiate through her own body. And her body had met and matched his, anticipating his actions and moving in rhythm as if they'd performed that sweet dance before, as if they were one.

She'd never experienced anything like that with Jean Claude. At first, Marguerite had always felt uncertain of what she was doing and how to please her husband . . . and then, later, after centuries of his control, she hadn't cared to know. There had never been any in-between with them in her recall.

This then was what it was like with a lifemate. No wonder her children were all so happy.

Smiling at the thought, Marguerite let go of the

last of her reserve and reached out to wrap her hand around Julius's erection. Her smile widened when she saw the silver leap to life in his eyes, eating away the black, but when he opened his mouth to speak, she silenced him with a kiss, thrusting her own tongue into his mouth.

Julius moaned in response, closing his arms around her to draw her tight against him as his hips pushed forward, urging his erection more firmly into her hand as she caressed the length.

Marguerite smiled against his mouth, then broke the kiss and dropped abruptly to her haunches before him, making Julius blink his eyes open and peer down with a start. She grinned up at him, but when he started to bend, reaching for her, she knew he intended to stop her and quickly took him into her mouth. The action worked as she'd hoped and he froze at once, his hands moving over her shoulders and head, but not trying to stop her anymore. Marguerite ran her tongue around the tip of his shaft, excitement pooling between her legs as his pleasure and excitement began to invade her. It grew with every stroke or flick of her tongue, rolling through her in amplifying waves as the pleasure echoed between them growing with each return.

Marguerite was moaning now too, the vibration simply adding to their pleasure. She could feel the muscles of Julius's legs quivering under the hand she'd placed there to help her keep balance and quivered herself in response, her own legs growing weaker and weaker until they were both trembling. She became unsure which would come first, the final pleasure or collapse, then Julius suddenly tangled the fingers of one hand in her hair and forced her head away even as he caught her arm with his other hand and dragged her to her feet.

Marguerite opened her mouth to protest that she wasn't done, but he didn't wait to hear it. Covering her mouth with his own he kissed her almost violently and forced her backward until the back of her legs bumped against the bed, and then they were both tumbling onto it. Marguerite gasped into his mouth as his weight landed on her, but he quickly shifted to the side, his upper body sideways on the bed and leaning against her. He had one leg thrown over both of hers and used it to urge hers apart and keep them from closing as his hand slid up her thigh.

Marguerite cried out, her hips jerking as he found her slick, heated flesh. She sucked frantically on his tongue and caught at his upper arms, digging in with her nails, scoring him as he caressed her. She was already excited from what he'd been doing to her, but now he was pushing them both further, his fingers dancing over her briefly before sliding inside until they were both panting and desperate. Only then did he slide over her, replacing his hand with his shaft and driving into her with a violence born of need. Marguerite met and matched that need, raising her knees and planting her feet firmly on the mattress to raise her hips into the action until he was buried to the base.

As excited as they were, it didn't take much to drive them both over the edge. The mounting tension had Marguerite in a frenzy and when she felt her teeth begin to shift and slide forward, she broke their kiss to keep from biting his tongue, only to turn her head and sink her fangs into his shoulder. Julius growled, and she felt his own teeth pierce her neck, then they both pulled away, screaming as they went over the edge together plummeting into the whirlpool of release that waited below.

Nine

Marguerite woke up to find her head cushioned on Julius's chest and his arms wrapped round her. She lay still for a moment, simply enjoying being enveloped in his warm embrace and inhaling his scent. It was a sharp, tangy aroma that made her wonder what cologne he wore. She'd like to buy several bottles of it and use it as air freshener as well as throw it in her laundry so she could enjoy it all the time.

Smiling at the foolish thought, Marguerite eased out of his arms, moving slowly and carefully in an effort not to wake him. The clock on the bedside table read five P.M., a little more than an hour before sunset, and she'd like to take a bath before the other men were up and about. The townhouse had only one full bathroom and she imagined it would be in high demand when the rest of their small group started to stir. If she went now she could be done and out before that happened.

Her gaze slid around the room as she stood up and Marguerite grimaced as she realized she had no clothes here but those she'd worn the night before. A robe would have been handier, but she didn't have one with her, so had to drag on her skirt and blouse from the night before. She didn't bother with her bra and panties, however, simply scooping them up along with her shoes to carry to her own room.

Much to her relief, Marguerite didn't run into anyone on the way to her room. She slipped inside and dumped the clothes she carried on the foot of the bed, and then quickly stripped off the skirt and blouse. Leaving them where they fell, she took her robe from the wardrobe and slid into it, and then fetched fresh clothes and grabbed her hair dryer before heading into the bathroom.

With only an hour before the room would be in demand, Marguerite didn't take as long in her bath as normal. She rushed through it and then quickly dried off, dressed, and dried her hair. Once ready to face the day, she slid out of the bathroom, coming to a startled halt when she saw Tiny leaning against the wall in the hall.

"I'm sorry, were you waiting long?" Marguerite asked in a whisper.

Tiny shook his head as he straightened. "I just came out. I heard the hair dryer turn off as I did and figured you were about done so thought I'd wait and grab a shower before everyone else is up and about."

"Oh." She nodded and then offered, "If you tell me how to make coffee I'll put it on while you're showering."

"Hooked on caffeine already?" Tiny teased with a grin, and then shook his head. "It's okay. I fixed it before we went to bed this morning. It just has to be turned on."

"I'll do that, then," she said, moving toward her door. "And then I'll call Martine and see when we can talk to her."

"Sounds like a plan," Tiny said as he disappeared into the bathroom.

After leaving her things in her room, Marguerite jogged lightly downstairs to do as promised. She flipped on the coffeepot, then moved to the phone, grateful that she knew Martine's number by heart. Jean Claude's sister had had the same number for at least ten years, ever since moving back into her York home after one of the necessary breaks most of them were forced to take to prevent anyone noticing that they didn't age. Still, she had to pause and rethink the number since she had it memorized with the country code in the front. She mentally counted off the 011 44 and then actually punched in the following ten numbers, hoping she'd done it right. She didn't relax until she recognized Martine's housekeeper's voice saying hello.

Smiling, Marguerite leaned against the counter and asked for Martine, but her smile faded when the housekeeper announced that Ms. Martine was in London spending the weekend with her daughters. When the woman asked if she'd like to leave a message, Marguerite murmured no, thanked her, and hung up to scowl impatiently around the room. Honestly, they seemed constantly to run into roadblocks with this case. First there had been the three weeks of useless archive hunting, then the attack, and now when they thought they had a real chance of finding out something useful, Martine wasn't available to talk to.

"Why the long face?" Julius asked by her ear, his arms slipping around her waist from behind.

"Good morning," Marguerite said, her lips curving up into a smile as she leaned back into his embrace.

Julius caught her chin in his hand and brought her face around and up for a kiss that may have started as a gentle brushing of lips, but didn't end that way. Moaning as his tongue invaded, Marguerite turned in his arms to make the angle less awkward and then gasped in surprise when he immediately lifted her to sit on the counter.

"Julius," she laughed, breaking the kiss and trying to push him away. "Someone could come in."

"Tiny's in the shower and everyone else is still sleeping," he growled, his hands urging her knees apart so he could step between her legs.

"Yes, but— Oh," she breathed. He'd tugged her blouse from her skirt, raised it up to uncover the red lace bra she'd donned after her bath and immediately began to run his tongue along the flesh at the edge of the lace.

"But?" he asked against her skin.

"But," Marguerite agreed on a sigh, one hand sliding into his hair and the other moving over the smooth skin of his back. He wore only his jeans, leaving his chest and back bare for her to touch unhampered.

Julius chuckled and tugged one cup of the bra aside so that he could latch onto the excited nipple beneath and Marguerite groaned and unconsciously shifted her hips forward, groaning again as the core of her pressed lightly against his erection. Julius immediately let go of her blouse, letting it drop over his head as his hands reached for her hips and tugged her more firmly forward so that they ground against each other through their clothes. They both groaned then and he withdrew his head from beneath her blouse, abandoning her breast to kiss her again.

Marguerite kissed him back frantically, her hand slipping between them to find that while he'd donned the jeans, he hadn't bothered to fasten the button, simply pulling up the zipper. There was no need for fiddling with fasteners, she simply slid her hand inside and found him hard and eager.

Julius thrust against the caress, his own hands finding her skirt and beginning to lift it up and out of the way. It was the buzz of the coffeemaker announcing that it was done brewing and the coffee ready that brought her to her senses. Blinking her eyes open, she peered around the kitchen and immediately broke the kiss and caught at his hands to stop him as they slid between her legs.

"We can't," she gasped.

"We can," Julius assured her, running his lips down her throat as he brushed his fingers against her through her panties.

"Oh, noooo," Marguerite moaned and then shook her head firmly and redoubled her efforts to catch his hands, this time digging her nails into his skin. When he lifted his head to look at her, she said, "Tiny or one of the others will find us half dressed and unconscious on the kitchen floor."

"Oh, right." Julius sighed, dropping his head on her shoulder and letting her skirt fall back into place. Then he lifted his head abruptly and suggested, "We could go back to bed."

Marguerite smiled at his hopeful expression, but shook her head. "Work. I have work to do."

"Did I hear someone say work?" Tiny asked as he entered the kitchen and then his eyes found them and rounded. "That doesn't look like work."

Grimacing, Marguerite pushed Julius away and slid off the counter. "Good morning."

"Good morning, again," Tiny said with amusement, reminding her that they'd already met once that morning.

"Right," she murmured, then, hoping to distract him, said, "The coffee just finished."

The moment Tiny turned to glance at the coffeepot, she quickly reached under her blouse to readjust her bra, slipping her breast back inside. While her blouse had hidden the fact, she'd been uncomfortably aware that it was still out under there. Catching Julius's amused grin, she made a face and moved to collect cups, asking him, "Do you want coffee?"

"Not yet," he answered. "I think I'll go take a shower."

"Marcus was heading in next and Christian has already called dibs on following him," Tiny announced as he retrieved milk and cream for the coffee.

"Then I guess I'm having coffee," Julius muttered.

Marguerite smiled with amusement at his disgruntled tone as she collected three cups and moved to the coffeepot.

"So, did you call Martine? When are we going to see her?" Tiny asked as he joined her by the coffeepot.

"Yes, I called her, but there's a problem," Marguerite said on a sigh as she poured the coffees. "She isn't home."

Tiny looked as disappointed at this news as she'd been. "Where is she?"

"In London if you can believe it," she admitted dryly. "It seems while we were on the train here, she was on another train heading to London for a weekend with her daughters."

"Her daughters live in London?" Tiny asked with a frown.

"No. They're at university at Oxford. They were catching the train into London to meet up with her."

Tiny raised his eyebrows. "Impressive."

"Juliana and Victoria are both very bright," Marguerite said proudly.

Tiny nodded, but then shook his head with a wry expression. "So we headed up here from London to talk to her and she's gone down to London."

"Hmm," Marguerite murmured and then shook her own head and said, "You'll never guess where they're staying."

Tiny raised his eyebrows. "Claridge's?"

Marguerite shook her head. "The Dorchester."

He gave a short laugh at that, and then sighed and glanced from Marguerite to Julius before asking, "So . . . do we hop on the train and head back?"

"No," Julius spoke before Marguerite could voice an opinion. "Martine is only gone for the weekend, she'll be back tomorrow or the next night. I rented this place for a week, and besides with our luck, something would come up and she'd be heading back this way as we went down and we'd pass each other again."

Tiny nodded and then glanced to Marguerite. "You could call her."

"I'd rather talk to her in person," she said.

"Then maybe we should check the archives again while we're waiting," Tiny suggested. "We may have just missed —"

"You didn't miss anything," Julius said quietly. "Christian's birth was not recorded anywhere."

"Right. Good to know we wasted all that time," Tiny muttered, and then said impatiently, "You know it would make things a hell of a lot easier if you just told us her name."

Marguerite waited for Julius to tell the detective that he "couldn't" as he had her, but he merely smiled and said, "Where would the fun be in that?"

When Tiny scowled at him, he slapped his back on the way to the coffeepot to pour himself another cup and said, "Cheer up. It means you have at least two days to tour York before you have to get back to work. And it's on Christian."

"Leave it to you to find the silver lining, Father," Christian said dryly from the doorway.

"Good morning, son," Julius said with a grin. "Your hair's wet. Does this mean you've had your shower and it's now free?"

Christian shook his head. "Marcus is in there."

"I thought Marcus was showering after me," Tiny said with a frown.

Christian grinned. "So did he, but I'm younger and faster."

Julius shook his head mournfully. "The youth today, Marguerite. They have no respect for their elders."

Tiny snorted at the words as he moved to the refrigerator. "Five hundred and something isn't a youth, Julius."

"He's right," Marguerite said with amusement. "Tiny's the baby in the group."

"Yeah, and at thirty-five I look the oldest," he said with disgust as he removed bacon and eggs from the mini-fridge and set them on the counter.

"Are you planning to cook something, Tiny?" Julius asked with interest and then frowned as he moved forward and caught a glimpse of the contents of the small appliance. "Where is the blood?"

"Yes, I'm planning to cook. I'll cook enough for the three of us. And the blood is in the mini-fridge in the living room. There was no plug in here for it," he added to explain why it was in the living room and not the kitchen.

"You did manage to get another refrigerator, then?" Marguerite asked with surprise. "Where?"

"You don't want to know," Tiny said dryly, and then sighed when Marguerite raised an eyebrow in question and said, "None of the stores were open, of course. So, the guys 'convinced' the neighbor to sell us his."

"Oh, dear," Marguerite breathed.

"We paid him twice what it was worth and gave

him money to replace the groceries in it as well," Christian assured her quickly.

"Needs must, Marguerite," Julius said quietly when she merely shook her head.

"I hear Marcus on the stairs," Tiny announced. "Go shower, Julius, or your breakfast will be done and cold before you get back."

Julius didn't need any more prompting than that. Nodding, he kissed Marguerite on the cheek and headed out of the room with his coffee.

Marguerite watched him go with a smile, then started to turn to Tiny to ask if there was anything she could do to help, but paused when she saw Christian grinning at her.

"What?" she asked, grimacing when she felt the blush riding up her cheeks.

"Does this mean you'll be my mother?" Christian teased lightly.

Marguerite's embarrassment fled at once, her expression becoming serious, she said slowly, "I would be more than proud to claim you as a son, Christian."

The teasing in his expression leeched out of his face and he swallowed thickly, then nodded. "Thank you, Marguerite."

"Are you all right?"

Marguerite grimaced as Julius paused and caught her arm to keep her on her feet when she stumbled. Shaking her head at her own clumsiness, she laughed and said, "I'm fine. I shouldn't have worn these heels, though. I didn't even consider the cobblestone walks when I dressed tonight. It's uneven and they slip on the smooth stone."

"They look good, though," he complimented, his hand releasing her arm to slip around her waist. Letting it rest rather low on her hip, he squeezed gently as he peered down at the high-heeled silver shoes she wore.

Marguerite peered down at them herself, noting that they did look good, and they went well with the silver cocktail dress she'd donned for the show and dinner Julius had planned. Raising her head, she grinned at the interest in his eyes and ran a hand lightly across his chest.

"Mmm." Eyes beginning to glow as the silver flared in their depths, he turned her into his arms, his head lowering to kiss her, but Marguerite laughed and put a hand to his chest to hold him off.

"Behave. We are on a public street," she reminded him.

"We are," he agreed solemnly. "But as I recall there is a snickleway not far up the road. We could duck in there and—"

"Ruin our clothes when we both pass out afterward and probably be mugged while in a dead faint and helpless into the bargain?" she suggested dryly, then pulled free of his embrace and caught his hand to urge him to follow as she continued up the walk. "Besides, you promised me food."

"Food." He sighed with mock despair, but started to walk again, even as he muttered, "Passed up for a burger."

"Who said anything about a burger?" Marguerite asked with amusement. "When you said restaurant I thought you meant proper cuisine."

"That was the plan," Julius agreed. "But a burger

joint would be so much faster, and then we could go home and—" He paused when she turned and arched one eyebrow at him. A slow smile curving his lips, he murmured, "You look so cute when you get that look on your face. It just makes me want to—"

"Everything makes you just want to," Marguerite said on a laugh.

He raised an eyebrow himself now. "And you don't want to?"

"No," she assured him solemnly as she walked back the few feet now separating them. Placing a hand to his chest, she leaned up to kiss him apologetically on the lips and then whispered, "And the fact that my panties are wet right now is because it was so hot in that theater, not because I only have to look at you to want you."

Marguerite watched Julius's eyes widen, but the moment his hands reached for her, she whirled away with a laugh and started walking again, saying over her shoulder, "Feed me. Woman cannot live on love alone."

"You're a hard woman, Marguerite Argeneau," Julius growled, catching up to her quickly and taking her hand in his.

"Yes, I am," she agreed with a grin. "And I'm looking forward to trying the moules mariniere that Tiny mentioned he had last night when he, Christian, and Marcus stopped there."

"Hmm," he scowled. "That probably takes forever to make. We will be there hours."

"The anticipation will do us good," Marguerite assured him with amusement.

"You can go off a person, you know," Julius

warned, but squeezed her hand to let her know he was teasing.

Laughing, she paused at the door to the restaurant and reached for the handle, letting her hand drop away when he reached past her and opened it for her. She stepped inside, her gaze sliding over the busy restaurant with interest. The lighting was dim, romantic music played softly in the background, and the tables were arranged so that each had enough privacy not to feel intruded on by neighboring tables. They were met at the door, whisked to their table, and their waiter arrived at once, bearing two glasses of champagne to accompany their menus.

"So, did you enjoy the play?" Julius asked once they'd placed their orders.

"Very much." Marguerite smiled. It had been a modern comedy that had had her laughing from the start, even distracting her from the heat in the theater. Unfortunately, mind control didn't work over the phone and Julius had been forced to make do with what tickets were available. Their seats had been high in the back, nearly in the rafters. It hadn't been a problem, with their exceptional hearing and vision they'd seen and heard everything just fine, but it was a warm evening and the theater had been full, heat rising off the bodies and leaving them sweltering in the upper seats. It wasn't until the play was over that she'd realized just how hot. It had been worth it, though, but now that she'd been reminded of the free sauna they'd enjoyed, Marguerite thought a trip to the ladies' room to give her face a splash and check her hair might be in order.

Excusing herself, she stood and glanced around,

then stopped the waiter to ask where the ladies' room was. It turned out it was on the upper floor and she negotiated the building's steep, old steps with care, relieved when she arrived at the landing and spotted the sign over the women's bathroom door.

Slipping inside, she smiled at the pretty, young mortal at the sink and joined her. The walk had cooled her off after they left the theater, but as she had feared her face was a touch shiny and her hair looked a bit limp and sad. Marguerite fluffed her fingers through her hair, returning a bit of life to the stressed strands, then turned on the tap and splashed some cold water on her face.

Marguerite heard the door she'd just passed through open again, and assumed it was just another woman in search of the restrooms. It was a gasp from the woman beside her that made her blink her eyes open and start to straighten.

Catching sight of the mirror in front of her and the reflection of the figure in black, her eyes widened. It was the same person who had attacked her in her hotel room her first night in London, she was sure. The shape was the same; tall, broad shouldered, muscular, and covered from head to foot in black, including a black cape. He also had the sword, she saw and it was swinging toward her as she straightened.

Marguerite quickly ducked her head back down and stumbled to the side, away from the arc of the sword. Only the woman beside her kept her from falling to the floor. They both stumbled to the side and against the wall, and then Marguerite managed to regain her footing. She caught the woman's arm and pushed her toward the stalls along the back wall as she straightened to face her attacker, the action meant both to get the woman out of the danger zone and out of her own way so she wouldn't be tripped up at a critical moment.

"Go. Get out of here," Marguerite hissed at the woman, shifting to the side until the frosted windows were at her back as the figure in black turned to face her, his sword rising again.

Eyes wide with terror, the woman slid slowly along the wall of stalls, obviously terrified the man in black would hack at her with the sword at any moment.

Marguerite found herself worrying about that very thing herself when the man hesitated, his head turning the mortal's way, tracking her like a cobra about to strike. Desperate to distract him, she asked, "What do you want?"

Stilling, the black-clad figure turned back to her then, and Marguerite gave a little wave with her hand, urging the woman to make a run for it. Still, it wasn't until the man raised his sword and hurried toward Marguerite that the woman found the courage to scramble to the door. She pulled it open and slipped out of the room just as Marguerite threw herself to the side to avoid the oncoming sword.

She landed hard on the floor, her back slamming into the corner of the first stall with a painful jolt. Marguerite scrambled along the floor at once, sure that at any moment she'd feel the bite of the steel slicing into her flesh. It didn't happen, however, the sword had bitten deep into the wood of the windowsill and it took her attacker a moment to tug it free.

By the time he had and turned on Marguerite, she'd got back to her feet and was rushing for the door. He charged that way at once and knowing she wouldn't make it before him, or at least wouldn't get the door open and get out before he brought the sword down, Marguerite skidded to a halt and scrambled back toward the wall of stalls, her eyes darting around, searching for something to use as a weapon or shield. She very much feared that if she didn't find something and quickly, Julius would be eating his meal alone . . . as well as looking for a new lifemate to replace his headless ex-lifemate.

There was nothing to find however, nothing to hurl at him or block his blows. Sensing movement out of the corner of her eye, Marguerite drew her head back around to see the sword swinging again, and instinctively leapt back. The door behind her swung away under her weight, crashing into the stall wall as she stumbled back into the tiny cubicle.

Marguerite cursed herself for not diving left or right even before the back of her legs ran up against the toilet and she began to fall. She was trapped in the stall and had done it to herself, she realized with disgust as her attacker approached, the sword held high. He couldn't swing from side to side and take off her head in the small booth, but Marguerite had no doubt he'd simply give her a fearsome bodily injury, and then drag her out of the stall while she was too weak to fight and cut off her head then. She imagined he must be smiling with victory under that damned balaclava covering his face.

Furious with both herself and whomever this man was, Marguerite shot her foot up and out the moment he was close enough. She felt great satisfaction when it lodged firmly between his legs, the blow upsetting the man's aim, she saw just before the sword sliced down into her shoulder.

It was the clatter of high heels tapping down the stairs in a mad rush that drew Julius's attention. His first sight of the terror on the face of the woman even before her feet slid out from under her and she tumbled the last few steps was enough to send a shock of concern down his back and bring him to his feet.

Crossing the restaurant at a speed that would have startled everyone if their attention hadn't been on the jibbering woman now being helped to her feet by the maitre d', Julius didn't stop to hear what she had to say, but hurried up the stairs at once, taking them three at a time in his rush to reach Marguerite.

There were three doors off the landing at the top of the stairs. Julius rushed for the one with the ladies' room sign above the door, slamming it open with a crash that no doubt echoed through the building. He then froze in horror at the sight before him. A wounded and bloodied Marguerite was being dragged out of one of the stalls by her arm by a man dressed all in black. Julius's entrance had caught the man's attention, however, and the black-clad figure paused with Marguerite's legs still in the stall to peer around. The two men stared at each other briefly.

"Jesus," someone breathed behind him, telling Julius he'd been followed.

Julius charged forward, but the attacker was already moving to make his escape. Turning away, he ran in the opposite direction, charging the large square window at the end of the room, his sword out before him.

There was a shocked shout from behind Julius as

the man crashed through the glass and dropped out of sight, but he paid it no attention. Neither did he chase after Marguerite's attacker, instead, Julius stopped and knelt beside her, his hands moving swiftly over her to check her wounds. She'd taken a bad blow to the shoulder that had nearly severed her arm, and another to the chest. They were not killing blows to an immortal and she was already healing, but needed blood and a lot of it he realized.

Julius started to scoop her up into his arms, pausing when she moaned in pain.

"She's alive," someone breathed with shock by his ear.

Julius lifted his head to the speaker. It took him a moment to recognize the maitre d' and then he glanced toward the door with a frown as he became aware of the clatter of several people rushing upstairs to join them. Cursing, Julius slipped into the maitre d's mind, altering his memory of what he'd found here and sending him out into the hall to head off the oncoming crowd and assure them that everything was fine.

Once the door had closed behind the man, Julius scooped Marguerite into his arms and then hesitated. He could hardly carry her out of here past all the people out on the landing. He didn't have the time to wipe all their memories.

Marguerite moaned again, drawing his gaze down to her. She was pale, her face the color of the porcelain in the room. The blood was migrating to her wounds, repairing and regenerating and doing all sorts of miraculous things to save her life and limb. But it had a price and he knew soon she would be in agony as the nanos in her body attacked her organs in search of fresh blood.

Cursing, he moved to the shattered window and peered out. There was no sign of her attacker, but he hadn't expected there to be. More importantly, the walkway between the building and the river was completely empty, and that's what he'd hoped for.

Pressing Marguerite tight to his chest, Julius climbed up on the ledge and jumped through the opening, dropping one floor to the cobbled walk below. He landed awkwardly, his ankle twisting on the uneven cobbles.

Julius ground his teeth as pain shot through the abused joint, but ignored the pain and started quickly along the walkway in the direction of the townhouse, glancing at Marguerite with concern as she moaned again. This time she didn't stop.

Ten

"Hello?"

Julius tore his gaze away from Marguerite's pale face and glanced toward the door at that call. He'd been sitting on the side of the bed for the last half hour, just watching her as he waited for the men to arrive at the townhouse with the blood. Now he stood and moved to the door. Opening it, he stepped out into the hall and peered down at the men trooping into the rented townhouse.

"Up here," he said quietly, not wanting to disturb Marguerite.

Tiny was at the head of the trio and quickly started up, a cooler in hand. "We were as fast as we could be. What happened? Christian said we were to get as much blood as we could find and meet you back here. Is Marguerite all right?"

Julius didn't answer at once. His gaze moved past the mortal to Marcus and Christian as they followed the detective into the house. Each of the three men carried a cooler, all presumably crammed full of blood. He supposed they'd robbed a blood bank, and had probably brought back every last bag they'd found there.

Julius led the way to the bedroom where Marguerite was starting to stir again. He had known the two measly bags of blood he'd given her wouldn't calm her for long. Julius paused in the door and turned to Tiny as the man reached his side. He opened the cooler the mortal carried and grabbed a bag, then moved to the bed.

"What happened?" Tiny asked with concern as he set the cooler on the bedside table and turned to peer at Marguerite.

Julius didn't answer at first, his attention taken up with opening Marguerite's mouth and popping the bag to her protracted teeth.

"Jesus."

Julius glanced around at that whisper to see that Marcus and Christian had followed them into the room. Christian had shifted his cooler under one arm and bent to scoop up Marguerite's dress from the floor where Julius had thrown it after stripping it from her. The younger immortal held the dress up, his eyes moving over the blood-soaked and torn cloth with dismay.

"She was attacked at the restaurant," Julius told them.

"Where the hell were you?" Tiny asked, propping his hands on his hips.

"I was at our table. She'd gone up to the ladies' room. I should have gone with her," he added fretfully.

"That probably would have caused a bit of a stir," Marcus pointed out quietly.

"And you think this didn't?" Julius asked dryly, reaching for the cooler Tiny had set on the dresser as he saw that the bag on her teeth was nearly empty.

Tiny was there before him, opening the lid, and retrieving another bag for him. As he handed it over, he asked again, "What happened?"

Julius traded the empty bag for a full one before repeating, "She was attacked in the ladies' room. Fortunately, there was another woman in there with her and when she came rushing downstairs in a state, I headed right up."

"It was a woman who attacked her?" Tiny asked with a frown.

Julius shook his head. "No. It was definitely a man. He was an inch or so shorter than me, but just as wide; big arms, thick legs."

"Did you recognize him?" Christian asked, moving forward and placing the cooler he carried next to Tiny's.

"No. He was covered from head to foot in black; a black balaclava over his face, black clothes, even a black cape. He had a sword."

"Just like the guy Marguerite described the morning she was attacked at the Dorchester," Tiny said thoughtfully.

"Why didn't he cut off her head?" Marcus asked quietly. "Did you stop him?"

"I think so. She was badly wounded and he was

dragging her out of one of the stalls when I rushed in. I think he was trying to get her out where he could get a proper swing to behead her."

"Thank God you arrived when you did then," Tiny said, his worried gaze on Marguerite's face.

"You killed him?" Marcus asked and Julius felt his shoulders sag at his own failure as he shook his head.

"He threw himself out the window the minute I came in."

"So he's still out there somewhere," Christian said, and Julius glanced up to see all three men peering toward the window as if expecting a man in black to come crashing into the room at any moment.

"Did you lock the door behind you when we came in?" Tiny asked suddenly.

Marcus and Christian glanced at each other, and then Christian turned and hurried from the room.

"I'll make a quick search of the house while he's locking the door," Marcus muttered, following.

For a moment, Tiny looked as if he might follow to help, but instead he turned to Julius and said, "If this really does have to do with Christian's mother, you could put an end to it all by just telling him who the hell she is."

"It wouldn't keep Marguerite safe," he said quietly.

"The hell it won't. We'd go home then and she'd be safe."

"I don't think she would," Julius admitted at once, chilled at the very idea of her leaving.

"What?" Tiny asked with disbelief.

"I don't think she will be safe now no matter where she is," he said quietly, admitting the conclusion he'd come to while waiting for them. "I think whatever has been set in motion will continue to play out."

"Until what? Until she's dead?" Tiny asked angrily and bent to grab the sheet covering Marguerite. Julius reached to stop him, but the man only pulled the sheet down far enough to reveal the top of her shoulder. The wound there was already half healed but it was still a great, ugly gaping gash. "Just what the hell did Christian drag us into here?"

"I wish I knew," Julius muttered.

"What are—?"

"Leave," Julius interrupted wearily, and then slid into the immortal's mind to make sure he did so. He needed time to think without Tiny's worried and angry questions, so he sent him to his bed to remain there for the rest of the night. Julius knew the man would just ask his questions again in the morning, but hoped by then he'd have answers to offer him, or at least a good lie.

Sighing as the door closed behind the mortal, Julius retrieved a fresh bag and switched it for the empty one, then waited patiently as Marguerite's body drew it in. She didn't look quite as pale as she had been, more the color of parchment than porcelain now. She would need another three or four bags, but should be okay for a little bit after that, he thought. Of course, the healing would probably continue through the night. Even after the wound itself was no longer visible, the body would be busy repairing the internal damage and she'd need two or three more bags of blood before dawn, and then again when she awoke before she would be back to normal.

"The doors and windows are locked and there's no

one in the house but us," Marcus announced as he and Christian returned to the room.

Julius nodded as he switched bags again.

"This was the same attacker as at the hotel, wasn't it?" Christian asked quietly, moving around the bed to sit on the other side and peer down at Marguerite.

"I'm pretty sure it was, yes," Julius admitted.

Christian nodded. "And you still think my mother was behind it?"

"Her people most certainly," he answered and frowned at the guilt that swept over his son's face. "It is not your fault, Christian. Had I handled the matter differently at the time, none of this would have happened."

"What do we do now?" Marcus asked quietly, changing the topic. "Stay here and wait for Martine Argeneau to return from London?"

Julius hesitated, his gaze shifting to Marguerite. He wanted to show her more of York in the hope that she might remember something, anything of the past that she seemed to be missing from her memory, but wouldn't risk her being attacked again to do so. Next time, they might not be lucky enough to escape with her life.

"What time is it?" he asked suddenly rather than answer.

"Almost one o'clock," Christian answered. "There won't be any trains running now."

"No," Julius agreed. He was silent for a moment, and then said, "We'll discuss it tomorrow when we wake up. Marguerite can have an opinion then as well."

"I suspect she'll want to stay," Christian said. "So

long as we don't let her out of our sight she should be safe enough. Whoever it is who's attacking her seems to try to get to her when she's away from us."

When Julius glanced at him in question, he shrugged and said, "Otherwise why risk such a public attack? A public washroom with mortals in the room? The only benefit was that there were no other immortals in the immediate vicinity to help fend him off. That's probably the furthest you've been from her since we arrived."

"He's right," Marcus commented. "The man obviously followed us from London, and you two were out walking around the first night. Why didn't he attack then? He's avoiding attacking her when there are other immortals nearby."

"So if we keep her close, she should be safe." Julius's gaze slid back to Marguerite. If that were the case, he wouldn't leave her side for an instant until all of this was resolved. It wouldn't be a hardship. The hardship would be not trying to keep her in bed . . . naked for the duration.

Marguerite stirred as Julius took away the last empty bag, her eyes blinking open. Her gaze slid over the three of them with confusion, and then her memory of the attack apparently returned and she glanced down at herself.

"It's all right," Julius said. "You're safe now and almost completely healed."

Giving a slight nod, she raised her eyes to his. "Did you—?"

"He got away," Julius interrupted quietly.

"Was anyone else hurt?"

"No," he assured her and she closed her eyes with

a little sigh and seemed to drop back off into a heal-ing sleep.

Julius watched her for a minute, and then glanced at the other two men. "You may as well take the other two coolers of blood back to wherever you got them. There are still a couple bags in here and more is being delivered just before dawn."

Nodding, Marcus lifted the cooler he'd set on the foot of the bed, and Christian stood and walked around to the dresser to retrieve the one he'd carried in.

"Take a key and be sure to lock up behind you," he ordered as they left the room.

When they assured him they would and pulled the door closed, Julius stood up and started to undo the buttons of his shirt, grimacing when he realized that the cloth was sticky with blood and clinging to his chest. He glanced down at Marguerite, and then turned away. The blood had soaked into his pants as well as his top and he'd need to shower before slip-ping into bed next to her.

Julius left the bedroom and bathroom doors open, glancing through to Marguerite every few seconds as he turned on the shower and quickly stripped off his tacky clothes.

Unwilling to leave her alone for longer than nec-essary, he took the fastest shower he could manage, leaping under the cascade of water, splashing water on his chest, tugging the shower curtain aside to lean out and peer into the bedroom at Marguerite, then ducking back under the water long enough to soap up before sticking his head out to check on her again. The next duck under the water was his last and it was just long enough to wash away the soap, then he was out, grabbing a towel and wrapping it around his waist as he headed back into the bedroom.

Julius pushed the door closed behind him, and dried himself as he walked to the bed. He then dropped the towel and pulled back the sheet and blanket to slide into bed next to her.

Marguerite opened her eyes the moment she felt the bed depress beside her. She hadn't really fallen back to sleep, she just hadn't felt like talking while the other two men were there. She'd opened her eyes after she'd heard the door close, but had seen Julius undoing his shirt and the sight of her own blood staining the white top had been rather distressing. Marguerite had quickly closed her eyes again and simply listened to his movements, but had opened them with surprise when she'd heard the shower turn on. Realizing he was washing away the blood, she'd closed her eyes once more and waited patiently for him to finish and return. Now, he was back.

"You're awake," Julius said, stilling in surprise when he saw that her eyes were open.

"Yes," she offered him a smile.

Julius hesitated, his gaze concerned. "Do you want more blood?"

Marguerite shook her head. "Not right now, thank you."

He smiled faintly at her prim words, but asked, "A drink then? Or food?"

Marguerite shook her head. Despite not having gotten the chance to have their meal, she wasn't hungry. All she really wanted was for him to hold her close just then. She wanted his warmth and his strong arms around her to help her feel safe again.

Julius hesitated and she suspected he was searching his mind for something else he might offer, but apparently not coming up with anything, he finally lay down beside her, easing onto his back, careful not to jostle her. Marguerite waited until he was still, then rolled over and curled up against him, resting her head and arm on his chest.

"Don't hurt yourself, you're still healing," Julius said with concern even as he slipped his arm out from under her to wrap it around her back.

"It doesn't hurt anymore. It's mostly healed I think," she assured him snuggling into his chest.

They were silent for a minute, his fingers running lightly through her hair, her own toying with the hair on his chest, and then Julius suddenly asked, "Marguerite, will you tell me about your marriage to Jean Claude?"

She stiffened in his arms, her fingers stilling. Her marriage was not a topic Marguerite enjoyed thinking about, and while she'd revealed some of it to Tiny during the first three weeks here, it wasn't something she wanted to share with Julius. Marguerite was afraid if she revealed the humiliating details of her marriage, it might affect how Julius saw her. He might lose respect for her or see her as weak, or a victim because of how Jean Claude had controlled her. He might even begin to look at her with the same disgust Jean Claude had.

No, she wouldn't risk it, Marguerite would rather just leave her marriage as dead and buried as her husband was.

"Marguerite?" he queried softly.

Finally, she shook her head. "I would rather not."

Julius was silent for a moment, then sighed and said, "Marguerite, in another time and another place I would have respected that wish. I realize now it would have been a mistake. It would have left me at a disadvantage when— if anything happened."

"Anything like what?" she asked curiously.

Rather than answer, Julius seemed to change the subject, or at least shift it to the side. "Tell me about Jean Claude's death."

Marguerite breathed deeply, drawing in a great lungful of air. The question had taken her by surprise.

"I don't ask out of mere curiosity, Marguerite. There is a reason for the question."

When she tilted her head on his chest, to glance at him he stared solemnly back. Marguerite lowered her head again and began to pluck at the hair on his chest. "He died in a fire."

"How?" he pressed and she frowned, knowing that to explain how he had died she had to explain at least some of their marriage.

"Please, trust me," Julius said quietly.

Marguerite met his gaze, saw the pleading there and closed her own eyes on a sigh.

"Jean-Claude was . . . troubled," she began, and then glanced up through her lashes to see Julius nod. Swallowing, she continued, "I think he secretly loathed himself for marrying me, for the weakness in doing so when we weren't true lifemates."

"You knew you weren't true lifemates?" Julius interrupted quietly.

"Not at first. I knew nothing about immortals or . . . anything at the start. But I soon learned there was something wrong and that was what it was,"

Marguerite explained, and then said, "The first hundred or so years after we married weren't so bad. He wasn't cruel at least. He was just selfish and cold, indifferent to my feelings and needs. If he wished to go to a ball, or to travel here or there, I wasn't allowed *not* to want to go. He would insist and if I refused he would slip into my mind and make me compliant."

"I suppose it wasn't just restricted to attending balls and things," Julius said carefully. "Did he enforce your compliance in the bedroom too?"

Her expression must have been answer enough. Marguerite could feel the anger tightening his muscles. "It was just an occasional thing the first ten or twenty years. I was young and eager to please then, but . . ." She shrugged. "I grew up and became less so and the more I resisted, the more he took control, but there was no real cruelty. Just an indifferent determination for him to have his way no matter my thoughts or feelings."

"What changed that?" Julius asked, and she could feel his tension increasing.

Marguerite shook her head against his chest with bewilderment. "I don't know. It all followed our tour of Europe."

"Your tour of Europe?" he asked and something in his voice made her look at him sharply, but his expression was unrevealing and he prompted, "When was that?"

"It was a long tour, more than twenty years. It started somewhere around 1470 or so and went on until 1491," she admitted. "We left England and toured around Europe."

"Tell me about that."

The tension had entered his voice now, Marguerite noticed, but admitted, "It's all rather vague to me, although I recall it was pleasant."

"Pleasant?"

"Yes. I just remember having a good time. I know we visited country after country, city after city constantly moving, never really staying long enough anywhere to see anything." She gave a self-deprecating laugh. "I know it sounds silly to say that we spent twenty years of touring and not really seeing anything, but . . ." Marguerite shrugged against his side. "That's how I recall it."

Rather than seem confused by her words Julius nodded solemnly. "Go on."

Sighing, she began to pluck at the hair of his chest again. "To this day I don't know what happened to change things so suddenly. It just seemed like, overnight, Jean Claude became another person. He began to take to feeding off people who had imbibed too much, and people who had ingested drugs. He even hired servants who were alcoholics so that he could feed from them." She shook her head. "And the more he fed from such people, the more cruel he became."

Marguerite paused, and then admitted painfully, "And he couldn't even seem to look at me anymore without loathing in his eyes. He wouldn't allow me to leave the house alone, wouldn't allow me to have friends. Jean Claude said I was to be a mother to his children, and that was all I was to do." She shook her head with despair. "And yet for the longest time he refused me children."

"Refused you children?" Julius asked softly.

Marguerite nodded. "I wanted to have another

child. Lucern was a little over one hundred and I began to ache to hold a child in my arms again." She paused suddenly and realized, "In fact that too started directly after the European tour," she admitted with a little sigh. "I guess it somehow changed both of us."

"And you wanted a child," Julius prompted.

Marguerite nodded. "It was more than want. I needed a child in my arms, they felt empty. I felt as if . . ." She stopped and shook her head, knowing how ridiculous it must sound.

"Tell me," Julius said, and somehow she knew the answer was very important to him. The problem was, she didn't know why.

After a hesitation, Marguerite admitted, "I felt as if I had lost a child. As if there was a child who should be there, but wasn't. I yearned for a baby . . . So much so, I pestered him constantly." Marguerite flushed as she admitted that she'd begged her husband to share his seed and get her with child. "I had never begged for anything before that. I had too much pride. But I did then." She managed a smile and shrugged against him once more. "And eventually he did. It took a long time, but a hundred years later he came to me and Bastien was born."

"Were you happy then?" Julius asked.

"It helped," Marguerite said and then tilted her head to tell him. "I love children, Julius. I have raised my own, as well as nieces and nephews. I can't imagine any mother wanting any child dead, let alone her own."

"No. I don't think you can," Julius said solemnly and closed his eyes, but not before she thought she caught the sheen of tears in them.

"What are you thinking?" she asked quietly.

"I'm remembering . . . a dream I had."

"Tell me," she urged, tired of talking herself.

"It was of you and me in another time."

She smiled.

"We were lovers and true lifemates and so happy sometimes my heart hurt with it. But I seemed always to fear trusting that happiness, afraid that I would lose it. And then I did. I lost it to the actions of another, but mostly through my own lack of faith."

"Lack of faith?" Marguerite asked with a frown. "In what?"

"In you . . . and in my first instincts about you," Julius admitted. "In the dream someone told me something about you that really wasn't a lie and was the truth as they saw it, but wasn't the whole truth either. My first instinct was that it was not right, but I allowed my fears and doubts of others to convince me that exactly what I had feared had happened, that it had all been false, and I let you go."

Frowning at the sadness in his expression, Marguerite reached up to brush the hair back from his face. "It sounds a horrible dream. We must be sure never to allow it to happen in real life."

"Yes," Julius said huskily. "Never again."

Marguerite wanted to ask him what he meant by 'never again,' but his mouth was on hers and his hands were moving on her and she soon forgot the question. It felt as if she had lived the last seven hundred years just for that moment, to be in his arms, and to hold him in hers. She didn't think life could ever be so perfect again and understood his dream fears, because suddenly she was afraid that it would all be snatched away and she would wake up in her own cold bed, finding it had all been a dream or even worse, that it wasn't Julius in the bed beside her, but Jean Claude.

Julius opened his eyes sleepily and reached for Marguerite, scowling when she wasn't there. The other side of the bed was empty. Marguerite was up before him and gone again which was damned annoying when, like the morning before, he woke with a raging need for her. This may be their second time around—at least for him—but it appeared his need for her was going to be just as desperate as it had the first time he'd met and fallen in love with her.

Those thoughts drifted away as Julius recalled the attack the night before. Marguerite had nearly been killed and should be resting to recover. What the hell was she doing up?

Shifting up onto one elbow, he peered at the bedside clock, frowning when he saw that it wasn't even yet noon. What was she doing awake? Pushing the sheets aside, he slid his feet to the floor and got up, heading for the door without bothering with clothes. Other than Marguerite there were only men in the house. Besides, no one should be up at the moment anyway, including Marguerite.

Scowling, Julius pulled the door open and stepped out into the hall. The bathroom door was open, showing that it was empty and he had just turned toward her bedroom door to check there, to be sure she hadn't slipped off to her own room, when he heard Tiny's voice from below.

"Marguerite? What are you doing up?" the man

asked and Julius moved to the top of the stairs to peer down, eyes widening when he saw that Marguerite was just stepping off the bottom step. All she wore was one of his T-shirts, the garment large on her and reaching halfway down her thighs. He'd fetched it for her to wear on a trip to the bathroom last night before they'd gone to sleep and she hadn't bothered to take it off on slipping back to bed, claiming she liked the idea of wearing his clothes close to her body.

Julius had smiled at the time, but wasn't smiling now. While the cotton shirt covered the important bits, it was hardly decent enough to wear and walk around in front of Tiny, he thought with irritation.

"Marguerite?" Tiny was frowning now as well, concern drawing his expression tight as he stepped out of the living room and into the hall ahead of her. "Are you all right? Marguerite?"

The detective reached out to catch her shoulders to try to bring her to a halt as she continued forward without slowing, but rather than stop, Marguerite reached out, clasping him by the arms and tossing him to the side as if he were nothing more than a pillow that had fallen in her path. She didn't even glance in Tiny's direction as he crashed into the hall wall and fell, but continued on toward the door.

Shocked and confused, Julius hurried down the stairs.

"Are you all right?" he asked Tiny as he rushed past and barely caught his stunned nod before turning his gaze back to Marguerite as he hurried after her. She was at the door now, pulling it open and stepping out into the sunlit day and he shouted her name but she didn't even look around. She had taken several steps outside before he caught up to her and caught her arm.

Julius jerked her around to face him, then saw that her face was completely expressionless, her eyes dull and flat. She raised her hands to clasp him as she'd done with Tiny, no doubt preparing to toss him aside as she'd done with the mortal, but suddenly stopped and went limp.

Cursing, Julius caught her before she hit the sidewalk, and then scooped her up into his arms, but froze as he became aware of the people on the street. At least a dozen people stood around on the sidewalk, on both this and the other side of the street. Some were alone, some in groups, but every last one was gaping at him where he stood completely naked, an unconscious Marguerite in nothing but his T-shirt in his arms.

There were far too many for Julius to wipe all their memories on his own unless he wanted to spend several minutes there performing the task, minutes during which more people would approach and have to be wiped as well, so Julius muttered the only excuse he could come up with. "She sleepwalks."

Whether they believed the explanation for what they'd witnessed or not, Julius didn't care. Turning away, he carried her quickly back into the townhouse, grateful to find Tiny there to close the door.

"We heard you shout, Father. What happened?" Christian asked, hurrying down the stairs with Marcus on his heels.

Julius paused at the foot of the steps. He'd intended to take Marguerite straight up to his room and hold her close until she woke up. The men on the stairs prevented that. They also caused yet another problem. He didn't mind Marcus knowing what had happened, he even wanted to talk to the man about it and get his opinion and advice on the matter, but he definitely didn't want his son there. Or Tiny for that matter.

"Father? What happened to Marguerite? Is she all right? Was there another attack?" Christian asked.

Julius shifted his gaze from the woman in his arms to his son, then past him to Marcus. He briefly met the older immortal's gaze, hoping the man could read the message in his eyes and then gave the same excuse he'd used outside.

"Nothing. Marguerite was sleepwalking," he growled, turning on his heel to carry her into the living room. "Go back to bed."

"She wasn't sleepwalking," Tiny protested, following him. "She looked right at me, but there was nobody home, Julius. It's like she was drugged or hypnotized or something."

"What?" Christian asked as he stepped off the stairs and followed them. "Is that true, Father?"

Julius's only answer was a grunt as he laid Marguerite on the nearest sofa and grabbed a throw off the back of the couch to place over her. He then settled on the edge of the couch and brushed her hair off her cheeks, watching her face worriedly.

"It's true," Tiny insisted, "Marguerite would never hurt me, but she picked me up and tossed me aside like trash. She had to have been controlled like I was in California."

"Controlled?" Christian sounded shocked.

"Yes," Tiny muttered, and Julius felt the material of the mortal's corduroy pants brush against his hip as he moved closer to peer at Marguerite with concern. It reminded Julius that he was naked.

"I'm going to get dressed. You two stay here and watch Marguerite," he growled glaring at Christian and Tiny. "Call me if she wakes up."

He started from the room, glad when Marcus immediately followed. He wanted a word with him. Julius jogged up the stairs and strode straight into his room.

"I hadn't expected this. It was frightening to behold," he muttered to Marcus while dragging a pair of jeans from the wardrobe and stepping into them.

"What was frightening to behold?" Christian asked, and Julius nearly tumbled over sideways as he jerked around, jeans still at half-mast, to see that his son had followed them upstairs.

"I told you to keep an eye on Marguerite," Julius hissed dragging the jeans the rest of the way on and doing them up.

Much to his fury, the man shrugged the suggestion away impatiently. "Tiny can watch her."

"Tiny cannot watch her. Didn't you hear him? She threw him across the room like a bag of garbage being tossed in the back of a truck," Julius growled furiously. "He cannot stop her if she is controlled again and made to walk out the door."

"So, she *was* controlled," Christian said with triumph.

Cursing, Julius turned away to grab a T-shirt from the drawer where he'd put them and pulled it on as he strode quickly toward the door. He couldn't leave

Marguerite alone downstairs with Tiny and risk her being controlled again and sent walking out the door, probably to her death.

"There was a time you would have obeyed me without question," he growled at the boy in passing.

"Yeah, well, there was a time when you deserved that honor," Christian snapped back, following him into the hall.

Julius stiffened and paused at the top of the landing to peer at him narrowly. "Are you saying I don't deserve it now?"

Christian hesitated, and then sighed and said, "I don't know if you do or not, Father. You won't tell me anything and I'm not sure what's going on."

"I have told you why I won't tell you about your mother," Julius began wearily.

"Not telling me about her is one thing, but you have more secrets than that," Christian said grimly.

Shaking his head impatiently, Julius turned to start downstairs.

"Is Marguerite my mother?"

That blurted question made the blood freeze in his veins and Julius came to an abrupt halt on the stairs. He turned slowly to peer up at his son, noting that Marcus looked as shocked by the question as he felt.

"What would make you even think something like that?" he growled, avoiding answering the question.

"The picture in your desk drawer in your study," Christian announced descending several steps until he stood only one above him. "A miniature painted portrait of Marguerite or a woman who looks just like her. She's wearing clothes from the late fifteenth century . . . around the time that I would have been born."

Julius paled at the words. "When—? How—?"

"I found it when I was a boy," Christian admitted, and added unapologetically, "I was snooping. I looked in your drawer and found the painting. I thought she must be my mother because you kept it hidden and . . . because she had such a loving smile I wanted her to be." He admitted with a shrug, "I used to sneak in there often just to look at her and imagine that she would appear at our door one day and—" He swallowed and waved away whatever foolish child's dreams he'd had.

"When I met Marguerite in California, I knew at once that she was the woman from the painting." Christian smiled wryly. "Why do you think I hired her? Tiny may be a detective, but *she* isn't and I didn't really think they'd be able to find the answers I wanted anyway. Only you can give me those."

"Then why did you hire them?" Julius asked, suspecting he already knew the answer.

"Because I knew Marcus would tell you I had, even though I'd asked him not to."

When Marcus shifted uncomfortably, the younger immortal glanced at him and shrugged. "You are a loyal friend to my father, Marcus. You were raised together and are like brothers. You tell him everything," he said dryly and then turned back to his father and admitted, "I brought Tiny and Marguerite over to Europe knowing you'd hear about it and—as usual—try to intervene. I wanted to see your reaction when you met. I was sure I'd be able to tell if she was my mother."

Julius let out his breath on a slow sigh and leaned against the stair railing. Here he'd thought himself so clever keeping everything from the boy and he'd figured out most of it on his own.

"So," Christian said grimly, "is Marguerite my mother or does she just look like her?"

Julius shook his head and opened his mouth to answer, but some instinct made him glance toward the living room door as he did and he froze, alarm snapping his mouth closed. Their voices had obviously drawn Tiny. The detective stood in the doorway waiting for his answer with grim anger, but that wasn't what made the blood run cold in Julius's veins. Marguerite had awakened and stood behind the mortal, her pale face and horrified expression telling him that she too had heard everything.

Eleven

Marguerite stared past Tiny's back to the men on the stairs, her brain roaring with horror and drowning out any possibility of thought.

"Is Marguerite my mother or does she just look like her?"

Christian's question was screaming in her head, repeating over and over like a skipping record.

"Marguerite?"

She blinked her eyes, seeing that Julius was off the stairs and moving toward her with Marcus and Christian following. Pushing Tiny out of the way, he hurried forward, his eyebrows drawn down with frustration and concern.

Marguerite backed away as he approached, feeling as cornered as she'd been in that stall the night before. She moved back until she came up against the couch, and then flinched when he reached for her.

"Don't touch me. Leave me alone." The words were wooden rather than panic filled as they should have been. She felt disconnected, empty.

Julius let his hands drop, but didn't back off. Instead, he said calmly, "I can explain."

Marguerite stared at him, waiting. She wanted him to explain. She wanted him to have an answer that would fix everything so that her heart would stop breaking . . . and so she waited, giving him that chance, but he hesitated, and then said almost helplessly, "No, I can't."

Marguerite sucked in a breath, staring at the man she'd found such pleasure with. She'd thought he was her lifemate, had foolishly allowed herself to love him, to dream of a future together. But nothing was as she'd thought.

She knew she wasn't Christian's mother, which meant that she just looked like his mother. She looked like a woman Julius had obviously loved deeply and whose picture he'd kept near at hand for five hundred years. It was Jean Claude all over again, she realized and felt her heart crumbling to dust in her chest.

He reached for her again, but this time Marguerite struck out, slapping him sharply across the face. Julius stilled, eyes glowing black. He didn't try to stop her when she walked around him and pushed her way through the others to leave the room. She could feel their eyes following her as she walked upstairs.

Marguerite went straight to her room, closed the door behind her and just stood there for a moment, the silence crowding around her . . . and then the chittering began in her brain.

"You look like Christian's mother," it taunted. *"Julius must have loved her dearly to still have her picture. She was his true lifemate, you just look like her."*

"He can probably read you and was simply saying he couldn't because he wanted you . . . because you look like his lifemate."

"Every time he made love to you he was thinking of her."

"Every time he touched you, he was touching her."

"It's not you he wants at all. You're just a stand-in."

"It's Jean Claude all over again."

She should leave, Marguerite thought numbly. She should go . . . somewhere. Find someplace where she could be alone to lick her wounds and think. She moved away from the door and peered around the room, her eyes landing on the bed. Memories of their lovemaking immediately rose up in her mind, making her long for his arms around her, his lips on hers, him inside her . . .

Maybe it would be different than it had been with Jean Claude. Maybe . . .

Cursing, Marguerite hurried to the closet to find something to wear. She dressed quickly, paused to take a shaky breath, and then peered around the room. She needed to get home, but didn't have the energy or any desire to pack. She'd leave her clothes, she decided, they'd just remind her of Julius anyway.

She started to cross to the door, but then paused. The men were in the living room. There was no way she was going to be able to slip downstairs and out the door without their notice.

Sighing, she glanced around. When her eyes landed on the dark curtains on the opposite wall, she crossed to the window and drew open the heavy material. Sunlight immediately splashed into the room and she took a step back, her eyes lifting to the sky. The sunlight was blinding overhead. Her gaze slid to the digital clock on the bedside table to see that it wasn't even one o'clock yet.

No wonder she was exhausted, she'd had hardly any sleep at all, Marguerite thought absently as she peered down at the narrow alley behind the townhouse. It was an easy jump to the ground and would save her running into Julius on her way out and possibly being stopped.

Marguerite glanced back toward the bedroom door as she thought of Tiny, but she was rather hurt that the mortal she'd come to think of as a friend hadn't followed her upstairs to be sure she was all right, and, instead, had stayed with the Nottes. It felt like betrayal to her.

Her attention shifted back to the window. While the building was terribly old, the windows were new, probably installed for energy-saving purposes. Marguerite released the lock and slid the window open. She cast one nervous glance skyward, climbed to sit on the window sill with her legs dangling outside, and then pushed herself off. She landed on the stone below with a small jolt, her knees bending to ease the impact, and then started to stand up straight again.

"You'll explain and do it now! Marguerite deserves that much at least."

The faint words were spoken in Tiny's angry voice and she turned her head, and then ducked to the side as she realized she'd landed in front of the kitchen window and the men were now entering the kitchen.

And Tiny was confronting Julius Notte on her behalf, not conspiring with him, she realized. The fact almost sent her marching back into the house to collect the mortal and take him with her, but Marguerite decided against it. She really didn't want to have to face Julius again. She'd call Tiny on his mobile as soon as she got somewhere with a phone and have him meet her.

The sun was beginning to warm the back of her head. Marguerite moved quickly away from the window to head up the alley.

"Are you going to tell me what the hell's going on?" Tiny asked, following Julius into the kitchen.

"I told you, I can't," Julius snarled, dragging the door of the mini-fridge open and then slamming it closed with a curse when he recalled that the blood was stored in the mini-fridge in the living room.

"The hell you can't!" Tiny snapped. "You'll explain and do it now. Marguerite deserves that much at least."

"So do I," Christian added grimly from the door.

"Perhaps it's time," Marcus said quietly.

Julius glanced at him silently, then sighed and dropped to sit at the table. He spent a moment trying to sort out where to start, then decided the best place to start was the beginning and said, "I met Marguerite here in York in 1490."

"She *is* my mother," Christian breathed, dropping into one of the other chairs.

"No, she isn't," Tiny told him apologetically. "She can't be."

"She is," Julius corrected quietly and the mortal turned on him.

"If she met you before, why didn't she say so? Why have you both been acting like you didn't know each other? And why the hell would she agree to go hunting for Christian's mother when it was her?" The mortal shook his head with disbelief. "You're lying and you'll have to do better than that. She sure as hell didn't spend the last three weeks going half blind looking through archives for kicks."

Christian's eyebrows drew together in confusion. "That's true."

"I'll explain if you can both sit down and shut up long enough to allow it," Julius said patiently.

Tiny scowled, but moved to take a seat at the table, then raised his eyebrows.

Nodding, Julius started again. "I met Marguerite here in York in 1490. Marcus and I came here to . . . er . . ."

"Carouse," Marcus filled in dryly.

"Carouse?" Tiny asked with bewilderment.

"Gamble, lift the skirts of the prettier wenches and feed on the locals," he explained and then shrugged. "We were young . . . er. Younger."

Julius smiled faintly at the correction, but then continued, "I met Marguerite our second night here and that was the end of the carousing for me."

Marcus shook his head at the memory and commented, "Spoiled all the fun."

"Why doesn't she remember?" Tiny asked, and when Julius turned a scowl on him, sighed and said, "Right. No interruptions. Go ahead. I'll shut up."

Julius nodded, and continued, "Marcus and I were hunting when we spotted her."

"Hunting?"

"Looking for dinner," Marcus explained when Julius sighed in exasperation at yet another interruption.

"You aren't talking deer are you?" Tiny asked dryly.

Marcus shook his head solemnly and when the detective grimaced, reminded him, "There were no blood banks back then."

"Right." He sighed. "So you were hunting and spotted Marguerite."

"She was beautiful," Julius continued with a smile. "She had on a burgundy gown with the lowest décolletage a lady of quality would dare to wear, a matching cape, and this ridiculous little cap perched on her head that looked like a bird in its nest."

While Christian remained silent, Tiny grunted, apparently not seeing the charm.

"She was on the hunt too, though she'd found her quarry and was leading him into a snickleway. I waited until she had finished her meal and then approached."

"And was lost," Marcus said mournfully.

Julius smiled faintly at the words, but his smile faded as he said, "She had been widowed twenty years earlier and had a grown son. She'd just moved into Martine's home to live while Martine moved away for a bit to prevent anyone realizing she did not age."

"Widowed?" Tiny asked with surprise.

"Her son's name was Lucern," Julius continued, ignoring him and the man held back his questions, though his confusion was plain on his face. "Fortunately, he was one hundred years old when she became pregnant with our child and there was no issue with carrying him to term.

"We were both extremely happy. Then, shortly before she was to give birth a messenger arrived. My father had been at the English court arranging a marriage for my sister, Mila, to her true lifemate, Reginald."

"He was an English baron, still is I suppose," Marcus told Tiny. "And Mila is short for Camilla. She and Reginald are Dante and Tommaso's parents."

When Tiny nodded, Julius continued, "Mila was visiting with Marguerite and me, but was now ready to join our father at court. Marcus and I escorted her to him." He shook his head sadly. "I wish now I had left Marcus to accompany her alone."

Tiny opened his mouth, no doubt to ask why, but Julius didn't wait for the question and continued, "While I was gone, Jean Claude Argeneau had returned from the dead. Marguerite—"

"Wait, wait," Tiny protested. "I know you didn't want interruptions, but you have to explain this Jean Claude bit. What do you mean returned from the dead? Was he or wasn't he dead? Can you guys die and come back? I don't understand."

Julius frowned. "Don't you know about our people?"

"Yes, yes," Tiny said impatiently. "Your ancestors are from what is now referred to as Atlantis. They were advanced scientifically, and combined nano technology and bioengineering to create little biters who run through your blood repairing and regenerating everything so you never age and never grow ill. But they use more blood than a body can create, so you need blood. There were blood banks in Atlantis, but when it fell, your people were forced to flee and live among the rest of us more primitive types in squalor. Without blood banks, the nanos altered you to hunt and feed and survive off mortals." He paused and raised an eyebrow. "Right?"

"I meant the healing part, not our history," Julius said dryly. "But never mind, it is easier just to answer your question. Jean Claude was supposed to have died in the Battle of Edgecote in 1469, beheaded in battle," he explained wearily. "And, no, immortals cannot come back from a beheading, we will not regrow a head. Marguerite, as well as the rest of the immortal community, was led to believe that Jean Claude had died in battle and was gone. She lived as a widow for more than twenty years before we met."

"But Jean Claude wasn't dead?" Tiny asked with a frown.

"No," Julius said. "I returned home to find Marguerite missing and I was raising a search party for her when Magda, her maid, stumbled through the gates with a newborn Christian in her arms. She said Marguerite had given birth to our son earlier that same night and gave the child to her, ordering Magda to kill him and bring his body to me in the home we'd shared . . . along with the message that she had chosen to return to Jean Claude, a lifemate but also her true love. She regretted ever becoming involved with me and wished never to see me again."

Christian sagged in his seat, pain twisting his face, but Tiny's reaction was the opposite.

"No," he said firmly, leaping to his feet. "There is no way that happened. Jean Claude wasn't Marguerite's true lifemate, she told me that herself. He made her life miserable. Some of the things he did to her . . . " Tiny shook his head. "And she would *never* kill a child, especially not her own. She loves her children. You've got the wrong woman."

"It was Marguerite," Julius said quietly, but acknowledged, "I didn't believe it myself at first. I thought the maid must be lying, trying to cause trouble between us for some reason. But both Marcus and I read her and we saw the memory of Marguerite telling her to kill Christian and bring him to me and say those things. We *saw.*"

Tiny sank back into his chair, shaking his head with stunned disbelief. "But she wouldn't do that."

"We weren't convinced either until she murdered the maid," Marcus announced quietly.

"Murdered the maid?" Tiny asked with renewed horror.

Julius merely nodded and continued, "She was pushed down the stairs. After that I took Christian and fled back to Italy to keep him safe. I never set foot in England again until now."

"And then that trouble happened in California and Christian insisted on going over to find out who had killed his cousin." Marcus picked up the story. "We knew it would mean some interaction with the Argeneaus and tried to talk him out of it, but when he refused to be swayed from hunting down Stephano's attacker, Julius asked me to accompany him to keep him safe."

Marcus grimaced and said, "I was shocked when I first met Marguerite again and she didn't appear to recognize me. I thought it was a ploy and read her mind, but she really had no recall of me," he said with remembered dismay. He shook his head. "Even more amazing was that she had no recall of Julius or anything that tied them together. There was a lot happening in California at the time, but I searched her thoughts when she was distracted and there simply was *no* memory of her ever being in York, meeting Julius, living with him, or having Christian."

"How is that possible?" Christian asked quietly.

Julius exchanged a glance with Marcus, then sighed and admitted, "Marcus and I discussed that when the two of you returned from California and he told me all he'd learned. We think her memory has been wiped."

"But she's an immortal," Christian protested. "Our memories can't be wiped."

"And yet the memories are gone," he pointed out. "She doesn't recall me, Marcus, or even the period when Jean Claude was missing. Instead, Marcus found some vague memory of a tour of Europe during the twenty-two or –three-year period encompassing his death and our being together."

"How?" Christian asked with bewilderment.

"We don't know," he admitted with a sigh. "It's possible a three-on-one might have done it."

"A three-on-one?" Tiny asked.

"A procedure where three immortals merge together and wipe away memories of a fourth individual," Julius explained.

"A mortal," Christian insisted with a frown. "That only works on mortals. You can't wipe the memories of an immortal."

"But if they're telling the truth then Marguerite's

memories have been wiped," Tiny pointed out, and then added, "and I believe it."

Julius nodded, glad at least that he didn't have to convince the detective.

"So," Tiny continued, "the question becomes, why would they wipe her memory of that specific period if she willingly did all you just recounted?"

"That is what we wondered," Julius admitted. "It seemed obvious to us that all was not as it had been presented at the time. We needed to find out what really happened five hundred years ago. If she'd had her memories still intact, Marcus could have read them, but she had no memories to read. So, the best bet seemed to be to get her to York and hope that being here sparked some memory in her that would unravel the rest and we would finally find out what happened."

Tiny snorted disparagingly. "If she did order Christian killed, Jean Claude controlled her and made her do so."

"I agree," Julius murmured.

"You do?" Christian asked and the hope on his face that his mother hadn't wished him dead made Julius's heart ache for him.

"Yes, I do," he said firmly. "The Marguerite I know now is the same woman I fell in love with all those years ago, and she is not a woman who could kill a child, any child, and most definitely not her own."

"Well, then—" Tiny began but Julius interrupted him.

"But that doesn't explain her killing the maid who saved Christian."

"Jean Claude must have controlled her and made

her do that as well," Tiny said with a shrug that suggested this was obvious, but Julius shook his head.

"She was alone when she entered the house. Jean Claude was not with her, and he wouldn't have been able to control her from a distance any more than I can control someone out on the street from here."

"I was controlled in California and made to unlock Vincent's door by someone outside," Tiny pointed out.

"Then the immortal must have been looking in the window. They have to be able to see where they are sending you."

Tiny frowned over this news and then said, "So whoever controlled her was in the house today?"

Julius stiffened and stared at the man.

Tiny was frowning. "Did you see anyone? I don't recall seeing anyone in the house, but I could have been controlled. *Did* you see anyone?"

"Dear God," Julius breathed as he realized he hadn't seen anyone in the house. Someone had controlled her from outside. But how was that possible?

"How can anyone possibly control her like this?" Christian asked with a frown. "She is an immortal. No one should be able to control her so completely."

"What do you mean?" Tiny asked curiously.

"She's seven hundred years old," Christian explained. "Mortals and newly turned or young immortals are easily controlled by all and sundry, but the older we become, the better we become at erecting guards in our mind to protect ourselves. She shouldn't be controlled so easily. In fact, Jean Claude should have lost his ability to control her after the first hundred years or so."

"I wondered about that too," Marcus admitted. "It troubled me that he still controlled her so completely right up until his death."

"You were able to read her, Marcus," Tiny pointed out. "Could you control her as well?"

"No, I tried to control her and make her sit beside Julius on the train when she started to move to the opposite table," he admitted. "But she didn't even hesitate in step."

"But you can read her easily enough?" Tiny asked, trying to understand.

"Reading is different," Julius explained. "Marcus and I are much older. We can read most immortals younger than ourselves if they are distracted, and Marguerite was undoubtedly distracted in California and then again here."

"Can *you* read her?" Tiny asked Julius, eyes narrowing.

"No. She's my lifemate," he said without hesitation. "We cannot read lifemates, that's what makes them—"

"I know. I was just checking," Tiny interrupted and then sighed. "So, Jean Claude shouldn't have been able to control her for so long, but somehow managed to. And someone controlled her today, but it couldn't be Jean Claude because he's dead, right?"

"He was supposed to be dead five hundred years ago too," Marcus pointed out dryly.

That comment had a stultifying effect on everyone. Three pairs of eyes turned to him as if he'd suggested they hold an all-male orgy.

Marcus shrugged. "Well, it's true. He was supposed to be dead for more than twenty years when he returned and reclaimed his wife. And," he added grimly, "the man supposedly died in a fire this last time. What if it wasn't him they buried?"

"Dear God," Julius breathed with horror and stood up. "She's not safe here. We have to take her back to Italy."

"I doubt she'd be any safer there than here," Tiny argued. "Besides, we need her to remember and you need to keep her here to help her do that."

Julius considered this briefly and then shook his head. "There is security on my estate. It would be difficult for anyone to get close enough to control her there. It is more important to keep her safe. We can resolve everything else later if necessary."

"You're going to have to tell her everything," Tiny warned. "Right now she's probably packing her bags and ordering a taxi," he said and then frowned and asked, "Why the hell didn't you just tell us everything from the beginning?"

Julius snorted at the idea. "That would have worked well, I'm sure. What should I have said, "Hello, Marguerite. I'm Julius Notte, your long lost lifemate. I know you don't remember me, but we met five hundred years ago when you thought you were a widow. We're true lifemates and love each other more than life. We even married and were expecting our first child when Jean Claude, your husband who was supposed to be dead, showed up. You dumped me for him, ordered our child murdered and then killed the maid for not killing him. Oh, and by the way, those twenty-two years or so you spent in Europe? Never happened. And maybe your husband is alive now, we're not sure, but heck, let's be lifemates and live happily ever after, huh?"

Tiny grimaced. "I guess it would have sounded pretty farfetched when you first showed up in London. Especially after you attacked me and everything."

"You were in bed with my lifemate," Julius snapped. "As for telling her now, despite everything that has happened, she will probably still find it too farfetched to believe. That's why I didn't even try to explain to her just now when she asked me to. She is never going to believe me. She'll think I'm mad, or lying, or . . ."

"Another Jean Claude," Tiny suggested quietly when he shook his head helplessly.

"Yes," Julius said miserably. "That bastard hurt her terribly. She has trust issues because of him and I don't know if our love is enough to help her get past her fears and believe in me . . . in us."

They were all silent, and then Tiny said tentatively, "You might be able to convince her. There is that painting in your desk that Christian mentioned.

Julius was considering that and wondering if it would help convince Marguerite of the truth behind the seemingly wild tale when Tiny suddenly straightened, his expression excited.

"Was Martine here when it all happened?" he asked.

"No. I told you, when we met, Marguerite was living here while Martine—"

"Oh, right-right," he said on a sigh and was silent for a moment before asking, "Where was her oldest son, Lucern?"

Julius sighed. "He was here in York with her for the first couple of weeks after she moved in, but I didn't meet her until after he left. Marguerite sent messengers out to look for him when we decided to marry, but he was a mercenary and moved around a lot and it took a while to reach him. Then we realized she was pregnant with Christian and decided we couldn't wait for his return. I gather he popped up back in York a few days after his father returned."

"Lucern was a mercenary?" Tiny asked with disbelief. "I thought he was a romance writer?"

Julius sighed. "I'm sure he has been many things, Tiny, he's over six hundred years old. When he was young he was a warrior. Now he's a romance writer. Five hundred years from now he may be a scientist. Interests change when you have the time to explore them."

"Right," Tiny muttered and then asked, "Wasn't there anyone around from her family who could help back you up?"

Julius started to shake his head and then paused. "Her brother-in-law."

"Lucian?" Tiny asked with dismay.

"Intimidating fellow, isn't he?" Julius asked dryly. "He gave me the *talk*."

"The *talk*?"

"The *If you hurt her, I'll kill you* talk," he said dryly.

"Yeah?" Tiny grinned.

Julius sighed. "He's a hard bastard and he was Jean Claude's twin brother. I don't think he'd be very helpful."

"I don't know," Marcus said suddenly, and Julius

glanced at him in question. "Well, despite their being twins, Jean Claude let Lucian think he was dead along with everyone else. He obviously didn't trust him to keep the secret."

Tiny shook his head. "No, he wouldn't. From what I know of the family, Lucian's a hardcore, by-the-book type. He'd have turned Jean Claude in to the council."

"That doesn't necessarily apply to his brother, and doesn't mean he'd help me out now," Julius pointed out.

"No," Tiny agreed on a sigh.

"I think we should leave the issue of finding a family member to help back up your story until we see if Marguerite needs the extra convincing," Christian announced. "The picture and your word might be enough."

"Do you think so?" Julius asked uncertainly.

He shrugged. "There is only one way to find out."

"Right." Julius stood . . . and then sat back down. "What do I say?"

"Just tell her everything," Tiny advised. "Be honest. We'll back you up if necessary. And if it doesn't convince her, ask her to at least come home to Italy with you so you can show her the picture and perhaps call Lucian to get him to back you up."

Nodding, Julius straightened his shoulders and stood up again. He strode purposefully up the hall, reached the stairs and then turned back, turned to the stairs again, then hesitated once more. This was the most important thing in the world to him. He was about to ask her to trust him on blind faith. Something *he* hadn't managed to give *her* five hundred years ago. He didn't want to spend another five hundred years without her. He didn't want to lose her for a minute. He had to do this right.

"Father," Christian said quietly, walking up the hall toward him.

Julius glanced at him, relieved for the excuse to delay.

"Get your ass up there and talk to the woman. I've spent five hundred years without a mother because you were too stupid to talk to her back then and find out what was going on. And she spent that same time in a marriage that was hell for the same reason. It's time to fix things."

Well, as support went, it rather sucked, Julius decided with disgruntlement and began to trudge upstairs. The hall was silent when he reached the landing. Julius forced himself to cross to the door, reached for the knob, then hesitated. What if he got it wrong and messed up yet again?

"Go."

He glanced over his shoulder, scowling at his son. Christian was now at the foot of the stairs glaring at him. Turning away, Julius shook his head and opened the door. He didn't panic when he found it empty. Marguerite had obviously returned to her own room. The message was "*No more nooky for you, mister.*" He supposed he should have expected that, he probably wouldn't be able to lure her back to his bed until all of this was straightened out.

Wincing at the thought, he moved to the next door, but didn't hesitate this time. Julius could actually feel Christian's beady little eyes glaring into the back of his head, so he opened the door at once and then stepped inside to peer around, only to realize this room too was empty.

Turning away he peered at the open bathroom door, and then checked the last bedroom despite the fact that she would have no reason to be there. Of course, she wasn't there either. Marguerite was gone.

Marguerite's eyes widened at the hordes before her as she paused at the mouth of the alley. It opened on to a busy street filled with shoppers moving every which way. While she'd thought the streets were busy at night, they were nothing like the mass of humanity before her now. It made her glad she normally only came out at night. This was madness.

Terribly aware of the sun overhead, Marguerite forced herself to move, thrusting herself into the herd, her nose quivering as she was pressed from every side. Now that she was out of the house, Marguerite was becoming aware of a need for blood. The attack last night had caused a lot of damage and used a lot of blood to heal it, and while Julius had fed her several bags at the time, she knew she should have had three or four more bags on awaking. Instead she'd had none. That was going to be a problem.

She was already paying the price, cramps starting in her stomach.

Marguerite sighed to herself. Her heart was breaking and she was a hungry vampire surrounded by several hundred, or even thousand, living, breathing blood bags with legs. She could feel her teeth shifting in her mouth as the smell of them hit her.

Feeling like a fox dropped in the center of a hen house, Marguerite forced her fangs back into place and hurried up the street, doing her best to weave around people to avoid contact. Unfortunately, they didn't seem to have the same concern. They were brushing, bumping, and knocking her at every turn. It seemed that personal space wasn't a consideration here, she thought with annoyance, withstanding the urge to grab the first plump mortal she passed and drag them into the nearest snickleway for a nibble. She had to get out of there.

Much to Marguerite's relief, the crowd began to thin as she reached the end of the street. She'd broken free of the town center, she realized and paused to peer around. The roads here were wider, allowing vehicles and the first thing she spotted was a row of taxis at a stand. Breathing out with relief, she hurried to the first one in line and leapt into the backseat.

Pulling the door closed with a slam, Marguerite glanced toward the front of the taxi, only to frown when she realized the driver was missing. She twisted on the seat, peering about until she saw a handsome young man break away from a small group of men gathered by the third car. He nodded at her as he hurried toward the taxi and Marguerite relaxed back in the seat.

She eyed his throat as he slid into the driver's seat in front, and then blinked as his voice sounded over the little intercom system between the glass separating front and back of the vehicle.

"Where to, love?"

Marguerite hesitated, and then asked, "Can I fly from York to Canada?"

He shook his head and turned in his seat to peer at her through the glass. His smile was engaging as his eyes slid over her with interest. "Sorry, love. You'd be wantin' an international airport for that. The nearest one is—"

"Take me to the train station," Marguerite interrupted, uncaring where the nearest international airport was. If she couldn't fly out of York, she'd return to London and fly out of there. She just wanted to get moving. While being in the taxi was better than being outside, the windows weren't curtained and sunlight was still reaching her. The sooner she was indoors, the better.

Nodding, the man turned to face front and started the engine.

Marguerite noticed his eyes finding her repeatedly in the mirror and looking her over, but didn't speak. Her own attention was fixated on the tan skin of his neck beneath his short-cut dark hair. She was hungry and not for food. Her cramping was becoming more insistent and painful.

She felt her teeth shift again in demand, and slid her tongue forward to touch the tip of one as she stared hard at the man's neck, an image coming to mind of her leaning forward and burying her teeth in his throat. Of course, she couldn't, the glass barrier was between them, but that didn't stop the image from replaying through her head along with an imagining of the relief she would feel were she to do that. The pain would ease, and the clamoring in her would be reduced to a less frantic din. All she had to do was—

"Here we are."

Marguerite blinked and glanced out the window at the people moving in and out of the doors he'd stopped in front of; the York train station. The idea of having to move through that crowd while she was in such a state was a scary one.

"That'll be—"

The driver's words died as Marguerite turned back and slid inside his mind. Turning in his seat, he shifted gears and pulled out onto the road again, steering them out of the busy traffic and onto a quieter street. He pulled into a parking lot and parked, got out of the front seat and climbed into the back, his expression blank as he settled on the bench beside her.

Marguerite didn't waste time. Shifting, she climbed onto his lap facing him, her knees on either side of his hips on the seat. She tilted his head to the side and sank her teeth into his neck. The driver's body went stiff and he jerked as her fangs pierced skin, but then he moaned with excitement and raised his hands to grasp her hips as she began to share her pleasure and relief with him. Closing her eyes, Marguerite sighed and ignored the way he clutched at her hips, pulling her hard against him, her concentration was on the blood flowing into her body, easing the pain.

Twelve

"I thought you were going to let me buy you a drink?"

Marguerite smiled dryly at that laughing complaint from the man she was leading by the hand, and assured him, "I am."

"Well, forgive me for saying so, love, but leading a man back here is like to make him think it's more than a drink yer wantin'."

"And what would a man think of that?" she asked with amusement, releasing his hand and turning to catch him by the tie instead as she backed farther into the quiet corner of the locker area where she'd brought several others over the last half hour.

Vampire on a rampage, she thought with self-mockery. It had been a long time since she had fed off the hoof. She'd forgotten how exhilarating it could be; choosing your prey, stalking him while allowing him to think he was stalking you, then luring them into a dark or deserted corner and . . .

"He'd be thinking he's one lucky son of a bitch," her prey admitted, his voice going low and husky as she bumped up against the lockers.

Chuckling, Marguerite ran one hand down his chest as she drew his head down with her hold on his tie and whispered, "Would you like me to tell you a secret?"

A slow smile spread across his face and he said, "Go on then, tell us."

Smiling, she leaned up by his ear. His arms immediately closed around her, his hands roaming.

"I'm hungry," Marguerite whispered. She felt his hands still in confusion, then clutch at her as she sank her teeth into his throat. In the next moment, he moaned and pulled her tight, pressing his body into hers as she fed. He was the sixth man she'd bitten since the taxi driver. Marguerite only took a little from each, but wished she could take more, she needed it. Her people were allowed to feed on mortals in an emergency, and this was an emergency. Unfortunately, the York train station had skylights overhead and no matter where she went, the sun seemed to follow. She doubted it was going to be much better on the train with all its windows. She couldn't seem to escape the sun today and hoped it wasn't an omen for the trip ahead.

Of course, one thing had gone right at least. Marguerite had borrowed a phone from her first blood donor and called Tiny's mobile, managing to reach him when he was alone and her call wouldn't draw the suspicion or attention of the Nottes. He was going to slip out of the house and catch a taxi to the train station. They'd take a train back to London, and then catch a flight back to Canada. This whole episode of her life would be over and done with and she could start the miserable business of trying to forget it.

"Are you quite done? I'm growing tired of watching him squeeze your ass."

Marguerite froze at those sharp words, her eyes popping open and landing on Julius Notte's furious expression. Panic struck, followed by anger, but she controlled both and concentrated on retracting her teeth and her mind from the man she'd been feeding from, then released her snack and sent him on his way, the whole incident wiped from his memory.

Marguerite concentrated on him until he was out of sight before turning to face Julius.

"What are you doing here?" she asked grimly.

"Looking for my lifemate," he snapped.

"Well, keep looking," she said coldly and turned to walk back out into the station proper.

"I don't have to, I found her," Julius said, keeping pace with her and taking her arm.

"Sorry, I'm not your lifemate, I just *look like* her," Marguerite said, shaking off his hold and then added sarcastically, "Lucky me. I must have the most common face in history. First Jean Claude and now you." Pausing abruptly, she scowled at him. "What did you do with Tiny? I suppose you read him to find out I was here?"

"No. He told me."

Her eyes widened in alarm, then narrowed and she hissed, "Liar."

"I don't lie," Julius said quietly. "Tiny *did* tell me, and he's here looking for you too along with Marcus and Christian. The four of us split up to search the station when we didn't find you by the magazine shop where you were supposed to meet him."

Shaking her head, she turned to walk away and he said, "Marguerite, we are lifemates. I can't read or control you. I wish I could," he added in a mutter. "I'd take control right now and march you out to the first taxi I could find and give you a good spanking for letting dirty old men touch you."

"Dirty old men?" Marguerite cried, swinging around in disbelief. "He was a businessman, well dressed and clean-cut and he was no more than thirty-seven, a damned sight younger than you."

"But he *looks* older," Julius said smugly. He looked less than smug, however, when he added, "and he's mortal. Probably disease ridden."

Marguerite stared at his disgruntled face, the realization slowly dawning that he was jealous. Jean Claude had *never* been jealous. He'd enjoyed watching her feed on male mortals. In fact, she suspected he would have liked to see her do more than that and just hoped to God he hadn't taken control and made her do so. If he had, she just didn't want to know.

"Please, Marguerite," Julius said quietly. "Just come with me and let me explain things."

She shifted uncertainly, the request tempting, very tempting in fact. Marguerite wanted him to be able to explain all her worries and fears away. She didn't want to lose him, but fear and pride made her shake her head and turn away. "I have to catch a train to London."

"Good, we're heading that way too, we'll accompany you," he said taking her arm again.

"I don't want accompanying," she said firmly, shaking off his hold.

"We have blood."

She stopped abruptly.

"Nice, fresh, clean blood. Bags of it. You won't have to hunt."

Marguerite didn't really care about bags of blood. She actually had been enjoying the hunt, but the blood might be a good face saver so it didn't look like she was giving in for any other reason. She glanced around, noting that Christian and Marcus were making their way toward them from either side, and then she spotted Tiny hurrying toward them from straight ahead. He obviously wasn't being controlled by anyone or held against his will and she frowned, wondering if Julius was really telling the truth. Had Tiny gone over to the other side?

Determined to find out, Marguerite slipped into his mind briefly, touching on his anxiety and worry that she would be angry at him, but also his determination that she give Julius a chance. He thought it was in her best interests. In fact, he was afraid it was the only way to keep her safe from . . .

"Jean Claude?" Marguerite murmured with confusion as she read the name in his mind, and then cried out as she was suddenly snatched up, hefted over Julius's shoulder and being carted through the station at a dead run.

"Julius had your best interests at heart."

Marguerite stopped pacing to scowl at Tiny. The

detective was sitting on her bed, eyeing her warily, both of which he'd been doing ever since entering her room at the townhouse several moments ago.

"Tiny," she said with the slow care of someone who thought they were talking to an idiot, "he has kidnapped me."

"No, he hasn't," the detective assured her quickly.

She snorted and arched an eyebrow. "He grabbed me, threw me over his shoulder, and charged through the train station like he was fleeing a burning building."

"Yes, but—"

"And then," Marguerite cut him off, "he continued to run all the way back here to the townhouse with me over his shoulder like a sack of potatoes. I'm sure everyone was staring . . . although I couldn't say for sure since I couldn't see through the back of my skirt, which had fallen over my head," she added acidly. "My butt must have looked like the full moon rising over his shoulder in the white lace panties I'm wearing. Thank God I didn't put on a thong."

"Your panties are very pretty," he assured her soothingly. When she turned sharply on him, his eyes widened in alarm at the violence in her face and he said quickly, "I only saw them for a second when he first picked you up. I was running way behind after that. Even carrying you he's inhumanly fast and I couldn't keep up," he added with disgruntlement, "Marguerite, he had your best interests at heart and you really haven't been kidnapped."

"I believe the definition of kidnapping is taking someone by force and holding them against their will and I am definitely unwilling."

"Yes, but I'm sure you wouldn't be if you'd just let him explain."

"I don't see him offering explanations," she snapped.

"Because the minute he put you down in the townhouse, you stormed up here . . . and then you started screaming and throwing things at him when he followed you," Tiny said with exasperation.

"I was upset," Marguerite snapped.

"Yes, I know that and so does he, so he left you alone to calm down."

"I'm calm," she snarled.

Tiny merely pursed his lips doubtfully. "Look, you haven't been kidnapped. The bedroom door isn't locked, you can leave the room any time you want."

"And if I tried to leave the townhouse?" she asked archly.

"He'd probably try to stop you," Tiny acknowledged. "But it would be by reasoning with you. He didn't mean to kidnap you. When you said Jean Claude's name he thought you'd spotted him in the crowd and was just trying to keep you safe from him. Cut the guy some slack, Marguerite. He loves you."

Her mouth twisted bitterly. "He doesn't. He can't. We hardly know each other."

"Are you going to tell me you don't love him too? Because you sure seemed pretty happy there for a day or so."

"As I said, I hardly know the man, Tiny," she said impatiently. "It can't be love. It's just a squash."

"A squash?" he asked blankly.

She sighed. "An infatuation?"

"Oh, you mean crush," he realized.

Marguerite waved her hand impatiently. "Crush, squash, it means the same thing."

"Well, actually no, it doesn't. I mean it does in that you can squash or crush a bug, but you can't have a squash on someone. It's—"

"Tiny," she interrupted shortly.

"Right. Not the issue at the moment," he muttered and cleared his throat. "Look, just let him explain everything, okay?"

"I don't have to."

He rolled his eyes impatiently. "I know you don't have to, but a grown-up person would—"

"Tiny," she interrupted dryly. "I wasn't being childish, I meant I don't have to because I've read it all out of your head already."

His eyes widened incredulously. "Cut that out!"

Marguerite sighed and lay wearily back on the bed beside him, saying without apology, "I needed to know I hadn't been wrong in trusting you. I wanted to be sure you hadn't betrayed me. After all, you appeared to be running with the enemy."

"I wasn't betraying you," he said sharply.

"I know." She opened her eyes long enough to find his arm and pat it, then closed them as she added, "Well, at least not on purpose. I know you really believe this nonsense story of his."

"It's not nonsense," Julius said quietly.

Marguerite's eyes shot open and she sat up abruptly at the sight of a solemn-faced Julius standing before her. She hadn't heard him enter the room, the man moved as silently as a thief, which was an apt description she decided, since he'd stolen her heart.

Sitting up had put her eyes level with his waist and

they immediately found the bags of blood he held. They were undoubtedly peace offerings, she thought, ignoring the hunger that immediately leapt to life in her. She needed the blood, but was too stubborn to take it from him. Instead, she forced her hungry eyes away from them and found herself staring at his zipper. Marguerite scowled, briefly considering punching him there, then stood to move quickly away from him and both temptations.

"It *is* nonsense," she muttered. "From what I've read of Tiny's thoughts, you told him we'd met before."

"We have."

"We haven't," Marguerite countered firmly. "I'd remember. And I'd certainly remember if I gave birth to Christian."

"You—"

"As for ordering him *killed*— A defenseless little baby?" she asked with disbelief and then shook her head firmly. "Never."

"I agree," Julius agreed quickly and crossed to set the bags of blood down on the dresser beside her. "We don't think you would have done those things either. At least not willingly . . . not without someone controlling you."

Marguerite tsked impatiently and shook her head. "There is no way I would have forgotten twenty some years of my life, including meeting a lifemate and giving birth. I'm sure it isn't even physically possible for an immortal to—"

"I know it's hard to believe. I've been struggling with it myself, but we *have* met before, and we discovered then that we were lifemates, and those things *did* happen." When she started to shake her head again, he sighed and said, "Just tell me this, if it were possible for an immortal's memory to be erased, was Jean Claude the type of person capable of using it against someone?"

Marguerite glanced away from him, her mouth flattening. After a moment, she admitted, "If it suited his purposes, yes."

"Then—"

"*If* it were possible," she interrupted grimly. "But it simply isn't possible. It can't be."

Marguerite heard the desperation in her own voice and turned abruptly away, biting her lip painfully. The truth was she didn't want it to be possible. She didn't want to believe that she'd lost something so precious and been forced to order her own child's death.

Turning back sharply, she asked, "And if this is all true, then who has been trying to kill me since London? You said you thought it was Christian's mother's family. If what you say is true, that would be my family and no one in my family would try to kill me."

"Jean Claude m—"

"Jean Claude is dead," Marguerite said with exasperation.

Julius was silent for a minute and then asked, "Who else besides Jean Claude could control you?"

Her eyes widened at the seeming change in subject, but she said, "No one. He's the only one. Thank God," Marguerite added in a mutter.

"But Marguerite, this morning—" Tiny began and then snapped his mouth closed at a look from Julius.

Her gaze slid between the men warily. "What about this morning?"

"She'll just read my mind," Tiny muttered apologetically to Julius.

Marguerite turned toward Tiny to do just that as Julius snapped, "Well, think of something else then, dammit."

Marguerite frowned as Tiny began to recite *Three Blind Mice* in his head, and then gave up with a small shrug and said, "I'll just read him when he's distracted."

Julius sighed and ran a hand through his hair. "It will just upset you."

She turned on him sharply. "I am over seven hundred years old, Julius. Deciding what is best for me is not your place any more than it was Jean Claude's."

"You're right, I'm sorry," he said at once, looking rather shocked to realize that's exactly what he'd been doing. He gave his head a shake, then sighed and said, "What do you remember about this morning here at the townhouse?"

Marguerite frowned at the question. "I remember waking up in the living room. I was on the couch and Tiny was in the doorway looking out. I got up and came up behind him and saw you and Christian and Marcus on the stairs and heard what you were saying."

Julius nodded and then asked, "How did you get to the couch?"

She stared at him blankly and then started to shake her head with confusion.

Nodding again as if expecting that reaction, he asked, "What's the last thing you remember before waking up on the couch?"

"Last night," she said slowly, searching her mind. "We went to a play, then a restaurant. I was attacked in the ladies' room and woke up in bed with you. We talked and . . . er . . ." Marguerite glanced at Tiny. The mortal was grinning like an idiot. Sighing, she said, "Then we talked some more and then I put on your T-shirt to go to the bathroom and when I came back we went to sleep."

He nodded. "You remember everything . . . about last night. Then there's this morning."

Marguerite frowned. "I think I got up at some point to get blood. I was very sleepy, though, and don't recall how I got to the couch . . ." She shook her head with confusion. "Did I lie down to sleep?"

"I can only tell you what I know," he said. "This morning I woke up at a little before noon and you were up and gone. I was annoyed," he admitted. "I got up to find you. When I came out of the room I heard Tiny asking you if you were all right. I looked down the stairs and saw you walking toward the door. You were heading outside in nothing but my T-shirt."

Marguerite's eyes widened incredulously at this claim, but he continued, "Tiny stepped in your way and you picked him up and threw him into the wall."

"What?" she burst out, her eyes shooting to Tiny to find him nodding that it was true.

When she turned back to Julius, he continued, "And then you just walked outside into the sunlight, in only the T-shirt. I ran out after you."

"He was naked," Tiny informed her, apparently determined she understand the sacrifice he'd made.

Julius ignored him. "I picked you up and brought you back inside and laid you on the couch. That's why you woke up there. After I laid you down, I drew a blanket over you, and then ran upstairs to pull on some pants and that's when Christian started grilling me. You know the rest."

"It's true, Marguerite," Tiny said quietly. "Every word of what he just said is true. You just walked right outside in that T-shirt. But it wasn't you. Your face was blank, no expression at all. Someone was controlling you."

Marguerite leaned weakly against the dresser behind her. She was stunned by this news. No one but Jean Claude had ever controlled her, and she hadn't thought it possible anyone else could. She'd reassured herself that he was only able to do so because he was so old and had been the one to turn her, but now someone else had done it. Or Jean Claude was alive as Julius seemed to think.

Marguerite didn't know which possibility was worse, that someone else could control her as Jean Claude had done, or that he might still be alive.

"I'm sorry I didn't tell you everything from the start, Marguerite," Julius said, then shrugged helplessly and pointed out, "But, look how much trouble you're having accepting it after knowing we are true lifemates. Can you imagine your reaction if I'd blurted it all that first night we met?"

She'd have thought him mad, Marguerite acknowledged to herself.

"I don't know how I can convince you I'm telling the truth. I was hoping that being here in York, where we met and lived for the short time we were together, would help you remember, but . . ." He shrugged unhappily.

"You have the portrait," Tiny pointed out.

"Yes," Julius said and then explained to Marguerite. "The portrait in my desk at home in Italy, the one you heard Christian talking about. It is you. It's one of two portraits I had commissioned of you that year. I had a large one painted to hang over the fireplace, and a miniature made so I could carry it with me when I traveled. The large painting was gone from the castle when I returned to find you missing, but the miniature was with me and I still have it.

"I would like you to come home to Italy with me to see it. You would be safer there anyway. My home has a high-tech security system including a wired fence. That should help keep anyone from getting too close to control you," he added quietly.

Marguerite shifted. She was so tempted to believe him. Julius seemed sincere and if she did believe him she could have him back, but it was so hard to believe. How could she have forgotten? How could her own memories be false?

"Why would Lucern never have mentioned this to me?" she asked suddenly. "He would have been around one hundred at the time. He—"

"You sent men to look for him when we decided to marry but he didn't return until after it was all over and you were back with Jean Claude," Julius said quietly. "I am not sure what story he was told then, but we never got the chance to meet."

Marguerite would have called her son right then to demand he tell her what he knew, but he was traveling with Kate and thanks to some stupid, grubby little

London thief, she didn't have his cell phone number.

"I did meet Lucian," Julius suddenly blurted.

Marguerite's head jerked up. "Lucian?"

"Yes. He apparently checked on you often after Jean Claude's death. He knows all about the two of us and knew we were expecting," he assured her and then added, "I don't know if he'd admit to it all since it paints his brother pretty black, but he might."

"Let's call him now," Tiny suggested abruptly, getting to his feet.

Marguerite nodded with relief. She was finding herself more confused and frustrated by the minute, part of her believing, the other part afraid to. But if Lucian knew about this, the whole matter could be cleared up in minutes.

"Use my cell phone," Julius offered, taking it out of his pocket and giving it to her.

Marguerite accepted it and punched in the number, grateful that she knew it by heart. Raising the phone to her ear, she listened tensely to the ringing, her eyes following Julius as he moved to sit on the foot of the bed. He looked a bit anxious, but not exceptionally so.

She stiffened and turned away from him as the phone was answered, but sagged as a recorded message informed her that Lucian and Leigh weren't available and to try again later. Marguerite felt a moment's pleasant surprise that Lucian and Leigh had apparently turned out to be lifemates and worked things out. She'd had a good feeling about the pair the moment Lucian had called her about the woman, and she was happy for them, but would have been happier to talk to Lucian at that moment.

Marguerite glanced toward the clock on the bedside table as she listened to the instructions to leave a message and sighed as she saw the time. Two P.M. That made it nine A.M. back home, and Lucian didn't pick up the phone during the day for anything. He turned it off while he slept. He did have a cell phone that he kept by the bed in case of council emergencies. That phone he would answer during the day. Unfortunately, Marguerite didn't know the cell phone number off by heart. She didn't need it, she didn't often have emergencies and it was programmed into both her home phone and cell phone anyway.

"Lucian," she said wearily when the beep sounded. "I wish you were there. I need your help. I'll try again later."

Marguerite closed the phone and turned to the men, noting that both Tiny and Julius were looking about as disappointed as she felt. She started to hand the cell phone back to Julius, and then paused as an idea occurred to her. "Martine."

Julius shook his head. "I never got to meet her either. You were staying in her home while she had a break. She couldn't return for fear someone would recognize her and note she hadn't aged."

"Yes, but she could at least tell me if I really had stayed here in York, couldn't she?" Marguerite said with triumph. "And then I would know if I have missing memories, wouldn't I?"

His eyes widened at the suggestion and he smiled. "Yes you would."

Smiling now, Marguerite flipped open the phone, punched the number for directory inquiries and asked for the number to the Dorchester Hotel in London, noting that Julius had begun to pace, as had Tiny. She could feel the tension in the room mounting.

When the number was rattled off to her, Marguerite quickly hung up and punched it in, then began to tap the fingers of her free hand impatiently against her leg as she waited. She breathed out a little breath of relief when the phone was answered by a cheerful female voice announcing the hotel. Marguerite asked for Martine's room, waited through a couple of clicks, and then almost groaned when she heard yet another recorded voice. Of course, Martine would have requested they not be disturbed during the day while they slept and any calls directed to voice mail.

Marguerite didn't bother to leave a message this time, instead, flipping the phone closed with an impatient snap. "I'll have to wait until sunset to try again."

They were all silent for a moment, and then Julius sighed and said, "You look exhausted. Why don't you have some blood and take a nap until then?"

Marguerite hesitated. She *was* exhausted. She'd only had a couple of hours of sleep that morning before everything had happened. And she definitely needed the blood. She nodded acquiescence.

Rather than look relieved by her easy acceptance of the suggestion, Julius seemed to look a little more tense as he announced, "Marcus and Christian went back to bed just before I came up here and I would like a couple hours of sleep too, but I don't want to leave you alone."

"That's all right, I'll keep an eye on things," Tiny said. "I slept last night for a change. That's why I was

Thirteen

"Wake up, partner."

Marguerite's eyes jolted open as she was poked in the backside. Blinking away the sleep in her eyes, she rolled to her side and peered over the edge of the railing along the top bunk, scowling at Tiny for kicking the underside of her bed from where he lay on the lower bunk bed.

He merely grinned and rolled out of the lower bunk. "It's sunset. Actually it's later than sunset," Tiny admitted apologetically. "I'm afraid I fell asleep reading."

Eyebrows drawing together, Marguerite glanced around the room, but it looked no different than it had when she'd fallen asleep. The curtains on the window kept the room dark, the only light coming from the small lamp Tiny had moved beside his bunk so he could read while the rest of them slept.

Her gaze moved to the double bed where Marcus and Julius were still asleep. Christian had moved to Julius's room so that they could take over the room that he and Marcus had shared until today, but Marcus had offered to stay to be on hand in case there was trouble.

Marguerite had been surprised when Julius had suggested they disturb Marcus and Christian and switch rooms with them. She'd been waiting for him to suggest that he climb into bed with her to be close in case there was trouble. However, he hadn't. It showed he was smarter than she'd given him credit. While Marguerite was coming around a bit, and even beginning to believe there may be some truth to his story thanks to his encouraging the phone calls earlier, she hadn't swung so far that she would be willing to let him back into her bed. She needed some evidence to back up his story first.

"Are you going to lie there all night?" Tiny asked dryly. "I thought you wanted to call Martine?"

Nodding, Marguerite sat up and then maneuvered herself around to climb out of the bunk. Tiny moved over to the bed to wake up the men as she did and by the time she moved toward the door, Julius was up and following her with Tiny and Marcus on his heels. They trailed her downstairs, but Marcus broke off from the party to duck into the living room to retrieve blood for all of them while the rest of them continued into the kitchen.

Marguerite walked straight to the phone and placed the call, having to dial directory assistance first to get the number again. She had dialed the hotel number and was waiting for the phone to be answered when

Marcus entered the room and offered her a bag of blood.

"Thank you," she murmured as he handed another to Julius. She watched enviously as the two men then leaned against the counter side-by-side and they both popped the bags to their teeth.

Her mouth was watering by the time a dignified male voice answered her call and announced that she'd reached the Dorchester Hotel.

Marguerite straightened at once and asked for Martine's room and then cursed under her breath and hung up when she was told that she'd already checked out.

"I'm sorry, it's my fault, Marguerite," Tiny said quietly. "I fell asleep."

"It doesn't matter," she muttered, trying to sound like she meant it. "Martine will be on her way back to York. I'll just have to call her when she gets home."

Marguerite saw Marcus and Julius exchange a glance as she popped her own blood bag onto her teeth, and then Julius said, "Yes, of course you can, but it will have to be from Italy."

Marguerite couldn't speak thanks to the bag in her mouth, but she narrowed her eyes with displeasure.

"You aren't safe here," he pointed out apologetically.

"We could stay in the townhouse and not go anywhere just until we talk to Martine and *then* head to Italy," Tiny pointed out.

"Yes, we could, but it means Christian, Marcus, and I will have to watch her like a hawk in case she's controlled again. At least one of us will have to be with her at all times. Even in the bathroom."

"What?" Marguerite ripped the bag from her teeth. Fortunately, it was now empty.

"You slipped out the bedroom window," Julius pointed out.

"Yes, but—"

"Fortunately, whoever controlled you earlier apparently wasn't watching the back of the townhouse, otherwise they'd have you now. But if they saw us chase after you and bring you back, they'll figure out you must have slipped out a window and it might just have given them the idea to try to make you leave that way next time so no one stops you. There are windows in every room of this house, Marguerite, including the bathroom. You cannot be left alone. Not here. In Italy we will still have to watch you, but not quite as closely."

Marguerite stared at him blankly, unfortunately not able to argue the point. And—also unfortunately—suddenly realizing she needed to go to the bathroom. The idea of doing so with either Marcus, Julius, or Christian standing guard a few feet away was horrifying.

When her wide eyes turned to Tiny, he moved to her side and took her hands, giving them a reassuring squeeze. "I think we should go."

"We? You'd come with me?" she asked with relief.

"Well, it's our case isn't it, partner?" he said lightly, then more seriously. "I'd be happy to be your backup. I think you need to go, Marguerite. Not just because it would be safer, which it would. But for your own peace of mind. I know it's driving you crazy not being able to ask Lucian or Martine about the past. The trip would help pass the next several hours until you can reach one or the other of them. You can call them from Italy. *And* you can see the painting when we get there."

"And I can go to the bathroom there without an escort," she muttered.

"That too," he agreed with a grin.

Marguerite didn't join him in grinning. The longer they stood there talking about going to the bathroom, the more she had to go. However, she refused to go while one of the men stood guard. She could call from Italy.

"Let's go," she said abruptly, pushing herself away from the counter and heading out of the kitchen.

"Wait a minute," Julius said with a surprised laugh when she headed straight for the front door. "We have to pack and wake Christian and check the train schedule and call to Vita to have her arrange to have my pilot meet us in London."

Marguerite turned to eye him with exasperation. "Well, hurry up then. I have to go to the bathroom and if I can't until we get to Italy, I'd like to get there."

There was a moment of silence as the men glanced at each other and then Tiny cleared his throat, "Marguerite—"

"I am not going to the bathroom with one of the men standing in there watching me," she said coldly before he could suggest it. "So everyone can just get moving."

"You won't have to wait until Italy," Julius assured her, struggling to hide his amusement. "I'm sure it's safe enough on the train if one of us stands outside the door. There are no windows in the train bathroom as I recall."

She felt herself relax a little at his words. It was better than having to wait until she got to Italy, anyway. Nodding, Marguerite turned and headed upstairs. "I'll pack."

"I'll stay with her while you wake up Christian and pack," Marcus offered. "Then you can stay with her while I pack."

Sighing to herself, Marguerite ignored the conversation and started upstairs, leaving the man to follow as he liked. She heard stirring from Julius's room as she slipped into her own and quickly closed her door for fear that Christian would come out and see her. She hadn't spoken to the younger immortal since she'd learned the story Julius had told Tiny. She'd walked straight to the bunk beds and climbed into the top bunk while Julius had woken Marcus with news of the new sleeping arrangements, avoiding even looking in the young immortal's direction as she settled in the bed. It hadn't been easy since he'd been asleep in the lower bunk at the time, but she'd managed it and had been pretending to sleep when Julius had then woken Christian.

The door opened behind her and Marguerite hurried toward her suitcase as Marcus stepped inside and leaned against the wall to watch her. He didn't say anything, but neither did she. Instead she busied herself with packing as she listened to the murmur of Julius and Christian's voices next door and wondered how on earth she was supposed to act around him. She was starting to believe Julius's story. Her memories of that time were so vague in comparison to the memories of the rest of her life, that it made her wonder.

Marguerite had lain in that top bunk straining her mind, trying to recall more of their European tour than that it had been pleasant, but that was all there was in her mind. She didn't recall any individual events such as the journey itself, stopping in one city or another, or even whether she'd been saddle sore from the journey. And that was wrong.

And then there was the hope that had been on Julius's face in the kitchen while they'd waited for her to call the Dorchester and talk to Martine. Yes, Marguerite was starting to believe Julius. And if she believed him, then Christian was her son. A son she had given birth to and then handed over to a maid to kill. Dear God, the boy must hate her. And even if he didn't, she hated herself.

"Christian doesn't hate you," Marcus said quietly, and Marguerite stiffened, realizing he'd been reading her thoughts.

Annoying man, she thought with irritation and heard him chuckle softly.

"Of course I'm reading you," he said unapologetically and then added, "I love Christian like a son, and Julius like a brother. I'll do what I can to be sure they aren't hurt again in this."

Marguerite straightened slowly and peered at him. "Why am I so easily read and controlled? Other immortals aren't."

Marcus hesitated, a troubled expression crossing his face. "I don't think you're that easily read."

"You can read me," she pointed out and he nodded.

"But you're upset right now," Marcus pointed out. "You weren't as easy to read in California. You were distracted the night we met because you were worried about Jackie and Vincent, and that's when I discovered you didn't remember me or anything about meeting Julius and me in York."

"You were here at that time too?" she asked with surprise.

Marcus nodded. "I lived with the two of you that year. I'm the one who suggested we find a place in the city when the two of you realized you were lifemates."

Marguerite frowned, searching her mind for memories of him. All she succeeded in doing was making her head ache. Giving it up, she glanced at him resentfully and asked, "Can you control me?"

He shook his head firmly and her eyes narrowed.

"You've tried?"

Marcus nodded, again unapologetic. He didn't explain further and her lips twisted with displeasure as she returned to packing.

"Julius said to tell you he'll come relieve you in a minute," Tiny announced entering the room. "He's done packing and is just calling about the plane."

When Marcus nodded acknowledgment, Tiny hesitated then moved to join Marguerite at her suitcase.

"How are you doing?" he asked, and she could tell by his concerned expression that he wasn't referring to her packing.

"I'm not sure," Marguerite admitted quietly as she finished placing the last article in her suitcase and began to zip it up. Once that was done, she glanced at him and asked suddenly, "Do you really believe all this?"

The detective considered the matter seriously and then nodded. "Yes."

When she closed her eyes, he added, "I think you do too."

Marguerite blinked her eyes open to peer at him as he continued, "You just need time to accept it. It's a lot to take in. A past you didn't know about, a life-mate, a child, being a bigamist."

"What?" she asked with shock.

"You married Julius while you thought you were widowed," he pointed out. "That means you have, or had, two husbands."

Marguerite just gaped at him as he tilted his head thoughtfully. "Although, legally, I don't think you would have been a bigamist. I think a person is legally considered dead if they are missing more than seven years. At least they are now. The laws might have been different then." He shrugged the matter away as unimportant and then glanced at her to tease, "So are all your sons as grumpy as Christian?"

When she just stared at him with disbelief for teasing about something so distressing, Tiny raised a hand and pushed her mouth closed, his expression serious as he said, "You either laugh or you cry in this life, Marguerite. And I think you've had enough to cry about up to now, don't you? It's time to laugh."

"Damn."

Marguerite stopped gaping at the house they were pulling up to and glanced at Julius at that curse. He was eyeing a car parked in front of the house with a combination of worry and dismay.

"Well, you called him," Marcus pointed out with amusement, apparently understanding Julius's upset.

"I left a message. I didn't expect them to head over,"

Julius muttered and then catching her concerned gaze, he offered her a smile. "It will be all right."

Marguerite nodded slowly, but didn't say anything. She hadn't been saying much of anything since leaving the townhouse. Mostly what she'd done was stare. She stared at Julius, trying to find these memories they said were missing, imagining him in fifteenth-century dress in a fifteenth-century York. And she stared at Christian, trying to see herself in him and wondering if he really was her son. And through all her staring, both men kept giving her little reassuring smiles, as if to say it was all right. Everything was all right.

It made Marguerite feel bad. She felt bad for not remembering Julius, if there was anything to remember. She felt bad for apparently trying to kill Christian, and she didn't have a clue what to say or do or even how to interact with either of them now, so all through the train ride to London and then on the airplane to Italy, she'd just kept staring at them both.

The car pulled to a halt in front of what was apparently Julius's house and they all got out and moved around to the trunk to retrieve their luggage. They were moving toward the front door of the house when it opened and a tall, dark-haired man stepped out.

If Julius hadn't seemed pleased to know this man was here, the man looked no more pleased himself. His face was cold, his eyes filled with loathing as they fixed on her, and he growled, "Julius!"

"Hello, Father," Julius said calmly, taking Marguerite's arm in his free hand and starting forward. "How—?"

Marguerite glanced at him with surprise when he

suddenly snapped his mouth closed mid-greeting and stopped walking. She knew it was the appearance of the dark-haired woman who suddenly hurried out of the house that made him pause, but didn't understand why. She thought the man was much more intimidating . . . until the woman burst out furiously, "How could you bring that—that *woman* here, Julius? Here! After what she did!"

Marguerite stiffened, confusion rife in her. She wanted to be angry at such a rude welcome, on the other hand, if she'd done what they all said she'd done, well, she kind of deserved it.

"I'm sorry," Julius said to Marguerite with a sigh, and then he handed his own suitcase over to Christian and turned to head toward the couple. "Mother, Father. Come inside, we need to talk."

He took their arms and began to lead them back into the house, but paused at the door to glance back to the rest of the party. None of them had moved. Marguerite didn't really want to, and Marcus, Christian, and Tiny had only moved as far as to position themselves around her, offering silent support.

Julius nodded as if it was as it should be and said, "Marcus, could you come with me?"

"Do you want me to take your suitcase?" Tiny offered when the man nodded and started forward.

"Thank you, no. I'll just leave it inside the door," Marcus responded.

"You can leave mine inside the door as well, Christian," Julius said and then added, "Please see Marguerite and Tiny inside and get them settled and then give them a tour of the house so they know where everything is." He started to turn away again but paused to swing back and add, "Put your mother in the room next to mine."

Marguerite felt a jolt of shock roll through her at the word *Mother*. Not that she'd never been called that before, she had four children—other children, she corrected and frowned with confusion.

"I think he means you," Christian teased softly, apparently spotting her confused expression.

Marguerite forced a smile, but couldn't manage any more than that. Her mind was drawing a complete blank. Apparently her intelligence had run off to hang out with her missing memories wherever those were, she thought wearily.

"It's okay," Christian said quietly. "It's a lot to accept, I know."

"You seem to be handling it all well enough," she pointed out unhappily.

"Maybe," he said, slinging his overnight bag over his shoulder so he could take her arm and urge her forward. "But I've spent five hundred years sneaking into Father's desk to look at your picture. Your face has always been my mother's face in my mind." He squeezed her arm gently. "I know it hasn't been the same for you. You didn't even know I existed and probably aren't even yet sure it's true."

Marguerite swallowed. He was being very kind to her considering she'd ordered him killed at birth.

"Maybe you could show her the picture now," Tiny suggested as they entered the house.

"What picture?"

The question made them pause inside the door and glance at the woman moving up the hall toward them. She was oddly attractive in an austere way, at least until she smiled in greeting, then the austerity dropped away, becoming a memory.

"Marguerite, this is my Aunt Vita. She's my father's oldest sister."

Vita Notte laughed at the introduction. "You never call a woman old, Christian. And oldest is even worse." Shaking her head, she turned to Marguerite. "Hello, Marguerite, is it?"

"Yes," she accepted the hand held out and shook it with a small smile.

"My mother," Christian growled, and Marguerite couldn't decide if it was pride, or warning, or both in his voice. She saw the surprise flicker in the woman's eyes, and braced herself for an attack as the mother had launched, but Vita merely released her hand, her smile becoming a little stiff.

"Of course, I should have realized . . . the name. Well . . . isn't this nice," she said and then seemed to be either unsure what to say next, or unwilling to say any more.

Marguerite herself was at a loss as to how to fill the silence that followed and it was Tiny who finally said, "Christian was about to show us to our rooms."

"Yes, of course." Vita immediately stepped aside for them to pass and as they began to continue forward, said, "The Rose Room is quite nice, Christian. Marguerite might like it."

"Yes, it is, but Father wants her in the room next to his," he responded and then he was leading them around a corner.

Marguerite felt her shoulders relax the moment they were out of the other woman's sight. This was looking to be an unpleasant stay indeed if she was constantly waiting for Julius and Christian's family to attack her. Not that Vita had seemed intent to do so. She hadn't seemed to know how to react to her presence. Marguerite could sympathize. She was a little lost herself.

"Here we are," Christian said after leading them upstairs and along the hall to a door almost at the end. Pausing, he opened it, and then reached inside to switch on the light before waving her in.

Marguerite walked inside, pulling her suitcase behind her. The room was large and airy and decorated in cream colors that made it bright and cheerful and soothing.

"If you want to unpack, I'll take Tiny to his room and then dump my own suitcase in my room before giving you a tour around."

"I wouldn't mind a shower before the tour," Tiny admitted. "It's been a long day."

Christian hesitated and then glanced at Marguerite in question.

"That's fine," she said.

Nodding, Christian turned back to the door. "Half an hour, then. I'll collect you both in half an hour for the tour."

"And the picture?" she asked.

Christian hesitated, and then shook his head. "I think it's probably best if my father shows you that."

Marguerite nodded in understanding.

"Come on, Tiny. I'll show you to your room so you can get that shower. I wouldn't mind one myself now."

Marguerite followed them to the door and closed it behind them, then turned and paced restlessly across the room to peer into the en suite bathroom. It seemed obvious it was shared with the next room, the master bedroom she realized and turned away to pace to the windows. Tugging the curtain aside, she looked out on the dark yard. It was large, well kept, and surrounded by a high wall with wire running along the top that Julius hoped would keep out anyone who wished to control her.

Marguerite let the curtain drop back into place and began to pace.

She wanted to see the painting. She also wanted to call Martine and Lucian. She was restless, and impatient and wanted answers.

Mouth firming determinedly, she strode to the door of her room. Julius had said she could see the painting and make the calls when she got here and that was what she was going to do. Marguerite simply couldn't wait.

The hall was empty when she slipped out of her room. At the stairs she paused and peered nervously down, not eager to run into Julius's parents or even his sister on her own. She didn't see anyone, however, so—straightening her shoulders—started silently down.

She reached the main floor, and went searching for the study, peering into each room as she passed. All of them were empty and then she heard voices coming from an open door at the end of the hall. They were growing louder with each word, telling her that someone was approaching the door.

A frisson of anxiety sliding up the back of her neck,

Marguerite opened the door she stood beside, the first she'd come across with the door closed and slid inside. She eased the door quietly closed, just catching a glimpse of Julius as he stepped out of the room at the end of the hall. She didn't think he'd seen her, though, and breathed a little sigh of relief that she hadn't been caught snooping by Julius and his parents as she released the doorknob.

Turning, Marguerite leaned against the wall to wait for the hall to be empty again, deciding that she'd head right back to her room. She didn't mind Julius knowing she was poking around looking for the painting. She really didn't think he'd be angry, but she was less than eager to have his mother or father know. Their opinion of her was bad enough alread—

Marguerite's thoughts died as she glanced around the room and realized that it must be Julius's study. She stared at the desk arranged in front of the windows across the room and let her breath out on a slow sigh, then forced herself to move away from the wall and walk to the desk.

Fourteen

"Oh, that's a likely story!"

Julius and Marcus exchanged a speaking glance as Marzzia Notte threw her hands in the air and began to pace the library. They had known the woman would be difficult about this. Of his two parents, she was the most volatile. In contrast, Nicodemus Notte, Julius's father, was always calm. His mother's reaction was the reason he'd hoped to keep them out of the matter until he had everything resolved. It had never occurred to him that they'd show up at his home before he was ready for them. He'd only called his father, to ask if it was possible for a three-on-one to be done on an immortal and what the results might be. Unfortunately, his parents had been out when he'd called and Julius had been foolish enough to leave a message that had piqued his father's curiosity sufficiently that he'd come to see what it was about.

His mother clucked with disgust and said, "The truth is now that her precious Jean Claude is dead she has decided to make do with you."

"He was not her precious Jean Claude. They were not even true lifemates," Julius insisted, though he didn't know why he bothered. He'd already told her this.

"How would you know?" she asked sharply, whirling to glare at him. "You cannot read her."

"But I can," Marcus said, drawing her furious gaze.

Nicodemus had been silent through all this, a stark contrast to his wife. Now he moved to Julius's mother and slid an arm around her, drawing her to his side in a manner that seemed to calm her at once. Turning to Marcus then, he asked, "And you are positive her memories are missing?"

Marcus nodded.

"How can that be?" Marzzia asked with a frown and then suggested, "Are you sure she was not simply guarding her thoughts?"

"No." Marcus shook his head. "I have read her repeatedly both in America and since we flew to England. In California, I even crept into her room while she was sleeping to read her while she could not put up any guards."

Julius scowled at this news. Marcus had neglected to mention that fact. Before he could say anything, Marcus continued.

"Marguerite Argeneau has no memory of any of us or that time," he added firmly. "Including the twenty years when Jean Claude was missing and presumed dead. Which begs the question, why wipe her memory of the incident if she really did turn Julius away and return to Jean Claude?"

His mother was silent, her expression becoming troubled. It was Nicodemus who asked, "The memories are just not there? Or is it that she has other memories in their place?"

Eyes narrowing, Julius glanced to his father. The tone suggested he was considering something.

"She has other memories in their place, a vague recollection of traveling Europe with Jean Claude. Very vague," Marcus added dryly. "More like a thought than experience."

"Her mind has been wiped and new memories put in to replace them," Nicodemus growled thoughtfully.

"But it would take a three-on-one," Julius's mother protested. "That is dangerous enough on a mortal, but on an immortal? No." She shook her head. "It could have killed her. No immortal would agree to do that to another."

"Don't be so sure," Nicodemus muttered with disgust.

Marzzia frowned at the possibility, but sighed. "It matters little. Not remembering what she did does not make up for the doing."

"*If* she did it," Julius pointed out quietly, and she looked at him with surprise. An expression that was quickly followed by pity.

"My son," Marzzia said sadly. "I know you loved her, but she wasn't who you believed her to be. She had all of us fooled. And while she may have been your true lifemate, you were not her only lifemate. She chose Jean Claude over you and then tried to kill your child. He probably demanded it of her to prove her loyalty to him."

"I told you, they weren't true lifemates. Jean Claude Argeneau could read and control Marguerite from the day they met."

"Why the devil did he turn and marry her then?" his father asked with outrage.

"Apparently, she is a mirror image of his wife before the fall of Atlantis," Marcus explained.

"Sabia," Marzzia murmured and then her eyes widened and she began to nod. "Yes. Yes. She did look like her. Very like her."

"You knew Jean Claude's first wife?" Julius asked with surprise.

"Of course," Marzzia said with a shrug that seemed to say it should be expected, and then added thoughtfully, "And you are sure they were not lifemates?"

"It is well known among her family," Marcus repeated. "I read it from Vincent's mind."

"And Jean Claude controlled her?" Marzzia asked, definitely looking troubled.

"Yes," Julius affirmed on a sigh. "It is no secret among her clan that he made her life miserable all the years of their marriage. Especially the last five hundred years."

"Punishment," Marzzia said with a wise nod. "Punishing her for loving you."

Nicodemus raised his eyebrows with amusement at his wife's words. "Now you think she maybe didn't do those things? Throwing over our son? Ordering her own child murdered?"

Marzzia shrugged. "Why erase the memory if it was true? Besides, she did love our Julius. Who could not love him? And he was her true lifemate; no woman would choose Jean Claude over our Julius, especially when he was her lifemate. No." She shook her head. "Jean Claude could control her and he did. He made her do those things and then wiped her memory of the whole incident," she decided firmly and then clucked her tongue, compassion claiming her expression. "Oh, the poor girl! She is an innocent in all this . . . torn from her love and child . . . suffering all these years. I must go see her!"

"No! Wait, Mama," Julius growled with frustration, hurrying after her.

"And I am going to welcome her to my bosom as my own daughter," she announced striding toward the door. "Marzzia," Nicodemus said quietly, and she stopped, "let Julius explain. There is more going on here than we yet know."

Julius eyed the man warily, wondering if he'd read him. It was a problem with parents. They were harder to keep out of your thoughts.

"What don't we know?" Marzzia asked, moving back to her husband.

"The only reason I called you was to find out if it was possible to do a three-on-one to an immortal," he explained with a sigh. "Marcus and I have never heard of it being done."

"Most think it impossible," Nicodemus said with a nod. "And are encouraged to think so to prevent it from being done. It is a very dangerous procedure. It takes much longer than with a mortal, sometimes days. The three involved must be old and strong with the stamina to finish it. They must completely supersede the working of the victim's brain to do it and if they take too long about it or make a mistake . . ." He shrugged. "They will die."

"But there would be nothing wrong with them afterward except that the memories are missing?" Julius asked with concern. "They couldn't suddenly be read and controlled by all and sundry?"

"At first they could," he admitted slowly. "It is a great trauma on the one it is done to. Even if they survive they are usually not the same directly afterward. Often they are catatonic, easily controlled until their mind heals and they recover their ability to think and make decisions again."

"How long would that take?" Julius asked, suddenly worried for Marguerite.

Nicodemus narrowed his eyes, knowing there was a reason for the question, finally he asked, "You say Jean Claude controlled her throughout their marriage?"

"Yes," Julius said quietly and asked, "Is that because of the three-on-one?"

Nicodemus smiled. "You always were a clever boy. Yes, that is why. He may have been able to control her when he first turned her, but it would have become harder and harder over time as she grew stronger and developed the ability to guard against it. By the time he supposedly died, and perhaps another fifty years or so afterward, he would have found it very difficult indeed to control her unless he was making physical contact or she was tired and vulnerable. However, in the normal course of things, these last four hundred years or more, he shouldn't have been able to control her at all, and yet you say he did." He shrugged. "That is another symptom of the three-on-one. It is as if once they have been inside the mind, tinkering around with it, they leave an opening they can reach through at any time afterward to take control of her mind. She could easily have been controlled when she gave the maid the order to kill Christian."

Julius nodded, he'd already come to that conclusion. Now he asked the other question he'd wanted to ask his father. "Could she have been made to kill the maid?"

"Certainly. They could completely take over her will, just as we do with mortals."

"But without being in the townhouse at the time?" Julius asked. "Jean Claude was not in the townhouse when Magda was killed."

"And there was no one in the townhouse in York when Marguerite tried to walk out this morning," Marcus added when Nicodemus started to shake his head.

Julius's father paused at this news. "Marguerite has been controlled since Jean Claude's death?"

Julius and Marcus exchanged a glance. He had only told his parents what Marcus had discovered in California, that Marguerite didn't recall anything. He hadn't brought up the recent attacks on her, but now he told them about the attacks at the hotel and restaurant and Marguerite's being controlled that morning in the townhouse.

"I do not know," Nicodemus admitted on a sigh. "I have never heard that they can be controlled from a distance, but I suppose it is possible. The question would be who is doing the controlling now?"

"We think it is Jean Claude," Julius said quietly.

"What?" Marzzia gasped, giving up the silence she'd kept through the last part of the conversation. "But you said he was dead."

"He was supposed to be dead five hundred years ago too," Julius pointed out.

"Do not settle on him and forget the other two," his father warned. "They too could control her. You must consider all three as possibly being the threat now."

"But we don't know who the other two are," Julius said with frustration.

"They would have to be people he trusted, who were old and strong like he was."

Julius nodded slowly as he considered who the other two might have been.

"Martine and Lucian are old enough," Nicodemus said thoughtfully.

Julius's head shot up at this comment from his father, and his eyes widened with horror.

"Well, they aren't likely to back up the truth about that time, then," Marcus said dryly.

Marguerite set the phone back in its cradle and dropped back into the desk chair with a groan. The fates were against her. She was sure they must be. It was the only explanation for her continued inability to reach Martine and Lucian. She had approached the desk intending to look for the picture, but then she'd spotted the telephone and decided to try to reach Martine and Lucian again instead. The answering machine had picked up at Lucian's on the second ring. She hadn't bothered to leave a message this time, simply hanging up. Marguerite had then tried Martine. The housekeeper had answered and assured

her that yes, indeed, Martine was back from London.
Unfortunately, she'd gone out to visit a friend. She
shouldn't be out too much longer, though, did she
want to leave a message?

Frustrated by these repeated attempts and misses,
Marguerite had left the number listed on the phone
she was using and asked her to have Martine call her
back. With her luck, the number on the phone was
probably the wrong one, Marguerite thought. She
seemed destined to remain in this limbo of not knowing. It was driving her mad.

She made a face and glanced at the desk before her.
It wouldn't surprise her if she tried every drawer and
came up empty; it really was one of those days. Shaking her head at her doomsday attitude, Marguerite
sat up and reached for the top drawer. She was so
positive she wouldn't have any success that when she
pulled it open and saw the painting, she just stared at
it for several minutes.

There were papers on top of the painting, obscuring
most of it, but it was definitely the bottom corner of
a painting sticking out. Taking a breath, Marguerite
reached for it, pausing when she saw that her hand
was trembling. Closing her eyes, she squeezed her fingers into a tight fist, holding it for a moment before
releasing it, and then she opened her eyes and lifted
the picture out from beneath the papers.

Marguerite dropped back in the seat, her eyes swim-
ming over the image on the canvas with amazement.
It *was* her . . . and not her. At least not a her she knew.
The features were the exact same, the shape and color
of her eyes, the shade and wave of her hair, the full,
bowed lips, the straight nose . . .

But this was not the woman she saw in the mirror each morning. That woman could feign a smile with the best of them, but they rarely reached her eyes. Only her children could really make her smile, and then that was only recently. For the last six hundred to almost seven hundred years, the eyes that had met hers in the mirror had been sad and lonely. Neither description fit the Marguerite in the painting.

Her clothes were fifteenth-century wear, a long forest green gown. And the artist had been a true artiste. He'd caught the sparkle of laughter in her eyes and had somehow made happiness radiate from every brushstroke. The woman in the image glowed with love and joy . . . and she was heavy with child.

"Christian," she breathed, brushing one finger over her swollen stomach in the portrait. He hadn't mentioned this bit of information, but it was now obvious why he'd assumed the woman was his mother.

Her gaze drifted over the image again, this time stopping on her throat. A medal hung there from a chain. It was a gold St. Christopher's medal, portraying a bearded man with a staff in his hand and a bundle on his back. Well done as it was, Marguerite couldn't make out these details in the portrait. She knew because she recalled the medal. She'd worn it every day of her life from the moment her eldest son, Lucern, had given it to her when he was a boy of eighteen. He'd purchased it with his earnings from his first mercenary job and presented it to her on her birthday. She'd never taken it off, not to sleep, to bathe . . . never. And yet one day she'd noticed it was missing. That was about five hundred years ago. The loss had upset her greatly at the time.

"It's in the drawer."

Marguerite gave a start of surprise and glanced guiltily toward the door as Vita closed it and crossed the room.

"The necklace," she explained, "it's in the drawer as well."

Marguerite glanced down into the drawer and spotted the end of a gold chain sticking out from beneath the papers. Reaching out, she tugged it forward with her finger, and then picked it up.

"You gave that to my brother the day he left to take my sister, Mila, to court. You told him it would bring him back safely to you."

"I thought I lost it," she whispered, peering at the medal.

"I suppose in a way you did," Vita murmured.

They were both silent for a minute, and then Marguerite cleared her throat and said, "Julius said he would show me the painting when we got here, but he was busy with your parents, so I came . . ."

"Snooping?" Vita suggested, the words softened by a smile. "I'm afraid I would have too. I am not the most patient soul. I come by it naturally. My mother isn't very patient either, though she'll deny it to her death." She made a face. "It is unladylike to be impatient, you understand."

Marguerite smiled wryly and admitted, "Then I am afraid I'm not very ladylike."

"We should get along well, then," Vita said with a laugh. "My parents despair of me. My interests are too masculine; hunting, riding, battle, and the business. They were terribly glad when Julius was born and could take over helping Father to handle family business. They were sure I would come to enjoy more feminine pursuits then."

"And have you?" Marguerite asked.

"No," she admitted with a laugh. "I love business. I think fate cheated me and I was meant to be a boy."

"Business," Marguerite said softly, a memory clicking into place. "Of course, you are the sister who was helping Julius with the business while he was in England."

Vita grimaced, a flicker of anger flashing briefly in her eyes. "Helping with the business? Is that what he called it?" she asked with disgust. "I could build a castle singlehandedly and a man would say I *helped* out." She heaved a sigh. "Men! You can't live with them and you can't kill them. What can you do?"

Marguerite bit her lip and glanced down at the picture in her hand to hide the sparkle of amusement in her eyes. She'd often heard similar complaints from her daughter and supposed she'd made a few herself.

She sensed Vita leaning over her shoulder to peer at the picture as well. They were both silent for a moment, then Vita said, "Everyone knows about this picture and the necklace in the drawer. It's hard to keep a secret in this family."

"Does Julius know you all know?"

Vita straightened, her expression thoughtful as she considered the question. "I don't think so. At least, no one has said anything to him as far as I know, not in all the five hundred years that he has kept your picture here." She glanced at the portrait again and said sadly, "You were both so happy back then. Julius had always been happy by nature, but . . . when he found you. . ." She shook her head. "I have never seen him like that." She gave a little sigh. "It was all so tragic when we thought you'd broken his heart and tried to kill his child."

Marguerite winced at the words.

"Julius changed overnight. There was no more laughter, no more smiles. He was so unhappy. We thought it would ease with time, but it has been five hundred years."

Marguerite swallowed unhappily and made an effort at changing the subject. "Did I know you too?"

"Not well," Vita said, her eyes still examining the picture. "You and Julius were a bit wrapped up in each other at first as is natural. Actually," she gave a laugh and said almost apologetically, "it was kind of sickening at the time. You were constantly making eyes at each other and touching each other. You couldn't stand to be apart. I was half jealous and half appalled to think that I might someday behave like that when I met my lifemate."

Marguerite didn't take offense at the comment. She'd borne witness to her own children's discovery of their lifemates and knew exactly what she was talking about. She had found herself both happy for them in their joy, and at the same time, a touch envious and almost depressed that she didn't have that. It was hard to be alone when there were happy couples around. It made you wonder what was wrong with you.

"But then," Vita continued, "when it all fell apart, I almost found myself wishing for a return of the lovey-dovey business that came before."

"God, he was so in love with you, and so miserable without you. The man moped endlessly." She frowned then glanced at Marguerite and said, "I overheard Julius telling Mother and Father that you don't remember anything from that period. Is that true?"

Marguerite nodded unhappily, her gaze sliding back to the picture as she tried to recall posing for it.

"Nothing at all?" Vita pressed.

"Nothing," Marguerite admitted unhappily.

Vita patted her shoulder. "I'm sure they'll return in time."

"Do you really think so?" she asked, eager to believe that.

"Well, Dante and Tommaso were saying that you named all your dogs Julius."

"Yes, I have," Marguerite realized. In all this excitement and upset it hadn't occurred that she'd named her dogs Julius, every one, over several centuries. It was a lot of dogs.

"And dogs are faithful and loyal and give love freely much like my brother," she pointed out and then nodded. "I think you must have memories still in there somewhere. Perhaps they're just locked away where you can't reach them at present."

Marguerite hoped that was true. Not that it would make much difference to her feelings. She had fallen in love with the man all over again and now that she had seen the portrait, she was quite sure what he'd said was true. Jean Claude had somehow wiped her memory, made her leave Julius, and tried to make her have her own child killed.

Thank God for the maid, Magda, Marguerite thought and then frowned as she recalled she had apparently murdered the poor woman for failing her.

"He was really angry about that," Vita commented, and when Marguerite glanced at her with wide eyes, she said, "I'm sorry. It's rude to read you, I know, but he is my little brother and I wouldn't want to see him hurt again. He was crushed when you returned to your husband the last time. You aren't going to do that again, are you?"

"Jean Claude is dead," Marguerite said, but wondered if it was true.

"Yes, well, he was supposed to be dead the last time too," Vita pointed out.

"So I've been told," she murmured, beginning to fret. Jean Claude was dead. He had to be.

"So, you wouldn't return to him if it turned out he was still alive?" Vita pressed and then added quickly, "It is just that I know what Julius can be like in a fury and while he was heartbroken for himself, he was furious about Christian. But he isn't naturally cruel, so if he was a bit mean to you when the two of you first met again in England—"

"He wasn't," Marguerite assured her quickly, but thought he would have had every right to be.

"Good." Vita nodded and turned away. "I should go see if they're done talking yet. We were on our way to the office to discuss a project I want the company to bid on when Father insisted on stopping here to see if Julius was back yet."

Marguerite waited until the door had closed behind the woman and then peered down at the portrait and necklace in her hands. Her gaze slid over the woman in the image and she thought to herself that she could be that woman again . . . glowing with love and happiness. The possibility made her heart ache with yearning.

And then her gaze slid to the St. Christopher's

medal and Marguerite thought that she'd been right when she'd given it to Julius. It was going to bring him back safely to her, because it convinced her more than the portrait that he'd told the truth. The medal had meant a great deal to her. She wouldn't have given it to just anyone, and she'd never taken it off. Giving it to someone she loved and who was heading out on a journey was the only reason she would have willingly taken it off. St. Christopher was the patron saint of travelers, or at least he had been back then. He had been decanonized during the late twentieth century she knew.

But Marguerite had no problem believing she'd taken it off and placed it around the neck of the man who had made her as happy as the woman in the portrait.

Now she just had to tell him that.

Closing her hand around the necklace, she slid the painting back into its spot under the papers, then closed the drawer and stood up. Marguerite hurried for the door, slipped into the hall and was rushing back toward the stairs when she nearly crashed into Tiny and Christian coming around the corner from the opposite direction.

"Marguerite!" Tiny looked relieved to see her as he caught her arms to steady her. "We were worried when we couldn't find you in your room. You were supposed to wait for us."

"Yes, I know, but I—" She shook her head, unwilling to take the time explaining. Instead she glanced to Christian. "Where is your father?"

"I'm not sure," he admitted. "We were going to look for him if we couldn't find you. His luggage is missing from the hall. Maybe he took it up to his room after my grandparents left."

Nodding, Marguerite tried to move around them, but Tiny held on.

"Wait a minute. What about the tour Christian was supposed to give us? I've talked him into showing us the portrait."

"I've seen it," she admitted. "It's lovely. Go take a look. I have to talk to Julius."

Breaking free then, Marguerite hurried upstairs and along the hall to her room. She slid inside, crossed to the connecting bathroom and hurried through it to the door to his room and then paused, suddenly unsure how to proceed.

What should she say? Marguerite stood, biting her lip and simply staring at the door for a moment, then let her breath out on a small tsk of annoyance. She believed him. The painting and necklace had convinced her. Surely that was a good thing and what he wanted?

Everything will be all right, Marguerite assured herself and reached for the doorknob. She would know what to say as soon as she saw him.

Fifteen

Julius laid his suitcase on the bed, and began to unpack with a sense of relief. He was glad to be home, he was glad to have Marguerite here with him, and he was glad that he'd managed to convince his parents to leave and not interfere. It was a good day.

Smiling at his own thoughts, Julius began tossing dirty clothes into a hamper in his dressing room, and setting what still clean clothes were left on the shelves. He'd promised to keep his parents informed as to what was happening and what he learned. The problem was he didn't really know where to go from here. His main concern was to keep Marguerite safe. Beyond that he wasn't sure what to do. He needed to find out who was behind the attacks in London and York. His instincts told him it was that damned Jean

Claude. The man had stolen his happiness more than five hundred years ago, and Julius was sure he was trying to steal it again. But his father had warned him not to focus on Jean Claude and ignore the possibility of another being behind the attack. So he had to try to find out who it was.

If the incident where Marguerite had been controlled was connected to the other two attacks, then the person behind these assaults had to be one of the three people who performed the three-on-one on her. His father thought the most likely suspects were Martine and Lucian. That was a problem. Marguerite was supposed to call one or both of them for back-up proof of his claims, but if they were involved, they weren't likely to back him up. They'd hide it. He supposed that would be proof that they were involved, but it was also likely to make Marguerite decide he was lying and leave.

Julius wasn't sure of the motive for the attacks either. Jean Claude hadn't tried to kill her back then, but had taken her back like a toy he'd abandoned and then regained interest only when he saw someone else playing happily with it. What reason would the man have to want her dead? As far as Julius could tell, the other two involved wouldn't have any motive at all . . . unless it had something to do with the past and the fact that she was snooping into it now. Did someone want the past to stay buried? Or did they want to keep him and Marguerite apart? Or perhaps both?

These were all things Julius had to sort out and he hadn't a clue how to go about it. He wasn't even sure how to find out for certain whether Jean Claude was dead or not. The only thing he could think was to have someone dig up his grave, although that wouldn't prove anything if he was a pile of ashes.

Julius sighed with frustration and returned to his suitcase for another stack of clothes, his concerns turning to the more immediate problem of keeping Marguerite from calling Martine and Lucian.

The click of his door opening made him pause and glance about, his eyebrows flying up when he saw Marguerite standing in the door of the bathroom between his room and the one she occupied. They then lowered with concern when he saw her stark expression.

"Marguerite? Are you all right?" he asked, laying the clothes back in the suitcase and starting toward her with concern.

"I was in your study," she announced. "I saw the painting."

He waited, uncertain what was coming next.

"Did I tell you where I got this?"

Julius shifted his gaze to the chain she dangled from her fingers. The St. Christopher's medal. His muscles slowly relaxed.

"Did I?" Marguerite asked, starting slowly forward.

"Your son," he said, "it meant a great deal to you because of that. You said you never took it off, but when I left with Marcus to take Mila to court, it was our first time apart. You took it off and asked me to wear it to ensure I returned safely to you."

Julius saw a tear slip out from under her lashes and frowned. Moving forward, he placed a finger beneath her chin and urged her face up. When she opened her eyes, he told her, "I took it off when I brought Christian back to Italy, and I threw it out the window in a fury."

Her eyes widened slightly at the claim and he admitted, "Which was foolish, because it took me two nights of crawling around in the grass with a candle to find it again." Her lips began to spread in a smile and he shrugged. "I couldn't throw it away. I felt like it was throwing us away and I guess I hoped it would bring us safely back together again someday as you promised."

"And it has," Marguerite whispered and leaned up to kiss him.

She believed him, Julius realized with relief. The necklace and portrait had been proof enough for her and Marguerite trusted him. He let his breath out on a silent prayer of thanks to God and slid his arms around this precious woman. He had gamboled through life until he'd met her the first time, enjoying all it had to offer, but never really fully experiencing any of it until meeting her. With Marguerite the nights had sparkled, and life had seemed filled with endless possibilities. And when he'd lost her, all that light and sparkle and possibility had seeped away, leaving life a sepia silent film. But he had her back now, and he'd never let her go, Julius thought . . . and then they both stilled as a knock sounded at the door.

"Ignore it," he murmured, drawing her toward the bed and pushing the suitcase off.

"Marguerite? It's the phone for you," Tiny said through the door.

"I didn't hear the phone," Marguerite said with surprise.

"I don't keep one in my room. Too many telemarketing calls during the day disturbing my sleep," Julius explained.

"It's Martine," Tiny added.

Julius felt the blood in his veins freeze. Marguerite believed him now, but if she talked to Martine and the other woman said it was all nonsense as he feared she would . . .

"Oh!" Marguerite pulled away with an apologetic smile. "I'd better get that. I called and left a message for her to call back."

She'd slipped out of his arms before he could stop her. By the time his brain started to work again and he reached for her, she was out of reach.

Julius stared after her with growing horror, sure that his world was about to collapse again. By the time he was able to shake himself out of the stupor that had claimed him she was slipping through the door.

"Wait, Marguerite." He hurried forward, but she was hurrying now too and when he burst out into the hall he was just in time to see her disappearing down the stairs. Tiny, moving at a much slower pace was only halfway up the hall.

"Is something wrong?" the detective asked with concern when Julius cursed. "I thought talking to Martine was a good thing?"

"Not if she was one of the three," Julius said grimly as he hurried up the hall. "She might tell her it was all nonsense."

"Martine?" Tiny asked, running to keep up with him. "You think she—?"

"The other two had to be old, strong, and people Jean Claude trusted," he explained.

"So your father verified that three-on-ones on immortals are possible?" Tiny asked jogging down the stairs next to him.

Julius nodded, then burst ahead, breaking into a dead run as he reached the main floor. He skidded to a halt at the door to his study just in time to see Marguerite pick up the phone.

"Hi, Martine," she sang happily into the phone, offering him a smile when she turned to lean against the desk and spotted him in the door.

Julius sagged against the doorframe, his eyes fixed on her expression. He sensed when Tiny arrived and joined him in the door, worried and out of breath, but ignored him as he waited for the betrayal to appear on Marguerite's face.

"Yes, I did," Marguerite said. "Actually, I called Friday night as well, but you had left for London to spend time with the girls. Did you have a good time?"

Julius felt his teeth grind together at her chatty tone. Dear God, the fates were going to drag this out.

"Oh, that sounds lovely," Marguerite laughed. "Yes, I quite liked the Dorchester too. Did the girls have a good time?"

"Jesus," Tiny breathed next to him, apparently as impatient as he.

"Really?" Marguerite laughed again. "I shall have to try that the next time . . . Yes . . . What? Oh, well it's not really important anymore, and I was calling to ask a question that might seem silly."

Julius held his breath.

"Yes, well . . . I was wondering . . . I didn't happen to stay at your home back in the fifteenth century? Say around 1490 to 1491?" Marguerite paused, listening, and then said, "Martine?"

Julius felt his hands clench.

"Yes, I know it is and I'll explain when next we meet, but the answer is important to me and—" She paused and listened, her expression going solemn. He couldn't tell if that was a good thing or not and wished he could hear the woman's answer.

"Really?" she asked quietly and then shook her head slightly and said, "No."

Marguerite listened again and Julius was beginning to experience pain in his chest. He wasn't sure of the cause until he realized that he was still holding his breath. He let it out slowly and started across the room.

"I— I'll come see you soon and explain, I can't . . . No, everything is . . ." Marguerite paused, her eyes widening on Julius. He supposed his expression was probably expressive of his feelings at that point and he wasn't feeling very happy. It sounded to him from this end as if Martine had lied and told her no.

"I have to go, Martine," Marguerite said quickly and hung up. She then reached for his arm with concern. "Are you all right?"

"What did she say?" Tiny asked abruptly from the door before Julius could answer.

"Oh." Marguerite glanced at the mortal and smiled. "Yes, I did stay in her home in York."

Julius blinked in surprise. He'd been positive she was echoing Martine's no when she'd said the word.

"Martine said I sent her a message about being with child and planning to marry 'some Italian' as she put it," Marguerite said wryly. "But then shortly afterward she got a letter from Jean Claude telling her that he wasn't dead as everyone had presumed, that I'd lost the child, and you had left me and he and I were sorting things out. He told her it was a delicate subject and never to bring it up to me as it upset me greatly."

"The bastard," Tiny muttered.

Julius simply sank to sit on the edge of the desk, his legs suddenly weak from the scare he'd had. Martine hadn't lied to her. She'd backed up his story.

"I guess the good news is that this means that Martine wasn't one of the three," Tiny commented thoughtfully.

"Martine?" Marguerite asked with surprise. "No. She never would have been involved in something like that. We are friends."

When Tiny glanced his way with raised eyebrows, Julius turned to Marguerite. "My father suggested that the other two who had performed the three-on-one with Jean Claude would have to be old, strong, and people he trusted," he explained. "He suggested Martine and Lucian."

Marguerite shook her head slowly. "No. They both have too much honor."

"But he was their brother," Julius pointed out.

"Yes, but . . ." She grimaced and then said, "Marcus is like a brother to you. Would you do it for him?"

Julius snorted at the very suggestion. "Marcus would never ask it of me."

"Yes, but—Never mind, the point is, they would

not have supported him in this. Besides, Martine said he informed her in that letter that he wasn't dead as everyone presumed, and you said Lucian thought I was widowed too?"

When he nodded, Marguerite shrugged. "Then Jean Claude didn't trust them with that information did he? If he didn't trust them to accept that behavior as all right, he'd hardly trust them with something like a three-on-one. And rightfully so, I should think. Lucian would overlook a certain amount of bad behavior from Jean Claude, biting drunks and so on even after blood banks were instituted, but only so long as he didn't really see it. He knew Jean Claude was doing it, or suspected, but avoided *really* seeing it, because then he would have had to do something about it. He told me that himself," she admitted. "But something like this?" Marguerite shook her head. "He couldn't be involved with it and still overlook. Lucian and Martine were not involved," she said with certainty.

Julius peered at her silently, not at all convinced and thinking she was a bit naïve. Twins were different. He had seen it in Dante and Tommaso. They might not always like what the other twin did, but they were as close as could be and would defend each other to the death.

That was a concern for another day, however. Right now, Marguerite had seen the painting and the necklace and talked to Martine and was convinced of the truth. All would be well. So long as she was here with him and safe, everything else would fall into place eventually. Julius really believed that.

Smiling, he straightened from the desk and scooped her into his arms.

Marguerite merely smiled and wrapped her arms around his neck as he started across the room.

"I gather we aren't going to talk about this anymore?" Tiny asked dryly as he stepped out of their way.

"No," Julius agreed as he started up the hall. "Later."

"Right," Tiny said wryly. "I guess I'll go find Christian and finish the tour."

"Good thinking," Julius called as he started up the stairs.

Marguerite peered up at Julius as he carried her along the hall. She started out smiling, but then it slipped away and she said solemnly, "I'm sorry."

"For what?" he asked with surprise.

"For making you prove what you said was the truth," she explained. "For not believing you without evidence."

Julius snorted at the words. "I can hardly complain since if I'd believed in you back then and hunted you down for answers I would have realized there was something wrong and we would have been together these last five hundred years."

"But that's exactly it," Marguerite said quietly. "You told me about your 'dream,' which was really our past wasn't it?" When he nodded, she continued, "You said that someone had come to you with a tale that was false and you didn't have faith in me and let me slip away. And I said then we must never let it happen in real life and then I did."

"Marguerite, trust is—"

"Important," she insisted, reaching out to open the door to his room when he paused before it.

"Yes," Julius agreed, stepping through and kicking

it closed. "But it is also something that takes time to develop. You knew we were lifemates, or believed we might be, and you gave yourself willingly to me, but we still only knew each other a matter of days this time as far as you were concerned. Back then, I had known you for almost a year, surely long enough to develop some sense of who you were, and yet apparently not long enough. At the first test of my love and faith, I failed. Mine is the greater sin, and we have both paid for it."

"But—" Marguerite began, but he silenced her with a kiss.

"But nothing," Julius said when he lifted his mouth. He released her legs and she clutched at his arms as she came upright before him. "I have found you again. Hopefully, we are both wiser for the experience. Now I want to enjoy us."

Marguerite peered up at him silently, tilting her face into his palm when he cupped her cheek. Suddenly recalling Vita's question earlier, she asked, "Why were you not mean to me in London when we first met? You should have hated me for leaving you for Jean Claude and ordering Christian dead."

"I could never hate you," Julius assured her and then grinned. "Well, for the first hundred years afterward I hated you, but when Marcus came to me with the news that your memory seemed tampered with, it was like an answer to a prayer. I decided at once you hadn't done those things we'd thought and I wanted you back in my life.

"I wasn't mean, because I love you," he said solemnly. "And because without you, I have no soul, and life is just a trial to get through. But with you, it holds untold joy."

"I think I must have loved you back then," she said quietly. "I look like a woman in love in the portrait and I want to be that woman again."

"It's enough to start with," he assured her and lowered his head to cover her mouth with his.

Marguerite opened to him and unlike the mad, desperate passion that had claimed them before, this time the caress was tender and sweet, slowly deepening until she moaned and stretched her back, her body arching into his. When Julius broke the kiss, she blinked her eyes half open and he smiled.

"You will never know how many mornings I lay awake remembering this look on your face and yearning to see it again," Julius whispered, his hands undoing the zipper of the peach-colored dress she wore. "I've dreamt of your smell, your touch, your lips, and your breath soft against my cheek as I claimed you."

Marguerite lowered her arms from around him as he drew the dress forward off her shoulder and down her arms. It promptly slipped down to pool around her feet. Free of it, she reached for the buttons of his shirt, but Julius brushed her hands away.

"No. I didn't have the patience or ability to go slow in York. It had been too long. Let me do this as I've dreamed all these centuries."

Marguerite lowered her hands to her sides, meeting his gaze as he ran his hands slowly up and down her arms.

"I recognized your scent the moment I entered your hotel room that first day and it smelled like heaven."

She shivered and closed her eyes as he leaned forward and inhaled by her neck, and then he kissed her there and Marguerite shivered again. Her hands came up to his waist as he unclasped her bra and then she was forced to lower her hands again as he removed it.

"You're even more beautiful than I recalled in my dreams."

Marguerite opened her eyes in surprise because this wasn't the first time they'd been together, but then she realized they had been in such a rush in York, he'd never really taken the time to look at her. Julius was looking now, his eyes flaming silver as they slid over her skin. Her body responded as if it were a physical caress, her nipples hardening and reaching out eagerly, liquid pooling low in her stomach and sliding lower. And then he kissed her again, his hands and fingers roaming over the flesh he'd revealed, following the curve of her waist, the flat of her stomach and then mounting the slope of a breast.

Marguerite groaned deep in her throat and slid her arms around his shoulders again, then groaned once more when her breasts lifted with the action, scraping across his chest. Julius caught her under the legs and carried her to the bed, only ending the kiss as he straightened from laying her down. She didn't get a chance to complain at the loss. In the next moment his mouth was sliding over her neck and down her collarbone to her breast. Marguerite clasped his head and twisted her own on the pillow, her legs shifting restlessly as he drew on the sensitive bud before sliding lower.

Her stomach muscles rippled as his mouth trailed over it, quivering under the caress and then Julius nibbled his way to the top of her panties. She gasped and writhed as he ran his tongue along the lace edge, and then reached for him desperately when he caught his fingers under the waist and drew them slowly down.

Marguerite caught her fingers in his hair and tried to urge him back for another kiss, but he merely caught her fingers in his, and shifted between her legs. Her body arched of its own accord as his mouth trailed over her thigh, her breath coming in small breathless pants, and then wooshing out of her on a cry as he found the center of her. She bucked into the caress, her hips jerking without her consent. She caught her fingers in the comforter she lay on, clawing at it desperately as he pleasured her.

Marguerite felt his fingers dig into her thighs as Julius lavished her with attention and knew in what little bit of her mind was still coherent that he was experiencing her pleasure with her and using the knowledge it gave him to direct him in what felt best, what would make her cry out, or shudder or writhe. He used it to drive them both to the edge repeatedly, always easing back before they could find release.

When the sound of tearing cloth reached her ears and she realized she was rending the comforter, Marguerite released it and grabbed for his shirt, tugging it up around his head until he lifted his head and arms to allow her to pull it off. But then he simply dropped between her legs and continued his sweet torture until Marguerite was trembling and nearly sobbing with need. Only then did he finally rise up and shift over her, shedding his pants as he went before settling his hips between her thighs.

Marguerite felt his erection bump against her and

wrapped her legs around his hips as Julius drove into her. She cried out as he filled her, her body tense and quivering and then he kissed her and began to move and she clutched him close and rode the storm until it broke overhead.

She woke some time later to find they were both under the covers and he was on his back in bed, holding her in his arms.

"Have I mentioned that I think you're fabulous?" he asked, his chest moving under her head.

Marguerite smiled and pressed a kiss to his chest. She then raised her head to peer at him. "I think you're pretty fabulous too."

"I guess we're just a fabulous pair," Julius said, lifting his head to press a kiss to her forehead.

"Does Mr. Fabulous have any food in this house for Mrs. Fabulous?" she asked hopefully.

"Mmm, I was just thinking of food too," he admitted and then laughed. "We were like this the last time too. Make love, eat, make love, eat, make love."

"I hope there was the occasional bath thrown in there," Marguerite said with amusement.

"Many of them," he assured her. "Some of them we even took separately."

She laughed again and his expression softened.

"I love it when you laugh."

"I love it when you look at me like that," she answered promptly.

They stared at each other for a moment, and then he kissed her quickly and he jumped out of bed.

"Food," Julius announced when she peered at him with surprise. "We won't have any here. Christian hasn't eaten for centuries, and Vita and I for longer than that."

"Vita?" she asked with surprise.

"She stays here often," he explained striding naked and unselfconscious to his dressing room. His voice floated out, distracted and easy. "It's closer to work than her own home so when she's going to be spending a lot of time at the office, as she has this last week while I was in England, she usually just stays here. She'll probably head back to her own place in the next day or two."

"Does Christian live here with you?" Marguerite asked curiously. He'd mentioned taking his things to his room when they'd arrived, and she wondered if he still lived with his father after five hundred years.

"No. He has an apartment in town, but he keeps a room here and stays on occasion." Julius reappeared wearing a dark burgundy robe, and carrying a fluffy white one he held open for her.

Marguerite slid out of the bed and slipped into a robe.

"We'll have to hurry," he said heading for the door as she tied it. "If we want food we'll have to order in and it's getting late."

Pausing at the door, Julius glanced back as she crossed the room to join him and smiled. "I've always been intrigued by those commercials on television. Now I'll get to order in."

"We should check with Tiny. He's probably starved by now."

Julius nodded and grinned as they moved out into the hall. "You think like a mother."

"I *am* a mother," she pointed out with amusement. "Four times over."

"Five," he corrected gently.

Marguerite froze midstep, her eyes widening with alarm. "Yes, of course. I—" She paused helplessly, feeling just horrible that she had neglected to include Christian, but it was all still so new.

"It's all right, Marguerite. It will take some time," Julius said gently, rubbing her back through the fluffy terry cloth robe.

Marguerite nodded, but she wasn't really feeling any better. Christian Notte was her son, but a veritable stranger.

"Marcus told me on the train back to London that you were feeling awkward and unsure of how to act with Christian."

She grimaced as she recalled the man reading her mind in her room. It was a bad habit she would have to start putting up guards against, Marguerite decided.

"It will get easier once you get to know each other and spend some time together," Julius continued, urging her to start walking again.

"*Time together*," Marguerite said softly, grabbing at the idea. "Yes, I should spend time with him. Get to know him."

"I'm sure he'd enjoy that," Julius said with a nod.

"What kind of things does he enjoy?" she asked.

"Hmm." He considered the question as they started down the stairs. "Archery, downhill skiing, swo-"

"Downhill skiing?" Marguerite asked with amazement. "At night?"

Julius grimaced but nodded. "He says it adds to the challenge and the enjoyment."

"I'll bet," she said with a laugh. "How about something less physical?"

"He loves music," Julius said and then told her proudly, "He plays several instruments and used to play with an orchestra."

"Really?" she asked with interest.

Julius nodded, but his smile was replaced with a grimace as he added, "He has recently switched to more modern music. Hard metal or alternative something." He shrugged, obviously not sure what it was called, and then added, "He plays with a band in town most weekends."

Marguerite bit her lip to keep from laughing at his obvious distaste for the music in question.

"The three of us could go to a concert and—" Julius paused when she stopped at the foot of the stairs and placed her hand on his chest. Raising his eyebrows, he asked, "What?"

"I—It might be better if I could spend some time alone with him, Julius. Just the two of us," Marguerite said seriously, and then quickly explained, "I'm afraid if the three of us go out, I would just be distracted by your presence and that would defeat the whole purpose."

Marguerite waited anxiously for his reaction, afraid she'd offended him, but he considered the suggestion briefly and then, much to her relief, nodded solemnly. "You're right, of course."

Relaxing, she smiled and slid her arm around him as he steered her up the hall.

"I'll check with Dante and Tommaso for you and find out what he would enjoy and arrange tickets if you like."

"I would appreciate that, thank you," Marguerite said. "And perhaps he could tell you the name of a good coffee house or something too. I know Christian doesn't eat or drink anymore, but it would be nice to stop in somewhere quieter afterward so we could talk."

"Good thinking." Julius hugged her to his side. "You'll get to know him in no time."

Sixteen

"*What did you think?*"

Marguerite smiled at Christian as he threw himself into the chair next to her at the table. It was their night out to get to know each other, but rather than getting tickets to a concert, she'd decided she'd rather hear him perform, so Marguerite had asked him about his band and if she might attend the next time they performed. Christian had seemed a little uncomfortable when she'd first suggested it, but had agreed and told her they were playing at a local spot in a couple of nights and she was welcome to come.

She'd spent the time between then and this evening looking for any little signs of herself in Christian, and she'd actually found some. Where his father had black hair, Christian's was a dark auburn like her own. He had his father's eye color but her large almond-shaped eyes. He had his father's jaw but her high cheekbones. It was nice to note these things, but hadn't made her more comfortable around him, and, despite her desire to get to know him, Marguerite found herself feeling and behaving in a stiff and unnatural manner around the boy.

Julius had reassured her over and over that everything would be all right and just to relax and be herself, but while Marguerite had a sincere desire to feel and act with Christian as she did around her other sons, he wasn't her other sons. She had centuries of shared experience with them and virtually none with Christian. On top of that, Marguerite was suffering under a burden of guilt and regret for the time lost with him. She was struggling.

Right this minute, however, some of her stress had lifted. Marguerite had always loved music and found it soothing, and had realized as she watched and listened to her son play that here was something they had in common besides hair color. Here was something they could discuss. Christian played violin in his rock band, and he played well.

"You hated it," Christian guessed when she remained silent so long.

Marguerite shook her head quickly. "No. I didn't. I quite liked it. This is the first time I've heard violin rock live, but I've always thought it added a fascinating sound to the mix, and you play very well. I enjoyed it."

When he looked doubtful, she insisted, "It's the truth. Actually, I was just thinking that you must get your musical talent from me. Your father is tone deaf."

"Yes, he is," Christian agreed with a grin, then said, "You play?"

"Yes. Piano, violin, guitar, drums—"

"Drums?" Christian interrupted with disbelief.

Marguerite shrugged. "If it makes music, I've probably played it. I have always loved music and it filled up my time. Being a housewife is extremely boring, especially when you have servants to actually do the work," she said wryly and then breathed out a little sigh and admitted. "I used to play all the time, but haven't as much since Jean Claude died. I was finally free to come and go as I liked and I've been going a lot, but tonight has made me want to play again."

Christian glanced toward the stage as the next band began to warm up. "They're going to start up. Would you like to go somewhere quieter for a coffee or something before we go home?"

Marguerite nodded at the offer, knowing it was purely so they could continue to talk. Christian didn't eat or drink. When she realized she was smiling and that it felt more natural than any of the other smiles she'd given him since finding out he may be her son, Marguerite felt herself unclench a little inside. Perhaps it *would* be all right after all.

"There's a coffee shop around the corner," Christian said as they stepped out into the night. "I don't know if it's any good there, but it's close enough we can walk."

"I'm sure it's fine," she said as they started along the street.

"Hey, lady, you dropped something."

Marguerite and Christian paused and glanced back to see a man pointing to a small purse lying on the sidewalk.

"I'll get it," Christian said, releasing her arm to hurry back along the street.

"But I didn't bring a—" Her confused words came to an abrupt halt as Marguerite became aware of movement out of the corner of her eye. Turning sharply, she realized they'd stopped at the mouth of an alley and someone—two someones, she realized—in dark clothes and masks were rushing out at her.

Marguerite instinctively turned to make a run for it, but didn't have a chance. Before she'd taken two steps, they were on her.

Cursing, she struggled briefly but they were immortals, and both larger and stronger than she, she soon found herself caught against one of the men, a long, wickedly sharp knife at her throat. For one moment, Marguerite thought he intended to cut her head off right there in the street, but he merely pressed it to her throat until he drew blood, forcing her to stop struggling.

Breathing shallowly and trying not to move to prevent the knife from sinking any deeper into her flesh, Marguerite saw Christian stop halfway back to the purse and turn. He froze at the sight of her predicament. The man who had called out that she'd dropped something was scuttling away up the street. No doubt he'd been paid to distract them with the purse business, she thought on a sigh, then met Christian's angry gaze.

"Run," Marguerite ordered, uncaring of the knife at her throat.

When Christian stared at her silently, his expression unreadable, she knew he was going to be stubborn about this.

"Christian, do as I say, dammit!" she snapped, stomping her foot furiously and ignoring the bite of the knife as it slid deeper. "I'm your mother!"

"Yes, you are," he said, a smile slowly curving his lips upward, and then he raised his arms in surrender and walked forward.

"Turn around," the fellow behind her ordered when Christian paused a few feet in front of them.

Christian tossed her a reassuring glance and turned around, asking cheerfully, "So, where are we going?"

Instead of answering, the second man stepped up behind him. Marguerite cried out in warning, but it was too late, the man had driven his knife into Christian's back. As he twisted and jerked the knife upward, she began to struggle, uncaring of the damage she was doing herself, but paused when a shout sounded from the entrance of the restaurant.

All three of them froze, only Christian continuing to move and that was only to collapse to his knees. Marguerite peered toward the restaurant to see Dante and Tommaso rushing forward, but the twins stopped abruptly at an order in Italian from the man holding her.

Marguerite wasn't surprised to see the pair. Julius had told her that he wanted the twins to follow them and keep an eye out tonight and she'd agreed so long as they kept their distance so she and Christian could talk freely. They'd been sitting at the other side of the bar and she'd seen them get up to follow when they left, but the bar was crowded and they'd had farther to go to reach the door. She and Christian should have waited at the door for them, Marguerite thought unhappily.

When the man holding her said something else in Italian, his comrade nodded and immediately lifted Christian, hefting him over his shoulder. He then came to stand beside them.

Marguerite stumbled and nearly beheaded herself when the man holding her suddenly began to back toward the alley, but she quickly grabbed his arm and managed to keep her feet. Her hold didn't ease the pressure of the knife against her throat however and it was a tense few minutes as they backed into the alley.

Dante and Tommaso followed slowly, eyes narrowed, bodies tense as they waited for an opportunity to intervene, but that never came. Marguerite was backed up to a van, and held still while the second man opened the side door and dumped Christian's unconscious body inside. While he then rushed around to leap behind the steering wheel, Marguerite was dragged back into the van by her captor. The knife remained at her throat until he threw her aside to close the door. Marguerite took that opportunity to crawl to Christian and try to check on him, but the next moment pain radiated through her head and unconsciousness claimed her.

Julius stood, staring out the window of his office, his gaze lifted to the stars overhead. Somewhere out there, under those stars were his lifemate and son . . . and he may never see them again.

That thought had been running repeatedly through his head for the last two hours since Dante and Tommaso had returned to the house and told him that they'd failed in watching his son and Marguerite and that the pair had been taken.

Julius had wanted to crawl across his desk and rip both their hearts out, but he'd calmed somewhat since then. At least, he didn't blame them anymore for what had happened. They'd done their best. The fault lay with him. He should have refused to let Marguerite out of the house. But she was so uncomfortable around their son and had been so eager to spend time getting to know him, and the previous attacks had always taken place when she was alone without another immortal nearby to aid her, Julius had thought she'd be safe.

He'd thought wrong, and now it could cost him both Marguerite and his son. Damn Jean Claude Argeneau! He had to be behind this.

"Julius?"

He turned sharply, his gaze moving eagerly to Vita as she entered his study, hoping for news. Waiting for a ransom demand that he knew would never come was driving him wild, but Marcus had pointed out that they had called in everyone who worked for them, mortal and immortal alike, to search for the pair, or some sign of the van that had taken them, or even for Jean Claude Argeneau. And if there was a ransom demand, he should be there for it.

It was possible, Marcus had suggested, that this was a different matter altogether. After all, the other attacks had been outright murder attempts on Marguerite alone and they hadn't really had to take Christian at all once he was disabled, but had. Also, while his son had been stabbed he could recover from that and Marguerite hadn't been harmed much before being dragged off.

Julius didn't think even Marcus believed these suggestions, but he was hoping the man was right as he watched Vita cross to him.

"What is it? Is there news?" he asked, hoping that if there was, it was good news.

"No," she said apologetically. "I just thought you should know, some of Marguerite's family are here."

Julius's eyebrows rose with surprise and then he frowned. "Which ones?"

"I'm not sure," she admitted. "The only one who introduced himself was Bastien. He's one of her sons, isn't he?"

"Yes." Julius nodded. Bastien Argneneau was the one who ran Argeneau Enterprises.

"There are three others with him."

Sighing, Julius moved around his desk and headed for the door.

"Well, that was a cheap shot."

Marguerite opened her eyes and peered down at her son. She'd woken up several moments ago to find that they were locked in some kind of cell or dungeon, both of them with chains around their ankles, tethering them to the wall. But their upper bodies were free and the length of the chains allowed some movement. The first thing she'd done was check Christian.

Marguerite had been alarmed by the state he was in. His wound was already healing of course, but he'd lost a lot of blood. She'd known he'd be in pain when he woke up and had left him to sleep while she'd taken a look at the chains around her ankle.

Marguerite had tested their strength, tugging at the chain between the wall and her ankle. When the links hadn't shown any sign of stress, she'd then tried to pull the fastening out of the stone wall instead, but that hadn't given any either. They wouldn't be able to break the chains.

Marguerite had then shifted back to Christian and lifted his head into her lap to whisper soothingly and brush the hair back from his face as he moaned in pain. She could sympathize with him. Marguerite was in a bit of pain herself. The head wound she'd taken must have been a serious one. Her head was throbbing, the side of her face caked with dry blood, and her body was screaming with a need for more blood to replace what had been lost. She thought that the man must have caved in the back side of her head. No doubt, her body had used up a lot of blood to repair it. They were both in a bad way, which had, no doubt, been the intent of their attackers. In this state, they weren't likely to cause too much trouble or have the strength to break their chains.

Frightened for their future, Marguerite had begun to sing a lullaby she used to sing to her other children when they were young. The sound had seemed to soothe Christian. At least, his moaning had slowly quieted, leaving him sleeping peacefully. She'd sung until her voice began to crack from a dry throat, and then had fallen silent and bowed her head as exhaustion had claimed her. Marguerite had finally closed her eyes, dozing in and out of a fitful sleep that had ended the moment Christian spoke the wry complaint about being stabbed in the back when he'd surrendered.

Now she opened her eyes and peered down at him with a relieved smile. He was pale from loss of blood and there were lines of pain around his eyes and mouth, but he was alive and awake and she could have wept with relief.

"Yes, it was a cheap shot," she agreed. "And completely uncalled for since you'd given up."

"But smart," Christian murmured.

When she raised her eyebrows, he shrugged mildly in her lap. "I may have appeared resigned, but even a tame cat can turn."

Marguerite smiled faintly and brushed her fingers through his long hair. It was as soft and silky as a baby's and her smile faded as she said, "I wish I had seen you as a boy."

"I wish you had too," he said solemnly.

"I bet you were adorable."

"Undoubtedly," he agreed tongue in cheek.

Marguerite closed her eyes as pain radiated through her head. Once it had passed, she smiled at him in what she hoped was a reassuring manner and said, "Tell me what your childhood was like. Were you happy?"

Christian hesitated, but then his smile faded and he began to try to sit up. "I think we would do better to try to find our way out of—" Christian's words ended on a quick inhalation of breath as he got halfway upright and then froze before dropping back to lay against her.

"I think we are both still healing and you should

stay put until you can move without turning green," she suggested quietly.

"Green, huh? At least my head is not misshapen." The words were said lightly, but there was concern on his face as he peered at her. "Does your head hurt very badly?"

"Yes," Marguerite answered simply, and then added, "now stop changing the subject and tell me about your childhood. It'll distract us both from the pain. Was it a happy one?"

"Happy," Christian echoed the word thoughtfully and then nodded. "For the most part. Father was a good father."

"Did you always call him Father?"

"No. I called him Papa when I was young, but you know, after a hundred years it seems a bit undignified so I switched to Father."

Marguerite chuckled softly and leaned back against the wall, closing her eyes to try to imagine what he spoke of as he continued, "I lacked for nothing, except for you, of course. But Gran and the aunts spoiled me rotten to try to make up for it. Naturally, I took full advantage."

"Naturally," Marguerite murmured, forcing away the guilt she felt for not being there for him.

"Father was always there for me," he added solemnly. "He played with me when I was young and trained me himself."

"What did he train you in?" Marguerite asked, trying to keep the pain out of her voice.

"Battle, hunting, feeding . . ."

"Were you a good student?"

"The best," Christian assured her. "I was always

trying to please him, to make him smile. He always seemed so sad. I thought if I could just be perfect, the sadness might leave his eyes."

Marguerite swallowed thickly and kept her eyes closed to keep back the tears gathering behind her closed lids.

"I remember asking Gran once why Father was always so sad, and she said it was because he missed my mother. That she'd hurt him terribly. It's the only thing she ever really said about you, and she seemed angry when she said it, so for the longest time I didn't ask about you anymore. But of course, the older I got, the more curious I became and when I was a teenager I think I drove them all crazy with questions about you."

"Not that it got me any answers," Christian added, a wry note to his voice. "They had a pat line they gave me. Your mother is dead and that is all you need to know."

"It wasn't enough. I wanted to know what you were like. I thought you must have been wonderful for him to miss you so much, and I was sure everything would have been all right if you were just there with us. Father would smile and be happy and I would have the smiling woman from the picture as a mother, and she would love us both and make everything all right."

Refusing to let them fall, Marguerite blinked away her tears, and then peered at Christian with fear in her heart. His honesty was frightening to her. It told her he thought they weren't likely to survive. She didn't think he'd be this forthright otherwise. She had her own fears in regard to their survival. The previous attacks on her had been outright murder attempts and she doubted their captors had much better intentions now despite having included Christian this time. But they couldn't afford to give up. So long as there was hope, there was a chance, but if he gave up . . .

"Christian," she said quietly. "We're in a spot of trouble here, but we aren't done yet. Don't tell me anything you will regret when we get out of here."

He peered at her, solemn and unblinking. "I have had a million imaginary conversations with you over my five hundred years. Let me tell you. I might not get another chance."

Marguerite bit her lip, but held her tongue.

"I always believed them when they said you were dead," he continued quietly. "Otherwise you would be with us. But I often daydreamed that you were there and proud of me."

"I'm sure I would have been," Marguerite assured him. "And I wish I . . ."

"What do you wish?" Christian prompted.

Marguerite frowned. She'd been about to say that she wished she'd been there to tell him so, to love and mother him as he deserved, to help raise this handsome young man, watching over him proudly as he grew to manhood. But she had stopped herself because that would be a betrayal of her other children. If Jean Claude had not done what he'd done, and she had stayed with Julius and Christian, then Bastien, Etienne, and Lissianna would never have been born. She couldn't wish for that, not even for a moment. Marguerite loved and cherished all her children.

"Mother?" Christian whispered.

Marguerite felt a thickness in her throat when he called her that, but forced a small smile and a shrug and said, "I wish for the impossible."

"I understand," he assured her solemnly.

Nodding, she blew her breath out, forcing the sad mood with it and then teased lightly, "So you were spoiled rotten by your aunts and Gran?"

"Of course," Christian said, matching her tone. "I am an only child. Only children are always spoiled rotten. They get all the attention and all the goodies."

Marguerite smiled wryly and murmured, "Oh, dear."

"Oh, dear?" he echoed curiously.

"Well, you are not an only child anymore, Christian. You have three brothers and a sister and will soon be an uncle."

A startled look entered his eyes at her words, and he admitted, "I hadn't thought of that. I mean, I knew you had other children, of course. But my mind never made the leap to . . ." He shook his head in wonder. "Brothers and a sister."

"They will love you," Marguerite assured him. "Bastien's nose will be out of joint at first because he will drop in ranking from second son to third, but they will all love you."

Christian snorted at the claim. "It is more likely they will resent having to share you after all this time."

Marguerite gave a dry laugh. "Trust me my dear, they'll be grateful to have someone else for me to interfere with and take some of the heat off of them. I have driven them mad for years, sticking my nose into their business. They will be glad for any respite."

"I don't believe that," Christian assured her.

"No?" she asked with amusement. "Well, you wait until I'm dragging home the check-out girl from the grocery store for you to try to read." Marguerite shook her head. "No. I have no doubt they are enjoying their break from me while I am over here in Europe."

Seventeen

"Julius Notte?"

Julius came to an abrupt halt halfway across his study as the doorway was suddenly crowded with men. The Argneaus.

"I'm sorry, Julius." Vita moved to his side. "I did ask them to wait and said that I would bring you right along."

He waved her apology away, knowing it wasn't her fault, and then arched an eyebrow at the men still crowded in the doorway.

The man at the front of the group moved forward, a hand extended.

"Bastien Argeneau," he introduced himself.

Julius nodded and accepted the hand in greeting.

"I apologize for not waiting as requested." His

gaze encompassed both Julius and Vita, and then he smiled wryly and added, "But we couldn't. We're all a bit worried about Mother. She was calling home every day for the first three weeks she was in England, and then the calls suddenly stopped. Thomas flew to England to look for her and we were tracking her cell phone to try to find her, but it turned out we were tracking someone who mugged her and stole her purse and the cell phone with it."

"She was mugged outside the Dorchester the night we moved from there to Claridge's," Julius said wearily, thinking it seemed so long ago now, though it had barely been a week since it had happened.

"Ah." Bastien nodded. "Well, when Thomas was able to find her, the rest of us flew over to help. We were scouring York when we found out she'd called our Aunt Martine and left this number. I managed to use the phone number to get this address. Is she here?"

Julius hesitated, wishing he could reassure the younger immortal, and wishing he didn't have to tell him what he did, but finally blew his breath out and admitted, "She and our son were kidnapped off the street earlier tonight."

There was a stunned silence, and then one of the men behind Bastien said, "Kidnapped?"

Another said, "*Our* son?"

Julius opened his mouth to explain the "our son" part, but such a long and convoluted explanation was beyond him at the moment, so, he merely nodded and said, "Yes. Kidnapped. I have men out looking for the van that took them, as well as any sign of Je— the man we think is behind it," he said, avoiding mentioning their father for now. "I have had to stay here waiting in case there is a ransom demand."

Bastien's eyes narrowed and Julius felt a slight ruffling in his thoughts. Mouth tightening as he realized the immortal was trying to read him, he immediately slammed his guards up into place to block him out.

"You said 'our son'?"

Julius turned to glance at the speaker, his eyebrows raising in question.

"I'm sorry," Bastien said quietly. "This is my brother, Lucern."

Julius nodded, and offered his hand, saying, "Marguerite's oldest son. The writer."

And the one he'd never got to meet back when he'd first found Marguerite and married her.

"And this is our cousin Vincent," Bastien introduced the next man.

Julius raised an eyebrow. He'd expected the man to be the youngest son, Etienne, but he supposed that must be the man standing glowering behind the others. They all looked like their father, or at least their father's twin brother since he'd never met Jean Claude himself. But while the rest of the men were dark-haired and the resemblance to their father could be seen, the blonde at the back bore the most striking resemblance.

Vincent held his hand out, recapturing his attention and Julius accepted it, saying, "You're Marguerite's nephew. The one who produces and acts in plays. My own nephews Neil and Stephano work for you."

Vincent's eyes widened. "I thought you must be related to them when I heard the last name."

"Yes. I'm Christian's father," he said.

"Christian's father?" His eyebrows went up and then he frowned with concern. "Christian isn't the one kidnapped, is he?"

"Yes," Julius admitted unhappily.

"But you said 'our son,'" Lucern growled with confusion. "Yours and whose?"

Julius ran a weary hand through his hair as he realized he simply couldn't avoid explanations. "Mine and your mother's."

There was a dead silence as three pairs of male eyes all widened in shock. Only the man at the back of the group didn't react so. Instead, his eyes narrowed and that made Julius's eyes narrow on him and he suddenly got the feeling this was not Etienne Argeneau, the youngest son. In fact, he realized, this man was much older than the others. He could sense his power and strength and he carried himself like a king.

"Yours and our mother's?" Bastien echoed slowly. "I'm sorry, you seem to have us at a slight disadvantage here. What—?"

"Your mother and I are true lifemates. We have a son together," Julius muttered with distraction, his eyes still on the man at the back of the group. Finally, his voice cold and flat, he asked, "Who are you?"

The man arched one arrogant eyebrow and growled. "It's been a long time, but I'm still surprised you've forgotten me. I didn't think you'd forget our talk."

"Lucian Argeneau," he growled, fury rising within him along with the realization. Julius had no idea who the third person must have been in the three-on-one, but he was positive Lucian must have been one of them . . . which made him one of only three suspects involved in the attacks on Marguerite. He hadn't given up on Jean Claude being the culprit behind this whole affair, but didn't doubt Lucian knew something about it. The pair were twins.

"Yes." Lucian arched one arrogant eyebrow and opened his mouth to speak, but never got a word out. Instead, he snapped his mouth closed with amazement as Julius launched himself at him with fury.

Julius didn't land a blow. The moment he rushed forward to attack, the other three men moved to stop him. Bastien and Lucern were quicker than their cousin, and he suddenly found himself being held before Lucian by the brothers, his arms out at his side crucifixion style. The two men weren't hurting him, but he couldn't move . . . except for his mouth. Struggling against the men holding him, he spat, "What have you and that stinking no good brother of yours done with Marguerite and Christian?"

Lucian's eyebrows flew up with apparent bewilderment. "What?"

"You heard me," Julius snarled, renewing his efforts to shake off Marguerite's sons. He nearly managed it in his fury, but Vincent moved around in front of him and braced his chest, standing as much to the side as he could so that Lucian and Julius still faced each other.

Lucian nodded at the man, then glanced at Julius and said, "I haven't a clue what you're talking about."

"The hell you don't," Julius snarled. "You know something. He's your twin."

"Who is?" Vincent asked with confusion.

"Jean Claude," he said through teeth that were grinding in frustration and fury.

There was silence as the men glanced at each other with confusion and then at their uncle. Julius could have gnashed his teeth. The man had to know something. It was his only hope. Otherwise he'd have no idea where to look. He'd lose her, lose them both. "God dammit. You have to know something. I can't lose her again."

"Lose who? Our mother? What do you mean *again*?" Bastien asked. "And what does Uncle Lucian's being our father's twin have to do with this?"

Julius snarled with frustration, his gaze sliding over the faces of the men around him. Bastien and Vincent looked thoroughly confused; Lucern, however, was now looking thoughtful, but Lucian was stone-faced.

"I'm afraid we aren't following you," Vincent admitted quietly. "Who has Aunt Marguerite?"

"Ask *him*!" Julius nodded his head toward Lucian. "He and his brother are behind this."

"What is he talking about, Uncle?" Bastien asked with some frustration of his own.

Lucian Argeneau was silent and then gave a slight shrug. "I don't know."

Julius snorted bitterly. "Just like you didn't know that Jean Claude was really alive when he went missing for those twenty years?"

"What? Father was missing?" Bastien asked with a start and then glanced at his brother. "Do you know what he's talking about, Luc?"

"It was before you were born, Bastien," Lucern said. "He was missing for twenty years. Morgan said he was dead, beheaded in battle."

Julius nodded toward the head of the Argeneau clan.

"Lucian knew better. He knew he was still alive."

When the men all turned to Lucian, he shook his head. "I thought he was dead too. Jean Claude didn't even let *me* know he was still alive during those twenty years he was missing. And he would never discuss it. He just said he'd needed time to himself."

"Right," Julius said sarcastically. "And next you'll say you had nothing to do with stealing Marguerite from me and wiping her memory?"

"What?" The head of the Argeneau clan peered at him sharply.

"The three-on-one. You, Jean Claude, and someone else wiped her memory," Julius said. "We've figured it out. We know she didn't really order our child killed. She must have been controlled and that's easy to do after a three-on-one, isn't it. We've figured out everything."

"I was told Marguerite lost your child and you left her because of it. I was told you said she must be poor stock if she couldn't produce a living child."

"That's a lie."

"Then why did you leave her?" Lucian asked.

"I didn't leave her," he said furiously. "I had to go to court. When I returned Marguerite was gone. And our child didn't die, but it's no thanks to your brother. Jean Claude controlled her and made her order the maid to kill him, but the woman brought him to me instead."

"Christian?" Vincent asked, his expression still confused.

Julius nodded. "He is my son with Marguerite."

"Let go of my son!"

Julius glanced past Lucian's shoulder, his eyes widening on his father's furious face. Nicodemus Notte was noted for his calm. Julius didn't think he'd ever even seen him lose his temper . . . before this. The man was definitely not calm now. At least, his expression wasn't and his eyes were flaming silver black, but his voice still sounded steely calm as he said, "If you gentlemen wish to see Marguerite again I suggest you release my son, cooperate, and talk. You need to work together, otherwise we will lose both her and Christian."

There was a moment of silence, as the men holding him glanced at each other. When they then glanced to their uncle, he nodded. Julius was immediately released.

"Son," Nicodemus growled in warning when he tensed, preparing to attack Lucian and beat the information he wanted out of him.

Julius ground his teeth, but forced his muscles to relax.

Bastien glanced from Nicodemus Notte, to Julius, and then finally to Lucian before saying, "Do you three want to fill the rest of us in on what the hell's going on? Who has our mother? And what is this about our father being missing, and—" He waved a hand with frustration. "All the rest of it."

Julius glared at Lucian, daring him to speak and start sprouting lies, but the man was staring back, narrow eyed. It was his father who said, "I think we should all sit down. Julius, you will explain everything from the beginning, and then these gentlemen can tell us what they know and, hopefully, between the six of us we can come up with something to help us find Marguerite and Christian." He glanced past

Julius and said, "Vita, tell my driver I won't be leaving right away after all."

Julius glanced around with surprise. He'd forgotten his sister was even there, but now saw her nod and move dutifully to do as his father asked.

"And make some coffee, please," his father added as she headed out of the room. "These gentlemen eat and drink mortal food."

"How did you know?" Vincent asked with surprise.

"I can smell it," Nicodemus said calmly, and then glanced at Julius. "The living room?"

Sighing, he nodded and led the way out of his study.

"It isn't working."

Marguerite released her end of the chain and dropped back to sit, leaning against the wall beside Christian. They'd talked for quite awhile as they'd waited for the worst of the healing to be over. But once they could both move without terrible pain shooting through them, they'd taken stock of their situation and begun to try to see if together they could break the chains that bound them. It wasn't working, however. They were both weak and Marguerite was now suffering the gnawing pain of blood hunger. She knew Christian would be too. They were wasting their strength on the endeavor.

"We'll have to think of something else," Christian muttered, his gaze shifting around the small, dingy cell. There were no windows, but a barred one in the thick door. Light from the hall beyond was spilling into the room through the small embrasure, and he frowned at the opening. "This place looks familiar."

"It looks like every dungeon I have ever been in,"

Marguerite muttered with disgust. There was a time when they had slept in such dark, dank dungeons to avoid the sunlight that crept through small cracks and fissures in old homes. "Perhaps we should come up with a plan to overtake our captors when they return."

"Why haven't they returned?" Christian muttered.

She'd wondered that herself. In truth when she'd been dragged into the van, she'd expected to be killed right away, not left to wait in a dingy little cell. She was grateful for the extra time. It had given her and Christian a chance to bond. There was nothing like a crisis for bonding, Marguerite thought wryly. She was no longer uncomfortable with him and had even called him son a time or two without feeling awkward about it. But she'd give that up in a heartbeat to have him somewhere else and safe.

"You should have run when I told you to," she said on a sigh.

Christian glanced at her, and then reached out hesitantly to cover her hand with his and squeeze it briefly before quickly releasing it as if afraid of offending her. His voice was husky as he said, "I'm glad I didn't. I finally got to know my mother."

"That's hardly worth dying for," Marguerite muttered, her eyes on the hand he'd touched. She wanted to take his hand back and hold it. She wanted to wrap her arms around him as if he were still a boy and rock him gently as she assured him they would be fine, but she wasn't quite that comfortable with him yet, and wasn't at all sure they were going to be fine. It made her sad. Not for herself so much. While Marguerite regretted not getting to be with Julius to enjoy their love and bear children with him, she had at least had children, and experienced some of the beauty of a lifemate. Christian, however, had not. She could die more peacefully knowing that he would live to do those things.

Of the three of them, however, Marguerite was most concerned for Julius. He would lose her again, but more importantly, he would lose his son, and she didn't think the double loss was something he would recover from easily.

"What does Jean Claude want?" Christian muttered suddenly with frustration. "First he was trying to kill you and now he has taken us both."

"I don't think it is Jean Claude," Marguerite said with a frown. When he glanced at her, she shrugged helplessly. "I just don't. He's dead. He has to be dead."

A look of pity crossed Christian's face at the desperate sound to the words and she sighed and tried for reason.

"Why would he kill me?"

"Perhaps he was trying to stop all this from coming out. Grandfather says that the three-on-one was outlawed some time in the sixteenth century. It's a dying offense now. Perhaps he was trying to keep what he'd done from being discovered."

"But it wasn't outlawed when it was actually done to me and I don't think they can punish him for it. Besides, killing me now isn't going to stop that from coming out. Your father knows, Marcus knows, your grandfather . . ." She shrugged. "He'd pretty much have to kill your whole family to keep it from coming to light."

"Maybe he plans to," Christian said, his expression turning grim at the possibility.

Marguerite shook her head. "I just don't think it's Jean Claude. We buried him."

"Did you see the body?" Christian asked.

Marguerite frowned and reluctantly shook her head. "They said it was too destroyed for an open casket."

Christian arched an eyebrow, and then stiffened and glanced toward the door as they heard the clang of keys twisting in the lock. They both shifted and began to get warily to their feet.

"It looks like we're about to find out who it is," Marguerite said grimly.

"It isn't Jean Claude."

Julius peered at Lucian suspiciously when he made that comment. He was the first to speak after Julius had finished explaining the events of the past, and what had occurred since Marguerite had stayed at the Dorchester in London.

"Are you sure, Uncle?" Vincent asked solemnly.

"He's dead," Lucian insisted.

"But everyone apparently thought he was dead before," Vincent pointed out dryly and shook his head. "I never liked the way the old bastard treated Aunt Marguerite, but I never thought he'd sink that low; wiping her memory, ordering a child killed, and making Aunt Marguerite kill the maid? If he wanted the maid dead, he should have at least had the balls to do it himself."

"He is dead," Lucian repeated firmly. "And he

couldn't have made Marguerite kill the maid without being able to see her to control her."

"He made Marguerite walk out of the townhouse and wasn't in there when that happened."

Julius glanced around with a start at Tiny's voice and stood abruptly, but paused when the detective shook his head in answer to the question on his face. The mortal and Marcus had teamed up to join the hunt for the van that Marguerite and Christian had been taken in. Apparently, without success.

"I'm sorry. It's like trying to find a needle in a hay-stack, Julius," Tiny said with frustration as Marcus entered the room behind him with a tray with coffee, cream, and sugar in his hands. "We're all out there just driving aimlessly around, checking every van when the one they were taken in may not even be on the streets anymore. Marcus and I came back to brainstorm with you and see if we couldn't think of a better way to pursue this."

"Vita gave me this to bring in," Marcus said as he set the tray on the coffee table.

Julius nodded, but his attention was on Lucian as the man said, "If Marguerite was controlled and made to walk out of the townhouse in York, then the person doing the controlling must have been looking in a window, or otherwise able to see her. They can control her mind, but cannot see through her eyes, it would be like trying to steer a car blind."

"Yes," Nicodemus said with a nod, "that is what I thought, but when they said there was no one around, I wondered if I'd been mistaken."

"So Jean Claude must have been at a window or something to be watching her while he steered her out of the house?" Vincent asked, apparently thoroughly convinced of the man's culpability. Bastien and Lucern on the other hand were remaining silent. Bastien appeared troubled. Lucern just grim.

"It wasn't Jean Claude," Lucian insisted. No one paid him attention.

"Are you sure you didn't see anyone outside the townhouse when you went out after Marguerite?" Tiny asked Julius.

He shook his head. "There was no one there. And no one saw Jean Claude near the townhouse back when Marguerite killed the maid, Magda."

"There are curtains on the windows of the townhouse in York, but not on the door," Vincent said suddenly, and when Julius peered at him with surprise for knowing this, he explained, "We've been staying there the last couple of days. When Thomas came looking for Aunt Marguerite, he and Inez found out that a townhouse was rented under the name Notte in York. "He shrugged, we thought it was Christian. They rented the place to stay there while they looked for more information. We've all been staying there."

Julius nodded and said, "You're right, there are no curtains on the window on the front door, but Jean Claude couldn't have got away from the window that quickly. I didn't see him on the street when I went out, and I did look around. All there was were rather horrified mortals."

"Julius was naked," Tiny explained.

"Perhaps Jean Claude was watching from a building across the street," Vincent suggested. "Binoculars would have allowed him to keep his distance and see her at the same time."

"Jean Claude is dead," Lucian repeated.

Julius ignored him and pointed out, "But he couldn't have seen up into our room where she was sleeping and made her come below."

"But she wasn't in bed," Tiny reminded him. "Marguerite said she got up to get more blood and then the next thing she remembered was waking up on the couch."

"She would have had to walk up the hall to get to the kitchen, that's when Jean Claude must have got control of her. He must have been watching the house. When he saw her through the window, he took control and made her turn and head out the door," Vincent decided, not knowing that they'd kept the blood in the mini-fridge in the living room. It didn't matter, though, Julius supposed. Marguerite would have had to walk through the hall to get to the living room as well.

"It wasn't Jean Claude," Lucian growled.

"It must have been something similar when Magda was killed," Lucern announced suddenly joining the conversation. "Because I guarantee Mother would not have killed the maid. She adored her. Father must have been at the townhouse that day too."

Julius peered at the man. He'd thought from his silence that Lucern hadn't believed what he had told them, but now recalled Lucern had known about his father being missing, and had received a letter from his mother about their plans to marry, though he knew she hadn't mentioned being with child in it. Julius now wondered what the eldest Argeneau boy had been told when he arrived in York back in 1491 to find his father returned from the dead and his mother back with him.

Leaving the matter for now, he considered Lucern's words and frowned as he said, "Vita didn't mention seeing Jean Claude at the time."

"Vita?" his father asked with a start.

"She was the one who told me Marguerite was at the townhouse. She said she saw her go upstairs and wondered if we'd got back together. She didn't mention Jean Claude, however, and I'm sure she would have if she'd seen him there."

"God dammit! It wasn't Jean Claude!" Lucian roared, and when everyone turned his way, he scowled and admitted more calmly, "I cannot say for sure it was not him in 1491, but he certainly isn't behind what is happening now. He is dead."

"You don't know that for sure," Vincent said quietly. "None of us can be sure. The funeral was closed casket."

"Uncle Lucian is the one Morgan called when he woke up to find the house in flames and Father dead," Bastien said quietly. "He went and handled the firemen and police and retrieved Father's body. He would have seen it."

"Yes, but Jean Claude's body was destroyed in the fire. He was nothing but ashes. That is why it was closed casket. There was *nothing* to see," Vincent pointed out. "Even Lucian can't be sure it really was him."

"Yes, I can," the head of the Argeneau clan insisted.

"How?" Julius asked suspiciously. "If he was only ashes—"

"He wasn't ashes," Lucian admitted, his mouth twisting.

Vincent's eyes widened. "Then he could have survived. You might have buried an empty casket."

"No we didn't."

"You can't be sure," Julius insisted.

"Yes, I can."

"How?" Julius demanded again.

Lucian hesitated, and then propped his elbows on his knees, dropped his head into his hands and began to rub his forehead as if it were paining him.

"If you have some proof that Jean Claude is dead, you best share it," Nicodemus said quietly. "Because if he is dead, then we are looking to the wrong person and wasting time."

Lucian nodded in resignation and said, "I know he is dead, because . . . I beheaded him myself."

No one moved. No one spoke. Julius wouldn't have been surprised to be told that no one breathed. They all simply sat staring at Lucian with wide, stunned eyes.

"As Bastien said, Morgan called me that night," Lucian said wearily. "Jean Claude was badly burned but he wasn't dead. He was a blackened and charred mess and wasn't healing quickly. His system was full of a drunk's useless blood and he refused the blood I brought with me. Instead he asked me to kill him and end his suffering. He said he loathed himself for hurting Marguerite and everyone else around him, but he couldn't seem to help himself. He said he had nothing left inside him and he begged me to give him peace."

"So you killed him?" Julius asked with disbelief.

Lucian shook his head. "I couldn't . . . until he admitted that he had been feeding on mortals and had actually set fire to the house. He'd intended to die in the fire, but Morgan had dragged him out."

Sighing, Lucian lifted a haggard face to look at Julius. "Feeding off mortals is against our council laws in North America. It is a killing offense that has to be taken before the council for pronouncement. Feeding on them unto death, however, gains instant death and the hunter doesn't have to take them before the council for pronouncement." He shook his head. "But Jean Claude was my brother. I would have taken him before the council and had someone else commit the deed, but he begged me to kill him and then pointed out that if this mess was put before the council, everyone would know. He said he'd done enough to hurt Marguerite and the children and asked me again to kill him and then to arrange a closed casket funeral so no one would ever know." Lucian shrugged helplessly. "And so I honored his wishes."

Julius sank back with horror, not at what Lucian had done, but because he believed him. The expression on his face as he confessed to taking his twin brother's life had been too stark with pain and guilt for him not to believe him. Jean Claude was dead . . . and now Julius had no idea who could be behind the attacks and taking of Marguerite and Christian.

Bastien cleared his throat. "Then it has to be one of the other two who has Mother and Christian now."

They all looked to Lucian and then Vincent asked what they were all wondering. "Uncle, do you have any idea who the other two could have been?"

Lucian straightened abruptly, his expression turning cold as he forced himself to consider the problem at hand. The change was almost shocking, though it shouldn't have been, Julius supposed. The man was a warrior, a hunter and did what had to be done.

"Morgan would have been one," he announced abruptly. "While I had no idea Jean Claude was still alive when he went missing for those twenty years, Morgan did. He was the one who carried back the tale that Jean Claude had been beheaded in battle."

When Julius sat up, hope on his face, Bastien frowned and told him, "Morgan is dead. He went rogue and Uncle Lucian had to hunt him down. He was captured and put to death by the council."

"Who else then?" Vincent asked, settling on the arm of the sofa beside his uncle and awkwardly patting his back.

Lucian didn't seem to notice the attempt to comfort him, his face was taut with concentration. Finally he shook his head. "There is no one else I can think of that he would trust with this type of thing."

The words made everyone in the room sag with disappointment.

"All right," Tiny said firmly. "Then we have to think of people who would want Marguerite dead and could have been around back then."

"No one would want Mother dead," Lucern said firmly. "She never had the opportunity to make enemies. She was always forced to remain at home."

Tiny shook his head with disgust and then suddenly paused.

"What are you thinking?" Julius asked, desperate for any suggestion.

Tiny hesitated and then admitted, "It just occurred to me that perhaps we are thinking about this wrong."

"How do you mean?" Vincent asked the detective.

Tiny pursed his lips and then said tentatively, "Maybe Marguerite hasn't been the target here."

"What?" Julius asked with bewilderment. "But she is the one who has been attacked each time."

"Not each time. She was made to order your son's death back at the beginning," he pointed out and then asked, "Why?"

Julius stared at him blankly.

"Think," he said grimly. "There was no reason for Jean Claude to want Christian's death. He had wiped Marguerite's memory of the baby. Why not just give Christian to you along with the message that she wanted nothing more to do with you both? Or even dump him with a band of Gypsies?"

"Perhaps he was jealous of Julius," Vincent suggested, but didn't sound as if he believed.

Tiny shook his head. "It couldn't have been jealousy. He wandered off and let everyone, including Marguerite think he was dead. He would hardly be jealous if she then started a new life with Julius."

"Then why did he come back?" Vincent asked. "He was gone for twenty years. Why suddenly come back?"

Tiny shook his head again. "I don't know, but I'm pretty sure it wasn't to reclaim Marguerite. They weren't lifemates. They were miserable together, and he didn't even love her if you judge by the way he treated her. Something else must have caused his return."

When no one commented, he added, "And now Christian has been involved again. The kidnappers could have just left him there on the sidewalk and taken Marguerite if they'd wanted, but they took him as well."

Julius was frowning at the truth of this when Tiny glanced at him solemnly and said, "And if Marguerite wasn't the true target, that leaves you."

"Me?" he asked with surprise. "They haven't done anything to me."

"Yes, they have," the detective said solemnly. "Marguerite's being wiped and taken away by Jean Claude hurt you, not her. She didn't remember you . . . just as she didn't remember Christian. His death would only have hurt you. And now Marguerite and Christian's being taken is hurting you again."

"You're saying all of this has been done to hurt Julius?" Nicodemus asked slowly. "That Marguerite and Christian are just the vehicles to do so?"

Tiny shrugged helplessly. "I know it's hard to imagine, but if Marguerite has no enemies and Jean Claude is dead, she can't be the real target. Julius is the only other person being hurt in all this."

"And us," Bastien said staunchly.

"But you weren't alive back then," he pointed out.

"Lucern was," Vincent pointed out.

"But Christian's kidnapping wouldn't affect him at all," Lucian said slowly and then glanced to Julius. "Who are your enemies? Ones who would have been around back then as well as now."

"Wait a minute," Julius said. "If someone wanted to hurt me, why wait five hundred years? Why not attack or try to kill Christian before this? And why not attack me outright? Why go the circuitous route and attack Marguerite and Christian?"

"Perhaps it's someone who couldn't attack you outright without revealing themselves," Marcus suggested, jumping on the band wagon. "And perhaps your misery and unhappiness was enough for them all these centuries."

Julius was shaking his head in disbelief when he heard his father sigh. He glanced toward the man with a frown. Nicodemus Notte was standing at the window, separate from the group, a troubled expression on his face as he peered out into the night.

"What is it, Father?" he asked with trepidation. "Have you thought of someone who would want to hurt me and was around back then?"

"Yes, I'm afraid I have," he said wearily.

Eighteen

"Aunt Vita?"

Marguerite saw the betrayal on her son's face as he stared at the woman leaning on a sword in the doorway, and reached out tentatively to take his hand in hers. She squeezed in sympathy, but when she tried to release him right away as he had done earlier, Christian clutched her hand and tugged her slowly closer and a little behind him.

It was a protective gesture and while it touched her, Marguerite was the parent here. If there was any protecting to be done, she would do it. She'd done little enough for him prior to this. Pulling her hand free, she stepped around him, placing herself squarely in front of Christian as she demanded, "What's going on, Vita?"

"Yes. What's going on?" he echoed, dragging Marguerite abruptly behind his shielding body.

"Christian," Marguerite said with exasperation, hurrying around to stand in front of him again. "I am your mother. Let me handle this."

"Mother?" he muttered with not a little exasperation of his own. Pulling her back around, he placed himself between the two women and turned to take her by the arms. "I know Vita, you don't, and I am the man."

The last word ended on a gasp as he suddenly stiffened, his eyes going wide. Marguerite grabbed his arms, her own eyes wide with horror as she saw the end of a sword sticking out of his chest.

Christian cried out as the blade suddenly disappeared, and then he began to fall. Marguerite tried to catch him, but he was heavy and all she managed to do was twist him around so that she was between him and Vita. Marguerite lost her balance at the end, landing on her bottom, but did manage to cushion his head.

"That settles the argument nicely, doesn't it?" Vita commented, and Marguerite glanced over her shoulder to see that she was holding up the sword, peering with interest at the blood staining the blade. She glanced at Marguerite now and said, "I do hate the 'I'm the man' argument. So sexist."

Marguerite glanced down to Christian and saw his eyes briefly flicker open. He peered at her silently, gave his head a very tiny shake, and closed them again. Aware that her upper body hid his face from Vita's view and that she had no idea he was conscious, Marguerite eased her hand out from under his head and stood up.

"Will you tell me what this is all about now?" she asked, the chain on her ankle jangling as she moved slowly away from Christian. "I presume you're the one behind the failed attacks in London and York?"

She was hoping that the "failed" part would prick the woman's pride and get her attention. Much to her relief, it worked. Vita ignored Christian and glanced at her sharply, fury flickering in her eyes.

"I planned them, and if I'd carried them out myself, they wouldn't have failed," Vita snapped, her mouth twisting with displeasure. "The saying really is true that if you want something done right you should do it yourself."

"The man in England worked for you," she said.

"Did work for me," Vita corrected. "I put him in charge of keeping your family distracted and away from you, but he failed that too."

"My family?" Marguerite asked, her eyes narrowing.

"Your nephew Thomas arrived in London several days ago looking for you. Fortunately, he went haring off to Amsterdam. I had another one of my men follow him around and try to keep him from returning, however, he too failed." She grimaced and said, "Men can be so useless at times."

When Marguerite didn't comment, she shrugged and continued, "Your dear nephew returned to England and caught a train to York. I was afraid he might pick up your trail and follow you here to Italy, and I definitely didn't want the Argeneau clan interfering so I put my man in York onto Thomas and told him to keep him chasing his tail, or kill him if he had to, but not to let him find you."

"What did he do to Thomas?" Marguerite demanded, fear clutching at her chest. She'd raised the boy. He was like a fourth son to her, or fifth, she corrected herself with a glance toward Christian.

"Nothing," Vita said with disgust. "Once again he failed, only this time he got himself caught as well. Your sons and nephew handed him over to a council escort. I had to send men over to kill him before they managed to get information out of him."

Marguerite felt her muscles unclench as she realized Thomas was safe, and then frowned. Julius and Marcus had nearly convinced her that she was not easily read and controlled as she feared, that only whoever had been in on the three-on-one could do it, but if the man in York had done so . . .

"Was it your man in York who controlled me?" she asked reluctantly.

"Oh, God no!" Vita laughed at the suggestion. "That was me. After he failed to kill you in the restaurant, I hopped on one of the company planes and flew to England to handle you myself. And I would have too if that mortal hadn't interfered." Her lips quirked with amusement as she added, "I was sitting in a townhouse across the street when Julius called me on my cell and asked me to arrange for the pilot to take you all back to Italy. I did, of course. I also flew home at once."

So you were one of the three who took my memory when Christian was born?"

"Yes, I and Jean Claude and Morgan."

"Morgan?" Marguerite's eyebrows shot up at the name of Jean Claude's best friend. "I should have known."

"We wiped those years, your child, and your true lifemate from your memory like so much dust brushed off a table top," she said with a smile and then shrugged. "But you weren't the one I wanted to hurt. Julius was. I took away everything you loved to hurt him . . . and now . . ." She smiled widely. "I get to take you away from him all over again."

"Why do you hate him so?" Marguerite asked with bewilderment. She just couldn't imagine Julius doing anything to deserve this much malice. She had seen him with his sister and he always treated her with respect, but Vita Notte hated her brother with a passion.

"Do you know what it's like to be the eldest Notte daughter?" Vita asked, mouth compressing with displeasure as she moved forward and began to circle her.

Marguerite turned warily, afraid Vita was approaching Christian and would hurt him again, but Vita just kept walking, circling her like a shark. "I'm one thousand years older than Julius. I'm as old as Lucian, but while he holds power and position and the respect of his family and others of our kind, I do not. I'm just a woman." She veered off to pace the room now as she went on, "Oh, it was all fine at first. Those first thousand years, I was feted and trained to accept responsibility and position. I am the one my sisters looked up to, I am the one they turned to in times of crisis, I was the one expected to take over the reins of the family . . . but then Julius was born."

Her mouth was twisted bitterly as she turned to pace back.

"Julius," she growled. "The great male heir my father had really always wanted. "He would carry on the family name. I was smart, but he must be smarter, after all he was the feted male. Suddenly, I was nothing.

"You'll never know how much I hated him. I tried to kill him as a baby. I sent his nursemaid off to fetch something and set his room on fire," she admitted. "Cutting off his head would have been obvious murder and I couldn't risk that."

"Unfortunately, his nursemaid returned sooner than I expected and ran in to save him. It was all very heroic. She died the next day from her burns. Of course, he was terribly burned too, but he was immortal and lived. If the woman had been delayed by just a couple more minutes, that wouldn't have been the case, but . . ."

She drew in a slow deep breath, and then released it, her expression grim. "My father visited her before she died. I think she must have told him I'm the one who sent her away and promised to watch the boy. I can't be sure, of course, but she told him *something* that made him suspicious of me. He grilled me endlessly about what had happened and I admitted that I had sent her on the task, but insisted I hadn't bothered to stay to watch Julius because he was sleeping. That I thought he would be fine for the few minutes." She grimaced, and then sighed and said, "He let me off the hook, but I soon came to realize he hadn't believed a word I'd said. After that, I wasn't allowed anywhere near Julius. I was suddenly persona non grata in the family home, forever being sent here or there, always far away to tend to this or that."

"And he was constantly guarded by at least two immortals after that. They guarded him openly as a boy. Once he reached adulthood, Julius chafed at having guards and they were removed. At least he thinks so, but the truth is he still has them. They simply watch from more of a distance now."

"He knows what you tried to do?" Marguerite asked with confusion.

"No, of course not. Father never mentioned it to anyone. Julius just thought Father was overprotective because he was the only male."

Vita paused by the wall and scraped her nails angrily down the dirt-covered stone. "I couldn't kill him after that. The little prince survived to manhood and took his place on the family throne. He led his charmed little life, having everything given to him that should have been mine, and laughing his way through life as happy and jovial as an adult as he had been as a baby."

"Vita?" Julius asked, a frown drawing his eyebrows together. "But she has never acted cruelly to me, never been mean or shown this jealousy you speak of."

"Your sister is a master at hiding her feelings. So much so that I often wonder if she has any at all . . . besides her own interests, that is," Nicodemus said quietly. "I should have tended to her back then, but I couldn't prove anything, so I just had to watch you, and keep her as far away from you as possible." He sighed. "As the centuries passed and there was no more trouble, I allowed myself to be convinced that all was well, that she had got over her jealousy and accepted your presence."

"Not completely or you wouldn't be bringing it up now," Julius pointed out.

He nodded acknowledgment. "When Jean Claude reappeared and Marguerite left, Vita came to your side immediately. At first I thought she was just being a good sister. But more than once, while she was comforting you I thought I saw a flicker of unholy glee on her face, as if she was enjoying your suffering. However, it would be gone so quickly I thought I must have imagined it." He sighed. "But I have seen that same glee flicker on her face since you went to England and this trouble began."

"Maybe she is just happy that I have found Marguerite again," Julius said with a frown.

"Maybe," he allowed. "But this was when Dante and Tommaso returned and were giving an accounting of what they knew of the attack on Marguerite in the hotel. They were saying that you were terribly upset and obviously loved the woman. I would swear her happiness was over your upset. And I saw it again today when I arrived and found you confronting and being held by these men. She was standing back, watching with apparent delight. I was troubled too when you said it was Vita who told you that Marguerite was at the townhouse just before you found the dead maid. No one mentioned this to me before." He allowed Julius to absorb that and then added, "But it was Tiny's suggestion that it was someone who could not attack you personally for fear of revealing themselves that convinced me. Had you been found murdered at any time after that attack on you as a child, I would have looked to her at once."

Julius frowned. He didn't want to believe it could be his sister, but this was the only lead they'd had. Surely it wouldn't hurt to talk to her and see if he got a sense that something was wrong? Glancing around he asked, "Where is Vita? She was here earlier."

"She was leaving as we came in," Marcus announced. "She gave me the tray to bring in and said she had to go home to get more clothes, she may be needed here for a while."

Aware that the Argeneaus were all now looking at him, Julius frowned. He found it hard to believe that his big sister could be behind all of this, and could wish to hurt him like this. She'd always been fond of Christian, he'd thought. But it was the only lead they had at the moment and if his father was right . . .

Heading for the door, he muttered, "I'll go to her place and talk to her now."

"Not without me," Lucian declared, standing to follow even as Tiny and Marcus fell into step on either side of Julius.

"We're all coming," Bastien announced as Lucian and Vincent stood up. "We rented a passenger van at the airport. We should all fit in it for the ride."

When Julius paused and turned around to argue that he'd rather go alone, Vincent slapped a hand to his shoulder and grinned. "Give in gracefully. This family takes no prisoners. Welcome to the family, by the way . . . Uncle."

Nineteen

"So Julius was happy and you couldn't stand it," Marguerite prompted.

"No, I couldn't. I wished him misery and torture every day of his life," Vita admitted grimly, but then smirked and added, "And then you appeared . . . the answer to my prayers."

"Me?" Marguerite asked with confusion.

Vita's smile was something unholy to behold. "Of course, you . . . and Jean Claude."

Marguerite's mouth firmed, but she remained silent.

Vita moved to lean against the wall by the door, looking incredibly pleased with herself as she said, "I'm afraid I didn't immediately recognize the beauty of his finding you. All I saw was that once again fate had slapped me in the face, giving him a lifemate before me, when I am so much older and had waited so much longer. I admit I was bitter."

Still are, Marguerite thought grimly.

"Julius, of course, was delirious, walking around with a foolish grin on his face, practically flying with his joy. You were his everything: his hope, his future, his lifemate." She grimaced. "You were no better. The two of you were constantly cooing like a pair of love-birds," she said with disgust.

"I couldn't bear it," she admitted. "I spent every minute of every day fighting the urge to lop off your heads, but of course I couldn't. My father would have known it was me. So I suffered in silence . . . but when Julius announced that you were with child . . ."

Vita ground her teeth together at the memory, the sound loud in the silent room. "I nearly did kill you then, consequences be damned. But then I learned something that made me realize there was a much better way to handle the matter. I could crush my brother like a grape without killing anyone, and without any blame coming my way." She smiled, and raised her eyebrows. "Do you know what it was? You should. You lived it. "She smirked and taunted, "Oh, that's right, you don't remember."

Marguerite ground her own teeth now.

"Jean Claude was still alive," she said finally. "After twenty years of thinking yourself a widow, you weren't." She glanced at her solemnly. "He really never should have married you. It was a foolish mistake on his part when he could read and control you. Who could resist doing so?"

"Who indeed," Marguerite muttered. Certainly

not Jean Claude. He'd tried at first, managing for the most part during their first five years together, but it had started to go downhill quickly after that. Her life had become a nightmare of his wants and needs. He could make her do absolutely anything. Not in the mood for sex tonight, wife? He was. And suddenly she was too . . . with one part of her mind at least. The other part was aware that she was being controlled and hated him for it. She'd become nothing more than a puppet to his whims when he was around, never allowed to show her displeasure or anger. If even a bit of it slipped out, he took control, turning her into a medieval Stepford Wife. Yes, husband, I'd love to rub your smelly feet. Yes, husband, it is my pleasure to go here, there, or anywhere you want.

"Of course, he couldn't control you forever," Vita continued. "You soon began to develop the ability to guard your mind and resist."

"I did?" Marguerite asked with surprise, because it seemed to her that he'd controlled her right up until the very end.

"Yes, he told me so in one of his drunken rantings. By the time you had Lucern, he had to be touching you to control you, and even that didn't ensure the ability. He could still read you clearly, but he couldn't make you obey all the time. And once that began to happen, he soon grew tired of you," Vita said as if it were inevitable. "Even the fact that you looked like his dear departed Sabia couldn't hold his interest when he could read your hatred and loathing but not bend you to his will. So, of course, he strayed. Apparently it was usually only for several months or so.

He'd find someone else to dally with and play with them for a while, then return to you."

Marguerite's mouth tightened. She'd suspected that of course, but it still hurt to have it affirmed.

"Then Jean Claude met a true lifemate," Vita announced. "A mortal he could neither read nor control. He was captivated. He secretly turned her and lived quietly with her for twenty years, leaving everyone to think he'd died."

Marguerite's eyes widened. "That's where he was those twenty years? Why did he not just divorce me and free us both? I could have been with Julius and he could have been with her."

"How could he?" Vita asked with a shrug. "We are allowed to turn only one. He used up his one turn on you. Jean Claude would have forfeited his life were it revealed that he'd turned another." She shook her head. "So, he let you all think he was dead those twenty years, and I imagine he would have continued to do so had it been up to him."

"What happened?" Marguerite asked curiously.

"I needed him," she said with a shrug. "So long as he was off in his little cabin in the middle of nowhere with his true lifemate, my brother was free to live happily with you. So, when I learned through my very dear friend, Morgan, that Jean Claude was still alive, I went looking for him. Of course, it seemed obvious to me without even speaking to the man that Jean Claude would have no interest in what you were up to. So long as his true lifemate lived, he cared about nothing else."

"So you killed her," Marguerite guessed unhappily.

"Yes," Vita admitted with a grin and then laughed

with glee. "It was perfect! No one would have reason to suspect me of doing it. No one even knew I was in the area. And what possible reason could I have to kill her anyway?"

Vita released a little satisfied sigh. "It all went as if it were preordained. Jean Claude rode into town for some reason or other, and I rode up to the cabin. She heard the horse and came out, saving me from even having to dismount. I simply lopped off her little unsuspecting head with my sword before she realized what was happening.

"I returned to England at once, expecting him to return home to find his lifemate dead and flee back to his family and you."

"I gather he didn't," Marguerite murmured, noting her unhappy look.

Vita shook her head. "The idiot buried his lifemate and crawled into a barrel of ale. Literally. He wasn't even just biting drunks, he was drinking himself. Months passed. You grew rounder and everyone got happier . . . except me. I finally had to go back to get him," she said with disgust. "It was not easy, I can tell you. Jean Claude seemed to have lost the will to live. All he was interested in was having another drink and moaning about his loss. It took a lot of whispering in his ear to convince him that he should return."

"How did you do it?"

"I gave him a reason to live," she explained. "Hatred of you."

"Me?" she asked with amazement.

"Certainly. I pointed out that it seemed terribly unfair that you were living happily with Julius when your very existence was the reason he hadn't been able to openly turn his lifemate and place her in the safe bosom of his family. It was all really your fault that his lifemate was dead."

"Your reasoning is really something to behold," Marguerite muttered.

Vita stood up to begin her pacing again. "I arranged it all, timing it to happen when Julius was away. It was very close," she confessed with a shake of the head. "Julius dallied about leaving that day, uneager to be away from you, and Jean Claude was early. They rode right past each other on the street. But it all worked out."

Vita tilted her head and smiled at her pitilessly. "You were not happy to see Jean Claude. You demanded explanations and cursed him to hell and back. But he convinced you to return to Martine's with him to hear him out. Once he had you there, of course, he wouldn't let you leave."

Marguerite shook her head, wondering how she could have been foolish enough to go with him in the first place.

"Eight months pregnant, though you were, you decided to flee." Vita paused to peer at her. "Jean Claude was particularly enraged about your pregnancy, by the way. Did I mention his true lifemate was heavy with child when I lopped off her head? They were both very happy, apparently. Well, until I killed her and the unborn babe."

Vita continued pacing. "At any rate, you waited until Jean Claude was deep in drink and then you ran out to the stables."

She paused and Marguerite waited for the other

shoe to drop. Vita didn't keep her waiting for long.

"Fortunately, I happened to arrive as you were hurrying out to the stables."

Truly the fates seemed to have been aligned against her, Marguerite thought.

"It was all rather pathetic," Vita went on with a smile. "You had no idea I was behind all your misery and were so happy to see me. I rode my horse up to you and looked oh so shocked at the news you babbled at me, then I held out my hand, you took it and I swung you up behind me on my horse.

"'*Thank you, Vita,*' you said with heartfelt relief. I was touched really," she assured her. "And then I turned the horse and rode you up to the front doors of Martine's manor, dragged you inside, and locked you in your room with a guard on the door. I then had to get Jean Claude sobered up. I spent hours convincing him that something had to be done. We couldn't risk you trying to escape again. I convinced him that the easiest solution was to perform a three-on-one cleansing of your memories."

Marguerite closed her eyes. She wanted to curse Jean Claude for being so weak and easily led, but this woman had taken from him too. He had been a pawn as much as she, and Marguerite actually felt sorry for the poor bastard.

"Of course the procedure brought on early labor and Christian was born, but we expected that. I hoped for it actually. I told Jean Claude to kill him, but he did not have the heart to do the deed himself. He was regretting the three-on-one, regretting interfering in your life at all out of his own bitterness. He handed the child over to me and told me to send it away and then stumbled from the room and back to his misery and guilt. I don't think he ever recovered."

"I should have killed Christian there on the spot with my own hands," Vita said grimly. "But I wanted to torment Julius just that little bit more."

"So you controlled me and made me order the maid to kill Christian."

Vita nodded. "With the message that you had returned to Jean Claude, he was your first love and lifemate, and Julius was never to trouble you again."

"But Magda didn't kill Christian," Marguerite said with triumph.

"No, she didn't." Vita's gaze slid to Christian. "My own maid would have done what I said out of fear of death had she disobeyed me. *Your* maid wasn't quite so biddable. You obviously don't instill the proper respect in your servants," she reprimanded then continued, "When I got to my brother's townhouse later that day, the child and maid were installed in a room on the second floor."

"What of the maid's murder?" Marguerite asked.

"Oh," Vita waved a hand vaguely. "I couldn't risk her recognizing me, so she took a tumble down the stairs as soon as I could arrange it. She died, and I managed to point the finger in your direction, first by saying I'd seen you there and then by putting your broach in her hand."

"I thought that was a masterful touch," she preened and then frowned. "I was sorry to lose the broach, though. I'd always liked it and had taken it from your box for myself. I did ask you first and you didn't protest. Of course, you were catatonic at the time." She burst out laughing at her own joke.

Marguerite ground her teeth as she waited for her to finish.

"Anyway," Vita said once her laughter died, "Julius had fits over you trying to kill your own child. It's most unfortunate that I couldn't arrange his death at the same time, but I was under a bit of pressure and couldn't think of anything to kill him as well."

She shook her head dismally and then continued, "Julius packed up the child and fled England, and Jean Claude bundled you up and took you to France while you were still in the catatonic state. We put a memory of a European tour in your mind to replace the memories we wiped, and he eventually moved you to Canada." She shrugged. "And so five hundred years passed, you in your miserable marriage and Julius in his own misery, mourning the loss of you." She smiled and admitted, "I quite enjoyed his suffering, but I fear I may have rubbed it in a bit."

Marguerite was not shocked by the admission. Growing tired of the woman's crowing about all the misery she'd caused, Marguerite said, "So the plan now is to cause Julius more misery, by what . . . ? Killing both of us?"

"And him," Vita said calmly. "Fun as it is to torment Julius, I'm growing tired of the game. And now that everyone is thoroughly convinced that Jean Claude is behind these attacks on you, my father will never suspect me." She smiled. "I can finally get the annoying little gnat out of my hair."

Marguerite tensed as Vita crossed the room to stand on the other side of Christian.

They took two vehicles in the end. Dante and Tommaso were just arriving as they walked out of the house and Nicodemus ordered them into his car with him and his driver. Julius, Marcus, and Tiny rode in the van with the Argeneaus. Julius spent the ride worrying. Judging by the silence of the rest of the men, they were too. It was a grim group that piled out of the van when they arrived at Vita's home, a centuries-old stone building that Vita had owned for as long as Julius could recall. He'd always thought it grim and cold and it still appeared that way to him now as he approached.

"There are lights on," Tiny commented, peering through the window beside the door when there was no answer to Julius's knock.

"She won't hear us if she's in the basement," Julius muttered. "She has rooms down there where she used to practice her swordplay."

"She still does practice down there," Nicodemus informed him quietly and held out a key.

Julius wasn't surprised to see the key. His father had keys to all his children's homes, in case of emergency. Taking it, he unlocked the door and led the way in, some instinct telling him not to call out.

"I shall make Julius suffer for a couple more days, just to twist the screw a bit, you understand," Vita said as she peered down at Christian's still face. "For old time's sake."

"Of course," Marguerite said quietly and wondered when exactly Vita had gone mad. Living so long without a lifemate could do that to an immortal and it had obviously affected this one. The woman was riddled with bitterness and rage and madness.

"Then I'll send him a letter telling him where he can find you both. I was thinking a small wooded area not far from his house, but I haven't completely made up my mind yet." She shrugged. "He'll arrive to find you both dead and be crushed of course. I'll enjoy that for a few minutes and then put him out of his misery, and mine." She released a little sigh of pleasure at the very idea.

"What now?" Marguerite asked quietly. "You leave us down here without any blood until you're ready to kill us?"

"No, I don't think there's any need for that," Vita said thoughtfully. "Now that I've told you everything, it's really rather risky to keep you alive. What if you escaped? No. I think it's better if I deal with you now."

Marguerite's eyes widened with alarm. "But you wanted to torment Julius some more."

"I will," Vita assured her with amusement as she swung her sword up over her head. "It is nice and cool down here. Your corpses should still be recognizable in two days' time."

Christian's eyes shot open and he started to roll toward Vita, reaching for her leg, but Marguerite had already thrown herself toward him to take the blow as the sword swung downward.

Three things happened at once. Marguerite landed on Christian's side with a grunt, Vita's sword slashed across her behind, and Christian pulled his aunt's leg from under her, sending her tumbling to the ground.

"Marguerite!"

She blinked her eyes open and when Christian started to turn under her, catching her by the arms to lift her slightly, she smiled weakly despite the white hot heat in her backside and said, "You sound so like your father."

"That *was* Father," he assured her, worry drawing his eyebrows together. "Are you all right? Why did you do that?"

"I was protecting you. It's what a mother does," Marguerite said, closing her eyes with a grimace as pain radiated through her posterior section. Her eyes then blinked open again almost at once. "It was your father?"

Christian nodded, and then glanced to the side. She followed his gaze to see Julius pulling Vita to her feet and passing her over to Dante and Tommaso to be restrained. The twins promptly began to drag her from the room and she saw Nicodemus Notte follow, his expression cold and closed. The woman was in a lot of trouble, she thought, and was glad for it. No one tried to kill her children and got away with it.

"Are you both all right? Marguerite, can you—" Julius had started to lift her off of Christian, but paused when she groaned in pain. "Where are you hurt, love? I didn't see where she got you."

Marguerite closed her eyes as he began to check her back. This was so humiliating. Apparently her black skirt was hiding the wound, making the blood impossible to see. Presumably the slice in her skirt where the sword had got her was hidden by the folds of the material, because his hands were moving over her upper back and she could hear the frown in his voice as he said, "I can't find it, Marguerite. You were hit, weren't you?"

"Yes," Marguerite said and then sighed and added, "I won't be sitting down for a day or two."

She felt cool air on her behind. When Julius cursed, Marguerite smiled crookedly at her son. "How is your wound?"

Christian released a little laugh and shook his head helplessly.

She felt her skirt being dropped down over her behind, and then Julius moved up beside them.

"This is going to hurt a bit," he warned, and caught her under the arms to lift her off of Christian.

Marguerite managed to keep from crying out as white hot agony sliced through her behind by biting down on her lip, but sweat had broken out on her forehead by the time she was upright and on her feet. Her legs immediately gave out, and she bit down harder as they buckled, sending another shot of pain through her, but then someone was immediately there at her side, dragging her arm over their shoulder even as Julius slid under her other arm.

"Lucian," Marguerite said with surprise as she peered at the man. "What are you doing here?"

"Looking for you," he said wryly. "You didn't think we'd let you disappear and not come looking?"

"We?" she asked and glanced around to see the room was now filled with men. Her eyes slid over Bastien, Lucern, Vincent, Tiny, and Marcus with surprise.

"And you said they'd enjoy the respite from you," Christian said on a breathless laugh as he struggled to get to his feet.

Marguerite smiled faintly at his teasing, but then

frowned as Bastien and Lucern immediately moved to help him and he suddenly stiffened up, looking uncomfortable as he muttered that he could manage on his own. She knew he was now experiencing what she'd been suffering for the last few days. Uncertainty and discomfort in the face of unexpected family.

"Christian," she said quietly, "let them help you. That's what brothers are for."

He hesitated, then seemed to relax a little and nodded, allowing Bastien and Lucern to take some of his weight.

"I found some keys in the hall. Let me see if I can find the one to get your chains off," Vincent said, crossing the room toward her.

Marguerite smiled as he knelt to try various keys on her chain, and then glanced around and asked, "Where are the girls?"

"They're in York," Vincent answered, glancing up to admit wryly, "They weren't with us when we got Julius's number. It seemed better to come straight here than to go back and collect them."

"Jackie won't take that well," Tiny commented dryly, speaking of Vincent's wife, Jackie Morrisey, the owner of the Morrisey Detective Agency and Tiny's usual partner.

"I know," Vincent said cheerfully as he found the right key and the cuff around her ankle fell away.

Marguerite raised one eyebrow as she watched him move to Christian's chain. "You don't seem too worried about it."

Vincent shrugged. "She'll have a fit, throw a tantrum, I'll grovel a bit, and we'll have make-up sex."

He glanced up from working on the chain on Christian's ankle and grinned. "It'll be great."

Marguerite shook her head as she noted that all the Argeneau men were grinning. She suspected there would be a lot of make-up sex when they got back to their women.

"There you go." Vincent straightened as Christian's chain fell away. "We have blood in the truck. We'll have you both back in fighting form in no time."

"Blood," Christian sighed. "Sounds good."

Marguerite watched as Bastien and Lucern began to help Christian toward the door.

"They'll accept him," Lucian said quietly and she smiled and nodded.

"Yes, they will. They're good boys."

"We should get you out to the truck too," Julius said urging her forward, but pausing abruptly when she tried to walk and gasped when pain shot through her backside and down her leg as she moved.

Julius and Lucian paused and glanced at each other. Taller than she, they were both crouched over to fit her arms over their shoulders, then she glanced from one to the other as Lucian raised an eyebrow and Julius nodded. Without a word they then both straightened, lifting her off the floor.

"Better?" Julius asked as they began to walk forward with her dangling between them.

"Yes," she admitted with relief. "Now tell me I don't have to sit on the bus," she pleaded, and grimaced as they both chuckled.

Epilogue

"Finally," Marguerite said with a smile as Lissianna placed her new granddaughter in her arms.

It had been two weeks since she and Christian had been rescued from Vita's home. Julius had spent the time since fussing over her like a mother hen, feeding her bag after bag of blood and coddling her long after she had healed. He'd also spent that time telling her more about the period when they'd first met, hoping to bring back the memories that were missing.

It hadn't worked so far. Marguerite feared she may never remember, but she had her lifemate and her son, and that along with her other children and the rest of her family was enough.

Lucian, Lucern, Bastien, and Vincent had stayed at Julius's home in Italy for a couple of days while waiting for the European council to pass judgment on Vita. Once they'd pronounced that she be executed and the deed was done, they'd returned to York to collect their lifemates and head back to Canada. Marguerite had talked to everyone on the phone since then, but had only returned home to Canada the night before, flying in with Julius, Christian, Dante, Tommaso, and Marcus.

Bastien and his lifemate, Terri, had met them at the airport and brought them home, but everyone had left them alone last night to allow them to recover from the journey. Tonight, however, her family had congregated at her home, a family gathering to introduce the two families. Even Jackie, Vincent, and Tiny had flown in for the occasion, and it *was* an occasion, this was her first sight of her beautiful granddaughter.

"We named her after Uncle Lucian," Lissianna announced as Marguerite ran a finger lightly down the baby's soft cheek. "Her name is Luciana, but we'll call her Lucy."

Marguerite tore her eyes away from the beautiful baby and glanced worriedly toward her son-in-law at this news. The two men had not got off to a grand start and she was surprised he'd allowed the name.

"Lucian and I have worked things out," Greg assured her with a smile. "Like the rest of the Argeneau men, he's really not so bad once you get to know him."

Marguerite smiled, her gaze slipping across the room to where Christian, his cousins, and the majority of the Argeneau clan were seated, talking. Christian had spent a lot of time with his half brothers, his new cousin, and his Uncle Lucian during the two nights they'd remained in Italy, and they all seemed very relaxed and comfortable around each other. But then she'd expected no less.

A gurgling laugh drew her gaze back to her sweet granddaughter and Marguerite smiled and whispered, "Little Lucy, you're perfect."

"Yes, she is," Lucian agreed, appearing beside her. He reached over Marguerite's shoulder to offer the child a finger and little Lucy immediately grasped it in her tiny fist and tried to draw it to her mouth. "And soon she'll have a playmate."

Marguerite glanced up wide-eyed at this announcement. "A playmate?"

He grinned and then drew a petite brunette closer so she could see her as he announced, "We're pregnant."

"Already?" Marguerite asked with surprise and then beamed on the pair, thinking how much happier Lucian seemed. Things were really looking up when Lucian Argeneau actually smiled. "I'm very happy for you."

"Thank you," he said solemnly, then reclaimed his finger from Lucy to lay his hand on her shoulder, cleared his throat, and said quietly, "Marguerite, I want you to know I had no idea what was going on back then. I believed that Jean Claude was dead. He didn't even contact *me* during those years and he never explained his absence to me. It was a bone of contention between us for centuries."

Marguerite frowned at the hurt in his eyes, knowing he felt betrayed by his twin's silence during that time. Squeezing the hand on her shoulder, she said, "He couldn't have told you, Lucian. It would have put you in an untenable position. You were a member of the council in Europe at the time. You would have been faced with the choice of turning in your own brother, or breaking some of the laws you helped put in place. It was better he didn't tell you. I know it must have been hard for him too."

Lucian nodded, but he wasn't finished. "I was happy for you when you found Julius back then. It had been obvious to me for some time that you and Claude were not true lifemates and he'd made a mistake there, so I was happy to hear you had found someone who made you happy. But when Jean Claude returned . . ." He paused and shook his head. "He said the two of you were working things out and had decided to stay together. He told Lucern the same thing. I had no idea about the three-on-one or the—"

"I know, Lucian," Marguerite interrupted quietly and assured him, "you have too much honor for me ever to have thought that you had known or been involved."

Lucian nodded and patted her hand, his gaze sliding to Thomas as he led a pretty dark-haired woman over to join their little cluster. "We'll get out of the way and go join the others. Thomas has something to tell you."

Eyebrows rising, Marguerite watched the handsome young couple approach, smiling as she noted the way they moved, their footsteps in sync. Thomas was measuring his longer stride, reducing it to match the woman's shorter stride.

"Aunt Marguerite, I'm so glad you're safe and feeling better," Thomas greeted her, bending to press a kiss to her cheek.

Careful not to crush the baby, Marguerite smiled

and hugged her nephew before letting him straighten.
She then raised a quizzical eyebrow as her gaze slid to
the woman at his side.

Thomas grinned at her expression as he drew the
girl forward. "This is Inez Urso."

"Yes, I know. She works for Bastien," Marguerite
reached out to squeeze her hand in greeting. "I met
Inez when she came to Canada for a tour of the offices after her promotion to the executive position. I
see Bastien finally introduced the two of you as I suggested," she added with satisfaction.

"You suggested he introduce us?" Inez asked with
surprise.

"I don't believe it," Thomas muttered when Marguerite nodded. His gaze shifted across the room to
where Bastien was laughing. "I thought I was the
first one to escape your famous matchmaking and
all the time he was in cahoots with you. Wait till
I . . ." Catching Inez's hand, he started to lead her
toward the group, no doubt to give Bastien an ear-
ful, but paused as he realized he was marching off
on his aunt.

Turning back, he opened his mouth to speak, but
Marguerite grinned and waved him on. "Go on, join
the others. We'll come over in a minute."

"Oh, give Lucy here, Mother. She's wanting her di-
aper changed," Lissianna murmured when the baby
began to fuss.

Marguerite gave up the baby, but watched with regret as Lissianna and Greg moved to the other side of
the room to tend their daughter. Her gaze then slid to
the group seated on the couches and chairs arranged

around the fireplace. They were laughing and talking as if they'd known each other forever.

"Christian seems to be getting along well with his new brothers and sister," Julius commented, moving to sit on the arm of her chair now that she no longer had the baby.

"I'm glad," Marguerite said, her gaze wistful as she watched the young man laugh at something that had been said.

"What's the matter, love?" Julius asked with concern.

Marguerite shrugged and then admitted, "I'm just a little sad thinking about how much I've missed of Christian's life."

Julius bent to press a kiss to her forehead and suggested softly, "We could have another Christian to make up for it. Or a Christina."

Marguerite peered up at him, "Would you like that?"

"I can't think of anything more wonderful than having a dozen bambinos with you, Marguerite," he said with a smile, and then added, "but maybe not for a couple years. I've missed out on the last five hundred years with you and want to make up for lost time first." He paused and frowned, then said fretfully, "I'm sorry. I should have known you wouldn't have done any of what they claimed. I should have come for you after the maid brought Christian to me."

"I wouldn't have remembered you," she pointed out quietly. "From what Vita said, I wasn't even conscious, or at least mentally competent, for quite a while after the three-on-one."

"But I could have—"

"Done nothing," Marguerite insisted firmly, and then added, "Julius, please don't ever feel guilty about the last five hundred years. We all did the best we could. Even Jean Claude. I've hated him so much and for so long, but in the end, Vita damaged him too, killing his true lifemate and child as she did. When I look back on it, I see the difference in him before the missing memories and after. He wasn't great but he tried before that. Afterward, he was so full of rage and bitterness all the time and I never understood why, but now . . ."

"His loss didn't excuse his behavior toward you," Julius growled.

"No," she agreed quietly. "But it explains it."

He shook his head. "I still think I should have done something."

"And then I wouldn't have Bastien, Etienne, or Lissianna," she pointed out quietly.

Marguerite saw the flicker in his eyes as he recognized the truth of her words. Had he taken her from Jean Claude five hundred years ago, her three youngest children wouldn't have been born. She also wouldn't have raised Thomas and Jeanne Louise and . . . There were so many ands.

"I love you, Julius," she said quietly. "But I love them too and everything in my life—good and bad—has led me to this point where I can have all of you. All those experiences have shaped and formed me like a blacksmith beats a sword into shape in the fire." Marguerite peered at him solemnly. "I like who I am, and I'm happy with what I have: my five lovely children and you. It wasn't always easy. Sometimes it was downright painful. But I wouldn't change a thing."

"Then neither would I, my love," Julius whispered and kissed her.

A burst of laughter from the group by the fireplace made them pull apart and glance toward them curiously.

"Our children are up to something," Julius said with amusement.

Marguerite nodded with a smile. *Our children.* It had a beautiful ring to it. Julius was opening his arms to her family too and that was as important to her as the Argeneau side accepting his family.

"She did!" Tiny was insisting.

"She didn't," Christian said with a frown.

"Yes, she did, and she will with you too," Etienne assured his half brother, slapping him almost sympathetically on the shoulder.

"No," Christian said, but was beginning to look worried.

"Who did, or didn't, or will do what?" Marguerite asked as she and Julius crossed the room to join the circle of younger people.

"We were just telling Christian how you 'helped' us get together with our lifemates," Vincent announced.

"I didn't interfere with you and Jackie," Marguerite insisted at once. "I helped you along a little, maybe, but that was all. I never interfere."

"Oh please, Mother." Bastien laughed, his arm around Terri, his hand absently rubbing her arm as he spoke. "You told me outright that you thought Vincent would be much happier with a lifemate and you were going to see what you could do to help him in that area. And you are the one who suggested I introduce Inez and Thomas. That's part of the reason I asked her to help him when he went to England to look for you."

"You flew to New York to convince Kate to come back to me," Lucern said quietly, reaching for his wife's hand.

Kate smiled and leaned into him as she pointed out, "And you sent me to England to talk to Terri so she'd give Bastien a chance."

"You made me play cupid for Etienne and Rachel," Thomas added.

"And don't even try to deny that you interfered with Greg and me," Lissianna laughed as she and Greg joined them with a freshly diapered Lucy.

"She didn't interfere with us," Lucian commented with satisfaction, relaxing back in his seat and pulling Leigh, who sat on his lap for lack of chairs, back against his chest.

"Actually," Thomas murmured and all eyes turned his way, "the day you arrived with Leigh, Aunt Marguerite told me to make myself scarce and leave you to deal with her on your own. She said she had a good feeling about the two of you."

"What?" Lucian sat up abruptly, nearly sending Leigh sliding off his lap. Catching her, he murmured an apology and then speared Marguerite with a dark look. "You're the reason I couldn't reach Thomas?"

Marguerite scowled right back. "Well, it all worked out for the best, didn't it?"

There was silence and then Victor Argeneau shifted and said, "I hate to even ask this, but did you have anything to do with Elvi and me?"

Marguerite glanced at Lucian and Jean Claude's younger brother. He was Vincent's father and she'd been glad to hear the two men had worked out their issues and were building a relationship.

"Marguerite's the one who suggested I have you answer the ad in the paper when rumors started flying about a vampire in one of the lakeside small towns," Lucian growled with disgust and then shook his head and added, "but she couldn't have known anything about Elvi's situation in Port Henry at the time. The council had only got wind of her a week or so earlier."

"Did you say Port Henry?" Lissianna asked with a frown.

"Yes," Lucian said warily. "Why?"

Lissianna peered narrowly at Marguerite then turned to Greg, "Isn't that where she had us stop to eat when we all drove down to the Mennonite store about the baby crib for Lucy?"

"Mennonite store?" Leigh asked with interest and then glanced at Lucian. "I love Lucy's crib, we should go check out this store."

"It's wonderful," Lissianna assured her. "The workmanship is beautiful. Mom found it. We drove down a couple weeks before she went to Europe and they made and delivered the crib just a week before Lucy was born."

"Oh, yes." Greg nodded with sudden recall. "You were hungry when we left the store and we stopped for dinner at a little Mexican restaurant on the way back. What was the name of that place? Bella something."

"Bella Black's?" Victor asked with horror.

"That's it!" Lissianna exclaimed.

"That's my restaurant," Elvi said with amazement.

Lissianna frowned. "Mom spent a lot of time talking to the owner, but it wasn't you."

"It must have been Mabel," Elvi murmured, glancing curiously at Marguerite. "Though you do look kind of familiar."

"You came over to ask Mabel something while I was read—er . . . talking to her," Marguerite corrected herself and then shrugged. "It was only for a minute."

"Just long enough for you to read Elvi and decide you'd have me send Victor her way?" Lucian suggested.

Marguerite ignored him.

"You mean to say there isn't one of you that Mar— Mother didn't get together in some way?" Christian asked with amazement.

They all glanced at each other, then Victor said, "Maybe DJ and Mabel."

"Oh!" Marguerite brightened. "How lovely. I liked Mabel and DJ's such a sweetie."

Tiny gave Christian a nudge and teased, "And now it will be your turn. She'll try to find you a lifemate."

Marguerite scowled at the mortal when she saw the worried look on her son's face. Then she smiled archly and said, "Actually, Tiny, I was thinking that you would make some nice immortal a good husband."

Much to her satisfaction, while the mortal's eyes widened in horror at the very suggestion, Christian seemed to relax a bit. But only a bit, she noted unhappily. The last thing she wanted was her own son wary around her.

Sensing her fears, Julius squeezed her gently, his arms tightening briefly around her waist and urging her closer back against him.

"Tell me something," he interrupted in a loud voice when everyone began to speak at once. The moment silence fell, he asked, "Do any of you wish she hadn't interfered?"

There was a moment of silence as the couples looked at each other, then they answered in stereo with quiet nos or shakes of the head.

"Well, there you are then." He glanced to Christian. "You have something to look forward to, Son." Smiling at the doubtful look on his face, he then glanced toward Marcus and the twins and added, "Actually, you probably all have something to look forward to now that Marguerite's here to manage you. Enjoy."

"Welcome to the family," Thomas said with a laugh as the four men peered at each other with horror.

Chuckling, Julius turned Marguerite away and began to lead her out of the room.

Despite his apparent good humor over what he'd just learned, she glanced at him worriedly, and murmured, "I'm not really a meddler, Julius. And I don't have any grand intention to start hunting up a lifemate for Christian right away or anything."

"It's not meddling to want to see someone happy, Marguerite," he assured her, slipping his arm around her waist.

"I do want to see him happy," she said, and then added, "But I also want to get to know him better myself. And I want to spend time with you as well."

"And we will." Pausing in the hallway, he turned her to face him. "We'll get to know each other all over again, and you can get to know our son too. We have the time, that's one thing we have plenty of. Time and love."

"Time and love," Marguerite agreed as his lips descended to her.

At Avon Books, we know your passion for romance—once you finish one of our novels, you find yourself wanting more.

May we tempt you with . . .

- **Excerpts** from our upcoming releases.
- Entertaining **extras**, including authors' personal photo albums and book lists.
- Behind-the-scenes **scoop** on your favorite characters and series.
- **Sweepstakes** for the chance to win free books, romantic getaways, and other fun prizes.
- Writing **tips** from our authors and editors.
- **Blog** with our authors and find out why they love to write romance.
- **Exclusive content** that's not contained within the pages of our novels.

Join us at
www.avonbooks.com